Meeting Mozart
in Venice, Vienna & Prague:
A Novel Drawn from the Secret
Diaries of Lorenzo Da Ponte

For mia dolcetta, Patricia Dixon,
without whom the creation of this book
would not have been possible.

Praise for Meeting Mozart

"Howard Jay Smith has written the musical equivalent of *The Da Vinci Code*. Deftly plotted and richly detailed, the novel spans generations and involves Mozart, mysteries, masquerades, opera, spies, and much more. How Smith managed to pull it all together is a mystery in itself. But he does, and he's written a deeply satisfying ending"
— Patricia Morrisroe, author,
The Woman in the Moonlight

"An entertaining tale inspired by Mozart and his operas, aimed especially toward Mozart lovers. Its mingling of fact and fancy includes a memorable portrait of Mozart's raffish and brilliant librettist, Lorenzo Da Ponte."
— Jan Swafford, author, *Mozart, The Reign of Love; Beethoven; Anguish & Triumph; Brahms, A Biography*

"Smith writes beautifully and with a wonderful command of language and a deep knowledge of history, music and opera. This is a fantastic story and an absolute delight to read."
— Nir Kabaretti, Music Director and Conductor of The Israel Sinfonietta Beersheba and the Santa Barbara Symphony

"*Meeting Mozart* is a journey of transcendence, an exquisitely constructed novel crafted by a compelling storyteller."
— Alan Riche, Producer of *Duets, The Legend of Tarzan, Bodies at Rest, Family Man, Mod Squad, Starsky & Hutch*

"In this tour de force, Smith vividly brings to life not only Da Ponte's challenges in navigating the challenges of life for Jews, but also those of his descendants who must also face the horrors of the Holocaust and eloquently rise above them. A warm and heart-felt novel."
— Gaelle Lehrer Kennedy, author,
Night in Jerusalem

"Howard Jay Smith brilliantly juggles, with bravura and virtuosity, Da Ponte's fascinating and epic life. And for the first time he brings to the forefront how Da Ponte's Jewish DNA helped to catapult him into immortality."
— Tom Greene, writer/producer, *Wildside*, *Magnum, P.I.*, *Knight Rider*, *Star Trek*

"A mesmerizing story with substantial impact. Deftly written with sensitivity and insight."
— Grant Gochin, author, *Malice, Murder & Manipulation, The Lithuanian Holocaust*

"Howard Jay Smith's splendid literary novels incorporate mystery and historical fiction. With *Meeting Mozart*, Smith takes readers from the stylish streets of Europe's most important musical cities to a Jewish deli in early modern New York. And he reintroduces us to captivating historical figures as varied as Mozart, Casanova and Clement Moore in a complex and often-riveting tale about creativity, identity, and purpose."
— Russell Martin, author, *Beethoven's Hair, Out of Silence, The Sorrow of Archaeology*

More Books by Howard Jay Smith

Beethoven in Love: Opus 139

Opening the Doors to Hollywood

John Gardner: An Interview

More Books from The Sager Group

Lifeboat No. 8: Surviving the Titanic
by Elizabeth Kaye

#MeAsWell, A Novel
by Peter Mehlman

The Orphan's Daughter, A Novel
by Jan Cherubin

Miss Havilland, A Novel
by Gay Daly

Shaman: The Mysterious Life and Impeccable Death of Carlos Castaneda by Mike Sager

Three Days in Gettysburg
by Brian Mockenhaupt

Senlac: A Novel of the Norman Conquest of England, (Book One & Book Two)
by Julian de la Motte

See our entire library at TheSagerGroup.net

Meeting Mozart

A NOVEL

By Howard
Jay Smith

This is a work of fiction. Many of the details, places, characters, and events were inspired by real life; many have been altered for the purposes of the narrative. Any resemblance to actual living persons is entirely coincidental.

Meeting Mozart: A Novel Drawn from the Secret Diaries of Lorenzo Da Ponte

Copyright © 2020 Howard Jay Smith
All rights reserved.

No part of this publication may be reproduced, stored in a retrieval system, or transmitted, in any form or by any means, electronic, mechanical, photocopying, recording, or otherwise, without the prior written permission of the publisher.
Published in the United States of America.

Cover and interior illustrations by Zak Smith
Cover and interior designed by Siori Kitajima,
SF AppWorks LLC

Cataloging-in-Publication data for this book is available from the Library of Congress
ISBN-13:
eBook: 978-1-950154-39-5
Paperback: 978-1-950154-38-8
Published by The Sager Group LLC
TheSagerGroup.net

Meeting Mozart

A Novel Drawn from the Secret Diaries of Lorenzo Da Ponte

By Howard Jay Smith

Contents

Part One: Venice 1

Chapter One: Dreaming of Mozart 3

Chapter Two: Dolcetta 25

Chapter Three: A Death in Venice 43

Chapter Four: A Night at the Opera 63

Chapter Five: Via Giudecca 85

Chapter Six: The Fires Down Below 95

Chapter Seven: The Hands of a Conegliano 113

Part Two: Vienna **135**

Chapter Eight: The Emperor's Mistress 137

Chapter Nine: Queen of the Night 157

Chapter Ten: Songs of Seduction 169

Chapter Eleven: Celebrations 183

Chapter Twelve: A Descent into Hell 199

Chapter Thirteen: The Marriages of Mozart 217

Chapter Fourteen: Diamonds in the Snow 235

Chapter Fifteen: A Night to Remember 249

Chapter Sixteen: Kartnerstrasse Siebzehn 259

Chapter Seventeen: Kartnerstrasse Siebzehn
    Revisited 271

Part Three: Prague **285**

Chapter Eighteen: Leopold the Second 287

Chapter Nineteen: The Velvet Revolution 299

Chapter Twenty: The School for Lovers............................. 317

Chapter Twenty-One: La via della Giudecca 333

Chapter Twenty-Two: La Rinascita di Emanuele
                                  Conegliano........................ 351

Chapter Twenty-Three: By the Rivers of Zion 365

Chapter Twenty-Four: The Coda: New York,
                                    New York...........................389

About the Author 406
About the Illustrator... 407
About the Publisher 408

Chapter One: Dreaming of Mozart

Sunday Morning, January 27, 1946
The Veneto, outside Aviano Air Base, Italy

Mozart. Corporal Jake Conegliano, US Army Intelligence, was sound asleep and dreaming of Mozart when he first heard a knocking on the door of his quarters. Not just any Mozart but *The Marriage of Figaro*. Yes, Figaro, with the count pounding on his wife's bedroom door while her suspected lover scurried off to hide in her closet.

What had started as gentle taps grew ever louder until Jake awoke enough to realize the door banging was not from any opera. Instead, it was the Abbé Luigi Hudal, a priest from Santa Maria dell'Anima, the local Catholic Church adjacent to the air base. Abbé Hudal, an Austro-Italian with a gruff baritone voice, was calling out, "Corporal Conegliano. Conegliano, *aufmachen!* Open up, open up." So much for Figaro, the count and the woman of his dreams.

Throwing on a robe, Jake went over and opened the door. Abbé Luigi Hudal was a lean and angular clergyman whose cold dark eyes reminded Jake of a reptile, ever ready to strike. Abbé Luigi Hudal, who oversaw the Santa Maria dell'Anima choir, did however admire Jake's polished tenor voice.

Beyond the sight of Hudal's profile filling the doorway, Jake could see a clear blue sky—a good omen for travel after days of rain had drenched the entire Veneto region of northeastern Italy. Jake's shoebox-sized quarters were once the storeroom of an old farm house adjacent to the airbase outside Aviano. At war's end, with the Nazis routed out of the surrounding countryside, the Brits had taken over Aviano. Jake, a communications and radar intelligence specialist who also spoke fluent Italian, had been lent by the US Army to assist with highly classified technical upgrades to their avionics command.

Working with the English was a far better gig than liberating Dachau as he had done the preceding April. That was as close to hell on earth as he could have ever witnessed, and those images of human savagery and evil—pure evil—were forever imprinted in his soul. If there was but one lesson he had learned during the war against Hitler, the Nazis, the Italian Fascists, and their allies, it was this: any society that depends on conscience has no defense against a sociopath who has none. But in a month when his enlistment was up, it would be over. Jake would be going back home to his family in the Bronx, a free man.

Abbé Luigi Hudal barked out an apology for waking him up, one that sounded more like a Nazi officer giving orders. Hudal needed a tenor to substitute in as the lead with the choir at church that morning for Sunday's prayer service. He insisted Jake join him in honoring *il buon Dio*.

Jake told Abbé Hudal that no, he didn't have time for church. He had a four-day pass for his first stretch of leave since the war had ended six months earlier. He and Lt. Foxx, the British officer in command of the intelligence unit, were soon to be heading off to see an opera in Treviso, a half day's drive south. Given that the roads had been battered by the January rain storms that had turned the local streams coming out of the mountains into pavement-devouring torrents, the lieutenant had insisted on an early morning start to ensure they reached Treviso by curtain rise that evening

"It's Mozart's birthday and we're going to see *The Marriage of Figaro*," Jake said. Fragments of his dream recirculated in Jake's mind's eye in anticipation. He'd seen the opera a number of times at the Met while growing up in New York thanks to his father, Abe, who supplied the opera house with much of its lighting and sound equipment and had been savvy enough to negotiate season tickets as partial payment for his services. Before the war, Jake not only heard stars such as tenor Beniamino Gigli, bass Ezio Pinza, and the legendary soprano Rosa Ponselle, he had also watched when his father helped record some of the Met's legendary radio broadcasts.

"*Ja*, Mozart, eh?" said Hudal in his thick Austro-Italian accent. "But a proper Catholic soldier ought to first pay his respects to the Good Lord above on a Sunday. I insist you come, my son."

Though Jake loved to sing in the choir—one of the few acts of normalcy he had experienced in his three years of war duty—he had a built-in antipathy to Hudal. He never trusted harsh and intolerant spiritual leaders who clearly lacked empathy, especially those who insisted on telling him how to act or behave.

"Sorry, not today, Father. But I'd be happy to join your choir again next Sunday."

"You will anger the Lord if you fail me today. And it will cost you in confession."

"Not so," said Jake unmoved by the notion of Catholic guilt. He pushed back on the priest's pressure. "I've sung in your choir since arriving here only because it pleases me to do so. It's got nothing to do with being Catholic."

"Watch your words, son. Don't stray into blasphemy. And Mozart is no defense. The man himself was a Mason, a heretic whom God punished for his sins with an early death."

"Really?" That Hudal had disparaged Mozart made his dislike of the priest and the tactic of guilt ever stronger. Jake adored Mozart's operas so much so that he even felt a kinship with them, especially *Figaro, Don Giovanni,* and *Cosi Fan Tutte,* the three comedies Mozart had composed with an Italian librettist and priest, the Abbé Lorenzo Da Ponte.

"Yes, son. Now get dressed *und komme mit.*"

"Don't bother yourself, Father. I won't be there today, but I will be happy to serve your Lord next Sunday."

"But I insist. You must. Get dressed. I'll wait."

"Father, stop. You need to know I'm Jewish." This was not something Jake generally shared or let on to with others. It was one thing to be battling the Germans who had murdered Jews all across Europe but quite another to constantly be confronted with anti-Semites among the Allies, a cruelty he witnessed all too often in his own barracks. He was glad for the relative anonymity his Italian surname, "Conegliano," gave him while in the army.

Hudal's eyes flashed a rage that emanated from deep in his soul as he shook his finger in Jake's face, "Don't lie like that to me. A good son of Italy . . . now that is blasphemy."

Jake pulled the Jewish star he wore around his neck out from under his robe. Though he wasn't very religious himself, after all he'd witnessed at Dachau, he'd become ever more determined to stand up to Nazis, Fascists, and bullies of all stripes, including the Abbé Hudal. "I'll be there next Sunday, but not today. Mozart awaits."

The priest blanched upon seeing that six-cornered star. It was as if the Abbé Luigi Hudal had witnessed the great Lucifer himself standing there with horns on his head and a pitchfork in hand. "Oh no you won't," Hudal spit out. "Not then, not ever. I cannot have a Jewish heathen in my church. You'd be bringing Satan himself right to my door."

Fed up, Jake let Hudal have it. "You're damn right, Father, I'm gonna bring the devil straight into your church and let him drag you down through the gates of hell." Jake slammed the door shut, continuing to curse, "you son of a bitch," under his breath as he did so. Yes, Mozart was waiting, but the depth of his own anger surprised even Jake.

And it was time to dress. Jake was in fact looking forward to the drive through the Veneto countryside, something he had not yet been able to do since his arrival at Aviano in September. His family, Italian Jews who hailed from this very region, had emigrated to the United States and settled in New York. All through his childhood, he had heard stories from his parents about their village, Ceneda, a place they considered sweet and magical, a land nestled beside a crystal-clear stream bubbling out of the mountains, with fields full of wheat, dairy cattle, grapevines, and home to the world's finest prosecco. It was tucked somewhere in the foothills of the northern edge of the Veneto. His mother, Rosa, and her family came to America around 1911 when she was but ten. Abe, his father, had left their village three years later when he was fourteen, just months before the start of the First World War.

Though Jake was able to spot on a map the nearby town that gave his family their surname, "Conegliano," try as he might, he remained disappointed that he could never find Ceneda anywhere. It was the one village in Italy he had been determined to visit before going home, if only to tell his folks he'd been there and experienced the magic of their childhoods.

It was about half an hour later that Lt. Enrico Foxx, a British intelligence officer with the Coldstream Guard—and a fellow opera lover—pulled up in front of Jake's cottage in a battle-scarred jeep that looked as if it had seen more combat than Patton's tank command. The roof was gone and the body was splashed with mud, dents, rust, and a few bullet holes. Foxx, a notorious Casanova who resembled the actor Errol Flynn, had two young Italian women with him in the jeep: a redhead in the back and a dark-haired one in the front passenger seat. The lieutenant was whistling the Guard's regimental theme, "Non più andrai," which Jake immediately recognized as not only being from *The Marriage of Figaro* but a song that British foot soldiers adopted way back in 1787 as their own self-deprecating equivalent of "You're in the Army Now."

Jake, who by this time had traded his robe for his dress uniform and a winter-weight wool overcoat, had not expected to see the two young women, but knew it shouldn't have surprised him. Lt. Foxx had a reputation as a skirt chaser around the base, particularly among the local ladies, many of whom found desperately needed work at Aviano as housekeepers, cooks, and such. With a collapsed postwar economy, times were tough, and as his mother had once said to him, "Work that puts food on the table carries no shame."

He didn't know what line of work these two young ladies were in, but not having been in the company of a female since enlisting out of college, Jake was not about to ask or even guess. The trip to Treviso was the lieutenant's treat, born not only out of their mutual love of opera, but more importantly Jake's successful implementation of their top-secret avionics protocols—actions that earned Foxx's unit a citation and put the lieutenant on the promotional path toward captain. Foxx had even booked and paid for two rooms at a hotel near the opera house for himself and Jake—and for Jake, just shy of turning twenty-one, even that was a new treat. In all his young life, he had never stayed in a real hotel.

Foxx finished up his whistler's version of "Non più andrai" by singing the last few lines in a rich and full baritone voice,

Alla vittoria!
Alla gloria militar!
Alla gloria militar!"

After his final breath of song, the lieutenant pointed to the young woman in the back seat. The wind from the drive over had blown her lengthy copper-red hair all about, giving her the appearance of the goddess in Botticelli's *Birth of Venus*—if you ignored the filthy jeep in the picture.

Ever the proper and fastidious officer, the lieutenant snapped an order for Jake to hop aboard the jeep and take a seat beside her. "That amorous little butterfly is your date, Corporal," said Foxx, pointing to his Venus. She was all smiles, amiable and zaftig, attributes that pleased the young GI.

"She goes by 'Greta.' Doesn't speak much English—not that Italian should be an issue for a fine feathered Adonis such as yourself. Take good care. And the 'Queen of the Night' upfront, that's mine: Dolcetta Spinoziano."

"Yes, sir." Jake saluted and on command he tossed his knapsack into the back and slid onto the bench seat beside the red-haired goddess.

His Botticelli may have worn a bit too much perfume, her stockings had a few runs, and her cloth coat barely looked warm enough for a four-hour drive in an open-air jeep, but if the poverty that characterized postwar Italy left much to be desired, Jake was not one to complain. Her skin was a delicate white, her face angelic, and her lips red and creamy. He felt a hunger, a passion not experienced since school days back in the Bronx.

Other than photographing the starving living skeletons of Dachau, Jake had not even been in the vicinity of a woman during his three years of enlistment. He inhaled Greta's perfume; "*Escada*," she said. Sweet as incense—and smiled to himself. It was indeed the first whiff since he had kissed his mother goodbye back in New York. To be sure, this indeed pleased him very much more.

Yes, for Jake a four-day pass, a hotel, an opera, and a lovely young woman beside him, all conspired to make this January day, Mozart's birthday, even more bright and festive. To hell with the Abbé Luigi Hudal. To hell with his anger.

After setting the jeep back in gear and on the road again, Lt. Foxx made the day a tad warmer by pulling out a flask of brandy from his coat.

"The heater's out, so this will have to do." Always the gallant officer, he offered it up to Dolcetta first. She took a hearty swig, then passed it back to Greta as Foxx toasted, "Happy Birthday, Mr. Mozart," which Jake, without thinking, immediately translated in Italian, "*Buon compleanno, Signor Mozart.*"

Greta strained to greet him in stunted English over the roar of the jeep's engine, an annoying racket that made talking and listening a challenge in any language. Her words emerged from those painted lips with a decided German accent. "Allo . . . *Ich, Io,* I Greta, Greta Tedesco . . . "

"*Piacere. Mi chiamo Jacopo.* Please to meet you. I'm Jake," he added continuing to mix Italian and English for the benefit of Greta. It was a childhood habit learned in the Bronx where his mother, Rosa, always spoke to him in Italian to ensure that he would grow up bilingual. By contrast Jake's father, Abe, insisted on communicating solely in English, "The language of business and the future." Jake's Italian nonetheless rolled off his tongue effortless, "*Mi chiamo Jacopo Conegliano.*"

His use of Italian immediately put Greta at ease. "*Italiano Americano, si?*"

"*Si,* yes. *Sono di* New York, but, *ma,* my family, *la mia famiglia* is from the Veneto, *è Veneta,* A village near Conegliano, *a vicino Conegliano.*"

In response and over the rumble of the jeep's engine, Greta explained to him that she too was now working at the air base. But when Jake asked her what she did there, Greta shook her head and refused to tell him. Instead she said she came from a small village near Bolzano on the Austrian-Italian border where most everyone spoke a mixed German/Italian dialect. As the eldest daughter in a family of seven and with her father, a church organist, who was drafted into the army, missing on the Russian front since 1943, she had to help support her family by working and sending home as much money as she was able. And as Jake was quick to notice, she had the bluest of blue eyes that verily sparkled in sunlight and contrasted sharply with her milk-white complexion and fiery hair.

There was definitely a story there that intrigued Jake, but the noise made further conversation near to impossible. And although the weather wasn't half bad for January, the wind chilled them all. Greta snuggled up next to Jake, and how could a lonely GI not appreciate that? He put his arm around Greta and pulled her tight, as tight as if they been longtime lovers out for a ride in a friend's convertible sports car.

This being Jake's first venture off the base, the sights of the northern Italian countryside his parents had so vividly described to him all through his childhood enthralled him. The land was indeed as picturesque and dreamy as the images his folks had fed into his imagination. The winter rains had turned fallow wheat fields green with new sprouts. Every village they passed was prettier than the previous one, and in the far distance the Alps, capped with snow, punctured the clouds and set a boundary between earth and the heavens.

As romanticized as the sights were for Jake, the roads themselves were rather the opposite. Fallen rocks, potholes and the occasional bomb crater filled with mud, shrapnel, and rainwater made it impossible for Lt. Foxx to drive in a straight line. He verily slalomed his way between the obstacles.

And it was not long into their drive that their troubles began, real troubles that would soon alter Jake's life forever.

As they neared the village of Sacile, signs posted in Italian warned them that the bridge ahead was out.

"Damn it!" snapped Foxx, who was determined to make it to Treviso on time. "I was dreading this." He pulled the jeep over to the side of the road and reached into his coat for a map.

Foxx spread out the map looking for a detour, but all he could see was a spider web of country roads, most of which were little more than dirt tracks. Frustrated by this turn of events, the lieutenant was all gestures and prime English curses.

Jake asked Greta if she knew the roads around here. She shrugged and told him, "*No, sono di Bolzano. Sono una pianista, non una navigatora.*"

"*Sei una pianista?* You're a pianist?" He asked with a touch of amazement in his voice.

Before she could answer the lieutenant cut in, "During the war she rehearsed the singers for *Teatro La Fenice* in Venice. But enough of that, Corporal, right now we need to find an acceptable detour."

Jake was astonished. *La Fenice*, "The Phoenix," was one of the most famous opera houses in the world. He wanted to ask her more, much more, but before he could do so, Dolcetta, who up until then had been totally silent on their drive, spoke up.

"I know. I tell you roads. We go *qui*. Take *strada li*. I know them," she said in hesitant and broken English and Italian. The young brunette could not have been more than seventeen or eighteen. Her hair was pulled back in twin braids. Under her worn overcoat she was wearing khaki trousers, combat boots and an olive green military issue turtleneck sweater.

Ever the officer, Foxx snapped an order at her, "Well, which one. Tell me so we can get the hell out of here."

Dolcetta pointed to a thin line on the map. "*Qui. Strada, qui.* Go *qui*. Take *strada li, a Caneva.*"

It was clear to Jake that the lieutenant understood little of what she said and sure enough, in frustration Foxx turned to him. "Corporal, I cannot make heads or tails out of what she is saying. Translate. And quickly."

"Yes, sir. She says we go here," said Jake pointing to a line on the map, "And then we take this road up to the village of Caneva."

"Then where?" snapped Foxx again.

Dolcetta turned back around to Jake. The two conversed rapidly in highly animated Italian while Dolcetta simultaneously indicated a route on the map. But it was Dolcetta's eyes that caught Jake's attention, dark portals that flashed an intelligence, wisdom, and strength deeper and more profound than her short years. It was then, with something Jake called his "peripheral memory," he recalled seeing this young woman, this khaki-clad girl actually, on the base coming and going from the intelligence unit. Though that explained her wardrobe, he could not help but wonder what sort of women Dolcetta and Greta actually were and how they ended up in the lieutenant's jeep.

When at last she went silent, Jake translated for the lieutenant. "We take this road through Caneva. There we turn west and go up through Silvella, through these passes to the railroad junction town of Vittorio Veneto. That's where she's from. It's her home."

"*Prende il nome da una battaglia molto famosa che pose fine alla prima guerra mondiale,*" added Dolcetta.

"Now what is she saying?" demanded the lieutenant.

"Oh, just that Vittorio Veneto is very famous. It was named for the last battle of the first World War."

"Corporal, I don't need a history lesson. Just get me on a road to Treviso."

"Yes, sir. Here." Jake again sketched out the route. "From Vittorio Veneto we turn south east to Conegliano, which is where she said my family surname comes from."

"Corporal, stop with the history lesson. Directions, man, directions, focus on getting directions."

"Yes, sir."

The roads Dolcetta had indicated on the map were as poor, if not worse than the roadway they had been on initially. War, neglect, and bad weather had conspired to make them ever unpleasant with endless ruts, bumps, rocks, and mud. They crossed bridges over raging streams that seemed held in place by little more than habit. At times they paralleled a rail line and at other moments they zigzagged across those same tracks.

Still they persevered. And while the driving may have been tough on the lieutenant, little could have dimmed Jake's pleasure at having Greta snuggled up against him. While his eyes devoured the scenery, he imagined that his parents, grandparents, and great grandparents had probably experienced and enjoyed it too. He felt at home. These were his roots; this was where he was from. He imagined what his life could have been here, tucked into one of those farmhouses they passed along the road . . . a glass of prosecco in hand, flames crackling in the fireplace, a simple piano with a Greta of his own at the keys, her copper-red hair flashing in the firelight. And playing Mozart, yes, playing his beloved Mozart on a Bosendorfer, the best piano in the world . . .

It was a sweet dream that abruptly crashed into reality as they passed through a seemingly deserted enclave too small to even consider it a village, just a small cluster of whitewashed buildings with red clay tiled roofs. Some were burned out, others had collapsed facades.

"Look there, Corporal," said the Lieutenant indicating a stone wall. At chest height were rows of bullet holes and dark brown stains, no doubt from blood. "The war reached deep into these hills."

"*Tedeschi* kill many *qui*" Dolcetta mimed shooting a machine gun. Yes, the Germans had executed many. And in his peripheral memory Jake realized that most of the buildings they had passed in the last hour had been similarly desecrated. War was indeed hell, and beyond the paradisiacal childhood his parents had so lovingly described, he wondered what his fate would have been had he grown up here in the Veneto. Would that have been his blood on those walls? Would the evil he witnessed at Dachau have repeated itself here? He was a Jew, so he knew the answer was unequivocally yes. And as his encounter with the Abbé Hudal reminded him, it was never easy to survive as a Jew in an essentially hostile Christian world.

As they drove on in silence, the blue sky clouded up. A dense fog hung over the foothills and above the mountains hung blackened storm thunderheads. Somewhere past the village of Sarmede, the parallel road and the rail line both started across a particularly steep gorge carved out by a tributary of the Piave River. The bridge for the road made it all the way across, the rail line, not so much. Lt. Foxx stopped the jeep in the middle of their bridge and pulled out a camera from beneath his seat.

"You do know how to use this, Corporal, I presume." Foxx passed the camera over to Jake and then eyed the wreckage. As the technology grunt in the intelligence unit, Jake was often called upon to be the man behind the camera who documented anything and everything the army required, even though his true specialty was as an analyst of electronics and radar data.

The railroad bridge appeared to have been blown apart many months, perhaps even a year, earlier. In the river gorge below was the rusted-out wreckage of a locomotive and a German army supply train, as many as a dozen cars all together. The river currents swirled around and through them, adding fallen trees, weeds, and rocks to the piles of debris.

"*Sono io. L'ho fatto.* That's me. I did that," said Dolcetta. She drew a line across her throat. "*Ho ucciso molti nazisti.* Killed many Nazis."

Jake was taken aback yet again by her claim. Who were these women Lt. Foxx had brought along? A classical pianist and a partisan warrior? This was unlike any trip to the Met with his parents to hear Mozart's *Cosi Fan Tutte*.

"Pictures, Corporal, get snapping. We've heard all about this attack at HQ. A fortunate detour after all. But be quick. We need to roll before those rains hit again."

Jake and the lieutenant walked over to the side of the bridge to examine the wreckage below. As ordered, he began to take recon pictures, while Foxx continued to explain.

"Yes, Dolcetta had described the attack by her team of partisans in her debriefing, but until now, no one at the base had seen it firsthand. Superior work. Took the bridge out just as the locomotive was crossing. Look there. A perfect demolition and the rest of the train followed her into the ravine. Can't tell you how many of our boys' lives she saved by taking out those Germans. The best battles in a war are the one you don't have to fight. Yes, a real work of art."

At least two Panzer tanks and a half dozen field artillery pieces were among the wreckage along with cases of what had probably been ammunition and small arms. Jake made certain he captured it all on film before returning to the jeep where Dolcetta sat stoic and quiet in the front seat. Who was this girl in green who blew up bridges and killed Nazis? Even Greta looked upon her fellow traveler with awe and respect. No frivolous "Dorabella" or "Fiordiligi," were these two young women.

They drove on. The road past the bridge was even more torturous than before. Old bomb craters filled with rainwater and mud, pockmarked what little asphalt remained and made driving even more dangerous as they were often filled with tire-shredding shrapnel.

Howard Jay Smith

And the closer they came toward Vittorio Veneto, Dolcetta's professed hometown, the nearer the holes and craters were to each other. Getting between them without driving off the road was akin to threading a needle at twenty miles an hour. The lieutenant's driving skills were truly put to the test, but as they passed an abandoned farm house just a single kilometer out of Vittorio Veneto, his luck ran out.

The right rear wheel of the jeep caught the lip of one such crater and a bit of shrapnel blew out the tire. The jeep spun violently into a ninety-degree turn, which snagged the left rear tire, blowing it out as well.

Ever the good soldiers, Jake and the lieutenant exited the jeep and surveyed the damage. Two tires gone and only one spare.

Dolcetta spoke up to tell them that there is a *meccanico*, a car mechanic, just ahead at the edge of the village of Vittorio Veneto. As always, Lt. Foxx took charge. With military precision, he ordered Jake to replace one tire with the spare and then, when he finishes, they'll attempt to have the jeep limp into town to have the other one replaced.

So as to preserve his good clothes as much as possible from the mud and dirt, Jake rolled up his cuffs and then taking off his top coat and dress uniform shirt, tossed them in the back of the jeep. In good order the lieutenant slipped rocks under the other tires to prevent the vehicle from rolling as Jake began to jack up the jeep.

Greta sat down on a boulder by the side of the road to watch and wait, but Dolcetta, their young partisan fighter, joined the men in their effort. Like any army motor pool grunt, she wrestled the spare off its mount and rolled it over to Jake just as he pulled the blown tire off its hub.

As Jake then worked at positioning the spare onto the wheel, he sensed Dolcetta over his shoulder staring at his two hands, an action that made him most uncomfortable and a little bit embarrassed. Jake had a birth defect or more accurately a family genetic trait that normally no one ever noticed except when he played the piano. His right pinkie finger was abnormally long, as long as his ring finger, while the left pinkie was abnormally short. His father had it as well and reputedly so did his grandfather and every other male in their family. Growing up, his friends in school had often teased him about this oddity, which made him highly self-conscious of the defect, so much so that to prevent it from being noticed he often curled his fingers under his palms. But mounting the wheel left him exposed so he made quick work of the repairs.

If she had noticed though, the khaki clad girl said nothing.

Just as Jake finished, a light drizzle began to fall. Speaking fluent German, the lieutenant instructed Greta to take over the driving while he walked ahead to direct her around the worst of the potholes. Jake and Dolcetta were assigned to trail behind the wounded jeep so as to push whenever that might become necessary. In this way they ever so slowly began to cover that last kilometer to Vittorio Veneto.

Each of the several times the jeep became stuck in a pothole, Jake and Dolcetta set their hands on the back of the vehicle and pushed with all they had. It was a messy task and both their trousers were splattered ever more by mud. And each time they pushed, Jake tried to hide his pinkie fingers from her gaze.

But Dolcetta, who was not the least bit self-conscious, rapidly changed the mood from tragedy to comedy by singing aloud in a crystal clear and powerful soprano voice, "Non più andrai." And as Jake and Dolcetta pushed the jeep out of the mud yet again, all four of them joined together like a chorus in belting out Mozart's soldier's song of self-deprecating humor.

No more, you amorous butterfly,
Will you go fluttering round by night and day,

> *Disturbing the peace of every beauty,*
> *A little Narcissus and Adonis of love.*
> *No more will you have those fine feathers,*
> *That light and dashing cap,*
> *Those curls, those airs and graces,*
> *Those womanish rosy cheeks.*
> *Among soldiers, by Bacchus!*
> *A huge moustache, a little knapsack,*
> *A musket on your back, a saber at your side,*
> *Your neck straight, your head erect,*
> *A big helmet, or a big head dress,*
> *Lots of honor, very little pay.*
> *And instead of the fandango,*
> *A march through the mud.*
> *Over mountains, through valleys,*
> *With snow, and days of endless heat,*
> *To the music of trumpets,*
> *Of bombards, and of cannons,*
> *Which, at every boom,*
> *Will make bullets whistle past your ear.*
> *Cherubino, on to victory!*
> *On to military glory!*
> *On to military glory!"*

When they finished, Jake asked her in Italian, "So you know the opera."

"Certo! Of course, I do. Every song from *The Marriage of Figaro*, most of *Don Giovanni*, and even some of *Cosi Fan Tutte*. The man who wrote those lyrics for Mozart, the Abbé Lorenzo Da Ponte, was an Italian priest from the Veneto. During the war, when we were camped up in the hills, we sang at night to keep our spirits up. And you, you remind me of Figaro himself."

"What do you mean?"

Dolcetta turned to Jake and said just above a whisper so none of the others would hear, "*Sei un Ebreo di Ceneda.*"

"A Jew from Ceneda?" Jake was taken aback and could not believe what she had just said. How had she known that?

She pointed to Jake's Jewish star that dangled out from under his tee shirt. "*Quella stella mi dice che sei ebreo e le tue mani mi dicono che sei un Conegliano di Ceneda,*" which Jake knew translated as, "That star tells me you are a Jew and your hands tell me you are a Conegliano from Ceneda. Those hands are like Figaro's birthmark."

Jake was even more astonished when Dolcetta pulled out a Jewish star from under her turtleneck that she wore on a chain around her neck. Her star was carved onto a crushed bullet casing. "*Sono anche un'ebrea di Ceneda*—I am also a Jew from Ceneda."

Thoroughly confused, Jake could only speak in fragments, "But you, but you . . . *Hai detto che eri di Vittorio Veneto*—You said you were from Vittorio Veneto."

By now they were close to town. Dolcetta nodded in the direction of the first building on the outskirts which was indeed the auto garage, a two-story building with an apartment upstairs. A faded sign read, "*Meccanico di Ceneda.*"

Dolcetta explained to him in greater detail that Ceneda, had been renamed Vittorio Veneto after that battle she spoke of earlier, the one that ended the First World War. "Vittorio Veneto is Ceneda. Welcome home, *Ben tornado.*"

She continued to describe how, before the war, there was once a thriving Jewish community of perhaps twenty families who had lived in the area for hundreds of years. A few still resided in the confines of the old ghetto when the war broke out, including the Coneglianos. All the males in that family for many generations had the same hand anomaly. As soon as she saw Jake's fingers she knew.

"Are there any Coneglianos still in Ceneda? My parents would be thrilled to know I met them."

"*No, nessuno.* No one." Dolcetta verily choked on her words as she wiped her eyes, the first display of emotion Jake had seen from her.

Jake wondered, were those rain drops or genuine tears? Though this tough partisan girl quickly composed herself, he guessed tears. "Were any Jews survivors?"

She held up two fingers, then used them to wipe her face again. "*Solo io e mio grande zio, il rabbino Spinoziano*—Just me and my great uncle, Rabbi Spinoziano."

Dolcetta went on to explain that she and her elderly uncle were away deep in the mountains delivering supplies to a remote monastery, Santa Ava della Stelle, where one of their distant cousins, a Benedictine monk, lived when the Germans took control of the town and its railroad hub at the end of 1943. Her uncle was sheltered by the Benedictines as one of their own until the war ended, and she joined the partisans and became a fighter at fifteen. Everyone else, including her own mother and father, sisters and brothers, aunts and uncles, cousins and neighbors, friends and strangers—all Jews—were either murdered on the spot or transported away to the Nazi death camps back in Germany. When the war ended, Dolcetta and her uncle returned to the village. They hoped other survivors would also come home. They waited months, but no one did. She and her uncle had become the last Jews of Ceneda—and when they were gone, five hundred years of history would disappear as well.

As Jake looked up at the village shrouded in fog on the hill before him, the very place where his parents had been born, whatever joy he might have felt to have at last found their hometown was vanquished by the horrors of the war and the truths Dolcetta had just shared.

The drizzle had turned into a light but steady rain by the time they were able to maneuver the jeep into an open garage bay. The *Meccanico di Ceneda* building was itself an ancient relic of a bygone era. Old wagon wheels and horse tack that hung on the walls, betrayed its origin as a livery stable and stagecoach stop. Jake reclaimed his dress shirt and winter coat while Dolcetta introduced her companions to the local mechanic, Ferruccio Fresia, a man whom she had known from the village since her childhood. He was with his granddaughter, Olivia, a highly curious girl of perhaps eight who delighted in being her grandfather's assistant. Ferruccio also owned one of the few telephones in the entire town, but only by virtue of the fact that his shop was the closest building to the main road in and out of town. Ferruccio, a veteran of the First World War, had a maimed left leg and walked with a decided limp.

Translating for the lieutenant, Jake explained their dilemma. With Olivia trailing close behind, Ferruccio examined the jeep and then the damaged tires, shaking his head all the while. Olivia mimicked him. There was nothing he could do, both tires had shredded sidewalls and were therefore impossible to repair. And when asked if there might be a replacement wheel in the village, Ferruccio told them no, "*La guerra ha preso tutto.*" The war has taken everything. But he was confident that he might find one in Treviso, as it was a big enough city with many cars and trucks.

Jake translated a back-and-forth conversation between the lieutenant and Ferruccio as to how to proceed. Finally, Lt. Foxx announced his decision and the logic behind it.

Ferruccio's truck only had room for three counting the driver. Jake was to remain behind with the jeep while the mechanic would drive with Foxx and one of the ladies in his truck to Treviso. After buying the replacement tire, the lieutenant would remain in Treviso while Ferruccio returned home with the new wheel. Jake would finish the repairs and then join him in Treviso.

Given that Greta did not know the roads in this region and Dolcetta did, Foxx decided that they switch partners for the moment: Greta would accompany him to Treviso now, while Dolcetta would remain behind so that she could help Jake navigate the roads later that day. They would leave immediately.

When Jake translated the lieutenant's plan to the two women, the switch caught Greta off guard. She was sincerely disappointed, a sadness she shared with Jake. For his part, Jake explained that it was only for a few hours before they would be reunited, and that he, as a mere corporal had to follow orders—even if those orders meant surrendering the pleasure of her company to Lt. Foxx for the afternoon.

Greta hugged Jake and kissed him on both cheeks. But after starting to walk toward Ferruccio's truck, Greta quickly turned back, grabbed Jake and wrapping him tightly in her arms, gave him a full on lip-smacking embrace. Out of the corner of his eye, Jake spied little Olivia watching as if taking notes.

And as this was Jake's first kiss in three years, the two of them did not break from their embrace until the lieutenant—his patience over—ordered them to finish up and get a move on. Time was wasting.

The rains were beginning to fall ever heavier as Ferruccio's truck pulled out of the garage and onto the road to Treviso. From somewhere off in the village, church bells rang out for the noon hour, shaking Jake out of his love-sick reverie and reminding him that it was indeed a Sunday.

Dolcetta motioned for him to follow her into the labyrinth of alleys and byways that constituted Ceneda, "Come, *mangiamo*, we eat."

Chapter Two: Dolcetta

Sunday afternoon, January 27, 1946
Ceneda, the Veneto, Italy

Mozart. Yes, it was Mozart's Birthday. As Jake followed Dolcetta, he reflected on the peculiar irony of being stranded on Mozart's birthday with a Jewish partisan fighter in the town of his parents' births listening to the chimes muffled by the fog of the very same church bells that had peeled off the hours all through a childhood they had once described as magical. But now, as the rain fell, they reminded him more of Mozart's *Requiem* for the dead, and all that had vanished in a cesspool of hate and violence.

Dolcetta led him on a path that climbed up through the village. Their track had so many twists and turns that Jake, a trained cartographer with an excellent sense of direction, could not fathom where they were headed. Built on a hill at the lower edge of the Alps, Ceneda eschewed straight lines. Everything was contorted. One house seemed piled upon another but at odd angles. And one family's attic would have been another's basement. Although Jake could not make heads or tails of where they were or even which direction they were facing, he imagined that his parents, growing up here as children, had known every brick and stone of this village.

About halfway up the hillside they passed through a gate that marked the entrance to the old Jewish ghetto. As they walked through, Dolcetta pointed out a rusted mezuzah nailed to the inner post below a street sign that read, "*Via Giudecca.*" She told him that in centuries past—up until Napoleon's victories over the ruling Austrian aristocracy—the gate would have been locked every night in order to separate Jews and their religious heresies from their Catholic neighbors. The unspoken truth, however, was always the real fear: the perceived need to prevent cross boundary romances and the exchange of bodily fluids. In reality she said, over five centuries there were many "mixed" marriages and other more secretive liaisons. Regardless of religion, she asserted, everyone in Ceneda was family, blood family. Everyone, even the Fascists who had sided with the Nazis.

Inside the ghetto all was quiet; most every corner was deserted save one light that shone from a building that was once the synagogue of Ceneda.

"The eternal light still glows?" Jake asked in Italian.

"No," she said, also in her native tongue, "That was extinguished three years ago when the Nazis ransacked the synagogue. What you see is my uncle working at his office next door." Dolcetta explained that since Rabbi Geremia Spinoziano, who was eighty-seven years old, had returned at war's end from hiding out at the monastery, he had dedicated himself to gathering up all the surviving records, photographs, books, furniture, musical instruments, and important papers that had been left behind by the former residents of the ghetto. The temple's main sanctuary, which had been desecrated by the Germans, had become in essence a storeroom. With no longer having any sheep in his flock to serve, the rabbi took on as his life's final work the sorting and preservation of every key element that documented the history of their community before it all vanished.

"What happens when he's done? Where do the records go? Who will look after them?"

"*Non lo so.* I don't know. He's almost finished, and it will probably fall to me to keep these records, these holy records, the genizah, but I . . . *Non ho più casa,* I have no home and cannot imagine living here in Ceneda much longer among ghosts."

"Then the history of Ceneda dies?"

The girl in green shrugged, "Perhaps." She looked at him straight in the eyes. "Perhaps you, Jacopo Conegliano, the last of the Coneglianos, you should bring the records of our town's history, our sacred genizah, to a new Ceneda that you will create in America."

Before Jake could even formulate or consider an answer, Dolcetta opened the door of the synagogue. Rabbi Geremia Spinoziano, a sprightly, but gray-haired man who wore a red beret and a black suit that was nearly indistinguishable from the garb worn by the Abbé Luigi Hudal, rose to greet them. He embraced his grandniece with a warm hug, and then after a quick introduction to Jake, he welcomed the young corporal with an ever more enthusiastic bear-hug.

"*Un figlio prodigo è tornato,*" said the rabbi, a prodigal son has returned.

Lunch with the rabbi in the kitchen of his apartment adjacent to the synagogue was an unusual affair for Jake. In addition to the four bottles of prosecco that Dolcetta brought up from a wine cellar cleverly hidden beneath the basement, it began and ended with a single dish, typical winter fare for peasants living in the mountains: heaps of pasta—in this case *gemelli*—prepared carbonara-style using eggs and a local soft cheese not unlike parmesan, mixed with grilled bits of ham and sliced almonds. Jake ate his fill and drank the prosecco with the same abandon any battle-weary GI would have done on the first hours of a four-day pass.

And it also marked the first time since he was a child at Van Cortland Park in the Bronx with his mother and her friends that he spoke exclusively in Italian as their host, Geremia, knew no English.

But it was the ham that caught Jake by surprise, not exactly kosher, he thought for a rabbi and so he asked him about it.

"Ah, white meat," laughed Geremia. "You're as curious as your father, Abe, was when he was a boy. A good trait. Did you know that I officiated at his bar mitzvah? That was when . . . before the First World War . . . yes . . . 1913. He was brilliant, a great student, one of my best ever—save, perhaps, for my grandniece here, Dolcetta. Abe not only knew the Torah but also the sciences, literature, poetry, and of course opera. He loved opera. He even sent me recordings from New York. It was in his blood, which doesn't surprise me. Everyone in Ceneda loves opera. And you say Abe still sells sound and lighting equipment to the Met in New York?"

"Yes, but what about the ham? You were going to explain?" Mellowed by the alcohol, Jake had taken an almost immediate liking to the Rabbi. Geremia had the countenance of a New York Chinese restaurant Buddha, a laughing, smiling happy *Ho Tai* who somehow, in the midst of hell and destruction, had found the means to preserve and maintain both spirit and dignity.

"Impatient too, just like him as well. Your father wanted to know everything—but yesterday. He devoured books as readily as you've vanquished your pasta and that prosecco," the rabbi said as he refilled Jake's glass. The walls of Geremia's apartment were insulated from the outside world by endless shelves, each stuffed with volumes of books. "Abe read all of them, as did she before the war," he added pointing with the bottle of prosecco at Dolcetta, who blushed. "An education is the one possession thieves can never steal."

Since their arrival at the synagogue an hour earlier, Dolcetta had changed out of her muddy clothes and into a turquoise cotton shirtwaist dress. She had untied her braids and combed out her long chestnut hair, but she still wore the only shoes she probably owned, those combat boots. And although images of Greta's blue eyes and warm lips flashed through his mind, Jake could not help but notice how much more attractive Dolcetta was, even in a simple A-line dress. And for him the concept of attractiveness went far beyond the physical. There was depth and intelligence, strength, and fortitude, all softened by an infinite sweetness. He wondered how Greta was faring in the company of the lieutenant. Still he'd never met anyone quite like Dolcetta, a dark-haired girl with whom he felt a kinship and familiarity that utterly surprised and caught him off guard. And speaking exclusively Italian with her and the rabbi made him feel even more at home—he knew with certainty he was among his own people for the first time since being shipped off to war.

"But you were inquiring about the ham, weren't you," asked Geremia over the drumming of the rain on the windowpanes. What had been a light shower had now become a major downpour.

"Yes, sir," said Jake, very much enjoying his prosecco.

"Please," said the rabbi, "None of this 'sir,' nonsense. We are all family here. You should call me Geremia. Even your grandfather and I were friends growing up here." He turned to Dolcetta. "In the genizah chest in my study, there's a package of photographs. Please, my dear, bring it here."

Dolcetta made her way through a wide archway into the rabbi's office, where a fire roared away in its hearth, keeping the entire downstairs of the house warm. The bond of affection between uncle and niece was clearly obvious to Jake, and Jake, well, Jake was a happy young man just watching Dolcetta walk wearing that soft cotton dress. He could not but help notice how she moved with the grace of a willow tree swaying in a soft summer breeze.

"How is it a reverent Jew can eat ham? That is what you want to know, yes?" asked Geremia.

"Yes, sir."

"Geremia. You must call me Geremia, just as you father and grandfather did. You have their hands, their fingers, but you also have their heart, their soul, and their intellect. Let me tell you then and never forget this: true religion has nothing to do with theology, liturgical ceremonies, sectarian dogma, or dietary rules. When I hid out in that monastery, I became for three years a monk. Not on the inside, but on the outside. I shared the life my cousin, Adriano, and his brethren had taken on, and in so doing, I survived the Holocaust that swirled around us. I wore the black robes of a Benedictine with no less authority than if I had been a Harlequin during Carnevale. It was a costume, one I wore to camouflage myself, one that allowed me to live and ultimately return home to myself. And now, I wear this red beret—a hat our ancestors were once forced to wear outside the ghetto—as my tribute to the dead and murdered among us. As soldiers in a uniform, you and my Dolcetta have done the same, yes?"

Dolcetta returned with the photographs and set them on the table before her uncle.

Geremia leaned in close to Jake. "Do you know what God is—if there is even such an entity as God after all we have witnessed these past few years? God is not the providential, awe-inspiring deity as claimed by the children of Abraham and Isaac. God is but the fundamental, eternal, infinite substance of reality, the first cause of all things, and the substance of all things. God is not a judge who rules upon how well matters conform to his purposes. Nor is God a wise and just being who resides in a heavenly throne while making exceptions to the natural law because we either anger or please him. No, God, my God, the God I called my congregation to honor, is only the natural universe in all its unique, infinite, and eternal glory. There is no judgment. And this insight, which is openly available to all, leads us to the highest state of human accord. Happiness occurs when one understands and accepts the laws of nature and then experiences the peace of mind such knowledge brings. For me true religion only consists of one simple moral rule: love your neighbor. Yes, marry one another. And then practice justice and loving kindness with your fellow human beings on this lifeboat we call planet earth."

For Jake, the rabbi's simple but profound humanism stood in opposition from the Abbé Luigi Hudal's guilt laden and anti-Semitic tirades earlier that morning.

The rabbi opened up the portfolio holding a collection of faded black and white photographs. He flipped through them until he came to one taken more than thirty years earlier inside the synagogue of Ceneda. Four people stood below a glowing Eternal Light and in front of an open ark. In the center was Jake's father, Abe, at age thirteen, holding the Torah in his arms—his pinkie finger anomaly clearly visible. Behind him stood a younger Geremia dressed in his rabbinical robes and on either side of Abe, were his parents, Jake's grandparents.

"Here you see in the past your family, a splendid past, but when I look at you two on the cusp of tomorrow," he said glancing back and forth between Dolcetta and Jake as if they were indeed a couple. "I see the future of our people. Isn't that the true message of *The Marriage of Figaro* that you will see tonight? True love prevails over all threats and that the potential for a life of harmony and joy is infinite and must not be squandered?"

Such talk made Dolcetta uncomfortable. Nudging her uncle, she asked, "Will you tell him about the ham, already?"

Well into his fifth or sixth glass of prosecco, Jake— lightheaded as he had become—was anything but impatient, he hung on Geremia's every sentence as the rabbi continued.

"Yes, I will. The dietary kosher laws are no more sacred that this photograph. They were constructed in ancient times to protect people from eating food that was easily subject to contamination and disease. For someone today to hold these laws out as more important than life itself is nonsense. Those guidelines became law only to protect our lives, not destroy them. And so, when I was a monk, and when I was near to starvation and again when I returned home and there is still very little food about, I ate all the ham and pork I could to nourish this old body of mine and stay alive. To have done otherwise would be an aberration of the love and wisdom that is at the heart of Judaism."

The rabbi interrupted himself and turned to address Dolcetta, "And the manner in which you grilled those bits of chopped ham along with the slivered almonds was perfection itself. If there is a Heaven in my future, my dear Dolcetta, your cooking certainly opened the door."

"The secret, Uncle, was grilling them together until they turned a smoky brown, and then and only then adding them to the pasta, egg and cheese."

"It was fabulous," piped up Jake. "As magnificent a cook as my mother was, I have never tasted a carbonara as good as this."

"*Carbonara gemelli ebraico*," said Dolcetta.

"Ah, you see Jacopo, she cooks like an angel, she cleans up like a goddess, and she kills Nazis with bare hands. And one day my little niece will make a fine wife for some lucky man . . ."

Geremia let his last words hang in the air before continuing. "And do you want to know what Judaism truly is? I will tell you the secret, it is this: When you warm other people's hearts, you warm yourself. When you support, encourage and inspire others, then you will discover support, encouragement, and inspiration in your own life. And when you love and when others love and honor you, you create family and community. That, my children, is Judaism, that is love, and that is my blessing for both of you."

Geremia got up from his chair and walked over to a table in the study where a hand-cranked phonograph sat beside an upright piano and a rocking chair. He shuffled through a collection of records and finally, after loading one, he motioned for Jake and Dolcetta to come into the study and sit upon a couch near the fire. "I am going to play but one song, one I am sure you both know. The music was composed by Mozart, but the lyrics were written by a man who grew up here, a man who understood the longings and passions of the human soul, the Abbé Lorenzo Da Ponte. It is a duet from his opera, *Don Giovanni*, where it is used as a sly seduction song."

" 'La ci darem la mano,' " both Jake and Dolcetta immediately said aloud.

"Ah, yes, indeed. My two little scholars here are correct. But bear with me. Instead of picturing Don Giovanni singing this as a song of deliberate and wanton seduction over a hapless Zerlina, I want you both to close your eyes and hear it instead as if it were sung by a love-struck Figaro to his beloved Susanna. Listen here and then examine what is in your own hearts."

As the needle touched the vinyl the old 78 crackled alive with a *recitativo*. Jake instantly recognized the voices, "*Dio mio*, that's the Met's recording of *Don Giovanni*! Ezio Pinza and Rosa Ponselle. February 5, 1934. I was there. My father helped with the recording. I was just nine. It was my birthday."

"Wonderful. Yes. It is one of the albums your father sent me years ago," said Geremia, pausing the record. "Life comes full circle when we least expect it. But no, Ponselle played Dona Anna. Editha Fleischer sang Zerlina. Now, again, close your eyes. Both of you. Sit back and let your dreams rule the day."

Jake did as instructed and, warmed by the prosecco, he slid back into the same half-awake dream he had been in earlier that day when the Abbé Luigi Hudal first knocked on his door. Beside him he heard Dolcetta breathing softly as Geremia reset the needle to the *recitativo*. And as the rabbi had directed, Jake surrendered the image of the ever-sly Don Giovanni and found instead a madly-in-love Figaro singing to his beloved Susanna as the music began.

The male voice sang in *recitativo*:
> *With noble birth, noble manners*
> *Go always hand in hand;*
> *I'll show you an example;*
> *This very moment I will make you my wife.*

The female soprano responded:
> *You?*

He continued in *recitativo*:
> *I, for certain: Come to my little villa,*
> *Oh, come, my fairest jewel,*
> *There I will wed thee.*

In his mind's eye Jake became Figaro while a vision of Greta as Botticelli's Venus rose naked from the sea, her long red hair swirling around and caressing him as if the arms of a sea creature.

The male voice segued into full song:
> *There I'll give you my hand,*
> *There you'll say yes:*
> *See, it is not far,*
> *my love, let's leave, my beloved.*

Jake saw himself luring this dream Greta toward him; she's tempted but hesitant.

She sang:
> *I would like to, yet I would not,*
> *My heart trembles a little,*
> *It's true, I would be happy,*
> *But he may just be deceiving me!*

But he may just be deceiving me!

Jake's arms reached out toward Greta.

He sang:

Come, my beautiful beloved!

His vision of Greta leaned in and then retreated again into the fog—where he saw Lt. Foxx reaching for her.

She sang:

I'm sorry for Masetto.

He sang:

I will change your life.

Jake reached for her but Greta's image began to fade . . .

She sang:

Soon I won't be able to resist,
I won't be able to resist,
I won't be able to resist.

He sang:

Let us go!

Greta's arms reached toward him but it was too late. The lieutenant pulled her away.

She sang:

Let us go!

Greta vanished into the mists of illusion.

He sang:

There I'll give you my hand,
There you'll say yes:
See, it is not far,
My love, let's leave, my beloved.

And once more in his mind's eye he lured her back. But no, it wasn't Greta, it was Dolcetta. What was she doing there?

She sang:

I would like to, yet I would not,
My heart trembles a little,
It's true, I would be happy,
But he may just be deceiving me!

But he may just be deceiving me!
He sang:
I will change your life.

Jake reached for this vision of Dolcetta, but she too hesitates.

She sang:
Soon I won't be able to resist
I won't be able to resist.

Dolcetta swayed back and forth in her turquoise dress. He fell to his knees before her.

He sang:
Let us go!
Let us go!

Dolcetta took his hands in hers.

She sang:
Let us go!
Let us go!

She lifted him up and they sang together:
Come, come, my darling,
To soothe the pangs
Of an innocent love.
Come, come, my darling,
To soothe the pangs
Of an innocent love.

Hand in hand they moved off toward the fog of illusions.

He sang:
Let us go!

But as he looked into her eyes, one turned as crystal blue as Greta's, the other remained as dark as Dolcetta's.

She sang:
Let us go!
Let us go!

Who was this woman he saw taking him away? He felt sleepy and confused.

He sang:
> *Let us go!*

And he surrendered to her, whoever she was, as his eyes closed.

They sang together:
> *Come, come, my darling,*
> *To soothe the pangs*
> *Of an innocent love.*
> *Come, come, my darling,*
> *To soothe the pangs*
> *Of an innocent love.*

All three of them were asleep by the time the song ended, no doubt victims of excessive prosecco, Jake and Dolcetta on the couch and Geremia in his rocker beside the phonograph, which continued to go round and round and round.

They all remained inside their own private dreams until, for the second time that day, a knock at the door woke not only Jake, but Dolcetta as well. Jake looked down and saw his own hand wrapped around Dolcetta's.

She noticed it too and gently slid her hand free, but not before giving Jake a peck on the cheek. "You're sweet," she said as she stood up.

Jake blushed.

Dolcetta stopped the record player, and then started back toward the front door where she found Ferruccio's wife, Anna and their granddaughter, Olivia, standing there in the rain with a tattered *ombrello* shielding them from the storm.

Anna informed Dolcetta that Ferruccio had called from Treviso with a message for Jake from Lt. Foxx. "They're safe, they found a spare tire but the roads are flooded and they will not be able to return for a day or two or even three until the flood waters recede." And Anna, upon seeing Jake on the couch, spoke directly to him, "The lieutenant's last words were for you Corporal, 'Stay dry, enjoy Ceneda, and await further orders.'"

Jake thanked her, "*Grazie mille*, thank you for coming out to tell us this in such bad weather."

Olivia responded before her mother could, "*Prego*, you're welcome." The ever-curious girl then turned to Dolcetta, "Are you going to kiss him too?"

"I just did." laughed Dolcetta.

Olivia's eyes went wild, "Whoa! *Veramente?*"

"Yes, Said Dolcetta. "*Veramente.*"

Their exchange woke Geremia, who upon seeing his neighbors at the door, welcomed them in.

Anna declined, "Time to take this little devil to church," she said, referring to Olivia.

After they left, Geremia, Dolcetta, and Jake discussed the situation. The rabbi began, "Well, my young friends, it seems fate has conspired to bring us all together, hasn't it?"

"Since when do you believe in fate?" laughed Dolcetta.

"Of course, I do not believe in fate, certainly not more than I do superstitions, but . . ."

"But what, Uncle?"

"As I was saying, since fate has brought the three of us together on this most auspicious day, we should meet it head on, embrace it, and find glory in it."

"I don't understand," said Jake. All he could imagine was the odd calculus of Treviso: Lt. Foxx, Greta, and Ferruccio. Two hotel rooms and three guests, how would that turn out? Would the lieutenant try to seduce Greta? Would she succumb? Or would Foxx, Lt. Enrico Foxx, a man named for the great stage tenor, Enrico Caruso, be the gentleman and bunk with Ferruccio and leave the second room for her alone?

"Though fortune, my son, handed you a four-day pass, those same fates have also brought a great storm to wash you up upon the shores of your family's ancient home—it's straight out of Mozart's *Idomeneo*. And here you sit in the company of this dying rabbi and a beautiful young woman—one who has literally killed for her right to be alive here beside us. God works in mysterious ways and . . ."

Dolcetta finished his sentence, ". . . And even though you don't believe in God having mysterious ways to work, you believe Jake needs to take advantage of this opportunity, yes?"

"Ah, yes, but not just Jake, all of three of us have been handed raw gold to forge into beauty and wonder." The rabbi refilled all of their glasses with fresh prosecco. "*Saluti*, this calls for more celebration. First," he said turning back to Jake, "there is certainly no problem with you staying here until they return. It is after all, your birthright."

"What are you saying, my birthright? *Non lo capisco*." asked Jake.

"Oh, many years ago, long before even I was born, this apartment, my study, the downstairs anyway, was not always part of the synagogue. My family, the Spinozianos lived upstairs, and your family, the Coneglianos, lived right here.

Jake was stunned. "Here? Right here?"

"Yes, yes, for hundreds of years. In a village as old as this, homes and houses are always being renovated, remodeled, and changed around. Your family lived in these very rooms. Let this couch be your bed. And," he said upon opening a wardrobe cabinet and pulling out a thick feather quilt, "this should keep you warm as well. It too once belonged to the Coneglianos."

"Unbelievable," said Jake, his mind reeling. "Thank you. Thank you."

Dolcetta examined the quilt. "My God, it's beautiful, and judging by the fabric and design, it must be a hundred years old."

"Perhaps more, perhaps as old as Ceneda itself," said Geremia. "Assembling a single quilt took an endless number of feathers. Once made, it was kept forever, passed from one generation to another. It too would have been in the Bronx by now save for the fact your grandparents ran out of room to ship it to America. So here it is, yours again. And speaking of Mozart, I know you must be disappointed not to be seeing *The Marriage of Figaro* tonight, but I have something here in the genizah trunk that just might assuage your pain."

Geremia lifted out a cloth bundle from the open chest and set it on his desk. He untied the knot and let the cloth fall away, revealing five faded, yellowed, torn and water-stained leather-bound notebooks. One was labeled "Venice"; the next, "Vienna"; the third, "Prague"; the fourth, "London"; and the fifth and largest, "New York." "These are the diaries, the secret diaries of Mozart's librettist, the Abbé Lorenzo Da Ponte, the ones he dare not publish in his lifetime for fear their content would endanger . . . " Geremia stopped, shook his head with a grimace before continuing. "Consider them my gift to your family in exchange for all of those wonderful opera recordings your father has sent me."

Both Dolcetta and Jake were speechless and dumbfounded. They immediately crowded around the table to look at these frail survivors from the distant past. Geremia handed Jake the "Vienna" volume. He could not believe what he was holding in his hands, Da Ponte's diaries. He was almost too taken aback to even open it, but when he finally went to look inside, it fell open to a page in the middle where there was a sort of bookmark, a thin pointer made of twisted brass —very old itself—with a tiny hand at the end. Jake recognized it as a yad, a pointer one uses when reading the Torah so as not to contaminate the pages of that sacred book with human body oils.

Jake struggled to read aloud the crisp handwritten entries and it suddenly became apparent that though he spoke Italian fluently he lacked the fundamentals of reading. "*Dopo... aver... lasciato... il ristorante, sono... tornato... a casa ... da solo...*"

Sensing his troubles, Dolcetta stepped in and took over. "After leaving the restaurant, I returned home alone to work on the libretto for Don Giovanni. Not so for Casanova. Inspired, my aging lothario of a friend, departed with the two young nubiles, Magda and Mora, clinging to each arm. His adroit maneuver left Mozart—the ever-amorous Mozart—alone to pursue his affair with Storace. Yes, his wife, Constanze, was away again in Baden, not that it mattered a wit to Mozart. Her presence would have only altered his technique and timing. Mozart's seduction of Storace, our prima diva for The Marriage of Figaro, struck me then and there as identical to the manner in which he slid Angela Tiepolo away from me in Venice when we first met there on his birthday during Carnevale of 1771. I realized then, that Mozart himself, not Casanova, would be my true inspiration for the character of Don Giovanni. Yes, in truth, it was Mozart whom I pictured when I wrote the lyrics for "*La che darem la mano.*"

"Mozart? Casanova? Storace? Da Ponte? This is unbelievable," said Jake. "How is it possible you have these?"

"Tomorrow. Tomorrow I will give you the whole story; it's in my notebooks. Right now, I am a tired old man who needs to go upstairs to bed. But in the morning, oh, I'll tell you the whole megillah. It is a story perhaps more fascinating than the diaries themselves.

"*Per favore*, Uncle, not even a hint of how these came into your possession before you leave us?" asked Dolcetta.

"*Certo*. Father Adriano, my cousin who had sheltered me at the monastery; he was ninety. Adriano passed away right after the war ended but he left these treasures in my safekeeping," said the rabbi. His grandmother was a Da Ponte, and they had been handed down through the family.

The rest I will tell you in the morning over coffee and a good breakfast. Now they are yours. Oh, and Dolcetta, there's still some of that *crostata di pistacchio* you baked for me in the bread box."

After Geremia went up to bed, Dolcetta and Jake returned to the couch by the fire with. "Venice," the first volume in hand. There they wrapped themselves in the warmth of the feather quilt. And so as to facilitate their examining the diary together, Dolcetta slid close to Jake, but when her leg brushed up against his, it triggered Jake's memory of Greta from that morning. Jake envisioned her Botticelli hair, her perfume, her white skin, and how soft she felt snuggled up against him. Where was she now? Waiting for the curtain to rise on *Figaro* with Foxx?

Dolcetta opened the diary to page one and together they began to read.

Chapter Three:
A Death in Venice

Late on a Sunday afternoon, January 27, 1771
Sailing on the Venetian Lagoon, Italy

"Mozart." The young brunette sitting at the stern of our ship and under an outsized oriental-style rain ombrello asked me if I had heard of Mozart.

We had been only a few minutes out of the port of Mestre when this most lovely *Dona Brunetta* in a dark green Carnevale gown first motioned for me to join her under the protection of her ombrello. How could I resist? We were the only two passengers late that afternoon as a rainstorm had turned the normally routine passage by sail across the lagoon to the island city of Venice into a bit of an odyssey, one in which I would have been better served to be as blind as Homer, for she, the chestnut-haired beauty was indeed a temptation as dangerous as any of those a Ulysses or Idomeneo had ever encountered.

Yes, there I was, a priest, a recently ordained seminarian, the honorable Abbé Lorenzo Da Ponte, finding shelter beside her on this, a lumber *barchétta* with reefed sails that hung heavy and low in the churning seas. I confess, never was there a man more ill-suited to an ecclesiastical career than I, for in truth I loved women and could have never imagined a life without seeking solace in their arms or being soothed and comforted by the sweet softness of their flesh.

And though I said "No" and asked, "Who is he, this Mozart?" I must confess my own desperate straits. I was more intrigued by several drops of rain that were ever so slowly and most tantalizingly sliding toward the cleavage that separated her breasts, a pair of exquisite fruits barely constrained by the bodice of her Carnevale gown. Yes, two drops, one on each side of her neck traced a path my fingertips would have loved to follow.

"He's a composer, a very young composer of opera," she said. "He's not well known as of yet, but I am sure he will achieve the fame his talents deserve. He resides with our family while in Venice."

"You live there . . . in Venice?" I inquired, but in all honesty too distracted by an image of my caressing her sweet fruits to observe the foolishness of my own question. "This is my first voyage to the city," I hastily added as our boat bounced and fell across the waves.

We each scrambled to maintain our balance on the stern bench. I clutched the rail behind us; she in turn steadied herself by grabbing my cassock just above my knee and digging her fingers in deep. The water droplet on the left side of her chest gained speed as it raced toward the paradise I imagined it would find in victory. And oh, how my soul ached for such a triumph.

"Yes, we live there," she replied "my four sisters and I. Your first trip? Oh, my dear Abbé, I doubt you will be disappointed with our *La Serenissima*. Few men ever are," she added as she turned and looked directly at my eyes. Could she see through the windows to my soul? Would she uncover my secret desires? Did she already know what I truly craved?

Yes. No. Yes. No, I was hapless and helpless and a fool, who could not bear to take my eyes off of this vixen. Oh, such was my state of despair at my poorly chosen profession. Here I was on the last legs of a journey to the most Catholic hostel belonging to the foundation that had supported my education, *La Pia Casa dei Catecumeni*, and all this dunce of a priest could envision was discovering my own Garden of Eden in the company of this young Carnevale sprite. Discreetly, from under the brim of my hat, a *cappello romano*, I watched the water droplets shimmer and bounce across her chest. In my accursed imagination I envisioned her home, a brothel with each sister more beautiful, more seductive than the proceeding one. Yes, in my fantasy this fool of a priest conjured up a veritable garden of feminine delights, an Eden filled with the aroma of perfumes, wines, and incense.

And who was this Mozart she spoke of? And how jealous I was of the nights he must be enjoying in their company. My soul was burning as if already consigned to the fires of hell. Would that my ultimate destination in Venice be the gambling halls of the Ridotto or the masked balls of Carnevale, instead of the cloistered libraries and corridors of *il centro di ritiro*, the retreat center at *La Pia Casa dei Catecumeni*.

I despised this vow of chastity, a burden taken on only due to my having come of age in a poor village where the path to priesthood offered the only means to quench my thirst for an education, one that suited my true nature and abilities. And though I was consistently praised for being first in all my classes by the fathers who taught me, I could only rate myself all the more an idiot for surrendering to the church the essential core of my being and the affections of a young woman from my village who love and destiny would have had me marry. And now the mere sight of this new siren of the seas had me drowning under the burden of that accursed vow. Oh, how it constrained my soul and condemned it to hell, a hell I never believed in even as a child.

The sails rattled above us as our boat continued to roll between the waves. The young brunette let go of my thigh and took one of my hands in hers and commented on how I was far too handsome to be a clergyman. Little could she have fathomed the degree to which the mere touch of feminine flesh stirred my manhood—or perhaps she did? Though this was my virgin trip to La Serenissima, I was no innocent myself. Had she sensed that? Did she know that I had loved another before accepting the yoke and chain of priesthood? Yes, one so very deeply that I suffered to this day at the pain of separation? Did she see through my disguise, that of an abbé? Could she, would she, know me as just a man? These are the questions an unhappy priest asks.

And if I succumbed to temptations, gladly tossing my priestly garb into the lagoon and taking up the mask and costumes of Carnevale, would she or any of her sisterhood welcome me into what my feeble mind envisioned as their secret palaces of pleasure?

As I gazed back at her eyes, deep dark pools that revealed naught but mystery, she—in wonder and awe—spoke yet again of him, that composer, that Mozart. This man, this Mozart. Was I condemned to despise him in a degree equal to her rapture?

"Are you fond of opera?" she asked as our boat fought the tides.

I nodded to conceal my ignorance. How could I tell this Dona Brunetta that I have never ever been to an opera? What poor *paesano* turned priest had such opportunities, especially when the only world I had seen outside my home was the globe that hung inside our seminary at Portogruaro? And the only theater I had ever experienced were the puppet shows and *Commedia dell' Arte* plays performed at the back of itinerant gypsy wagons in my childhood village. They'd appear like a phoenix in our town square at the end of each harvest season when the crops were piled thick in the marketplace and newly uncorked prosecco would flow freely at every table to ease the pain of our labors. Would my ignorance of opera scores and libretti push this elegant lady away from me? Would I become ever so less attractive as man, as a partner, as one she might conceivably couple with? Was she even listening?

"Why, just a month ago on St. Stephan's Day, in Milano's Teatro Regio Ducal we attended the premiere of '*Mitridate, Re di Ponto.*' Mozart's first . . . *È un genio*, he's a genius. . . The acclaim, the applause, oh, my lord, it was overwhelming."

"Mozart, *un genio*? Truly? *Veramente*?" I asked in response, thus utilizing one of the few tricks of my priestly trade: always use inquiry to mask one's own ignorance and in so doing, appear far wiser than the dunce I accounted myself to be.

"Mozart's *genio*," she continued—and it was obvious to me she adored this man I now hated—"Mozart's *genio*," she repeated, savoring the way the word for genius gathered itself in her throat and then emerged through pursed lips. "Mozart's *genio* revealed itself immediately," she declared, "through the music he composed. Oh, he awed me to the point of rapture." She paused, inhaled deeply, her chest rose and fell . . . until at last, composed, she went on. "Purely by dint of his talents, ahh. . . Mozart conducted the orchestra from the harpsichord. As if by magic he transformed a dusty old libretto into a magnificent treatise of raw emotion. Such tender pain . . . Suffering . . . Characters of flesh and blood, love and tears . . . Men and women so alive with conflicts and anguish . . . My sisters and I alternately wept and cheered."

I feigned further interest so as to prolong our conversation and perhaps infiltrate myself into the good graces of this lovely young woman. "How so? Please, tell me more," I said as we neared ever closer to the city and the probable termination of our communion. But all she wanted to do was rhapsodize upon this Mozart.

"Yes, Mozart," she said, raising her eyes toward the rain clouds above as if to indicate how high this man resided in her judgments. "I was stunned and overwhelmed to discover his mastery of drama and, oh, what a keen sense of human emotions he expressed. It flowed so effortlessly from his music." She continued her exposition of his talents while I humbled myself to distraction by observing those lovely, sparkling water droplets caressing her skin. "Indeed, his *genio* granted him the power to depict even the most extreme scenarios with precision and grace. Oh, talent so rare it left me breathless and demanding more and more."

I too needed more, much more but felt powerless to express them to her aloud. Instead, "Your account, it's fascinating, go on, please go on." Ahead, the mists over the lagoon lifted ever so much above the water so that I could see the quay out in the distance where we would be docking shortly.

She, for her part, continued on with damnable enthusiasm, "Ah, for example, when Aspasia, our prima donna—a soprano played by none other than Antonia Bernasconi—in her aria, 'Pallid Ombre' . . . oh, just brilliant and tragic. She longs for death, verily begs for it. Mozart then contrasts that with her lover, *Sifare*, his aria, sung by that castrato, Pietro Benedetti. His desperate inner turmoil . . . truly *allegro agitato*. I wept openly. My sisters too."

What began as feigned interest, sweet honey to lure my Dona Brunetta, had by now, I confess, become honest and genuine fascination. Her intellect, yes, her intellect pulled my eyes from her flesh to her soul. Yes, not only was she a temptation, this siren calling out to my soul clearly had a keen eye for observation and a depth of knowledge, traits that only made me feel ever more humbled and ashamed of my own purely carnal desires toward her.

"There's no precedent," she added, "No other opera offers up such delicious anguish, nor such an outpouring of grief and betrayal. Oh, and Mozart's handling of the characters, his ability to focus on their true, deep, and profound emotions . . . oh, it swept me away, yes, swept me away. My lord, such virtuosity. The applause, thunderous. And afterward? Everyone shouted praise of Mozart. *Magnifico!* Bravo!"

The few shared minutes of our brief journey together would soon end, and then? I knew not. It was growing dark. A few lights flickered here and there on shore. I hurried to say something, anything, "Do tell, what style was the libretto?" I asked, knowing little more than the scripts of Punch and Judy comedies and the laughter that followed when such childlike plays were performed in my village.

"What style?" she asked, surprised and raising her head abruptly, which caused more of the water droplets to tumble uncontrollably toward her cleavage. "Do you know Metastasio?"

Victory at last, a name I recognized. Metastasio, the Italian Court Poet of the Hapsburgs, a writer beloved by all who shared our Italian tongue. As a boy, I had found a volume of his complete works in my father's tannery. Gaspare Da Ponte, the patriarch of our family, was a leatherworker who was frequently called upon to bind books. The Metastasio was an exquisite edition, bound with carefully worked hides dyed in a deep maroon hue and embossed with golden lettering and decorations.

Often when my father's work was complete but not yet delivered to the lord or lady or clergyman who had placed that order, I would ferret that volume up to the attic and bury my imagination, dreams, and visions between those pages. So it was with the Metastasio, a 1757 Torino edition father had redone for a bishop in Milano. We were so poor that I had no formal education until at fourteen I went away to the seminary in Portogruaro. Prior to that, I was entirely self-taught. In my village, I was known as the *Spiritoso ignorante*—the ignorant genius. Metastasio's volumes and others like it were my only salvation until as a teenager I began a formal and precise education into the ways and beliefs of the most holy Catholic Church.

Metastasio inspired me. I would even copy out passages from his book while hiding in the attic. I remember that particular volume most of all because I spilled ink, a lot of ink, from my pen on my favorite poem, "The Lovers' Descent," in which an old soldier sought to teach a young and brash army officer, who was feverishly in love with his friend's wife, that morality rests in our reason's ability to control those actions incited by our emotions. Those who were morally weak and thus lacked this control—such as this arrogant cavalier—will fall prey to emotional dictates and suffer the poor consequences that inevitably follow. Had my father known what damage I had done to that volume, he would have beaten me senseless, but he never found out. Metastasio's poems and stories fed my desire for an education so I too could be a poet and author—and this most passionate aspiration became the same blessing and curse that had led me astray and into the priesthood.

"I adore Metastasio," I said with confidence, "And you?" I asked in exchange as our *barchétta* eased into a berth adjacent to the Arsenal.

"The opera, Mozart's interpretation of the libretto that is, was in the style of Metastasio. Well structured, graceful, and full of import and verve. Mozart, why he's every bit as much a *genio* as Metastasio."

"*Veramente?*"

The crew dropped sail and made fast to the mooring. The neighborhood was otherwise dark and deserted. We both stood up to exit. My lady, seeking balance, again took my hand. My flesh tingled with nervous anticipation.

"While it is said that every man, even a priest such as you, Father, has the apparatus to please a lover, how few are those men, those inspired by *genio* . . . Ah, those, a Mozart, a Casanova, those are the rare ones that can truly excite a woman."

She stepped out onto the quay and released my hand. Had she judged me worthy of her favors or had she just ruled me out? Was I the *genio* she sought or just the fool I knew myself to be? Best wager on the latter. It was fully dark by now and the rains continued as if they were tears that measured the depth of my desolation. I followed her off the boat, praying against all hope and reason that our travels would continue entwined together.

"A Metastasio opera," I said, "Now that would be enchanting."

"Oh, indeed, Father, you are in luck."

"Why so?"

"*The Mercy of Titus* is performed tonight at *Teatro San Benedetto*."

"*The Mercy of Titus*? I don't understand."

"Metastasio's opera, *The Mercy of Titus*," she said as she leaned in toward me and gave me a quick kiss on the cheek, which teased me with ever more indecision and confusion. "You're very sweet, Father, and truly, truly much too handsome to be a priest. The curtain goes up in just a few hours. If at all possible, you must go."

With that she started to turn away to leave, but I tugged at her hand and turned her back toward me until our eyes met again. What was inside those dark and mysterious pools? Neither one of us moved until at last I broke the silent bond that held us inanimate. "Will you be there? I despise theater alone, especially when there is no one to share its joys."

"My dear, sweet *padre*, you are in Venice." She leaned in ever closer. "Anything is possible, even this . . . "

She kissed me and I fell from grace, willingly, happily, ecstatically. Our lips met and our tongues danced together for what seemed to this poor priest an eternity filled with sparks and flames. We pressed hard up against each other, so much so that I could sense our hearts throbbing in unison. Even the rain falling upon our faces did not quench the furnace burning inside my pitiable soul. And though neither one of us knew the other's name, it was then that I decided with certainty as to how I would spend my future days and nights in La Serenissima.

But when our kiss at long last ended, my Dona Brunetta abruptly pulled away. "Unfortunately, it's late. I must leave. My parents are home and waiting."

"Your parents?" I asked confounded, but she did not deign to answer.

Instead, without further hesitation, she scurried off under her *ombrello*. As I watched her disappear, my fantasies, foolish as they were, also departed, leaving me alone in the darkness of my own pathos on this forlorn quay. Yes, her parents are waiting. It was time for me to find a local *traghetto* or gondola that would deliver this clown of a clergyman into the cloistered confines of *La Pia Casa dei Catecumeni*.

There were no lamps on this deserted quay, and so I stood in near blackness. Even the crew of the *barchétta*, had, after securing their cargo for the night, left for what appeared to be a bar or casino about a block away, where the only illumination in the area was the light—and noise—spilling out through its open doorway.

As I reflected upon my situation, the evening rains dribbled off my *cappello* and overcoat. Several smaller canals all converged near the quay, each of which spun away into different parts of the city. One of them would surely lead me to *La Pia Casa*, but which? I scanned each of the waterways as best as I was able, to see if there was a gondolier about who could ferry me to my destination, but it appeared as if the evening's storm had kept everyone off the water.

I considered walking to the casino to inquire within for help, but stopped when I finally spotted a gondola coming toward the quay. It was a larger vessel, richly decorated, with glowing lanterns, a cabin athwart the middle and two gondoliers, one fore and one aft, which allowed it to move swiftly across the canals.

It docked at the quay and three people emerged from the cabin, which was also lit from inside by an additional lantern. In its glow I saw first, a woman with a scar on her cheek, perhaps a servant, in a plain hooded cloak, followed by a tall gentleman in the Carnevale attire of a Greek sage. And his mask, by use of small circular eye holes instead of the usual almond shaped slits, clearly created the visage of the blind poet, Homer. This sage carried a dagger with a silver hilt strapped to his waist. The third person to emerge, a woman, was a lady of some nobility, who was also garbed in Carnevale attire, a massive, flowing gown of vibrant purple satin. Her hair was flaming red, which tumbled like the fingers of a fire halfway down to her waist. She embodied the very image of the goddess Aphrodite born above the waves that I had once seen in a painting that hung on the walls of our seminary. Enchanting, I thought, enchanting enough to vanquish any reminder of my failure with that Dona Brunetta.

This goddess of the seas noticed me observing them. Turning to Homer, she whispered something to him. He nodded affirmatively and then made to leave the gondola behind the servant girl. My Aphrodite remained aboard and watched them exit. After they stepped onto the quay, she turned back in my direction, caught my eyes and smiled. Why, I don't know.

The servant girl under the hooded cloak hurried past me without looking up but I could see her scar, though, a horrid and fresh wound, running as it did from near her eye, across her check and down to her chin. She headed directly toward the casino. As Homer passed near me, the silver handle of his dagger sparkled in the lamplight. I stepped up to inquire if that gondola was for hire.

His abrupt and unexpected laughter could have shattered the walls of Jericho as it echoed off the surrounding buildings. The goddess aboard the gondola shared this laughter, and were it not for the comfort of darkness, all would have seen me blush with embarrassment.

And when Homer at last spoke directly to me, it was in a smooth perfectly accented patrician voice. "In La Serenissima, my dear padre, everything is for hire, the only consideration is cost." He pointed back at our Aphrodite's gondola, "But I sincerely doubt, Father, that a poor priest such as you can afford that."

Excusing himself, Homer set off after the servant girl and toward the casino. My Aphrodite eyed me up and down once more, and then, without explanation, she blew me a kiss. When I mimed catching it with one hand and then planting it on my own lips, she nodded affirmatively and then ducked back into the shelter of the cabin. She did however leave the door open. Was it for me, I fantasized? Or was she simply awaiting the return of her companions?

Turning away, I let a pinch of sanity prevail and dropped my lecherous dreams. Once more I began to search the waterways for a more plebian means of transport to my cloister.

Abruptly the quiet of the night was once again shredded, this time by loud shrieks and screams coming from outside the casino. Turning around, I saw a richly attired nobleman, masked and dressed for Carnevale as a *commendatore*, stagger out of the pub, yelling at the top of his lungs, "I'm dead, I'm murdered!"

He came running toward me, continuing to scream in anger and pain. The dagger with the silver hilt protruded from his chest. Before I knew it, the nobleman collapsed at my feet, breathing his last gasps. Removing his mask, I saw the meanest, nastiest face imaginable, one that reeked of cruelty and barbarism. I hastily pulled off my overcoat

and sheltered him with it. And then, but perhaps foolishly, I pulled the knife out. Blood spurted everywhere. I watched his eyes close and just like that, he was gone.

Suddenly behind me there were more shouts, those of an angry crowd spilling out the door of the casino, yelling, "There he is! There's the murderer!"

Yes, there I was frozen with confusion until another voice saved me. It was my Aphrodite.

"Quick, come away." She urged me toward her gondola. "Bring the knife! *Correre!* Run!"

Though panicked, I did not hesitate. Leaving my cloak behind but hefting the bloody knife, I scrambled over to the boat as fast as I could and jumped aboard. The two gondoliers had already doused the lanterns and were pushing off from the quay, which caused me to stumble. I fell flat on my face and dropped the knife. As I looked up, my Aphrodite grabbed the knife and waved me toward her open cabin door.

"Hurry!" she said.

The shouts were ever louder, ever closer, "*L'assassino! L'assassino!*"

I dragged myself into the cabin and collapsed on the floor. The red-headed goddess reached around me and locked the door.

"Your shirt, your hassock, quickly, give them to me," she insisted. "Your hat too."

Looking down, I realized I was covered in blood. I stripped down to my waist and passed everything over to my Aphrodite. She hurriedly bundled them up along with the knife and then opened a rear hatch. As she called to one of the gondoliers, my body began to tremble and shake from nervous shock and the chilly January night air. "Quickly, Tizio, into the lagoon with these." She pushed the bundle through the hatch and into his waiting hands and then in a rapid-fire guttural dialect which I did not understand, she barked a string of additional orders.

My Aphrodite then snapped the hatch shut and turned to face me. Though cold, shivering, and stunned by this sudden turn in my circumstances, I could not help but notice that this red-headed woman who sat opposite me in those tight quarters, was indeed a goddess—such beauty that it would melt the resistance of the most ardent celibate. Her skin was a smooth as buttermilk, her eyes devilish blue crystals, and her painted lips a Satanic red that was amplified by her fiery strands of hair. Instantly and instinctively my condemned soul craved her.

"In a few minutes one of the commendatore's boats will stop us. Tizio will tell whoever boards our vessel that I am about to give birth and that we are in search of a midwife. And you, Padre, you we must hide."

Where, I wondered as I looked about the cabin, half of which was filled with my Aphrodite's voluminous Carnevale gown. "But where?" I asked.

Without hesitation she shifted her legs and raised her skirts, "Here, come here, Padre, quickly, face down between my legs."

And that is how I met Angela Tiepolo, my Aphrodite, my fiery-haired Venetian goddess, and the woman who would soon become a mistress to this poor, miserable wretch of a priest. Yet, despite the severity of these events that occurred upon my arrival in Venice, I was clearly conflicted by the forces competing within me. Here I was, at the boiling point of my youthful vigor. Call it lust, if you must. Call it passion, call it sin. I was eager, willing, and lively by temperament, and, as many a woman had noted, attractive in person.

I further admit that by my own weaknesses and moral failings I would soon allow myself to be swept away over the next few months into a life dominated by the pursuit of amusements, carnal and otherwise, by this Angela Tiepolo, a woman whose appetites and desires matched my own. My obsession with this tempest would lead me to neglect—but not wholly abandon—my priestly obligations as well as my studies of literature and poetry. Of regrets, I had none, well almost none.

But our adventures that evening were far from over.

As I found myself returned to the womb, she doused the cabin lantern. All went dark. With her skirts well over me and masking my presence, Angela cradled my skull in her hands through the many layers of fabric as if my head were a baby ready to descend. Yes, I had fallen so far, so fast that in shedding my priestly garb, I had donned my very first Carnevale costume —that of an embryonic child.

And just as she predicted, when our boat was stopped by allies of the deceased commendatore, Angela began to moan as if on the verge of delivery. Our deception was immediately successful. After those pirates inspected our craft and thence departed, Angela released me from the happiest prison of my life.

Shortly thereafter Tizio and Sempronio, the two gondoliers in the employ of Angela, delivered us to a dock sheltered beneath the lower level of *La casa dei Tiepolo*, the house of the Tiepolos.

Once they had secured the gondola, Angela took my hand and led me out of the cabin and off the boat to a stairwell. There we were met by a bright-eyed seven-year-old girl, Barbarina, holding a lantern. We followed Barbarina up three flights and then entered the apartment belonging to her ladyship. Angela occupied the entirety of this upper level, while her twin brother, Girolamo, a gambler and drunkard whom I would unfortunately encounter all too soon, lived in a lower level.

A roaring blaze had already been set in the fireplace and so I warmed my half-naked body beside it while Barbarina delivered unto us a full dinner accompanied by two bottles of Barolo. She was an attractive child, well-mannered and efficient. On a table beside Angela's bed, she laid out several platters laden with cold cuts of meats, fruits, breads, and a few sweet desserts.

Truly I had conceived a most violent passion for not only one of the most delicious, but also one of the more capricious ladies of La Serenissima. In the several years that our affair would last, Angela and her shifting and often volcanic moods would quickly dominate all my hours with a variety of sordid follies and frivolities caused by love and jealousy. Yes, we engaged in such gambling and drunkenness, carousals and debaucheries, torrid affairs and bloody fights that one might ask how it is that a poor priest would have such a mistress, but the truth was, it was I who was in thrall to her. Angela's appetites for pleasure were ravenous. In that manner I can only proffer that we were equally matched, and as she was quick to inform me that first night, that I made her sing like an opera star in bed, with more sensitivity and skill than any other of her paramours—two attributes that pleased her enough to keep me around as if I were her lap dog. Given my prior years of deprivation, I was sufficiently satisfied by these conditions to remain obedient and by her side. However, with the exception of an occasional stolen minute at night devoted to some book or other, I do not think that I learned a single thing I had not known before— or which was worth knowing—except refining my skills while engaged in the art of *amore*. And it was those artistic skills I sought most to perfect.

But lest I get ahead of myself, I must return to that night. When I finally summoned the wits to inquire about the events on the quay, Angela shook her head, and bid me silent until Barbarina finally departed.

But even after the young girl left us alone and we began to drink and dine, Angela would not hear of my questions. "You saw nothing, you know nothing, and you were never there. There was no knife," she said as she continually refilled my wine glass.

"But . . ."

"*Ma niente*," she toasted me and we both drank ever more until the two bottles of Barolo were empty. "You suffered a hallucination or perhaps a nightmare, which I must now cure."

I was intoxicated enough to almost believe her. And when she bade me undress, I did so obediently until I stood bare before her. She then washed my skin down with a perfume scented cloth as if to remove every last vestige of the priesthood from my flesh. Approving of what she saw, she then had me undo her wardrobe as well. Normally, she said, this task was given over to her servant, the woman I had seen earlier at the quay wearing that hooded cloak and the mother to Barbarina. But given that her servant had not yet returned home, this task became mine.

Such a labor I undertook not only with the greatest of pleasure, but patience as well for it had been many a year since I had undressed a woman and I was determined to savor every moment not knowing when such an occasion would present itself again. Indeed, my Angela was in every curve of flesh a sculptor's dream, the very incarnation of an Aphrodite.

She led me into her bed and there we engaged in other more amorous forms of social intercourse until a few hours later, a nearby church bell chimed seven o'clock. Angela raised her head from her pillow and announced we must depart immediately for the Teatro San Benedetto.

"*The Mercy of Titus?*" I asked.

"Yes, you are familiar with it?"

"Metastasio's best," I stated with resolute, albeit puffed up confidence.

"Who?" she asked.

"Metastasio, it is his libretto that is to be performed."

My Angela could not have cared a wit. She declared that opera was commerce disguised as spectacle, and not the one upon the stage. It was rather more about those affairs in the boxes, private as they were, which fascinated her far, far more. Who was there, who was wearing what, who was with whom, who was sleeping with whom, and what deals, exchanges, and other transactions that could be negotiated. Yes, it was for her an entirely commercial venture, one that on the surface seemed to be all about the jewels, the champagne, the card playing, the gambling, and the assignations, including one in particular she had scheduled for later that evening.

Having had my priestly garb and thus my identity tossed away into the Venice lagoon, I soon found myself dressed in a Carnevale costume that Angela had summoned Barbarina to bring up from her brother Girolamo's wardrobe. The jacket, trousers, cape, and matching leather gloves were woven of satin in shaded patterns of red and black that resembled the feathers of a firebird, a Phoenix rising from the ashes of its prior life. The crowning piece was a *tricorno*—a three-cornered hat—that held the Phoenix's beaked half *bauta*-style mask in place. I welcomed the new identity Angela bestowed upon me as *Il Cavaliere della Fenice*, The Chevalier of the Phoenix.

As I took care to carefully examine my appearance in one of the many mirrors that graced the walls of Angela's apartment, Barbarina assisted Angela in reassembling herself into her evening's wardrobe. This required the young girl to climb a step stool so as to lower that massive purple gown over my goddess's multiple layers of undergarments. In one of the mirrors, I saw the child's white complexioned face in profile contrasted by her dark ringlets and eyes and could not help but think that this charming and efficient child reminded me of someone I had once known.

After the massive dress was in place, my lady sat back down upon the bed while Barbarina brought over Angela's matching purple stockings and shoes and assisted her mistress in putting them on. There was a slight tear on the right stocking above the ankle, which I pointed out to Angela, but she ignored it, noting that we were already late and that the gown would hide it anyway. She then finished off her costume with a matching *colombina* half-mask that covered only her eyes, nose, and upper cheeks. It was decorated with feathers as well as gold, silver, and purple crystals.

Thus attired, we followed Barbarina and her lantern back down the stairwell to where Tizio and Sempronio, waited for us. Angela whispered some instructions to Barbarina and then hugged and kissed her goodbye. I raised my mask to do the same but stopped when I realized the poor young child was crying.

I knelt down before her as a common parish priest and looked into those dark brown eyes that had watered up. "Are you sad, my child?"

"No," she said in a small, timid voice. "Not sad."

"Then what troubles you?" I asked.

"Not sad, happy." Barbarina kissed my outstretched hand. "Mistress says momma and me are safe and free. You killed the evil commendatore. *Grazie*, mio papà, *grazie*."

In my extreme naiveté I knew not what to think as this little child hugged me with such joy for being her savior.

Chapter Four: A Night at the Opera

Sunday Night, January 27, 1771
Teatro San Benedetto, Venice, Italy

Mozart . . . Yes, Mozart. Nothing in my lifetime had prepared me for what I, a poor priest naïve to the ways of the aristocracy, was about to experience when our gondola arrived at the Teatro San Benedetto.

A myriad of lanterns and torches illuminated the front entrance and portico along the Grand Canal where the glitterati of Venice—most costumed for Carnevale—mingled under a light drizzle while waiting to go into the theater, a theater whose private boxes were considered secure retreats from the noisy cafés and casinos scattered throughout the city. Standing tall and alone among those crowded about the entrance was my Homer, who represented a possible answer to the accumulating crimes and mysteries of my first night in Venice. But any questioning of this patrician would have to wait as our gondoliers, Tizio and Sempronio, did not stop there. Instead, they delivered us around to a side door off a perpendicular canal, the *Rio de l'Barcaroli*.

Beside that entrance stood a solitary figure, a man I would soon learn was Angela's twin brother Girolamo dressed in a black cloak—a classic *tabàro*—with his *bauta* mask pushed up and off his face. My lady had me wait aboard our boat while she went out to speak with him, a conversation that appeared anything but pleasant.

From Sempronio, the gondolier at the front of our craft, a handsome man with a long, wispy moustache who spoke with a thick Slavic accent, I quickly learned that masks, especially during Carnevale, were considered a necessity for most anyone who entered a casino or opera house. "These shields, principally *bautas* for men and *colombinas* for women, conceal one's identity, thus allowing the wearer to speak or act freely. Carnevale season, especially inside the theater and casinos, provides an escape from the rules and regimens of our daily life on a scale so grand that it offers up a virtual license to engage in anything, including anonymous yet consensual sex," he said as a wicked smile appeared on his face, by which I understood that Sempronio had a great deal of personal experience in these adventures.

"One can escape the past," Tizio chimed in with an equally exotic accent, "engage with the muses of pleasure now present, and suspend all consequences that come on the waves of the future. The private boxes at Teatro San Benedetto," he went on to explain, "are considered perfect for these assignations, or for politicking or plotting, or for any personal business that requires delicacy and discretion. Still, the theater is not without dangers for the elite who enter. Mixed among these costumed crowds are hidden innumerable charlatans, thieves, gamblers, and prostitutes. Our Council of Ten, which rules the Venetian Republic along with our Doge, considers all of these venues detestable, calling them mixing bowls of deceit, coins, cards, weapons, and wine, all of which corrupt customs and consume fortunes.

"Of course," he said with a laugh, "it is these very opportunities for licentious behavior that ensure that even our most prurient council members attend—but always well hidden by behind their own masks, capes, and disguises."

I thanked both men for their insights, for all too soon I would discover the virtue and necessity of preserving the secrets of one's true identity. And, though I was too far away to understand anything that Angela and her brother might have been saying to each other, their animated gestures made it clear that neither sibling was calmed by the other's words. Finally, Angela reached into a small purse she had secreted inside her gown and gave her brother a handful of gold coins. Girolamo carefully counted them out and then and only then, seemingly satisfied, he replaced his *bauta* over his face and walked off.

After Girolamo departed, Sempronio tapped me on the shoulder and motioned for me to leave the boat and join our mistress ashore.

I followed Angela through the side entrance of the Teatro San Benedetto and found myself backstage. Because of the canals and the high water table in Venice, no basements existed anywhere in the city. For an opera house this presented a design dilemma that necessitated shifting and squeezing all of the behind-the-scene functions—dressing rooms, rehearsal space, costume and make up rooms, prop storage, and so forth—into spaces behind and upstairs from the performance stage itself. Angela took my hand and with a sense of authority led me past a bustling sea of stagehands, actors, singers, and musicians, each in some form of prep work for the opera soon to commence. All stepped aside with deference at the sight of my lady as we maneuvered through the cramped spaces and up stairways until at last, we arrived outside the private boxes lining the hallway of the third tier.

Every public space was crowded and noisy with theatergoers coming and going in their finest Carnevale attire. They were attended to and trailed by uniformed servants and staff. When Angela paused as if to reconnoiter, I focused on listening to the conversations all about me. The snippets I overheard that spoke of the murder of the commendatore of the Casti family by a renegade priest, not only terrified me but made me all the more grateful for the protection provided by my costume and new identity as *Il Cavaliere della Fenice*.

Still, I did not feel secure behind my mask, nor did I know how far or how long my new persona would protect me from punishment for a crime I did not commit. As allies of the deceased man and the police officers of the Inquisition were apparently frantic in their searches throughout the city for the perpetrator, I thanked whatever gods there may be for the invisibility my costume provided.

With a hope to escape from these crowds and the fear I would soon be unmasked, I asked Angela, "Which booth is yours?" a question that set my lady laughing as loud as she had back at the quay.

"Oh, my dear sweet *Cavaliere della Fenice*. You truly are a holy innocent, aren't you?"

She had me there. I truly had no notion of what she was referring to nor why my question had set her off laughing.

"Which box, which booth, which seat? Which one is mine? Signor Cavaliere, they are all mine," she said with a sweep of her hands. "My family, the Tiepolos, we are the majority owners of the Teatro San Benedetto, and tonight we sit inside there." Angela pointed to the Royal Box, whose doors were the only ones emblazed with a gold crown and protected by two armed guards who stood with swords at the ready.

A servant, with a tray of glasses in one hand and a large ice bucket full of bottles of prosecco in the other, approached the Royal Box and was about to enter. One of the guards opened the door to the box for the servant which enabled me to glance inside. There sat a solitary man reading a book who was dressed in the Carnevale costume of a cherub. His mask was in the style of a three-quarters porcelain *volto*, which came down only as far as his upper lip. The china-smooth surface reflected the innocence of a child, and instead of hair, it sported grape vines in the manner of Bacchus, god of wine. The man's pants and jacket were of a patterned satin emblazoned with cupids and cherubim in all manner of behavior—erotic and otherwise—while his cape was festooned with brightly covered feathers as if they were wings held closely to the body.

"You will wait for me there while I attend to some business. I am told that our guest, *il Signor Cherubino* is also fond of your Metastasio, so you shall have a good conversation until I return, yes?"

"Yes," I said hoping she did not sense the fear that verily overwhelmed my entire body with a cold sweat. Angela gave a quick short whistle under her breath just sufficient to catch the guards' attention. One of them opened the door while the other motioned me forward.

As I walked the twenty paces to the box, I observed over my shoulder that Angela all but floated across the hallway in the opposite direction to where none other than that tall patrician man in Greek style robes stood out above the crowd. Indeed, it was my Homer. Beside him was a woman in a dark green gown. Initially her back was toward me, but when that woman turned about to greet Angela, I realized that it was, yes, despite her now wearing a matching emerald colored *colombina* mask, my selfsame Dona Brunetta.

How could this other woman I'd met by chance, my chestnut-haired beauty, be in league with these people? Yet another chill traversed my body as I considered the dangers. I understood nothing, not even whether to trust Angela. Had my infatuations with these sirens of Venice made me as blind as Homer to the threats around me? Or was this simply business as usual in La Serenissima?

Unsure of anything or anyone, I entered the box. The servant was in the midst of pouring prosecco into a glass for *il Signor Cherubino*.

The cherub nodded to acknowledge my entrance. "*Buona sera, signore*," he said. His voice was light, cheery, and youthful and I detected a slight Germanic accent.

"*Buona sera*," I replied as the servant proffered me a glass of prosecco.

The cherub and I toasted together, "*Saluti.*" The servant exited and shut the doors.

As I proffered an innocent question to the cherub about whether he knew of Metastasio, my eyes devoured the sights and sounds of the Teatro San Benedetto. As uniformed members of the orchestra drifted into position before the stage, wildly garbed patrons in all manner of brilliantly colored costumes filtered into the other boxes around where we sat and the seats below us on the main floor. Never, not even in my imagination, had I ever witnessed such grandeur, pomp, or beauty. Every architectural touch inside the theater was glorious and overwhelming, from the golden gilt columns to the plush red velvet seats and the massive stage curtain emboldened with interwoven portraits of heroes, gods, goddesses, and angels that matched the drapes that hung about each private box. Frankly, I was instantly mesmerized by the spectacle.

"I met the man himself two years ago when I was at the Hapsburg's court in Vienna," the cherub answered.

"Who?" I said. So distracted was I by the sights around me that I had forgotten I'd asked a question.

"Metastasio."

"Yes, of course, Metastasio."

"And you? You know his work? Are you an admirer? Or . . . ?" He let his question linger as he stared at me. Could he see my eyes, my identity, through my mask?

Fearful of everything at that moment, I answered quickly and thus shared with the cherub that indeed I was a great admirer of Metastasio's writings since I first discovered them as a boy, and in reading everything of his I could procure, I found my own inspiration to become a man of letters and literature.

"And you write what? Poems? Stories? Novels? Operas? Perhaps something I would know?"

I lied in response to hide my embarrassment at never having accomplished anything with my pen as yet, and thus suggested I was inspired by Metastasio to develop philosophical treatises and ecumenical works on romance, morality, and the frailties of human nature and that these essays were intended solely for a limited audience of scholars and churchmen.

Signor Cherubino nodded enthusiastically, stopping only to sip more of his prosecco, actions which led me to believe my deceptions had succeeded, but I was wrong.

"What then do you make of his poem, "The Lovers' Descent?" Will Signor Giulio's sense of loyalty and fidelity hold sway? Or will he shun the advice proffered by his mentor and take the opportunity given him to bed his best friend's wife?

Confident and perhaps a bit haughty in my response, I immediately replied, "Why my good, sir, is not the answer in the text? Is not his friend's bride, Signora Fiora, portrayed as a rock standing impervious to winds and tempest? A woman with a heart ever strong in faith and love? One who would never fall for such a seduction and betrayal? And does she not chase off her would be seducer by demanding that Signor Giulio not profane their hearts and affections with the unwelcome breath of his base words?"

I recited and rhapsodized upon Signora Fiora's text, which bubbled up from my memory. "In vain do you seek to seduce my soul whose unsullied faith is secured to that of my own dear love and shall not be unbound until death, despite all the world and fate. Between my husband and I, burns a kindled flame which warms and consoles us. Only the grave alone could alter my heart's devotion."

And as I continued into the poem's next stanza, the cherub surprised me by joining in with me for he too knew the words by heart.

"Respect this example of constancy, you abject creature, and do not let a base hope ever make you so rash or forward again."

Realizing—but perhaps foolishly—that I had naught to fear from this cherub I relaxed with a deep sigh, devoured the remains of my prosecco, and then refilled my glass.

The cherub lifted up the open book he had been reading when I first walked in and said, "This volume of Metastasio's collected works was gifted to me just last month by a bishop in Milano, but as you can plainly see, I am unable to discover the end of the story."

As he turned to the last page of "The Lovers' Descent," my hand began to tremble such that I dropped my glass of prosecco. The cause of my absolute and total shock? The ink-stained page I had ruined as a child in my father's attic. This volume the cherub held in his hands was indeed the very selfsame one my dear father had bound in leather a decade ago. Fortunately, my spilled prosecco landed on the floor and not the Metastasio.

"Are you well?" asked the Cherub.

Once more, I lied, replying that it was the shock of seeing such an exquisite volume so desecrated that had caused the accident. Hastily recovering my glass, I refilled it and took another sip to calm my nerves.

"But do you know the ending?" he asked yet again for, indeed my ink stain had obscured the last stanzas of the poem.

Gathering my wits about me, I offered that the answer was in the title, "The Lovers' Descent," which indicated the plural as opposed to the singular form, "A Lover's Descent."

"Ahhhh," said the cherub, most pleased with this explanation. "They all succumb to temptation, yes?"

"Indeed, yes, they do, cosi fan tutte," I replied.

"But such a contrast to *The Mercy of Titus* that we shall see before us tonight, where fidelity, loyalty, religious alliances, and friendship are severely tested. *Non è vero?*"

I shrugged and confessed to the cherub that my attendance here this night was because I did not know and had never seen this particular work of Metastasio, without of course revealing that in the entirety of my life I had never before seen any such performances. Still, I noted my profound fascination with the great poet's depth of wisdom and insight into the very struggles with love, romance, and morality that made us human.

In response the Cherub exclaimed that although the musical score for *The Mercy of Titus* was created by Christoph Willibald Gluck, a Bohemian composer of some note whom he admired, the libretto was pure Metastasio and based on the true historical life of the Roman Emperor Titus. Titus had sought to consolidate his power over the eastern portion of the empire through a proposed marriage to a Jewess, Queen Berenice of Judea. However, the prospect of a Hebrew woman potentially ascending to the throne of Rome as an empress was opposed so vigorously by the Senate, that Titus was compelled to send Berenice back to Judea. Into that power void, the opera commenced.

The performance was to open with Vitellia, daughter of Titus' deposed rival, who is torn between the opposite polarities of either seeking revenge against Titus or manipulating events such that she can marry him and claim the title of empress for herself. She riles up Titus's friend Sesto, who is in love with her, to act against Titus. In typical Metastasian dramatic form, Sesto is torn between his love of Vitellia, his friendship with Titus, and an added conflict that arises when Titus seeks to wed Sesto's own sister, Servilia, over Vitellia and make her his new empress. Yet ever more twists arise when we discover Servilia loves not Titus but her betrothed, Annio, and does not want to share the emperor's bed or title.

"The path of love is neither straight nor clear, and thus endlessly complicates our human condition," I said to the cherub, reflecting more upon my own circumstances than perhaps the plot of this opera set to begin shortly.

"You are a scholar, yes?" the Cherub asked, "And you have written treatises upon such matters?"

"Yes," I said, continuing to lie.

"And you have loved women?"

"Yes," I answered again, though in truth I had lain with only two, a childhood sweetheart in my village from whom I was torn when I was only a teenager and Angela Tiepolo, my Aphrodite, but an hour earlier.

"Can you explain women to me? I am surrounded by their wiles, whims, and fancies. Who are these creatures who bedevil us?

"What is it that confounds you, my son?" I asked. Once trained as a priest, always a priest.

To this, the cherub made a confession of his own, "I am but ten and five years this very day and truly believe I am the sort of conflicted man Metastasio writes about, thus my fascination with his poetics. When I am around a beautiful woman, I no longer know who I am or what I'm doing."

"How is that? I asked.

"First, I'm burning, blushing, changing colors, then suddenly chilled but hard as ice. To be beside a woman makes me tremble, and at the very word 'love,' my heart leaps and pounds and I am filled with longings I cannot explain."

"Is that not that hunger you describe, the condition of all men?"

"I know not all men," he said, "Only myself. I dream of romance and passion when I'm awake and find myself obsessed with loving women in my dreams. I am carried away by thoughts of their flesh and sweet affections and find the temptations of *amore* everywhere, in the air, the wind, the mountains, the streams, the valleys, even this opera house. My head spins and swirls around all these beauties, each one more delectable than the last. I want them all, yet only God above knows that this cherub mask shields a blushing face from those I find feverishly desirable."

"My friend, if I may call you that, is this not why Metastasio's poems and stories resonant?" I asked, "demonstrating as they do how true morality rests in our reason's ability to control those feelings and actions incited by our emotions?"

"Yes," he said with anguish, "but must it be so difficult? How does one endure such sweet torments?"

I lied yet again, a skill I was rapidly perfecting while in the company of this young man. "Those who are morally weak, those who lack such restraints, those are the men who inevitably fall prey to the dictates of emotions over reason and logic. Consequently, they collapse back into states of suffering where trouble inevitably finds them."

"Am I so weak that every woman who approaches causes me to tremble?

"Not weak, simply young and inexperienced. And I swear by this world, my friend, I do not jest. When it comes to women, you must breathe deep, abandon your fears, and remember above all else, these demons of the flesh that bedevil us are themselves mere mortals who suffer equal confusions. If they eat like us, and wear skirts, are they in fact, goddesses? Or women drawn and flustered by us in equal measure to our consternations?"

"This is true?" he asked.

"Yes," I said, "but be warned. By age fifteen a woman knows the ways of the world, from where the devil keeps his tail, to what's right and what is wrong. She knows the wiles that ensnare lovers, how to feign laughter or tears, and to make up good excuses. A woman will listen to a hundred men but speak with her eyes to a thousand men who desire her. She'll hold out hope to all, be they handsome or plain. She knows how to hide things without getting flustered and knows how to tell lies without ever blushing. Like a queen on a throne, she'll find a way to get her own way, for this is her schooling and thus her doctrine."

"Yes, it is true," the cherub said, answering his own question. "I knew that."

"Then will you promise me, my friend, to abandon all fear and hesitancy when opportunity next arises?"

"Absolutely," he answered, and I believed him.

From below, down by the stage the musicians of the orchestra were just beginning to warm up when the door to our box opened. In strode Angela followed by my Dona Brunetta, who did not appear to recognize me in the least, hidden as I was behind my mask and costume.

Angela did the honors of reintroducing me to the siren in green by graciously announcing, "Signorina Matilda Wider may I present to you my esteemed companion, and a great connoisseur of opera, *il Cavaliere della Fenice. Cavaliere,* Signorina Matilda Wider.

So, my Dona Brunetta had a name, Signorina Matilda Wider. Even with her mask on, Matilda could have looked no less fetching than she did only hours before on our storm-tossed *barchétta*. I stood, bowed politely and then lifting her hand to my lips, I kissed her flesh once again—sweetly and decorously—whilst holding my earlier passions in check. But I must confess, I still hungered for her and in my mind's eye I revisited every moment of our voyage that ended with that most passionate kiss on the quay—and all this despite my having exhausted myself that same evening with Angela. What is it they say, "One taste of sweetness only whets the appetite for a second or third bite?" I understood my inner self as licentiously incorrigible and left it at that.

"*Piacere di conoscerti*," my Signorina Matilda Wider said before she immediately turned to the cherub and added, "Signore, let me introduce you to Signorina Angela Tiepolo, *la regina della notte* in La Serenissima as she is the owner of this Teatro San Benedetto. Signorina Angela, this dear cherub is Signor Mozart."

Mozart? This fifteen-year-old boy who knew naught of women and love was her genio, Mozart? I watched in surprise as he stood up and then most graciously and with the sensitivity and skill of a well-poised courtier, lifted Angela Tiepolo's hand to his lips and kissed it as if she was a goddess and the only woman in the world. Even Angela, my Queen of the Night, was impressed. Perhaps I had taught the cherub too well?

Before I could even ponder the ramifications of those thoughts, the overture to act 1 of *The Mercy of Titus* began.

Angela bade us take seats, but she insisted on arranging us in a line for what I presumed were her own strategic purposes. In this row of four chairs, Angela had me sit to the extreme right, and she positioned Mozart on the extreme left. The two women sat in the middle, with Signorina Matilda Wider beside me while Angela positioned herself adjacent to Mozart on her left so, as she declared, "they could more effectively discuss business"—which in this case meant the possibility of Mozart writing an opera on commission for the Teatro San Benedetto.

Apparently, Mozart's father, Leopold Mozart, was supposed to have come to the performance this evening to meet Angela and negotiate such a contract, but Leopold had been taken ill. The elder Herr Mozart remained behind at the Wider palazzo, where both father and son had been residing during their stay in Venice. Matilda, my Dona Brunetta, had been sent along instead on short notice to deliver a proposal of conditions crafted by Leopold for the Tiepolo family.

Although my Angela and Signorina Matilda Wider were about the same age and had apparently been aware of each other's existence for most of their lives in La Serenissima, there appeared to be little warmth or friendship between them, a condition I was to learn that was not uncommon among women whose beauty and cunning made them naturals rivals for the affection of others.

The opera commenced and Signorina Matilda, whose attention was solely focused on the play at hand, gave no hint that she had in the least any idea that I was the man she had kissed at the quay only hours before. She sat still in rapt attention to the performance below, true to her nature as a genuine aficionado of the art form.

But yes, time for another confession or two by this poor priest. I still could not help but stare at Matilda as her chest heaved and sighed in harmony with the dramatics of the singers. Yes, I knew she had a brilliant mind, and as much as I might reprove myself for my base and carnal thoughts, I could not deny myself the pleasure of lusting for her as a woman, nor imagining her as an impassioned lover, just as I had dreamed on the *barchétta*. In this regard my state of mind was little different than the cherub's.

And still, despite the lovely distraction of these two sirens of Venice, I was nonetheless thoroughly entranced by the sheer spectacle of opera and *The Mercy of Titus*. The blend of music, song, and story was so compelling that I was completely unaware of the extent of the dramatic interplay going on in the other side of our Royal Box between Mozart and Angela.

Angela, my Angela, the woman who had just converted this priest into a willing sinner, constantly leaned in toward Mozart, allowing her bodice to brush up against him whenever she would whisper in his ear, which was frequently. Although the young composer was deeply attentive to the music of Gluck that underpinned the opera—so much so that I could see his fingers, which he rested on Angela's knee—dancing unconsciously in accord with the music. He would smile appreciatively and nod whenever Angela whispered into his ear. And given his confession to me about his fears of the feminine only minutes earlier, I suspected him taking deep breaths to contain the riot of emotions that must have been swirling about him. At this age Mozart was no match for Angela, or so I mistakenly thought all through the first act. I would later learn that for the second time that day Angela's massive Carnevale dress camouflaged a secondary performance that would have made the cherub's new teacher proud—most particularly had that scholar not been this clown of a priest I understood myself to be. Yes, Mozart was a quick study and indeed a genio, a genio with women.

Back to the opera, however, where the tumult of conflicts and emotions reached a dangerous climax. A sequence of poignant and enduring arias began when Vitellia learns of Titus's desire for Sesto's sister, Servilia. Vitellia insists that Sesto attack immediately, sack Rome, and assassinate Titus. Though Sesto feels shredded like a piece of meat between two wolves, and succumbs to Vitellia's wishes, he is in truth a victim of his own unchecked passions. Sesto leaves to rally his army for the assault on the capital.

Only after he is gone, does Vitellia discover the truth, an ever-changing truth: a merciful and good-hearted Titus will not tear Servilia from Annio. He instead announces he will ask Vitellia to be his wife and empress. But it is too late, Sesto and his legions attack Rome and set fire to the city as the curtain falls and the act ends. We four were left breathless, Mozart perhaps most of all.

The young artist turned to both Angela and Matilda. "Oh, the fury and fickleness of women confounds my senses. You two ladies, you who know what love is, please explain this all to me." He waved his arms toward the stage,

"Can you tell if what Sesto has in his heart is love? Or just infatuation that blinds him to Vitellia's manipulations? Such passions are all so new to me that I do not understand nor comprehend such behaviors devoid of reason."

Signorina Matilda spoke first. "Are these not the eternal questions we all ask? The very ones Metastasio has us struggle with?"

"Yes," I said, interceding. "I believe what Signor Mozart wrestles with is this: Why do these unchecked passions of Sesto that fill him with such potent desires, then blind him to the manipulations of a woman who only seeks to engage him as a tool for her own purposes?"

"Yes, why is it," Mozart asked, "that Sesto rages between pleasure and torment over a woman that loves not him, but vengeance and power? Vitellia's cold shoulder has Sesto shudder with indecision one moment and then a whiff of her perfume sets his spirits afire so much so he will betray his best friend. Why is this?"

"It is a woman's right, nay privilege, to behave as such, for how else in a world dominated by men can a woman exert power and control over her own destiny?" insisted Angela Tiepolo.

"But why," Mozart asked, "why do men lose all reason and surrender all rational thought when tempted by these feminine treasures that exist outside of our control? How is it we men are left as poor mortals, to sigh and groan without comprehension?"

"Is that love, you ask?" Angela said to Mozart. "Love is but a little thief, a serpent who acts according to his whim and leaves the heart no peace. Scarcely does love open a path between your eyes and heart before it chains your souls and takes away your liberty."

All too true I thought. We men have no control; we tremble and even flutter without knowing why when we are around women. By night and day, we find both heaven and hell in feminine companionship, yet whenever given the opportunity to linger in delight beside a woman, we do—regardless of the consequences.

"But Signor Mozart," Angela continued, "we have business to discuss, and not here." Angela then turned to me and Signorina Matilda, "Would you please be so kind as to entertain each other while I bring Herr Mozart to my office. We have a contract to sign."

Angela did not wait for an answer. She took Mozart's hand in her own and led him out of the Royal Box.

When they were gone and the door closed Signorina Matilda turned to me, her face red with anger.

"I hate that woman. Do you see her fawning all over him?" Matilda growled and grimaced as powerfully as if she had been Vitellia upon the stage seething about Titus. Signorina Matilda then proceeded to tell me all she had witnessed pass between Angela and Mozart in the course of the first act. Matilda insisted that Angela's amorous foreplay was just a prelude to a consummation in her office with Mozart. Did I know there was a bed in there? Matilda claims to have seen it half hidden behind a dressing screen when she and Angela had met earlier to review Leopold Mozart's proposals. And given Angela's reputation in Venice as the Queen of the Night, Signorina Matilda was convinced that they were engaged in conjugal bliss at that very moment.

"You are jealous?" I asked, wondering if I too should be concerned. But then I shrugged off all such feelings for I had not known Angela long enough to care. As for Matilda, the answer however was readily clear; she was raging. Her chest rose and fell and the thought of those sweet breasts in my hands made me want to appear sympathetic. Was I a cad? A licentious beast? A creature filled with carnal lust? Yes, yes, and yes. And was I concerned that the woman I had just engaged with, was off with another man? With Mozart? With the genio? No, no, and no. I did not care. The events of this day had so scrambled my sense of right, wrong, and reality, that I had lost all moral grounding. Thus motivated, I relied upon my priestly training to console Signorina Matilda and with luck, perhaps lure her back into my arms.

I took her hand in my gloved fingers and asked, "What is this man, Mozart, to you? Are you betrothed? Has he made promises to you?"

Though she was by now in tears and sobbing, she shook her head, and said, "No."

"Has he made advances upon you? Has he taken your honor?"

She wiped her tears with a handkerchief I offered. "No, *Cavaliere*, no. I only wish he had."

"You love him?"

"No, not love, but admiration, he is *un genio*, he is brilliant and his music so passionate that I wanted him to be my lover. Let him take me, not her. As for honor," she confessed, "I have already shared that with others. Which, dammit, is why I want him. I hate Angela Tiepolo. I have hated that *puttana* my whole life. That she should conquer Mozart before me . . . Oh, how she enrages me."

I took her hand in mine and once again brought it to my lips. I kissed it both tenderly and with the same passion I had shared with her rival in bed only hours before. And this gesture, born out of pure lust on my part for the woman who had earlier shared her ombrello with me—but did not yet know it was me—abruptly changed her mood.

"I suppose," she said, "there are other ways to extract my vengeance, yes, Cavaliere?" There was a wickedness in her smile that pleased this fallen abbé. After all, it is said that a woman's constancy is like the Arabian Phoenix; everyone swears it exists, but no one knows where.

Matilda Wider, my Dona Brunetta, stood up, pulled closed one of the two curtains about our box and then glided into my arms, arms that welcomed her back and fell tight around her. We kissed as we had at the quay and for the second time that day, my very first day in La Serenissima, this young fool of a priest captured yet another glimpse of heaven.

I cannot describe how we managed to consummate our passions beneath so many layers of costumes, gloves and masks—yes, we kept our masks on and our true identities hidden—but let it suffice to say that I never left my seat whilst she rode upon a wild sea until she could sail no more. Tizio and Sempronio would have been proud of me, asserting as they did that such secret sex behind masks was the essence of Carnevale in Venice. If one does not know one's lover, did it ever happen? In La Serenissima the answer was apparently no.

And when our adventure concluded she fell against my chest and sighed deeply. We remained still and content for I know not how long, but long enough for the musicians to have returned and begun their warms up for the second act.

"Mozart, do you still believe he's every bit as much a *genio* as Metastasio?" I asked unconsciously imitating her voice back on the *barchétta* when she said the word, "Genio." And that was a huge mistake.

"Who are you?" she demanded as she then pulled up my mask. I cannot tell you of the horrors I saw reflected in her face.

"You? You're the priest? The murderer! The murderer!"

I jammed the mask back over my face.

She abruptly looked past me toward the theater below and screamed as loud as any scream I had ever heard, one that was so blood curdling that it would have frozen the devil in his deceitful tracks, but the words were not the ones I had expected. "FIRE! FIRE! FIRE!"

For indeed the theater below us was in flames, flames that were leaping and spreading rapidly. In a moment sheer chaos erupted throughout the Teatro San Benedetto as shouts and screams came suddenly from every corner of the building.

Signorina Matilda ran for the door of the box just as Mozart and Angela Tiepolo came rushing back in. I knew they too had indeed sailed the seas of amore and been caught in flagrante delicto; the torn stocking that had been on Angela's right foot was now on her left. Signorina Matilda grabbed Mozart by the hand and pulled him out the door just as that tall patrician gentleman, Homer, fought to enter our box. Trailing behind him was that servant woman, the one with the hood over her head and that fresh scar that covered half her face. I quickly lost sight of Mozart and Matilda as they disappeared into the midst of the panicked crowds on the third tier.

Homer called to Angela, "We must escape! The commendatore's allies have set fire to the theater!"

Smoke began to envelop us all and with no time to waste, we pushed our way out of the box into the corridor.

"This way," shouted Angela, as she fought to lead our party toward the very same back entrance she and I had come up earlier that evening. Such was the degree of panic, fear, and terror among everyone there, that it made escape appear impossible. We were pushed, shoved, and jammed about as we made for that hidden passageway. But, just as Angela and Homer slipped into the passageway, a fleeing spectator knocked me down to the floor. I was nearly trampled in the stampede and lost my hat and mask. Fortunately, the servant woman was there to lift me up, and in so doing, she probably saved my life.

The woman and I ran into the back passage but before we could catch up to Angela and Homer, a wall of flames roared up in front of us, blocking any escape in that direction.

"This way!" screamed the servant. She grabbed my hand and led me the opposite way through what must have been Angela's office for there was the unmade bed behind a dressing screen along with two pairs of shoes, Angela's and Mozart's. Passing the bed, we found another stairwell that went up and up until at last we found a door. It was locked. I kicked at it with all my strength. It burst open, but everything was black before us except a pale moon straining to emerge behind the rain clouds.

I stood on the roof of the Teatro San Benedetto, four stories up above the Grand Canal. Behind and below me, the fingers of flames flared everywhere while hundreds of people, screaming and shouting, fled for the exits in panic. I knew that to remain here was to perish when the theater, a frail wooden structure, would soon collapse in upon itself.

There was no way out, except perhaps one, one that was as dangerous as running back into the inferno, and that was to jump four stories into the Grand Canal below. To succeed and survive the drop without shattering our bodies or drowning in the ice-cold water, we would need to fly far enough out from the roof into the night to avoid boats, buildings and structures below, before plunging into the black but very shallow waters of the Grand Canal.

Believing we were doomed, I turned back around and started to speak to Angela's servant, "There's no way . . . " but she raised a finger to her lips as if to quiet me.

"If we are going to die here," she began in a calm and steady voice that I immediately recognized from my past but her true face was difficult to see in the night shadows, "I want you to know that Barbarina is your daughter, and I am . . . "

Before I could react, she pulled the hood away from her face. Standing before me was my very first and only true love, the woman I had been torn from when I was but the youngest of young men, Zina Spinoziano.

Chapter Five: Via Giudecca

Before Dawn Monday Morning, January 28, 1946
Ceneda, the Veneto, Italy

Mozart. All through the night, Jake and Dolcetta had struggled to translate Da Ponte's handwritten diaries about Mozart. Though exhausted, they were so entranced by the narrative, nothing stopped them until Dolcetta, stunned by what she saw, read aloud the name, "Zina Spinoziano."

Dolcetta abruptly slammed the book closed and grabbed Jake by the shoulders. "Do you know who Zina Spinoziano is?" she demanded, shaking him so hard and with a strength he couldn't imagine this slight young woman possessed. "Zina, Zinabella Spinoziano is my grandmother's grandmother. I was named after her. We all know about her scar. It's family history. And her portrait is right there." She pointed to a painting above the piano that Jake had not noticed before. The portrait was one of several old oils that hung on the walls of the room.

Jake was dumfounded. "Zina is . . . is . . . is your family?" Other than the scar, the face he saw in that 175-year-old portrait could have been Dolcetta's.

"Yes, yes," she insisted. "*Mi chiamo* Dolcetta Zinabella Spinoziano." She jumped up from the couch and urged Jake to follow her back to Geremia's desk. There Dolcetta rifled through her uncle's desk drawers until she came to a large binder titled, "*La storia genealogica della comunità ebraica di Ceneda*"— "The Genealogical History of the Jewish Community of Ceneda."

Dolcetta hastily explained that completing this handcrafted volume was at the core of her uncle's work since he had returned at war's end from the Benedictine monastery where he'd been hiding. In it he had reconstructed as many of the family lines of Ceneda's Jewish community as possible. Most were descendants of one Israel da Conegliano, who moved there in 1597 with his new bride, Rosa Nuovaseta, from the larger nearby town of Conegliano. With the help of a local priest, Father Beccavivi, Geremia had begun his work long before the war but afterward, with the brutal extermination of the entire community, the rabbi felt an urge to complete it before his own death.

Geremia had laid out the book in reverse order, from back to front, right to left. The very last page began with the names of Israel and Rosa at the top with the next line below showing their eight children, the names of their spouses and their surnames when known, and the approximate dates of birth and death. Below that the format was repeated over and over with the names of their children and so on. Geremia had pulled all of this information from a collection of town and synagogue records as well as family prayer books, bibles, and other similar documents. Father Beccavivi's assistance was invaluable as it enabled Geremia to examine many of the diocese's records of the various mixed marriages and blended families that had occurred over the centuries.

What made the rabbi's charts unique was that he also color-coded each line of descent. Israel and Rosa da Conegliano's line was black. As new family lines appeared, other colors and "family chapters," were added. The Spinoziano chapter, for example, which first appeared around 1700 when a Jewish rabbi moved to Ceneda from Amsterdam and married one of Israel's great granddaughters, had a green line. Further, if the colored line was solid, it meant the lineage was confirmed. If the lines were dotted, it indicated that the connections were probable but not supported by any documentation. And when one page was filled, the rabbi continued the chart along with the colored lines on the next page to the left. Given that the Jewish families of Ceneda had shared but a dozen surnames, the charting was complex but manageable.

In fact, to Jake, who marveled at the simple brilliance of the model, it resembled the color-coded maps that detailed the many different New York City subway lines, lines he knew by heart. Conversely, navigating the charts for Dolcetta was for her as easy as Jake riding from the Bronx on the New York Broadway line to the Metropolitan Opera House in Manhattan.

On the first page, the newest page, she pointed out to Jake her name and those of her now murdered siblings. Their names all had a black line for Conegliano, a Spinoziano green, a Graziano orange, a Taormina gold, a Palumbo red, and even a dotted Da Ponte blue. She quickly flipped through the pages for Jake's benefit, pointing out the colored lines that ultimately connected her back to Zinabella and her father, Rabbi Baruccio Spinoziano.

Zina, she explained was a woman known not just for that scar but for her heroism and a great beauty that her wound could never diminish. "Zina fought back . . . and she was my inspiration to join the Resistance. I was terrified but thought if she could do it then, I could do it now. She gave me the courage to fight," she said as she stepped away to put up a fresh pot of coffee. "Your own family is here as well."

While Jake flipped back and forth through the pages and marveled at Geremia's work, Dolcetta got the coffee brewing and then she pulled that *crostata di pistacchio*, a pistachio tart, out of a bread box and cut off three slices. Dawn had begun to break through, and with it a warm sun erased the rain and the darkness of night.

"Whoa, I can see my own ancestry here," Jake said, "Though there appear to be several gaps, a number of dotted lines, and a few broken ones as well around 1800."

"You can blame the Napoleonic wars for that chaos," said Dolcetta. "There was a lot of fighting around here when Napoleon defeated the Hapsburgs and liberated all of the ghettos throughout Europe. But war always brings with it the usual bad results."

"Oh, yes, I understand. And what is this second name, 'Danielle Zinabella Spinoziano?' Jake asked as he pointed to a name with her same birthdate immediately adjacent to Dolcetta's.

His question froze Dolcetta. "My sister, my twin sister. *Gemelli angeli*, my mother called us, her twin angels . . . Dachau."

"I'm sorry. I was there for the liberation," offered Jake. "Maybe. Maybe, she was . . . "

Dolcetta shook her head. "We hoped, we waited. Even Lt. Foxx tried to help. We ran through every photograph in the intelligence archives. Nothing. No matches, no word. And no one, none of them came home."

"I'm sorry," Jake repeated, unsure of what to say to her in the face of such overwhelming tragedies. "Many of those pictures were probably the ones I took."

"You do not have to apologize," said Dolcetta. "The pain of their deaths is like Zina's scar. It never goes away, but we learn to live with it and move forward, just as she did. She was a hero who fought back and resisted the cruelty of our enemies."

Dolcetta went back to serving them both coffee and a slice of the crostata. She then filled a third cup and plate for her uncle. "Geremia should be getting up soon and he'll be excited to learn of this connection to Zinabella. He can tell you her whole history far better than I can. Wait while I bring this up to him."

She had been gone only a minute when Jake heard a crash upstairs and a muffled scream. He ran toward the stairway as she came stumbling down with a blank, thousand-mile stare on her face, a faraway look that Jake had seen all too often during combat when soldiers try in vain to distance themselves from a horror they have just witnessed. "What's wrong? What's the matter? What happened?"

Dolcetta shook her head. "Geremia's gone. In his sleep."

The funeral, or more appropriately the burial, took place later that afternoon up on *Montegiudecca* at the Jewish cemetery, a cemetery Jake realized would be populated with all of the many ancestors and relatives whose names had filled Geremia's book. As word spread through town about the rabbi's death, sympathetic neighbors—all Catholics—pitched in to perform the many necessary preparations, from preparing the body to digging the grave. Even the parish priest, Geremia's good friend, the sixty-year-old Father Beccavivi, insisted on helping. Ceneda was a town that, having lost nearly a third of its population during the war and the subsequent reckoning and retribution against the Fascist sympathizers in the months afterward, was all too used to burying its dead quickly.

Dolcetta, who had rummaged through trunks storing her parents' old clothes, found her mother's mourning dress, and wore black. Jake cleaned up his muddied uniform, but in tribute Geremia—and all the Jews who had come before him in Ceneda—he proudly doffed the Rabbi's old red beret instead of his brimmed army cap.

A horse-drawn mortuary wagon belonging to the parish church and driven by Father Beccavivi carried the coffin of the rabbi up a narrow alley known as *Via Giudecca*, Street of the Jews.

This passageway began in the old ghetto and ended at the fog-shrouded cemetery. Jake and Dolcetta, who were completely sleep-deprived for not having rested the night before, walked side by side in a daze behind Father Beccavivi's cart.

By the time their procession delivered the body of Rabbi Geremia up to *Montegiudecca*, a line of some two dozen villagers followed them there to say their goodbyes to a beloved and kindly man who had spent his entire life among them.

There were no prayers and no ceremony. Neighbors lowered the rabbi's coffin into an open grave, one surrounded by five hundred years' worth of Jake's own ancestral history: Coneglianos, Spinozianos, Taorminas, and Palumbos. Jake stayed close by Dolcetta's side as emotional support.

From where he stood, just ten feet away through the fog, was Zinabella Spinoziano's gravestone, which included a carved image of her face, scar and all. Though the etched letters were weathered and worn, he could still make out the epitaph under her name, a quote: "*Purtroppo, figli miei, devo andare via adesso,*" which Jake understood as saying, "Unfortunately, my children, I must leave now." That the epitaph spoke of "children," in the plural and not just the singular child he now knew to be Barbarina, meant that Zina had at least one other as-yet unknown child and perhaps more. But as he wondered, who that child might be, the oddest thing happened—something straight out of *Don Giovanni*. Maybe it was the exhaustion or the lack of sleep, but Jake could have sworn he saw Zina's carved lips move and that she spoke to him and him alone, "Leave the dead to sleep," she said. "Take the hand of the living. Laughter returns at daybreak."

Jake shook his head, as if to remove the cobwebs of confusion, but the voice came back again, this time ever more insistent, "Listen, time is short. Take her hand."

Not one to be a coward—nor one to believe in ghosts—Jake reached out to Dolcetta, who stood alone by Geremia's grave, and took her hand in his own. Her fingers wrapped around his. She turned and smiled. Then, in silence and one by one, each villager came first to Dolcetta and offered her a kiss, a hug, or a solemn handshake. In a half-whisper Jake also greeted the other mourners while introducing himself as *Jacopo, figlio di Abramo e Rosa Conegliano dall'America*, a gesture that brought small but discernable smiles to their faces on an otherwise sad day. Afterward, each respective mourner would toss a stone or a handful of dirt into the grave. The line began with Father Beccavivi and ended with Ferruccio's wife, Anna, and her granddaughter, Olivia.

When her turn came, Anna embraced Dolcetta, whispered something in her ear and then handed her a folded scrap of paper, which the young woman placed in her dress pocket without reading. Anna then faced the open grave and with tears flowing freely, she expressed her love of Geremia and her regret at not having come inside the day before to say goodbye.

When it was Olivia's turn, the young girl picked up a small stone, kissed it three times, and dropped it into the grave, saying as she did so, "Geremia, when you see *mamma e papa* in heaven, please hug them for me." They too had been casualties of war.

After everyone else save Father Beccavivi departed, Dolcetta and Jake were alone with just the wind, the sky, and the smell of freshly turned earth. The gray-haired priest asked Dolcetta if she would permit him to join them for the recitation of the mourner's Kaddish. "I ask not as a priest, but as a man, for your uncle was the dearest of friends."

"*Si, certo*," she replied and the three of them bid goodbye to Rabbi Geremia one last time by reciting the Hebrew prayer for the dead. When they were finished, Jake heard Zina's voice one last time, "*Non dimenticare mai, non dimenticare mai chi sei.*" Never forget, never forget who you are.

Dolcetta, who had remained stoic and unmoved during the entire burial despite her physical and emotional exhaustion, did not want to go home right away. She asked Jake to walk with her, which he did. Though he was glad to leave the ghosts of the cemetery behind, he kept a respectful distance from Dolcetta so as to allow her to remain inside her own thoughts and find the means to mourn one more loss. The more Jake observed Dolcetta, the more he admired her dignity, strength, and resolve.

They spoke no words as they climbed further up the *Via Giudecca* into the hills along *Il fiume Meschio*—the Meschio River—that flowed through town. In the years before electricity, the Meschio had powered Ceneda's mills and workshops. They followed a short trail through a patch of woods that opened up onto a fifteen-foot promontory that overlooked the river. Dolcetta scampered up to the top. Jake followed.

From the top of the point they could see not only the Meschio but the entire valley below that enfolded the village of Ceneda. Jake stared at the view in wonder, as his own parents and the nameless generations that had proceeded them, must have when they too were children, but he felt helpless not knowing how to comfort Dolcetta—if that were even possible. In less than a day she had become *famiglia*, his true family, with all the affection, angst, and ghosts that came with such bonds.

"When we were little," she finally spoke, "We called this place, *Monte Cervino* because it was high like the Matterhorn and we could see our whole world below us. I came here often in the summer with my brothers, sisters, and cousins to escape the heat. We would swim in the Meschio and the ones with courage would climb our *Monte Cervino* and leap from the top into the rapids."

"Did you jump?" asked Jake.

The question brought a smile to her face, the first he'd seen since the morning.

"Of course!" she insisted, picking up a stick of wood. "But not right away. When I was a child, I wondered if I would ever be as strong and courageous as the others. Look," she said, pointing to the rapids below them. "If you jump too short, you hit the mud below us. If you leap too far, the current will sweep you across into the marsh on the far shore. But if you land perfectly in the middle and then relax..." She threw the stick into the water, "The river will gently carry you all the way down to a gravel beach two hundred yards away." It was Gere . . . " She stopped, choked up, and the tears began to flow uncontrollably as Jake observed the stick float toward the beach. "It was Uncle Geremia who taught me and Danielle to act . . . to act with courage and wisdom. Be as brave as Zina, and to never ever fear anything or anyone. Those are the same words he repeated to me when I told him I had joined the resistance."

She collapsed into Jake's arms, sobbing. "I loved that man, I loved my family, I loved Ceneda. And they're gone, all gone." Jake embraced her gently and felt the tremors of grief wrack her body.

"Please," she whispered, "take me home."

They returned on the *Via Giudecca* to the house in the old ghetto. There, Dolcetta, still shaking, poured herself a glass of wine and collapsed on the couch. Jake followed and did the same.

"I cannot stay here any longer," she declared. "Everywhere I look I see ghosts, ghosts I cannot live with." She began to recite names, beginning with Danielle, trembling as she did so, her mother, her father, her other siblings and more, a seemingly endless compilation of the dead.

Jake felt even more helpless. "Where will you go? What will you do?"

She just began to shake her head, no, no, no. "I can't stay, I don't know, I don't know. Just away, maybe Aviano, maybe Treviso, maybe America. Far enough away from here to never see these ghosts again."

She turned to Jake and took his hand. "Help me, hold me, hug me."

He wondered, had she heard Zina too?

He let Dolcetta pull him close against her chest. She found his lips and kissed him. At first just gentle kisses, soft, sweet, tender kisses, but the pain, sadness, and exhaustion inside Dolcetta demanded more. Her kisses became deeper, intense, as if a dam had shattered and a formerly blocked river rushed through, an uncontrollable torrent. She pulled Jake down on top of her and every pent-up emotion inside her exploded into a frenzied passionate wrestling match on the couch, she clutching at Jake, wanting him, and he, hesitant and wondering if he should continue. His heart though, nourished on the hope of love, had no need of a greater inducement.

"But this is where it gets awkward," he finally whispered to her.

Dolcetta stopped and stared deep into Jake's eyes. "Come," she said, standing up. "Let's not be awkward." Dolcetta pulled off her mother's black dress and then, half-naked, led Jake upstairs to her childhood bedroom.

There they made love but not the love of lovers but rather the fire of two wounded, desperate people whose fearsome passion was a balm for each other's soul. And when they were done, they slept hard and deep without dreams inside each other's arms.

So great was their exhaustion neither woke until fourteen hours later when fresh morning sunlight poured into the room through an east-facing window and bathed them both in a warm light. Jake sat up and, turning to Dolcetta, he asked, "What's that noise?"

From somewhere off in the distance they both could hear the sound of a pianist playing the overture to the *Marriage of Figaro*.

"*Dio mio*, the note!" exclaimed Dolcetta jumping out of bed and rummaging through the pockets of the black dress until she found the scrap from Anna and opened it.

"What's going on?" asked Jake, genuinely perplexed.

"Get dressed," she answered. "Greta and the lieutenant are downstairs."

Chapter Six:
The Fires Down Below

Late Sunday Night, January 27, 1771
On the Roof of the Teatro San Benedetto, Venice, Italy

Mozart. Yes, Mozart.

As I embraced my beloved Zina for the first time in eight years and felt her arms around mine, my chest up against her beating heart, my distracted mind raced wildly, I could not help but wonder if that young *genio*, Mozart and the others had escaped the inferno? Would we live to see any of them again?

"We've done this before," Zina whispered in my ear with the same authority and certainty that had always characterized our conversations when we were young lovers. Her words pulled my thoughts back to surveying our own immediate danger. Yes, we had to escape and quickly.

"What? What did we do?" I asked. This was no time for puzzles.

"Jump," she said, "We did it holding hands in Ceneda, at *Monte Cervino* into the Meschio."

Yes, as children, we'd launched ourselves into the air, over and over again perfecting our ability to land in midstream and then ride the rapids to safety at the beach.

"But that was only fifteen feet down," I said, "This is four stories into a shallow canal."

"Listen," she said. The strength of her voice had always reassured me, "Take off your shoes, socks, coat and those ridiculous gloves. We only need run the length of this roof and jump together into the Grand Canal. And if we fail, if we perish, the world will know we died inside each other's arms."

Of course, she was right. Flames bathed the theater in their eerie midnight glow. With no time to waste, we shed our extra garments. Then clutching one another's hands, and with hope in our hearts, we ran as fast and as hard as we could toward the edge of the roof—and the canal below. But just as we leapt into the black void before us, I stumbled over a loose clay tile.

My slip caused Zina to spin out into darkness ahead of me and threatened to pull us apart. But even if it meant death, our fingers held tight. Glancing down, I feared we would not clear the flaming wreckage below. If only we could truly fly and be that Phoenix rising from the ashes of the Teatro San Benedetto.

It had been eight years—August 5, 1763, precisely—since we had last seen each other. I remember well that day. I was not yet fifteen and just coming into my own as a man. Zina was sixteen, a beautiful, mature young woman whose curves set my blood on fire down below. Our families had lived next door to each other in the ghetto of Ceneda. Zina and I grew up as close and tight as if we'd been siblings. After my own mother died giving birth to my youngest brother when I was but five, Zina became my rock, the big sister who kept my life going. All through my childhood we were inseparable and became ever more so when we were teens, a circumstance most families would have looked upon unfavorably, but not ours, for everyone in our community presumed we would eventually marry.

That August day when we said goodbye had begun as any other that season, the one we both called our "virgin summer." Zina and I would have secretly rendezvoused in the woods by the river and made love. Though we had been each other's first and only, together we taught ourselves well the arts of *l'amore*. By August, our passions were far more than just youthful lust. Oh, how we reveled in the joys of touch and being touched as the gods meant it to be when they created mere mortals. At that age of innocence, we rejoiced in the bonds of companionship and partnership, bonds we never envisioned shattering or existing without.

Shortly before noon on that warm and sultry day, I walked Zina and her mother, Anita, who had been fatigued by some undiagnosed heart ailment, down to the stagecoach stop at Antonio Fresia's livery stable at the edge of Ceneda. Zina was to accompany her mother to Treviso to see Dr. Malatesta, a renowned Jewish physician. The two women would be gone upwards of a week.

The coach arrived just as the cathedral bells tolled the noon hour. I loaded their bags with the assistance of Signor Fresia. After we helped Signora Anita step aboard, Zina hugged me goodbye with polite, respectful kisses on my cheeks. I replied with the same gesture. But, ahhh . . . After starting to walk toward the stagecoach, Zina quickly turned back around. She wrapped her arms around me and planted her lips directly on mine. I responded with the same joy and passion that had fired our lovemaking all summer long. Out of the corner of my eye, I spied her mother, Anita, watching and waiting with a smile she could not suppress upon her face. Signora Anita understood how much Zina and I thrived in each other's company.

We did not break from our embrace until Signor Fresia urged Zina to hurry up and board the coach before it left without her.

Watching them leave, I waved goodbye and continued to do so until the coach was out of sight. Signor Fresia then shook me out of my lovesick reverie, saying that my father had left word, that as soon as the coach had departed, he wanted to see me at his leatherworking shop, which was well outside the ghetto and in the heart of town.

Imagining that my father wanted to scold me for being late with his lunch or some other missed errand, or that he had somehow discovered that I had ruined his *Metastasio*, I headed back into the labyrinth of alleys and byways that constituted Ceneda. I was in love and having just kissed *la mia futura sposa* goodbye for the week, I did not care what complaints Papa had.

But when I arrived, I found my father, Gaspare, no longer wearing his red beret, a violation punishable under municipal laws for any Jewish male over thirteen years of age who was found outside the ghetto. When I asked him about this, my father had a different message for me. "Go home," he said, "And help your brothers pack everything into my handcart. We are moving out of the ghetto to a new home adjacent to the Cathedral of Ceneda. And you, you will no longer have to wear your beret either."

When I told him I did not understand, he reminded me that he had been alone since my mother had died ten years earlier. The bishop of Ceneda had granted my father permission to marry a young Catholic woman, Orsola Pasqua, who occasionally helped him at the shop, provided our entire family was baptized as new Catholics.

Those few words from my father caused my whole world to collapse as quickly as an old house in *un terremoto*—an earthquake. I knew all too well that a "*converso*," that is any Jew who became a new Christian, was forbidden by law for the rest of their lives—for the rest of their lives, mind you—to associate with or have contact under any pretext whatsoever with any other *ebreo*. The Catholic Church, which was terrified that Jews who converted would backslide into their old religion at the first opportunity, imposed the most stringent punishment to those who connived to practice as or associate with Hebrews in secret. Depending on the violation, offenders could be sentenced to any or all of the following: the whip, the pillory, indefinite prison, life as galley slave, or hanging by rope until dead.

If all this came to pass, my father's marriage would destroy any chance of mine ever occurring. Not only would Zinabella Spinoziano never become my bride, I would never be allowed to see her again. Stunned and in shock, I at first walked out in a daze and then, feeling as if this *terremoto* had shattered my heart, I ran all the way back along the *Via Giudecca* to the ghetto. There I sought out Zina's father, our rabbi, Baruccio Spinoziano.

We huddled together in his study for over an hour—me sharing my anguish, pain, shock; he consoling, counseling, and calming. Baruccio, a kind, compassionate and wise man, had already spoken with my father earlier that morning and knew about the conversion. Gaspare Da Ponte was not the first Jew in Ceneda to abandon our heritage and convert to Catholicism in search of a safer and less threatening existence, nor would he be the last. Being a Jew in a Christian world has always been difficult, if not downright dangerous. I never understood why we were always the object of hate and abuse simply for existing. Such was our world when I was young and is ever more so now as I endeavor to tell the true story of my life—truths I have heretofore been compelled to keep secret for these very reasons. And those truths are the reason I have written these diaries.

Rabbi Baruccio was a learned man who had spent two years preparing me for my bar mitzvah eighteen months earlier, and consequently understood my heart and the torment I was experiencing with far greater sensitivity than my own father. He urged me to seize the opportunity if it was presented that I could enter a seminary to get an education. "Knowledge is something," he reminded me, "That Jews have always valued as it was the one possession no one can ever take away from you." Baruccio knew too the suffering his daughter, Zina, would endure upon her return from Treviso when the rabbi would have to explain to his own child that the husband she was to have married, lived with, and given rise to a family, would now be absent from the ghetto and her life without recourse.

In the end, he advised me with tears in his own eyes: "Wherever you go, whatever you become, wherever your fate leads you, find peace inside yourself. Know your own heart, know thyself, and if you must, wear the vestments of your new life as lightly as if they were but a Harlequin's costume during Carnevale until such days as you have the strength to reclaim your own fate and return home to yourself."

He then handed me the little brass yad I had used to read the Torah at my bar mitzvah, and said, "Keep this with you, my son, and let it forever be a reminder of who you are, where you have come from, and where you have yet to travel."

After Rabbi Baruccio Spinoziano embraced me for what I believed would be the last time, I handed him my red beret and begged him to share this last part of me with my Zinabella. Looking at the yad, I finally said, "*Purtroppo devo andare via adesso.*"

I left my home later that day, not as the proverbial wandering Jew, but as a converso, with a shattered heart, destined perhaps to never return.

When Zina and I finally smacked into the dark surface of the Grand Canal, the water was icy cold, colder than the baptismal font that had plunged my very life into chaos years earlier. Our descent, which chilled my very soul, had come with such force that my feet smacked the hard bottom of the canal before I was able to push back and fight to reach the surface before my breath ran out. I gasped for air, then screamed aloud, "ZINA!"

We had landed only inches from the burning portico and wharf on one side and a boat filled with theatergoers fleeing the flames on the other. I searched the darkness for her in dread that she had vanished from my life again, but miracle of miracles, she surfaced right beside me.

"I'm here," she said in a whisper, while again raising a finger to her lips. "But we must escape and quickly. If the commendatore's family, the Castis find us, we are dead. Follow me."

As always, she was right. Danger, mortal danger existed if we were caught and even more so if we—a Jewess and a converso priest—were found together. Zina immediately turned and began to swim as quietly as possible toward the opposite shore, where there were a number of empty gondolas tied up to a dock. She had always been an adept and strong swimmer, and tonight was no different, even in the icy waters of the Grand Canal. I struggled to keep up and nearly lost sight of her. By the time I had reached the far embankment, she had already pulled herself into one of the deserted boats.

After climbing in, and careful to not make any noise, I helped Zina untie the boat. We pushed off and glided into the center of the Grand Canal downstream from the theater. Just then there was a huge roar behind us, the sound of the burning wreckage collapsing in upon itself. Though drenched and shivering in the January night air, we took up oars and with great stealth we began to paddle away.

"Where are we going to go?" I asked in a barely audible whisper, "To *La Casa dei Tiepolo?*"

Zina shook her head, "No," and continued to paddle hard as she could. In silence I did the same, in part to speed us away from the wreck of the *Teatro* and in part simply to stay warm. Zina, who knew the web of canals that defined

La Serenissima, took the point and led us off into the dark night.

Only when we were far, far away, and could no longer see the light from the flames, did she turn back and speak in a normal tone. "We need to hide the night before we are found out. Angela's apartments are too dangerous and her brother, Girolamo, is not to be trusted."

Trying to make sense of everything that had happened, I besieged her with a thousand questions as we pushed the gondola forward. And bit by bit, Zina's answers began to expose the mysteries surrounding my first night in Venice.

She began with the birth of Barbarina, whose arrival came here in Venice in the old ghetto just nine months after the last entwining of our virgin summer. When her parents, Rabbi Baruccio and Signora Anita learned of the pregnancy of their unmarried and no longer betrothed daughter, they arranged for her to stay with the Graziano family in Venice as they were also cousins to both Zina and me, my own long-deceased mother being a Graziano. There Zina gave birth to the child—our child—to avoid the shame or humiliation that would arise back in Ceneda.

When Barbarina was a year old, Signora Graziano who had once worked for the Tiepolos herself, arranged for Zina to become the maid servant to Angela. The Tiepolos were an old aristocratic family of Venice whose wealth was derived primarily from property holdings, including their majority ownership in the Teatro San Benedetto. Angela, who was about Zina's same age, took a liking to the young Jewess and her daughter. And though in Venice—as in Ceneda and across most of Europe—Jews were required to return to the locked ghetto each night, Angela made provisions to instead discreetly house Zina and Barbarina at her palazzo. In La Serenissima, women of wealth created their own laws.

The troubles—the ones that led to the killing of the commendatore of the Casti clan—began after Angela's brother, Girolamo Tiepolo, ran up massive gambling debts. Because he was a wastrel, a drunk, and completely unreliable, the family had prevented him from owning any of the family's interests in the theater and other properties. Nonetheless, to pay off his gambling debts to the commendatore, Girolamo gave the head of the Casti family fake certificates of ownership interests in the Teatro San Benedetto.

When the commendatore demanded Angela turn over ownership to him, she refused to honor the bogus documents. The Casti family then went after Girolamo. They kidnapped him and held him for ransom. When Angela heard about their demands for his safe return, she sent Zina to the Castis' palazzo with a note, refusing to pay the ransom and suggesting the commendatore keep her brother instead.

That infuriated the Castis even more, but Girolamo, ever the worm, suggested that Zina, a Jewess, meant more to Angela than he did, and was therefore a far superior hostage for the commendatore.

The commendatore, truly an evil presence, liked Girolamo's idea. Believing he could more successfully hold Zina as ransom, the head of the Casti clan sent Girolamo back to Angela with his new demands—pay up or he turns Zina into his personal concubine.

At this point Zina broke off her narrative. We were, by now, deep into the small canals that linked the city together. "Come," she urged. "Quickly, quietly, we must not be seen."

She slid the boat against a small wharf and tied it up. I followed Zina out of the gondola. She then led me to a nearby storefront, a tailor shop that also sold masks and costumes for Carnevale. Owing to the late hour, the shop was dark and shuttered. She rapped on the door in what struck me as some sort of coded secret knock. When the door opened, a woman holding a lantern and wearing a thick crucifix around her neck, poked her head out as if to ensure all was safe. Seeing Zina, she nodded affirmatively—but said nothing aloud—before letting us slip inside.

We two said not a word either, and I followed Zina's lead. As there was a warm fire burning in a pot-bellied stove, Madame Crucifix motioned for us to warm ourselves beside it while she scavenged up dry clothes. Zina stripped off all of her wet garments down to bare skin and with hand gestures indicated I should do the same. As I peeled off the last vestiges of my Phoenix costume, I could not help but glance over and over again at Zina and admire how beautiful she still looked to me. And, oh, how her curves and smooth flesh set the fires down below burning inside of me once again. Did she feel the same, I wondered? And, oh, the regrets I felt, the deep profound regrets and sadness I felt, realizing once again how much of my soul I had surrendered to the church. I cursed the day—silently of course—of my baptism.

Our Madame Crucifix returned with some undergarments, shoes and two black *tabàro* outfits, complete with capes, *bauta* masks and *tricorno* hats, one sized for a woman, the other for a man. We dressed in haste, all the while not uttering a word or making any unnecessary noise. Zina then had me toss our old garments into the fireplace. I watched the remnants of my Firebird costume and my identity as *Il Cavaliere della Fenice* go up in flames while she scribbled a message for Madame Crucifix to deliver that night to Angela at *La Casa dei Tiepolo*. Madame Crucifix then led us toward the back of the shop where she opened a false wall panel that revealed a small doorway and a secret passage with steps leading down a half flight beyond. She handed Zina a lantern and after urging us into the passageway with more hand gestures, she sealed the doors behind us.

Tunnels were as rare as basements in Venice and it was readily apparent why. Most of our passageway was wet or damp from the high-water table and the air inside the tunnel stank from persistent mold and rot. Nonetheless I followed

close behind Zina for several hundred yards until we came to yet another sequence of doors and false facades. Opening the very last one brought us into the open—and fresh night air—of a small triangular courtyard filled with carts and stalls. But no, not a creature was stirring so late at night.

"Where are we?" I asked in a whisper.

"The ghetto of Venice," she replied in an equally soft voice that nonetheless sent a shudder through my body. The Jewish ghetto of Venice was infamous in the Hebrew community for being the very first ghetto in all Europe where Jews were segregated and locked up at night. The roots of such oppressive tactics were old, long and deep in La Serenissima. And if I, a converso—and a priest at that—was caught seeking shelter here well after midnight when the gates were supposedly locked, that indeed was a major offense worthy of jail or even life until death as a galley slave.

Saying nothing, I stifled the terror in my heart and followed Zina. We crossed the main courtyard, coming at last to the side door of a three-story building. Up the stairs we went to a doorway on the second floor. Zina gave another coded knock and this time we were admitted into the home of the Signora Ricca Graziano, a middle-aged woman Zina describe as the cousin who had first sheltered her when Barbarina was born. Her tiny apartment was but two small, cramped rooms. Although we had awakened Signora Ricca and her youngest child, Celestina, from their sleep, she kindly fed us some warm soup that had been sitting on the stove, before returning to her room to doze off again. She knew better than to ask questions for which she did not need to know the answers.

Over this simple meal, Zina continued her narrative in a low whisper.

"When the commendatore tried to hold me captive, I fought back, as evidenced by my scar, one occasioned by his sword. And when he had me locked in a high room, I escaped by leaping out a window. Tonight, was not the first occasion when I had to swim to freedom."

"But what about the man who killed the commendatore, the one who was dressed as Homer?"

"By Homer, you mean the Chevalier de Seingalt? No, he did not kill the commendatore. I did."

Her answered so stunned me, that I could barely keep my voice down, "You killed the commendatore? But the chevalier, it was his knife."

"Yes," she said, "It was his knife but my hand that did the deed, and gladly." She tapped her scar lightly.

Zina went on to explain that after her initial escape from the Casti palaces, Angela sought out the assistance of an old friend, the chevalier, who was employed in secret as an agent of the Church Office of the Inquisition. The chevalier had a warrant drawn up for the arrest of the commendatore. When they attempted to serve the warrant earlier that evening at the casino by the quay, the commendatore pulled his sword on the chevalier . . .

"And that is when I snatched the knife from Casanova's belt and plunged it into the black-hearted commendatore."

"Casanova?" I asked. Zina continued to surprise. "The libertine himself?"

"Yes, of course, Casanova, your Homer, the Chevalier de Seingalt, and very dear to Angela."

"Her lover?" I asked, but Zina ignored me.

"Casanova's undertakings for the Inquisition and the church are done discreetly. You might say he is a spy, hence the blind Homer mask. In fact, no one in Venice even knows he has returned from his travels to La Serenissima. And," she added for good measure, "it is best for all of us if that it should remain as such."

"And the stories that the commendatore was murdered by a renegade priest? Was that also to throw off the Castis?"

"You, my love, you were in the wrong place at the right time. How were we to know that this priest fumbling about the quay was your high and holy eminence, the Abbé Lorenzo Da Ponte of Ceneda?"

"Must you mock me? I have enough self-loathing for both of us."

"You are the converso, not me," she replied. I could sense the disdain in her voice.

"I didn't plan to convert; it was all my father's doing."

"But nonetheless you embraced the church well enough to become a priest."

"I did that to get an education; it was the only way," I pleaded.

"And what did you learn?"

"That becoming a priest was the biggest mistake of my life, one that I will regret until . . . "

She cut me off. "Until what? Until you find another woman to seduce? I know all about your tryst with Angela. There are no secrets in La Serenissima."

At least she didn't know about my Dona Brunetta—I hoped.

"And in front of your own daughter!" she added for good measure.

"But I, but you . . ." I fumbled helplessly. There was little use in arguing.

"Enough, my love, my poor weak-hearted ancient love. What is it you truly want, what is it that his holiness, the Abbé Lorenzo Da Ponte, truly desires? Tell me, tell me now."

My head was spinning with a thousand confused thoughts. Summoning the courage to speak directly, I finally declared firmly, but in that same hushed whisper we'd both been using. "What I desire, what I have always desired is for you to be my wife."

Zina sneered at me, a gesture that was as devastating as that first *terremoto*, "You married the church. And me? What I desire is to sleep—alone." She pointed at the door to the other room. "My life," she said, "no longer belongs to you. We have been apart eight years, and in that time the passions we once shared have torn and faded like a curtain left out in the sun. That chapter of our lives is long over. Perhaps one day, who knows, matters between us will be different, but for now, I will share Signora Ricca's mattress, and you, you my love, you the converso, you who are still a priest, you my dear abbé, you will sleep there." She pointed to a straw bed near the stove.

Though profoundly disappointed, I knew Zina well enough to know that I would be wasting my time to argue further, so I did not even try. We bid each other good night.

Exhausted by the events and tumult of the day, my first and perhaps last day in Venice, I curled up on my mattress and fell soundly asleep.

Deep into the night, a dream, a particularly engaging one, carried me back to that virgin summer, in Ceneda oh so many years ago. There we were, Zina and I, kissing, hugging, touching, caressing, making love as we had done in the past when suddenly I realized that this was no dream. Zina, Zinabella Spinoziano, the greatest love of my life, had indeed slipped back into my bed.

There, on a straw mattress on the floor of a hovel in the ghetto of Venice, we made love as sweetly, as happily as we had as teenagers. When we were completed and exhausted, I cannot remember ever falling back asleep with such happiness and joy as that night. And to prove it was not a dream, Zina was still in my arms when Signora Ricca woke us in the morning.

The signora, who held her daughter on her hip, handed a message for Zina from Angela that had been slipped under the door during the night. After reading the note, Zina had us up and about quickly. "There is a plan for our escape," she said. "We must go now."

We donned our new disguises in haste. After thanking Signora Ricca Graziano for her hospitality, we immediately left the apartment. The public square of the ghetto was coming to life with shopkeepers setting out their wares. Anxious not to be noticed, we moved in silence. Zina had us retrace our steps from the previous night through the tunnel to Madame Crucifix's tailor shop. The madam had us wait there by the window until the sleek black gondola with Sempronio and Tizio manning the oars appeared in the canal before us.

Again, careful not to be seen, we hurried aboard and into the empty cabin. As the two gondoliers ferried us away from Venice and across the lagoon to the mainland port at Mestre where my odyssey in La Serenissima had begun less than twenty-four hours earlier, Zina revealed to me the rest of our plan of escape.

"Because of the fire, the story about town is that the Casti family destroyed the theater as revenge for the killing of the commendatore. However, since unknown numbers of people perished last night, the Doge's police force and those of the Inquisition are out in force today rounding up members of the clan."

"That's good, yes? You're safe, right?"

"No, only if they believe us dead in the fire, will the feud end. I need to leave Venice indefinitely. Therefore, Angela has arranged for a coach to meet us in Mestre and thence back to the safety of Ceneda."

"Your parents?"

"Oh, they will welcome us. Barbarina and I have been home numbers of times before. And I have friends there now who will take me in."

"But I, under penalty of death, I cannot return with you," I said.

"Correct," she said with absolute certainty. "No. No, you, my dear beloved abbé, you are not going to Ceneda. You are to stay here in Venice. Casanova, the Chevalier de Seingalt, has arranged an appointment for you to serve as a parish priest at the Church of San Luca."

Indeed, at the port of Mestre back on the mainland, we were received by none other than Casanova himself. This time the chevalier was garbed in black robes and a hooded cloak as a church officer of the Inquisition. Behind him was a private coach with four black stallions under harness. Barbarina, who sat inside by an open window, ran out to greet us as soon as she saw us emerge from the gondola.

As the young girl first hugged Zina and then me, Casanova informed us in no uncertain terms that the coach was there to transport Zina and Barbarina back to the safety of Ceneda, but that I was to return to Venice with him in the gondola. Casanova had brought with him as yet another costume for me to wear, that of a parish priest. He handed those to me along with a letter from the bishop of Venice, confirming my appointment as an abbé at the Church of San Luca.

"And if I refuse the appointment," I asked him, "and Zina and I run away together, to live somewhere free, and where no one knows who we are?"

I looked from Zina's eyes to Barbarina's and witnessed nothing but the love I had so desired for so long. As Barbarina stared up at me, I saw the hope in her heart that we would be rejoined. In that instant I imagined the life we would have together: husband, wife, mother, father, daughter. Oh, how I loved my Zina, my Zinabella Spinoziano. I flashed back to our virgin summer, then to our last kiss at the livery stable in Ceneda and finally to the joy of our lovemaking last night. A dream once denied was to become real.

Ever the diplomat, Casanova turned to Zina and asked her, "Will you run away with this man, forever living in the limbo of not knowing who will turn you in or betray your trust?"

Her answer was another *terremoto* that shattered my heart. "Absolutely not. I know who I am and where I belong."

"Well then," said Casanova, "if you run, Abbé Da Ponte, it appears you run alone."

I did not know what to do, what to think, or where to turn. Oh, I silently cursed my own hungers, for any man who builds his hopes upon a woman's heart is the same fool that believes he can snare the wild wind in a net.

"You may do so," Casanova continued politely but with a firm resolve. "It is well within your ability to run off alone. But if you defy us and put either Angela or Zina at risk, please know I will issue a warrant for your arrest. Someone needs to be held accountable for the murder of the commendatore and for torching the Teatro San Benedetto. It might as well be that renegade priest seen on the quay last night with a bloody knife in his hands."

"Is there no other way, no other options?" My eyes danced from Zina to Casanova to Barbarina, all the while looking for some glimmer of hope, for some way out, but there was none. I knew it. I knew the face of defeat. My sense of desperation and loss was as great, if not greater, than it was eight years before when I sat huddled with Zina's father, our Rabbi Baruccio Spinoziano.

Zina broke the silence. *"Purtroppo, dobbiamo andare via adesso. Lorenzo, torna con Casanova, si?"*

"Si," I said in full surrender. Her words were a good and proper poison. The cause was love and I swallowed it in a single gulp.

"Ti amo," She replied. "I love you. I will always love you, but today is not the day."

"Domani," I said with a forced smile. "Tomorrow I will find a way." What doctor, what antidote would save me from this death?

"*Domani,*" she replied. Zina kissed me on the cheeks. Though heartbroken, crushed, I kissed her back.

"*Anch'io,*" insisted Barbarina.

As I knelt down to say goodbye to this daughter who was whisked into and out of my life in a day, I asked her one last question. "How did you know I was your father? How was it you recognized me?"

"*Mani e dita,*" she answered. "Momma always said you would come for us one day. And when I helped you put on your gloves last night, I saw, I knew. *Hai le mani di un Conegliano*—You have the hands of a Conegliano."

Chapter Seven: The Hands of a Conegliano

Just Past Midnight, Sunday, May 13, 1962
Bayside, Queens, New York City

Mozart. Yes, Mozart. Greta was downstairs playing Mozart, only by now, more than sixteen years after they had first met, she was playing the overture to *Don Giovanni*, and Jake Conegliano could not have been happier. And why not? With the exception of one small incident earlier that evening at the Metropolitan Opera House in Manhattan—an incident he kept trying to put out of his mind until he could find a way to share it without upsetting his wife—everything in his life seemed to be working out perfectly.

And though the incident continued to nag at him, he remained determined to focus on all that was not only good, but grand, as if the dreams he had back in Italy had indeed become true. Yes, Greta, she of the milk white skin, crystal blue eyes and copper-red hair, and looking more alluring than ever in her mid-thirties, was downstairs playing Mozart, his beloved Mozart on the Bosendorfer in his den with all the style and grace of a professional concert pianist—which in fact is what she had become. And, of course, Mozart was her specialty.

But tonight, tonight was about family and friends. Crowded around Greta with glasses of prosecco in hand, would be the lieutenant, now British Cultural Attaché Enrico Foxx; Dolcetta, still lean and radiant at thirty-five; Jake's parents, Abe and Rosa Conegliano, whose private box at the Met they had all shared; Manny, Jake's nearly sixteen-year-old son whose college graduation they were all celebrating; Manny's girlfriend Pandorea, seventeen, who had also just graduated; and finally Pandorea's parents, professor of Italian literature Frank Cornetti and his wife, a cardiologist, Dr. Marietta Cornetti. And, yes, having just returned from the Met's performance of *Don Giovanni*, everyone was dressed to the nines, the women all in elegant summer-weight black gowns and bedecked with diamonds, pearls, and sapphires, while the men all wore the requisite tuxedoes.

Still upstairs and away from his guests, Jake hung his tuxedo jacket up in the bedroom closet and then loosened his tie. On the bed was the Conegliano feather quilt that once belonged to his ancestors in Ceneda. He had come up to the bedroom to find the cigars, hand-rolled Cuban Cohibas, that the former lieutenant had gifted him upon his arrival in New York a few days earlier. Enrico, as the lieutenant preferred to be known these days, had come straight to Jake's office in Manhattan directly after his flight from Tel Aviv had landed at Idlewild Airport with intelligence reports that had been coded as "Top Secret."

Yes, although Jake and his old compatriot, Enrico Foxx, were now closer to forty than twenty years of age, both colleagues still worked in the shadowy world of military intelligence. After returning to New York in May of 1946 with his Italian war bride, Jake had taken on a part-time job as a warehouse stock clerk for his father's electronics supply house while looking for full time employment more commensurate with the skills he had acquired in the army. Although he found clerking to be menial and unsatisfying, his mother reminded him that there's no shame in any work that puts food on your table—and his wife was pregnant with Manny.

When not at the warehouse, Jake knocked on many a door looking for work but without success. Then in September, just before the baby was born, a breakthrough came in the form of a transatlantic call from British Cultural Attaché Enrico Foxx. Apparently, the former lieutenant had made a recommendation on Jake's behalf for a position as an analyst with a rather secretive and private firm in Manhattan that did studies and research for the old Federal Office of Strategic Services. The OSS, as it was more commonly known, would eventually morph a few years later into the CIA.

Part of Foxx's portfolio included collaborating with the American intelligence agencies on hunting Nazis, who after the end of WWII were escaping to South America; however, on the call, Foxx alluded to Jake that their efforts were being stymied by anti-Semites in both the British and American services. Seems that in the early years after the war the Allies were more interested in employing hundreds of former Nazi scientists—such as SS Lt. Werner von Braun—to work on missiles and rockets than they were in chasing down those who had perpetrated the Holocaust. Foxx needed insiders who were smart enough and passionate enough to circumvent the obstructionists without letting on that they were Jewish. Jake jumped at the chance and landed the assignment.

The work of covertly tracking Nazis appealed to Jake far more than clerking in his father's warehouse. And much like his Conegliano ancestor, Lorenzo Da Ponte, Jake hid his Jewish identity and lived a life of secrets, masks, and disguises. He allowed everyone at the CIA to assume he was just another Italian-American Catholic. The trick worked. After a decade and a half, their efforts were now steadily and consistently bearing fruit.

The "Top Secret" reports that Enrico had brought him from the British MI6 spy agency, were the supporting notes from the trial in Israel of Adolph Eichmann, one of the masterminds of the Holocaust. Eichmann had hidden out for more than a decade in Argentina before his eventual capture by Israeli agents. The intelligence data could potentially help Jake expose the neo-Nazi network that helped Eichmann escape Europe through an underground network of Catholic monasteries. Among the prime suspects was the former abbé, now bishop, Luigi Hudal from Santa Maria dell'Anima. Hudal, whom Jake had been able to link to the German SS, was also suspected as being the mastermind of the raid on Dolcetta's village of Ceneda.

But tonight was not about secrets; it was about a celebration in honor of Manny—as much a genio as Da Ponte and Mozart—whose graduation, summa cum laude from Columbia University with a double major in linguistics and music, had been the focus of the weekend. Manny could read by age three, was bilingual with fluency in Italian by five, mastered the piano at seven, wrote his first concerto at ten, completed high school at twelve, and now his bachelor's. Watching Manny grow up and shatter academic boundaries at an unheard-of pace made Jake feel like Mozart's father.

As he searched for where their housekeeper might have hidden the box of cigars, Jake could hear the kids downstairs singing the wedding duet between Masetto and Zerlina, "Giovinette che fate all'amore," from *Don Giovanni*. Greta accompanied them on the Bosendorfer, while everyone else sang the chorus parts.

Zerlina/Pandorea:

> *You girls who have suitors,*
> *Don't wait until it's too late.*
> *If your hearts seethe with impatience,*

> *See, here is the remedy! Ah!*
> *What delight is in store!*

Chorus/All:
> *Ah! What delights; what delights are in store!*
> *Tra la la ra la!*

Masetto/Manny:
> *You feather-brained young lads.*
> *Don't go gadding about.*
> *The madcap's revelry has yet to begin. Ah!*
> *What delight, what delight is in store!*

There was such joy and optimism in the kids' voices and why not, he thought. Not only had they just graduated, they had both done so from Columbia University at an age when most of their peers were still struggling with high school algebra. Pandorea, who was also *un genio*, on a par with Manny, had an immaculately clean and strong mezzo-soprano voice that filled Zerlina's wedding eve song with exuberance. Manny's rich bass-baritone reminded him of Ezio Flagello's Leporello that they had heard at the Met only a few hours earlier.

Yes, both were prodigies. In a few hours they would be flying to Vienna for a graduate studies program in music and opera at the university there for the balance of the summer before returning to Columbia to complete their respective PhDs. Manny's major was to be in a newly created program in international affairs with the ultimate goal of carrying on in his father's field of espionage and perhaps become the next Wild Bill Donavan, but one who could also sing any of Mozart's arias from memory. Pandorea, whose talents were as multi-faceted as Manny's, was fascinated by the convergence of music, art, literature, and education, and she pictured herself as becoming either the youngest executive director ever for the Library of Congress or the chief curator at the Smithsonian. No, these two, with their astonishing talents, did not harbor small aspirations or dreams, dreams Jake believed they would easily accomplish.

Nonetheless, their innocence and enthusiasm recalled to Jake, Rabbi Geremia's words to him on that fateful weekend in Ceneda oh so many years past: "When you warm other people's hearts, you warm yourself. When you support, encourage and inspire others, then you will discover support, encouragement, and inspiration in your own life. And when you love and when others love and honor you, you create family and community. That my children, is Judaism, that is love, and that is my blessing for both of you."

Jake indeed felt blessed, not only by his son's extraordinary successes but also by his choice of a girlfriend, a young woman who in every way was his match, even culturally. Pandorea's parents were *Ebrei siciliani*—Sicilian Jews who had escaped the Nazi roundup after the collapse of Mussolini's regime by hiding out in a cave in the hill country near Siracusa and then assisting the American troops with invaluable intelligence during Patton's invasion of the island. The two migrated to America immediately after the war with support from HIAS, the same Hebrew Immigrant Aid Society that had assisted his parents when they settled in New York before the First World War. Frank, a professor of Italian literature, was also the new acting director of the Italian Language Library at Columbia University, and Marietta, a top tier surgeon, taught at Columbia's Medical School. Both were superb "old country" cooks, who enjoyed good wine and great opera, which only added to the charm and pleasure of being their friends.

When Jake finally found the box of Cubans under a stack of books his housekeeper had shoved under the bed before his guests has arrived, he opened it and inhaled deeply. Though he rarely smoked, Jake had developed a deep affection for the cigars. He pulled out four of the Cohibas along with a box of matches and a cutter and headed back out of the master bedroom and toward the stairs.

Chorus/All:
>   Ah! What delights; what delights are in store!
>   Tra la la ra la!

Zerlina & Masetto/Pandorea & Manny:
>   Come sweetheart, let's enjoy ourselves
>   And sing and dance and jump for joy!
>   Come, sweethearts, let's enjoy ourselves! Ah!
>   What delight, what delight is in store!

Chorus/All:
>   Ah! What delights; what delights are in store!
>   Tra la la ra la!

Earlier this year, Frank Cornetti, who knew from the kids that there was some sort of familial bond between the Da Pontes, the Coneglianos, and the Spinozianos, had lent Jake a copy of Da Ponte's *Memoirs*, from the Columbia library's collection.

Lorenzo Da Ponte's diaries had been translated from the Italian into English and published by one Elisabeth Abbott back in 1929, but they contained virtually none of the materials in any of the leather-bound volumes Geremia had gifted him. The discrepancies between the 1929 edition and these so-called *Secret Diaries*, puzzled Jake. Not once in Elisabeth Abbott's work was there even so much as a mention of the word "Jew." Nor did Da Ponte ever describe his hands as being those of a Conegliano; nor did he ever admit that he had been born in the ghetto of Ceneda in 1749 as Emanuele Conegliano and that he did not become a converso until 1763, a year after his bar mitzvah. Neither was there any mention of Zina Spinoziano, his Jewish girlfriend, nor their child, Barbarina. With his conversion to Catholicism came his new name, Lorenzo Da Ponte, the same moniker as the bishop who had presided over the ceremony, and the beginning of his unwitting journey toward becoming a priest.

And this purported Venetian encounter in 1771 of Da Ponte and Mozart? As best Jake could research, yes, they were both in La Serenissima on January 27, 1771, but there is not a single other historical record or document that could attest to their actually meeting there or then. The 1929 edition does not have them encountering each other until May of 1783, in Vienna at the home of Baron Raimund Wetzlar von Plankenstern, one of Mozart's benefactors, and like Da Ponte, a converso. Jake knew that the Teatro San Benedetto did burn down to ultimately be replaced by the now famous La Fenice, but did the "cherub" incident actually occur? Or was Mozart's presence there an invention of Da Ponte's? And if so, why would he lie? And if it was the truth, why were these autobiographical details about Da Ponte's life as a Jewish converso priest self-censored when he wrote and published his *Memoirs*? Jake had no answers, at least not yet.

And although Dolcetta had already determined that she was a descendant of Da Ponte through Zina and their daughter Barbarina, Jake's connection to Da Pontes was still not totally clear even though they were both born Coneglianos and that had puzzled him all of these years since those days in Ceneda. Unraveling the connection to Da Ponte and fully translating all of the *Secret Diaries* was something Jake had been determined to complete, but real life in the form of his job, a marriage and a child, especially a child who gobbled up knowledge at an unprecedented pace, had gotten in the way. Perhaps the answer lay buried in the genizah along with all of the other papers, documents, and volumes of the *Secret Diaries* yet to be translated. Or maybe it was in the missing history of Zina's other children, as suggested by her tombstone's epitaph. But for now, the genizah trunk, along with all of his old army uniforms and gear, was safely stowed away in the attic of his two-story garden apartment just blocks from Alley Pond Park in Queens, New York.

Though Jake was still unsure of his connection to Da Ponte, it did not stop him from naming his son after Mozart's librettist. Manny was after all short for Emanuele.

Jake sat down on the top step not only to listen but to reflect back again on all the good fortune that had happened to bring him forward to this time and place since those seemingly dark days in the Veneto. From the top of the stairway Jake had a bird's-eye view of everyone singing below. The scene reminded him of that morning sixteen years earlier in Ceneda, when he and Dolcetta, woke to Greta's playing Mozart's overture to *The Marriage of Figaro*.

On that fateful day so many years ago, both he and Dolcetta had not only raced to get dressed—she in her turquoise shirtwaist dress and he in his uniform—they did it with guilt, massive guilt, over what had happened the night before. They were each so nervous and uncomfortable that neither could speak nor look the other in the eye. Jake—in retrospect, naively—believed as Guglielmo did in *Cosi Fan Tutte* that his Greta could not have been as faithless nor succumb to temptations as he and Dolcetta had done. Maybe the lieutenant with his Errol Flynn eyes would betray their trust, but Greta? He fancied heaven had made her as constant and strong as her blue eyes had lured him in.

Ah, so when Dolcetta and Jake started to walk down those stairs back in Ceneda, they were startled to find not only the lieutenant, but Father Beccavivi, Ferruccio, Anna and grand-daughter Olivia Fresia as well, all crowded around Greta at the rabbi's old piano. And for some reason Father Beccavivi was wearing Geremia's red beret; the Fresias were dressed in their Sunday-best clothes, Olivia held a clutch of white crocus flowers and the double doors separating the rabbi's study and the synagogue had been flung wide open.

Dolcetta called out in disbelief, "*Che cosa?* What are you all doing here?"

The music stopped. Father Beccavivi spoke first. "Yesterday was one of sadness when I buried my best friend; today is one of joy. And 'why' you may ask? Well, now that you are both here, there's going to be a wedding."

"A wedding?" Jake asked, dumbfounded. "Here? Who? What?"

The lieutenant put his arms around Greta. "We are," The lieutenant said in English. "Greta and I, we decided to get married," which he then rapidly translated into German for Greta's benefit. Given Foxx's limited command of Italian, German was the only common language they both spoke fluently, "*Greta und ich. Wir haben uns entschlossen zu heiraten.*"

"*Ja,* yes, *sì!*" added Greta enthusiastically, but her eyes, also filled with guilt and a bit of remorse, darted back and forth between Jake and Dolcetta as if seeking their approval.

In rapid order the lieutenant explained that he and Greta had fallen in love in Treviso while watching *The Marriage of Figaro*, and though it might appear hasty, in fact they had known each other for some time now. Seems Greta's work at La Fenice also involved her being a covert agent for the British during the later stages of the war as it gave her cover to mingle with German officers. Foxx had long been her contact and control agent, but it wasn't until they were inspired by *Figaro* that he let go of fear and decided to propose.

"I confess," he said, "That whenever I spoke with Greta in the past, my courage at expressing my love and affection failed. My lips would stammer, and I simply could not say the words which had stayed locked inside me. But I am a soldier and in moments of the greatest stress, they say a hero must call upon all his strength. Between acts—finding my courage—I fell to my knees before Greta, 'In me alone you'll find a husband, lover, and more, if you agree,' and I smiled when she turned her most merciful eyes upon me and replied 'Yes.' "

"How could I refuse this man I had loved from afar for so long," said Greta. "Everyone blames we women if we change our affections," she added, looking directly at Jake, "but you, you must forgive me, for it is a necessity of our hearts." She turned then to Dolcetta. "We women are all the same, *non e' vero?*" Greta stroked the lieutenant's cheek. "Have you ever seen a nobler face, a sweeter mouth, or eyes more charming? If ever my heart changes its affections again, may that love cause me to live in pain instead."

Their news swept over Jake, leaving him not only speechless and dumbfounded but feeling as if he had been cast as one of the hapless lovers in *Cosi Fan Tutte*. All of Greta's earlier kisses, tears, and sighs? Two days ago. How could she forget them so soon? Nonetheless she had, and there was naught Jake could do about it.

However, whatever guilt, loss or confusion he may have felt, vanished as Dolcetta slipped her hand around his. He loved her touch; it made him happy in ways he had never experienced before in his own young life. Yes, Rabbi Geremia was correct, Dolcetta did cook like an angel, she did clean up like a goddess, and yes, she had killed Nazis with her bare hands. But one day, it only took one day for Jake to realize he had fallen wildly in love with her. And maybe, one day, he thought, Geremia's awfully cute and adorable niece, the first woman he had ever felt truly at home with, would become a fine wife for an extraordinarily lucky man named Jake Conegliano.

"And I am here wishing you all every happiness," said Father Beccavivi, hefting a basket filled with food and wine. "Let's jump to it, my friends. I am thrilled to perform the ceremony; We must light candles and prepare a table to celebrate in the style of our old nobility."

"But is all this legal, sir? Aren't there regulations, army rules and such?" Jake asked the lieutenant in English. "A British officer and an Italian civilian?"

"No, your assessment is correct, Corporal. No, it's not cricket, actually," replied Foxx, "But it is symbolic and something we both wanted to do before returning to Aviano. As you can well imagine, Corporal, the real paperwork will take months. But we have two more nights to honeymoon here in Ceneda." Foxx started to sing. "*To soothe the pangs of our innocent love. And after that, no more a soldier's life for me!*"

"Come," said Father Beccavivi, "Let's find a way of making matters right. In such times as we live, one must be philosophical. If it is acceptable to you, Dolcetta, I want the marriage ceremony for Greta and the lieutenant to be in your synagogue."

"*Certamente. Ma perché?*" said Dolcetta, perplexed. "You have a cathedral on the hilltop, no?"

"The stone walls of a cathedral are cold comfort to a man who has lost his faith. When your Uncle Geremia returned after the war," continued Father Beccavivi, "we spent much time together, both cleansing the synagogue and gathering the records of the Jewish community. I was deeply depressed by all I had witnessed during those years and the suffering inflicted, often in the name of our Lord. I struggled to understand how God could have allowed such horrors to occur. It was Geremia who taught me that true religion, that is God's insight, is divinely inscribed in the hearts of all people and has nothing to do with theology, sectarianism, or what house of worship one used for their ceremonies. True religion, Geremia would repeatedly assert, consists of a few simple principles: love your neighbor as yourself, and practice justice and loving kindness toward your fellow human beings."

"I understand, Father, but still I ask, why here?"

"Were I not a man of six decades already, I would renounce these robes and find a new occupation. But I cannot, nor would Geremia, were he still with us, allow me to do so. He would insist that I share my insights with my flock and comfort them in the knowledge that the highest state of human enlightenment and happiness occurs when we understand the laws of nature and experience that peace of mind such wisdom brings. It is to honor Geremia's memory that we should see a wedding here today."

"*Assolutamente!*" piped up Olivia. "I want to see a double wedding with lots of kisses!"

"A double wedding?" questioned Jake and Dolcetta in unison. Jake smiled at Dolcetta, and when she blew a kiss back at him, Jake fell to one knee.

"Would you marry me?"

"*Dio mio! Certamente!*" exclaimed Dolcetta. And just as Zina's ghost had predicted to Jake the day before, Dolcetta did laugh aloud in the morning, "Merciful heavens," she giggled like a young girl, "please, do with me what you will."

He took Dolcetta's hand and replied back with a line he recalled from *Cosi Fan Tutte*, "May the consolation for our sorrows be, to share our own sweet affection."

"*Certamente!*" she repeated as everyone moved through the open doorway and into the synagogue. The two couples paired off and stood beneath the chuppah.

Joining them under the wedding canopy were Ferruccio and Anna to serve as witnesses, with Olivia, of course, as the flower girl. Olivia separated the bouquet of crocuses into two halves and then handed one to each of the brides.

Father Beccavivi draped one of Geremia's rabbinical shawls, a tallit, over his shoulders. He then turned to Dolcetta and held out in his hand two gold rings, "I have these for you to use. They belonged to your mother and father. I cannot tell you now how it is I rescued them, but Geremia begged me preserve them for you, just for this very day. Will you now accept them as your own?"

Tears flooded over Dolcetta, realizing the priest had probably removed them from her parents' bloodied corpses before the Nazis looted them. "Si, certo. I accept."

Father Beccavivi looked at Jake as if to ask him as well.

"*Anch'io*," said Jake as he took the rings from the priest and placed the smaller one on Dolcetta's ring finger. She did the same for him with the other.

Anna then spoke up, "And we have a pair for the lieutenant and Signorina Greta. It would be an honor for us to have you married with them."

"Ecco," said Olivia, pulling two rings out of her dress pocket. "*Di mamma e papà.*"

Both Greta and Enrico thanked the girl and the little ceremony began with a benediction as unorthodox as the lives they each had endured through years of war.

Father Beccavivi intoned, "Blessed are the two bridegrooms and their lovely brides. May a kindly heaven smile on them. By these words as spoken by me and in the eyes of our friends, the following are joined in matrimony: Signorina Greta Tedesco with Lieutenant Enrico Foxx, and with Corporal Jacopo Conegliano, Dolcetta Spinoziano, her sister in spirit and affection. The two ladies are natives of our Italia; the gentlemen, an English aristocrat; and the other, an American soldier born of Italian blood. And to honor your mutual love, may the joy of matrimonial bliss be forever granted. And in the manner of roosters and hens, may you be prolific with progeny to equal you in wisdom, beauty, and courage. In the name of whatever gods that may be left to us, I pronounce you . . . "

Jake was abruptly shaken from his memories by a shout from his father, Abe, "Jake what about those Cubans you promised?"

And this was immediately followed by Enrico singing an a cappella spoof of "Bella Vita Militar" from *Cosi Fan Tutte*.

A cigar's life for me!
Every day a change of scent;
Cohiba today, calabash tomorrow,
Now on land and now but smoke.
The sound of matches and fires,
The sips of rum and brandy,
Lend strength to our charms and our spirits,
Longing only for victory.
A cigar's life for me!

Jake got the message. "I'm coming." He walked down the stairs past the portrait of Zina that hung on the wall, past a pile of suitcases on the floor and into the den where his father had already refreshed everyone's prosecco.

He handed each of the men—that is Enrico, Abe, and Frank—a cigar and took a seat beside his Dolcetta, a woman who brought him such joy and happiness every day of his life, that he could not envision even waking in the morning without her beside him.

"You're not going to smoke that now, are you?" Dolcetta asked. "The kids are still singing." In the years since coming to the States, Dolcetta had not only perfected her English, she actually worked as a part-time translator for the State Department's United Nations staff.

Jake nodded agreement. "*Domani*," he said. So deep was their trust of each other that he never argued with Dolcetta. Jake knew if she made a request, it was going to be honest, true, and sincere. Her ethics were impeccable. No games, no manipulations, just her core beliefs, and if she stated her feelings to him about some issue or another, he respected that and did his best to make her happy. She conversely did the same for him. They had flowed together so well for so long that he could not even remember the last time they had a fight about anything.

Frank thanked Jake, but added as he glanced at his watch, "I'll save this for another day, too. Our limo should be here pretty soon."

A stretch car had already been booked to deliver Frank and Marietta back home to Brooklyn after dropping both of the kids, as well as Enrico and Greta at the airport for a BOAC charter flight to Vienna, courtesy of the British Counsel's office. Vienna was home base now for Enrico, the British attaché, and wife, Greta, the touring concert pianist. Jake suspected Greta's travels were a cover for continued espionage work in Central Europe, but in his line of business, one never asked unless you absolutely required an answer. The Foxxes, who were also Manny's godparents, owned an extensive and grand style penthouse suite in the heart of Vienna on *Kartnerstrasse*. It was there that Manny and Pandorea would be staying over the summer as their guests.

"Me too," added Enrico pocketing his cigar, "*Domani.*"

"*Anche lui,*" said Jake's mother, Rosa, to Abe, as she gently—but firmly—took the cigar from him and dropped it into her purse. She still insisted on speaking Italian whenever possible, though by now it was far more habit than anything spoken for Jake's benefit.

"Oh, Rosie, must you?" Abe lodged a mild protest, but then blew a kiss to his wife of forty-five years.

"*Domani,*" replied Rosa. "*Domani, amore mio,* especially if you want to sleep in my bed tonight," a response that had everyone laughing.

With that exchange over cigars over, Manny and Pandorea resumed singing as Greta hit the piano keys. This time the kids alternated stanza of the infamous catalogue song, "Madamina," from *Don Giovanni*.

In his bold bass-baritone, Manny began by leaning in toward his grandmother and intoning:

Little lady, this is the record
Of the beauties my master has loved.

It's a catalogue that I myself compiled.
Come closer, read it with me.

But then Pandorea, jumped in, affecting a deep male voice she sang to Abe:

In Italy six hundred and forty,
In Germany two hundred and thirty one,
One hundred in France. In Turkey ninety-one,
But in Spain already one thousand and three!
One thousand and three,
One thousand and three,
One thousand and three!

As they worked through the lyrics, it triggered Jake's memory of the incident—Manny's incident at the Met during intermission, the one his genio son knew better than to share with mother, Dolcetta. As Manny had described it to Jake, Manny had spotted the woman he thought was his mother at the bar kissing another man. The woman's back was toward him, but in all aspects, he was certain it was his mother, right down to the black gown she wore and the red lace shawl draped over her shoulders. Even her hair had been lifted up into a French twist identical to Dolcetta's. Who, but twins do that, even one who had supposedly died of typhus at Dachau twenty years ago?

Manny had blurted out, "Mom!" and when she turned around to face him, he was even more certain it was his mother—but her eyes gave no hint of recognition. Her words came out in a thick Italian accent and hesitatingly as if she had some sort of speech defect. "Do . . . I . . . Do I . . . Do I know . . . know you?" the woman had said.

Manny realized she was a complete stranger. "I'm sorry. My mistake." Only when he turned and started to walk away did he spot the concentration camp numbers tattooed on her forearm. Although the first few digits were hidden by the embroidery of her red shawl, Manny remembered the rest, and later wrote them down, "9213474."

Was that woman Danielle? Jake was clearly torn. Over the years since the war's end, there had been a number of leads that indicated that Danielle might still be alive, that she had somehow survived Dachau. As before, he would run the information he had past the various Allied intelligence agencies, hoping to narrow down possible leads. And if they couldn't, maybe HIAS or one of the other resettlement agencies could.

In the past though, each time Dolcetta got her hopes up that her twin, the other half of the *Gemelli angeli*, was alive, those dreams were crushed. Dolcetta would then fall off an emotional cliff and swim in a sea of depression. And then, the ghosts of the dead would circle around her head—so much so that she couldn't function. Her withdrawals into darkness could last days, sometimes weeks. She'd stay in bed, skip work, and sleep fitfully, tormented by her memories. She'd wake at odd hours, exhausted and drained, only wanting to sleep more to get through it, but afraid to do so, knowing that the ghosts would reappear as soon as her eyes closed.

If there was one shadow over their marriage that pained him, it was this, for he knew that other than remaining loving, there was nothing he could do to banish those demons, demons that would be there for the rest of her life.

Meanwhile, the kids continued to sing. Manny jumped right back in with these lines to his mother, Dolcetta:

> *Here are country wenches,*
> *Chambermaids and city ladies,*
> *Countesses, baronesses.*
> *Marchionesses, princess,*
> *There are women of ever social class,*
> *Every shape and every age.*

Jake saw how happy Dolcetta was watching her son sing. He then and there decided he would wait until the morning, after everyone else would have left, except his parents. Jake was grateful his folks would be spending the night in the guest room before driving back to the Bronx the next day. He was certain he'd need their support with Dolcetta. Abe and Rosa knew and loved their daughter-in-law. They had welcomed Dolcetta into their hearts as family the moment she arrived in the States from Ceneda, pregnant with their future grandson, Manny. To them she was a living symbol of "home," a connection to their past and a treasured presence in their lives. Over the last decade and a half, Rosa had come to consider her as much her daughter as Jake was their son, maybe even closer. Dolcetta, for her part, had fully adopted them as the parents she no longer had and confided in them as such, especially Rosa.

Now Pandorea repeated the chorus as if a warning to her father, Frank:

> *In Italy six hundred and forty,*
> *In Germany two hundred and thirty one,*
> *One hundred in France. In Turkey ninety-one,*
> *But in Spain already one thousand and three!*
> *One thousand and three!*
> *One thousand and three!*
> *One thousand and three!*

Singing to Pandorea's mother, Manny then leaned in toward Marietta:

> *Here are country wenches,*
> *Chambermaids and city ladies,*
> *Countesses, baronesses.*
> *Marchionesses, princess,*
> *There are women of every social class,*
> *Every shape and every age.*

And then Pandorea and Manny both brought the song home with an impassioned duet where they not only alternated stanzas but also mimed out the actions as well.

Pandorea:

> *With a fair-haired girl his habit*
> *Is to praise her kindness,*

>*A brunette is always constant,*
>*A blonde is always sweet.*

Manny:
>*In winter he likes plumpish girls.*
>*In summer slender ones;*
>*Tall ones he calls majestic*
>*Short ones always dainty.*

Pandorea:
>*He seduces older women*
>*Just to add them to his list*
>*But his ruling passion*
>*Is for the young novice.*

Manny:
>*He doesn't give a hoot for wealth*
>*Or ugliness or beauty*
>*Provided she wears a skirt*
>*You know what he will do.*

Just then, the doorbell rang. As Jake got up to answer it, everyone else, presuming it was the limo and thus the end of their party, all joined in on one last round of the chorus.

All:
>*In Italy six hundred and forty,*
>*In Germany two hundred and thirty one,*
>*One hundred in France. In Turkey ninety-one,*
>*But in Spain already one thousand and three!*
>*One thousand and three!*
>*One thousand and three!*
>*One thousand and three!*

In a matter of minutes, luggage was loaded, fond farewells made, kisses and hugs given, tears shed and then, the six of them were gone, leaving Jake, Dolcetta, Abe, and Rosa behind.

As Jake helped his parents get set up in the guest room, Dolcetta straightened up in the den.

By the time Jake made it back to their own room, Dolcetta was already sitting up in bed with a book, but not any book. It was the "Vienna," volume of the *Secret Diaries*. In her hand was Da Ponte's yad.

"*Dio mio.* You're reading that?" he asked as he quickly undressed.

"Yes, I pulled it from out of the genizah trunk yesterday. If my only son is heading off to Vienna, I want to see what my great, great, great grand-*pappi* wrote about it," She said. Dolcetta patted Jake's side of the mattress. "Join me?"

"Si. Certo. Assolutamente." Jake slid into bed beneath the Conegliano quilt and snuggled beside the woman he adored and together, for the first time in many years, they returned to reading and translating, *The Secret Diaries of Lorenzo Da Ponte*.

Part Two
Vienna

Chapter Eight:
The Emperor's Mistress

Wednesday Night, After the Opera, January 4, 1786
The Burgtheater, Vienna

"**M**ozart?" asked Joseph II, the Hapsburg emperor. "Where is Signor Mozart?"

How could I tell him that Mozart was backstage engaged in an affair with Nancy Storace, who was not only the leading diva of our Viennese opera but also the emperor's own mistress?

Morals aside, these were delicate times indeed, not just for Mozart but for me as well. Clearly, I could not reveal the truth to His Majesty, our theater benefactor and perhaps the most powerful monarch in all Europe. One false step would bring about ruin for both of us. Any exposure of Mozart's affair with Storace would instantly threaten to derail not just his career but mine too, for in truth, we had been partnering in secret on a new libretto inspired by Beaumarchais' controversial French play, *The Marriage of Figaro*, that the emperor's own censor, Count Pergen, had already banned as a German language stage production. Our goal was to win not only His Majesty's approval to produce it as an opera for his Court Theater, but his blessings as well. Were we up to the challenge?

At age thirty, Wolfgang Amadé Mozart was no longer the boy genio, the cherub, I had met years earlier in Venice. Here in Vienna, Mozart was just one more struggling musician among many of significant talent, each jockeying for work as a composer of operas at the Burgtheater. He was married now, a father to an infant son and still took on live-in students to help pay off his debts. Despite his earlier accomplishments with concertos and as a pianist—and his predilections for dawdling with the sweeter sex—Mozart was desperate to produce an Italian opera for the Vienna Court Theater. So was I.

Our success or failure in this world filled with sycophants and snakes, hung in balance on the good will of Joseph II. The emperor was a knowledgeable, direct, and reasonable man without pretense. He played the clavier and flute, knew the complexities of musical compositions, took a direct interest in who crafted operas for his court and was not above employing all the leading divas of Europe, even if it meant sleeping with stars such as Storace.

I had to come up with an answer to "Where was Signor Mozart?" And quickly.

As the emperor and I faced off in the orchestra pit after the performance, Joseph II was surrounded by the usual coterie of aristocratic connivers and backstabbers: Count Franz Orsini Rosenberg, His Majesty's lord chamberlain and head of the Burgtheater; Antonio Salieri, the director of the court's Italian opera and a prolific composer in his own right; the Abbé Giambattista Casti, a fellow librettist and my potential rival; and the renowned composer, Giovanni Paisiello. Paisiello's fame came on the heels of his adaptation of Beaumarchais' prequel to *Figaro*, *The Barber of Seville*, for the Russian Empress Catherine the Great. Here in Vienna, Paisiello's *The Barber of Seville*, was a huge hit, and thus the composer was not above toadying up to Joseph II for a commission and bullying those that might stand in a queue ahead of him.

Only moments before Joseph II had inquired about Mozart, he and his entourage had, offered up warm congratulations on the most successful premiere of my opera, '*Il burbero di buon cuore,*' written for another friend and one of His Majesty's newly favored court composers, Vicente Martin y Soler. It was my first true success as a librettist and one I desperately needed to build upon. "*Abbiamo vinto!* We have won," Joseph II had declared after the performance. Such little victories helped to not only fend off my detractors and competitors but were also necessary to put bread—and wine—upon my table. And although I had earlier requested an opportunity to speak to Joseph II about our new project, this was not the right moment, especially in front of these serpents.

In this viper-ridden world, trust was something one garnered toward no man, for today's friend would no doubt be tomorrow's enemy. And as I raced to find an appropriate response to Joseph II's question, I studied the faces of his entourage for a clue to guide me.

Of those four, all of whom were Italian, the Abbé Casti, might have been my greatest threat, but to say that aloud would be to diminish the dangers presented by the other three. Casti, twenty years my senior and a friend of my friend, Casanova, had had great success along with Paisiello in St. Petersburg and aspired to do the same for Joseph II. When he arrived in Vienna, Casti presented himself to me initially as a colleague of the pen and a comrade of good cheer. Casti—like Casanova—also had a reputation as a dissolute womanizer. Even his face resembled that of a satyr. But what concerned me more despite his offer of friendship, was that Casti was a cousin—just a distant and uninterested cousin he claimed—to the now long-deceased commendatore of Venice and as such I was privately wary of his intentions. Revenge was as much a Venetian entree as were veal parmigiana and pasta.

Count Orsini, a close confident and trusted advisor to the emperor, as well as a longtime associate of Casti's, was yet another royal who held me in distain for my Hebrew heritage. Though I had never revealed the history of my birth and subsequent conversion for reasons that would be obvious to anyone with my Jewish background, I would still hear murmurs about the royal court that I was just *un diavolo di un sacerdote ebreo*—a devil of a Jewish priest, a slur I had good reason to suspect the count had his allies promote as one more subtle means to undercut my work.

And Salieri, what could I say about him? On the positive side, he was the court official who had initially hired me to be the Hapsburg Court Poet when I had arrived in Vienna a few years earlier with a letter of introduction from a good friend and scribe in Venice, Caterino Mazzolà. Perhaps feeling sympathy for a fellow countryman from the Veneto, Salieri inserted me into the court staff to polish various libretti in need of work, after winning approval to do so from Joseph II. Though the emperor called me a "virgin muse" at our first meeting, owing to my lack of experience writing operas, he had been an admirer and supporter of my efforts ever since.

But Salieri was a jealous composer who preferred his own operas to stand above the rest. I soon suspected my hiring was simply to create a scapegoat as each opera I was assigned to rework, ended up as fodder upon the stage, often owing to the relative incompetence of the second-tier composers who wrote those musical scores. And those failures had probably made Salieri as happy a man as Vicente Martin y Soler's success this evening no doubt infuriated him.

"Where was Signor Mozart?" I repeated aloud, cadging for time to think. Mozart had in fact been sitting with Martin y Soler and me in the box belonging to our friend, Baron Raimund Wetzlar von Plankenstern, during the performance of our *Il burbero di buon cuore*. Mozart slipped out prior to the completion of the last act so as to be inside Storace's dressing room before the final curtain—a fact I could not disclose to His Majesty.

"Yes, indeed, where is your friend, Herr Mozart?" repeated Joseph II. "I know the glory of this night belongs to you and Martin y Soler, but Signor Salieri led me to believe that you and Herr Mozart have been preparing something special for the court."

"Just a trifle," I replied, secretly curious as to how Salieri knew of our plans, plans we had discussed with no one, except. . . "*Niente di importante*," I quickly added. "I believe Mozart left with Martin y Solar for the party at Wetzlar's palace."

The Baron Raimund Wetzlar von Plankenstern, who was one of the most important bankers in Vienna and a great fan of both opera and the classical guitar, was throwing a bit of a bash for us at his palace to celebrate opening night. It was through Wetzlar's efforts that I first was paired with Mozart, and like me, the Baron was a converso, a new Christian whose changed status in Vienna vastly improved his social standing and ultimately, his wealth.

"And Madame Storace?" asked the emperor. Nancy Storace was not only the principal soprano in my *Il burbero di buon cuore*, Mozart and I had already written the lead part, Susanna, in our version of *The Marriage of Figaro* specifically for her. In addition to her voice, Storace possessed self-deprecating comedic skills that were rare among typically narcissistic divas. "Did she leave as well?"

"Oh no, I saw her backstage not minutes ago." offered up the first of two women who approached our group from behind. It was Catarina Cavalieri, a singer in many of the court's operas and a lady all Vienna presumed was Salieri's mistress. "Is there a part for me in your next opera, Signor Da Ponte?" she quickly added, resting a hand first upon my shoulder and then stroking my back—as if her affections would make me say, "Yes."

"Or me?" Joining Catarina, was the second woman, one I quickly dubbed "Lady Blue," for the stunning turquoise gown she wore that was cut in the latest Parisian style, a style I might add that hid all but teased everything. And, no, I had not lost my cravings for feminine delights, particularly after this Lady Blue snared my attention with but a single glance of her uniquely hazel-colored eyes.

"Of course," I said, echoing my own answer to a question every female singer in Vienna asked me every day, "There are parts you will love. . . . But you say Mozart's backstage?" Turning to Joseph II, I hastily added, "Your Majesty, let me round them up for you. And while I'm gone, perhaps Signor Salieri will share a bit more about my new libretto with you, Madame Cavalieri and . . . " I paused to meet Lady Blue's eyes with a welcoming smile.

"Adriana . . . Adriana Ferrarese del Bene," replied Lady Blue in a smooth and melodic soprano voice that to my profane sensibilities just oozed with sex. Even her jasmine-scented perfume rekindled my passions. And so, when she offered me her hand, I kissed her flesh with such regard that it made her tremor and smile discreetly. "You're leaving us, Signor Da Ponte? So soon?"

"Ah, my lady, the moon has just risen, and I have work to do before it sets," I said. Not only did I know I was susceptible to all her allures, I fully intended to succumb—and as soon as possible. Still, I forced myself to turn away from those enticements and without waiting for anyone's response, headed backstage.

When I arrived at Storace's dressing room, I knew exactly what I would find and did not bother to knock. I quietly opened the door and with some stealth, eased it closed behind me. Save for moonlight pouring in a half open window, the room was dark. Mozart, his back to me, was leaning over a supine Storace. Her skirts were up above her hips. Both were breathing heavily in the sort of rapture I instantly imagined I would have with my Lady Blue.

With regrets but wasting no time, I grabbed my friend, Mozart, by the scruff of his collar and yanked him backward.

"*Come?*" exclaimed a started Mozart in Italian.

"The emperor is on his way here."

"Joseph II? Now, *adesso*?"

"Si, adesso. You need to disappear before His Majesty arrives."

"And I was just about to sing my aria," said the quick-witted Storace as she stood up and straightened her skirts.

I turned to her, "You, you must get out front immediately and stall His Majesty."

"I certainly hope he doesn't expect an encore. One performance a day is all I can handle," she replied with a wink of her eye. Nancy, like many ladies and gentleman of the stage, had a reputation for juggling her affairs as adroitly as a magician.

But they say if you want to make the heavens laugh, tell the gods your plans. Of course, there was a knock at the door before Mozart and I could slip out.

"Signora Storace, may we come in? His Majesty is here." The voice was that of Count Orsini, addressing Nancy properly as "signora," for in addition to being the emperor's mistress, she was married to one John Fisher, a boor of an English musician and, if the stories Nancy had told us were true, a mean and violent drunk.

I mimed for Nancy to answer and then she of course nodded affirmatively as I then motioned for Mozart to follow me out the window and onto a ledge.

"*Solo un momento, per favore,*" Nancy sang out. "I'm still changing." Yes, our diva was indeed a skillful actress. As soon as Mozart and I climbed out, she closed the window, but left it ever so slightly ajar.

There we were, Mozart and I, in the middle of the night on a narrow precipice three floors up above *Löwelstraße*. It was snowing lightly and the chilly air bit into us both, as we edged out of sight and waited in silence.

Although their voices were now muffled, we could hear Nancy open the door, then greet the emperor and his entourage. There was a lot of chatter at first and then, just as it appeared that they were all going to leave, a hand, that of Count Orsini I suspect, reached out and sealed the window shut. Had he seen us on the ledge? Or was he just taking care of the theater he managed for the emperor? I did not trust the wry little smile that crossed his lips as he turned to leave.

When all was quiet, I tried to reopen the window from outside, but it was securely locked.

"Ah, the wages of sin," chuckled Mozart. "Well, my friend, here we are, again."

"Indeed," I said for it was hardly the first time since we had remet in Vienna that an assignation with a lover had gotten one or the other of us in trouble.

"If only my Constanze were here to rescue us," he added, joking about his wife, whom we both knew was far away at a spa in Baden.

As much as he appeared to be thoroughly in love with Constanze whenever they were together, Mozart was one of those men, who always seemed equally joyful when they were apart. It was a state of being, I personally did not understand.

Since Zina had rebuffed me and crushed my heart back in Venice, I had sworn off serious love and had become a philanderer, yes, but a serial one. Unlike Mozart, my affairs that began with my parishioners in Venice came one after another. Every Sunday at the Church of San Luca in Venice for seven years I said mass and heard confession, confessions I might add that guided me to whom I would kiss, gamble, or sleep with on Monday, Tuesday, and beyond. Call me sacrilegious, but I never betrayed or cheated on a woman, nor did I ever tread where I was not invited. Each woman I adored as a dessert to be nibbled upon with passion and affection. I remember their names, their faces, their eyes, their curves, their warmth, their touch as one does the beauty of a lyric poem. And hopefully their memories of this abbé, were just as sweet.

Of course, there was Angela Tiepolo and my Dona Brunetta, Matilda Wider; followed by Sofia, Guilia, Aurora, Giorgia, Martina, Chiara, Sara, Francesca, Ginevra, Noemi, Viola, Beatrice, and Anzelotta in Venice; and as I made my way north I first found fire with one Princess Patrizia in Parma; then onto Franziska and Tina in Treviso; Despina, Dorabella, and the Countess Ursula in Udine; Gretchen, Gaja, Geeta, and the Baroness Bella Gloria in Gorizia; Elvira and Anna, twins sisters of Dresden; Paulina, a duchess from Poland I had while passing through Prague; thence onto a nun, Zerlina from Zagreb in Bratislava; and in Vienna, ah, in Vienna, ah, in the choruses of Vienna, there was a Victorine from Vincennes; a Dorotea from near Dobling; a Maria Martini from Milano, and, oh yes, many more, a soprano here, a mezzo there, a wardrobe mistress, a costumer or three or four, and on it went. Yes, for every woman I found pleasure in loving, there was equally so a woman who found pleasure in loving this abbé, a priest to whom none would ever marry.

And, yes, whenever our regrets or despair overcame our delights, it was *tempo di partire*, time to say goodbye. We separated and moved on. Now, however, the issue was not the gentler sex but how to get off this ledge before we were found in the morning, two corpses frozen to death.

Down below on the street, *Löwelstraße*, despite the late hour, carriages and pedestrians alike were still out and about, though the usual noise and clatter was muffled by the softly fluttering flakes. In that era, Vienna, the capital of a vast empire, was a city that never slept. With luck, the royal carriage would soon be among them, well on its way to the soiree at Baron Wetzlar's.

"Tell me, my friend, what would our Figaro do?" asked Mozart, alluding to the protagonist of our libretto. "So, would our Figaro jump to his death? Smash a window? Or . . . "

"Or that," I said, pointing to an open window about thirty feet further along the ledge. "Our Figaro would escape through that window which, if my memory is correct, will lead us inside the costume room, and from there we are free."

Mozart nodded agreement; it was our only choice. Ever so delicately we began step by step to make our way toward that window, a feat far from easy. Not only was the ledge worn and narrow, here and there it was crusted with snow, the wind was blowing, the edges were slippery with ice, and there was a distinct lack of places for our fingers—numbed by the chill—to grasp onto.

I should have been furious with Mozart for how his womanizing jeopardized our work, but in truth how could I be? He was a genio and every note he composed rose so high above all other scribes in Vienna. True enough, I enjoyed my work writing for Martin y Soler's sweet melodies, but Mozart, ah, Mozart . . . The task ahead was convincing His Majesty, a skeptic about Austrian native Mozart's skill with Italian opera, that my friend could indeed create music of such sublime delicacy and depth that no other composer could compare and that the libretto we had created must be performed.

All of a sudden, as if on cue, Mozart began to whistle. I don't know if it was out of a nervous fear of falling or if he was just in the midst of composing. He was like that, one never knew. But it was a tune of such infinite beauty.

After a few bars I recognized it as "Porgi amor qualche ristoro," a plaintive aria from that opera we were working up in secret—or at least I thought it was in secret. Pierre Beaumarchais's original play of *The Marriage of Figaro* was a huge success in Paris though it also occasioned riots over its bashing of aristocratic privilege. Its German language stage version had been banned in Vienna as too revolutionary by Joseph II's court censor. Because of that ban imposed by Count Pergen, we did not want anyone at the court to know we were working in secret on this project as an opera until it was done. To write it on speculation was a financial gamble for both of us. I firmly believed that in transforming the play into an opera I had been able to edit out much of the verbiage that offended the very aristocracy it was meant to entertain, while retaining not only the essential plot lines but most of the comedic twists as well.

If my experience rewriting all of those dreadful operas Salieri had put before me taught me nothing else, successful operas are about what people feel, expressed through song; novels are about what people think; and plays are about what people say. The key to adaptation, was to read the source material, absorb its essence, and then throw the old book over your shoulder, which is what I did with *Figaro*. To slavishly force the words and structures of a novel or play into a libretto without re-envisioning them as elements of a musical score, was the quickest path to produce a failure; a path to which amateurs and small—but fiercely arrogant—simpleminded librettists still cleave, to this very day. How sad for them that they do not understand this core principle. Such pompous artists always act offended when their performances are scorned, and they usually blame the audience for not understanding their self-asserted masterpieces.

With Mozart, all I had to do was to provide him with the essentials of a scenario and then step aside and allow his magic to unfold. For "Porgi amor qualche ristoro," my lyrics were simple expressions of a young countess' disappointment at her husband's inattentiveness and philandering.

> *Oh Love, bring me some relief*
> *To all my sorrows, and for all my sighs!*
> *Either give me back my loved one,*
> *Or in mercy let me die.*

Mozart had already taken those lines and crafted them into a song of such grace and woe, that even the most cynical of audiences would be able to feel the pain of the countess's sorrows. To accomplish this consistently with each character in every scene took a genio of unfathomable talent, and that genio was the Mozart I had come to know, work with, and call my friend. Still, I could not blame Joseph II for being a skeptic. As gifted as Mozart was, he had not as yet—as the emperor would frequently point out—composed a significant or popular opera in the comedic Italian style that was all the rage. By contrast Salieri, Martin y Soler, Vincenzo Righini, Giuseppe Gazzaniga, and Paisiello had each already produced a half-dozen or more. Yes, the odds were indeed against achieving Joseph II's blessing, but if we were to succeed, ah.... Heaven, not hell, awaited.

When at last we reached the window, it was indeed ajar, but not sufficient enough for us to squeeze through. I tugged on the frame. It was frozen in place.

"Can't let that stop us," said Mozart. "Give it the old Figaro touch."

Indeed, I thought, our Figaro was an unstoppable force. Though just a servant, a common man—with a history not unlike mine, Casanova's or Mozart's—he possessed the brains, brawn, charm, and never-say-die attitude, essential to overcoming all obstacles and emerging triumphant. He was a man who lived in the world of aristocrats and nobility but was never awed or intimidated by them. Even in this Age of Enlightenment, such traits alone made him revolutionary.

Inspired by the fortitude of our hero, I yanked hard once more on the window frame. When the wood abruptly broke free and sailed out into space, I almost lost my balance and fell with it. Luckily Mozart grabbed my coat and held me fast to the ledge. The window plummeted three stories below toward the street. As we both looked down to follow its trajectory, the royal carriage—no doubt carrying His Majesty and his entourage—passed directly beneath us. The window shattered upon its roof and so startled the stallions pulling the emperor's rig that they broke into a run and dragged the carriage a block away before his guards had a chance to look up and discover the cause of their distress.

We, however, needed no further incentive to dive through the open space and into the wardrobe room as hastily as possible.

Inside among the many racks of theatrical costumes, we found a pair of basic black *tabàros* replete with capes and masks in the Venetian style, along with two hefty silver-handled walking sticks.

Thus attired, we slipped down and out unnoticed from the theater and onto the *Löwelstraße*. Although Carnevale in Vienna was nothing like the all-consuming madness of Venice during this time of year, one still found costumed revelers around and about at all hours and tonight was no different. We quickly made our way on foot over to *Renngasse* and were about to cut through an alley toward *Tiefer Graben* where Wetzlar's palace stood on the corner, when we heard the screams of a woman coming from a darkened recess.

Mozart and I ran towards the poor distressed creature, a uniformed servant, who was being forcibly attacked by two men, both of whom were well-dressed aristocrats. The first, in a long vermillion cloak, ran off at the sound of our footsteps, but the other—his back to us—persisted in his assault.

Rage, pure rage welled up inside me, Mozart too. It was the fury our Figaro must have felt upon learning his master, the count was conniving to rape his fiancée, Susanna, on their wedding night. Mozart speared the man first, thrusting his cane like a lance into the brigand's back. And just as the criminal howled in pain and twisted away from that thrust, I swung the heavy nob of my walking stick at him like a club and caught him with a hard smash on the side of his skull. He collapsed in a heap at the feet of the terrified girl, who could not have been more than sixteen or seventeen.

The blouse of this pretty young woman was torn and shredded from the assault, exposing her breasts and a silver locket engraved with a six-sided star that hung between them. Without hesitation I pulled off my cape and wrapped it around her to preserve what was left of her modesty. She was terrified and shaking uncontrollably—as was I. I had never felt such outrage well up inside me nor had I ever clobbered another man with such violence. What frightened me most though was that it felt good and satisfying, and if I had caught the other man, the one in the vermillion cloak, I would have struck him down as well. These were new emotions to a man of pen and paper.

"Did you know these brigands?" asked Mozart, tossing his mask aside to put the poor girl at ease. I did the same.

Her voice trembled, "N- N- No . . . No, Sir. I was just bringing, bringing wine back to my master's house. But that one," she said pointing at the limp body lying at our feet and speaking in a jumbled stew of German and Italian words, all pronounced with a distinctly Venetian accent, "That one, he called my name."

"Your name?" I repeated, "He knew your name?"

"Ye- Yes . . . he called to me just as I entered the passageway."

As she continued to thank us profusely for coming to her rescue, I turned the now unconscious miscreant over to see his face. And it was one I instantly recognized. It was Casti, the satyr himself, the Abbé Giambattista Casti, which left me wondering if his cohort was not his fellow traveler, Giovanni Paisiello. I regretted not being able to recall if Paisiello had been wearing a vermillion cloak earlier that evening.

"Did we kill him?" asked Mozart.

"Unfortunately, not. But I guarantee he will live to regret this night."

"Do you know this man, this face?" I asked the girl. When she bent down to look at him in the darkness, her locket with the engraved star fell outside the folds of the cape I had draped around her. Taking a closer look at her, I noticed that this poor servant was actually rather attractive, with the high cheek bones, dark complexion, deep brown eyes, and jet-black hair typical of the Jewish women, such as Zina, I had grown up with in the Veneto.

"No, sir, I never saw him before. Who is he?" she said.

When I told her, it was the Abbé Giambattista Casti, she fainted straight off into Mozart's arms.

Finding a box of snuff in my waistcoat, I put it under her nose to revive the poor girl. When she came around, Mozart opened one of the bottles of wine she'd been carrying and then gave her a sip to settle her nerves. Mozart and I each took a sip as well. Physical violence on the streets was not a common occurrence for either one of us, and I confess we were truly as shaken as she was by this incident.

When she was finally able to speak calmly, she identified herself as Celestina Grahl, servant to none other than our friend and soon to be host, Baron Raimund Wetzlar. She had been returning with a load of wine for our party when the two men attacked and dragged her into the alley. Celestina told us she had only come recently to Vienna from Venice to work for Wetzlar. She knew almost no one and was horrified that a stranger with ill intent would have known her identity.

"*Sei ebrea del ghetto di Venezia?*" I asked.

"No, no, no," she insisted, crossing herself. "Catholic. I am a good Catholic."

"You are safe with us, but this says otherwise." The six-sided star on the locket was that of a Jew.

"Si," she confessed with eyes downcast. It has never been easy to be a Jew in a hostile Christian world.

"And you know the Casti family, yes?"

"Si," she answered.

"What's this about?" asked Mozart, who was always amazed by my ability—one I did not quite understand myself—to identify a fellow Hebrew, regardless of whether they had become a converso.

"If my instincts are correct, this poor child is a pawn caught in an old Venetian blood feud. And she may be in more danger than we think," I said. "Let's get her home quickly. Had we not arrived in time, there was no telling what Casti would have done."

"And you wonder why my father warned me not to trust the Italians at court, even you, my friend," said Mozart as we dragged the still unconscious Casti into the darkest corner of the alleyway and propped him up against a wall. I doused Casti with the rest of that open bottle of wine and when it was emptied, I wedged it between his hands.

Celestina held up a money purse, plump with coins, and said, "Sirs, this just fell out of his coat." She handed it over Mozart.

He looked inside and laughed, before he handed it back to the still trembling girl. "No, it's not for us or him. It's your just compensation."

She was terrified to receive the pouch and turned to me for approval, "Should I, sir? I don't want any more trouble."

"This bastard does not deserve it," I replied, "Not even a copper *pfennig*. Go ahead, keep it all. Whatever is there, is now yours, provided you promise to spend it wisely and show kindness to others."

"Oh yes, sirs, I will, I promise I will, and I will be kind. Oh, thank you, thank you."

Casti, though still unconscious, groaned. I raised my cane to smack him once more, but Mozart stayed my hand.

"*Basta*, enough," he said.

Though I nodded agreement and I put down my walking stick, the thought of smashing that devil's face into pulp had great appeal.

We delivered a grateful Celestina and the balance of her wine safely to Wetzlar's palace by the servant's entrance. There we notified the majordomo, a man we knew well, of what had happened, before heading around to the main entrance.

"What was inside the purse?" I asked Mozart.

He laughed again as we entered. "A king's ransom. Enough gold and silver to buy Richard the Lionheart's freedom," he said referring to the ancient story of how the English king was once ransomed from a Viennese dungeon.

"Poor, Casti, you should have left him enough copper for a coach ride to Italy."

"No, this way they'll have to hitch the poor beggar to the wagon and let him drag it south through the Alps."

Inside the grand ballroom of Wetzlar's palace, we found the emperor and his full complement of lords and ladies all there, enjoying the baron's lavish hospitality. Imagine if you will the spectacle of me, Emanuele Conegliano, that poor ignorant child of Ceneda, a Figaro, a converso, being feted in one of the finest palaces in all Vienna by an aristocracy whose wealth, influence, and sophistication knew no boundaries. Yes, me, the Abbé Lorenzo Da Ponte, the court poet to Joseph II, me, the man whose journey through the corridors of power was just beginning—or so I hoped.

Among the ambassadors, princes of the realm, countesses of the court, baronesses, dukes and duchesses, I recognized Rasumovsky, Lichnowsky, Lobkowicz, Pergen, van Swieten, Esterhazy, and more. Musicians played, dancers danced, singers sang, waiters poured champagne, and uniformed servants brought endless platters of food. Everything was in honor of the success of the opera Martin y Soler and I had created. But all I wanted was a shot of brandy to calm my nerves. Later I'd salute those who had made my success possible.

Mozart set off in search of our beverages while I at last found Baron Raimund Wetzlar, our host, to whom I once more relayed the story of what had just transpired. Wetzlar was a good and sincere man who quickly ordered one of his personal guards to be on the alert for both Casti and for that man in the vermillion cloak, should he appear at the palace. And if found, Wetzlar added, the officer had instructions to make those miscreants aware of how sharp the terrible swift sword of justice was in Vienna. The incident was one he had feared might occur. Though a converso on the outside, Wetzlar was still very much a Jew on the inside who used his position of wealth and influence to discreetly help those Hebrews he knew who were in trouble or at risk, such as this young woman, Celestina.

Raimund was just about to tell me the story of how Celestina had been sent to him from the Venetian ghetto with a letter of introduction, but abruptly fell silent when Salieri, Caterina Cavalieri, and my Lady Blue, Adriana Ferrarese del Bene, came gliding over to offer their overflowing and effusive salutes to me for my success that night.

I simply smiled, nodded, and said nothing while my eyes did all they could to discreetly devour Adriana.

Salieri, who echoed the emperor's words and proclaimed the opera "a victory," went on to congratulate himself for having the insight, vision, and wisdom to hire me as a fledgling court poet despite my lack of experience because, as he now claimed, when he first met me three years earlier, he saw the "genio in my eyes." Yes, and as he rambled on, he announced that he and I, Salieri and Da Ponte, were soon to create a new opera masterpiece of our own.

"Assolutamente," I added, though I trusted nothing Salieri said or promised.

Just then Mozart returned not only with that tall glass of prosecco I needed, he brought the entire bottle, one he immediately pointed out was from a small village in the Veneto, Ceneda, the birthplace of tonight's hero, Lorenzo Da Ponte.

Never in my life had I ever been so celebrated, a condition that promised to become ever sweeter when Adriana Ferrarese del Bene, leaned in close as if to whisper. Instead, she bit my ear and then murmured, "Dance with me now, and I'll sing until tonight's moon bids us farewell."

Yes, an offer I could not refuse.

Chapter Nine: Queen of the Night

Sunday Morning, May 13, 1962
Bayside, Queens, New York City

Mozart's "Queen of the Night" aria from *The Magic Flute*, performed by Roberta Peters was playing on WQRX radio when Jake finally started downstairs for breakfast. He recognized Peters's recording immediately as the family had seen her perform the role numbers of times at the Met, and he had even bought her record album as a birthday present for his mother, Rosa, last year. It was no secret that his parents harbored a special affection for artists such as Peters who had achieved mainstream success in America and who were also Jewish.

No, he thought recalling the words Da Ponte had written in the diary pages that he and Dolcetta had translated last night: it was never easy being a Jew in a hostile Christian world. When you were part of an immigrant minority, one that had long suffered the indignity of discrimination, such pride for those who have succeeded came with the territory.

But this morning, Jake knew he would need Abe and Rosa's help supporting Dolcetta whenever it was that he would finally break the news about this latest possible sighting of her twin sister, Danielle. As he turned the corner into the kitchen, he went over in his mind, just what he would say first. Nothing came easy, but he was determined to find the means.

Dolcetta was sitting back in her chair, wrapped in her favorite blue terrycloth robe, her eyes closed, her hair down, and absent makeup. Her right hand was ever so lightly conducting in unison with Peters's voice. To Jake's eyes, she appeared more radiant than ever that morning. One only had to see her face in that moment to know the joy she felt listening to their beloved Mozart—and that look of pure contentment was one he was hesitant to shatter. It had been over ten years ago since the last possible sighting had proven false, and he hoped against hope that she would not slip into a depression again.

A mixed assortment of freshly washed breakfast dishes was already piled up in the strainer by sink. Jake looked around for his parents but did not see or hear them.

"Espresso?" asked Dolcetta when the aria ended. She opened her eyes and blew Jake a kiss. "It's fresh, hot, and just brewed—*proprio come me.*"

"*Assolutamente, mia amata,*" said Jake, stalling for time to think of how he should handle the conversation. A little caffeine first, he decided. "Where are Mom and Dad?"

"They left twenty minutes ago," replied Dolcetta. "Abe wanted to get back to the Bronx in time to watch a Yankees doubleheader against the Indians on TV, and Rosa didn't want me to wake you. We're seeing them at dinner Friday in the Bronx."

That was not going to make Jake's task any easier. Should he wait out the week? And maybe just kick back and watch the games himself?

Beyond opera, the Conegliano family passion was the Yankees. How could any Italian growing up in the Bronx not love a team that had featured DiMaggio, Rizzuto, Crosetti, Berra, and now a young Joe Pepitone. Good for Dad, Jake thought. He imagined Abe was also probably glad to have an opportunity to smoke that Cohiba cigar and drink a few beers. Yes, "Baseball and Ballentine" would rule the day. Still, with his parents gone, especially Rosa, he wrestled whether he should still bring up Manny's possible sighting of Danielle at the opera last night or stall until dinner on Friday.

"Do you like these cups?" asked Dolcetta as she poured one for Jake and refilled her own.

Last night Pandorea's parents had gifted them a pair of colorful hand-painted espresso cups from the town of Sciacca in Sicily. They just came alive in their kitchen.

"Yes. They remind me of being back home. I love 'em." Though no one in the family had enough emotional courage to return to Ceneda since Geremia's burial, everyone still referred to it as "home."

"Good. Because I'm thinking about buying an entire dinner set."

"You're going shopping in Sicily?" he mused.

"No, Manhattan. Marietta says there's a new Italian pottery store down the block from the UN. That's where she bought these."

"Listen," Jake said in that serious tone that abruptly got Dolcetta's attention. He had decided to just plunge in, no sense stalling or prevaricating. "There's something I need to talk to you about."

"*Che cosa?*"

Though Jake was challenged to tell her Manny's story of the encounter with her possible twin without upsetting Dolcetta, he proceeded slowly and steadily. Jake gave the same attention to each point as if he had been giving an intelligence briefing—only this time he was careful to constantly observe Dolcetta to gauge her reaction. He repeated Manny's description of the woman's black gown, her red shawl, the French twist, her accent and the concentration camp number on her forearm. Dolcetta listened attentively, but her face did not betray any emotions.

When at last Jake was done Dolcetta sat back in her chair, rocking ever so slightly, and repeating the numbers, "9213474, 9213474, 9213474," until she finally asked, "Do you believe it's her?"

Jake admitted he did not know. Manny was the only one who saw her, and he said as much as he carefully watched Dolcetta's face. Jake promised to use all of the resources of HIAS and the intelligence agencies to see what he could find out, but his wife's hazel eyes were far away, in another place, in another time.

He waited. Dolcetta said nothing. After a moment, she stood. She shut the radio. She sat back down. She sipped her espresso. She wet her lips. She looked at the face of the man she loved.

"Did you know," she finally began to speak but with long hesitant pauses. "Did you know . . . that the Nazis . . . the SS Command . . . they called me the "Queen of the Night" . . . and put a bounty on my head? I was fifteen, *Dio mio*, fifteen."

No, he did not. Jake did not know any of the details or stories of her fighting with *I partigiani*, the Italian partisans that resisted the Nazis in the northern mountains of the Veneto. After bringing his war bride back to the States in 1946, no one, especially Jews, spoke about what had happened during the Holocaust. It was all too horrific and memories were left unsaid. Jake was busy with his new civilian career, and Dolcetta was pregnant with Manny. Preoccupied with the present, their life moved ahead without referencing the past.

The details that the press published about the Holocaust after the war and during the Nuremburg Trials, and later the trial of Adolf Eichmann, were news to most Americans, but not to the Jewish community. Everyone had had family back in the old county, families such as the Coneglianos and Grazianos that now no longer existed. Stories of the gradual destruction of Jewish communities by the Nazis had been regularly communicated by the typical and routine letters sent by relatives that lived on both sides of the Atlantic. It was not until Kristallnacht in 1938, when Hitler launched his first overt attack upon Hebrew communities inside the Reich, that such communications started to break down. And it was only when the United States entered the war following Pearl Harbor that the flow of letters began to dry up completely. Yes, the details of the concentration camps, the SS killing squads, the ovens at Auschwitz might have been news to postwar America, but not to us, Jake recalled, as he waited patiently for Dolcetta to continue. And she did.

"Listening to Roberta Peters's aria just now," she said, "reminded me of those years of combat. I don't know why. Maybe it was hearing a woman, a Jewish woman at that, openly declare her absolute fury, a rage that has no boundaries, an anger so deep, so profound that it, unless checked, will drive you mad. Yes, *'The vengeance of Hell boiled in my heart, Death and despair did flare up about me!*'"

Dolcetta went on to describe how, when she initially joined up with the partisans in the mountains, they would not let her, a mere slip of a teenage girl, do any of the actual fighting against the Nazis. At first, she stayed behind in their camps with the other women, doing menial chores, but that quickly changed. Most all of the partisans were farmers and shepherds from the region who had little formal education. Few were those who could read or write in Italian, much less English, much less English, the language necessary to communicate with the officers in the British Intelligence that were airdropping supplies for them. That task, critical to the partisans for their survival against the heavily armed German troops in the region soon fell to Dolcetta. And when those supplies—including sophisticated armaments such as anti-tank bazookas, Browning automatic machine guns, contact mines, and plastic explosives—did arrive, she was the only one who understood the directions and guidelines as to how to use and maintain them. Though in the first few months of serving, she never had a chance to fight, she became not only the expert in the use of all of those weapons, but the instructor to all the other partisans.

In the early spring of 1944, just as the snows began to melt away in the lowlands around Ceneda, Conegliano, and the other villages at the base of the Alps, the German SS Command, began making its push into the highlands to root out the partisans and to continue their roundup of Jews. Their efforts on the ground were supported by the Luftwaffe's ME-109 fighter planes stationed at their base at Aviano. Fortunately for the partisans, the German planes could only fly when the weather deep in the mountains was clear—and that was rare, as a dense fog drifted off the mountains at this time of year. Her squad was tasked with ambushing the German patrols whenever they ventured north into the hills, an area that was not only extremely rugged but also had few passable roads.

"On April 8, 1944, the start of Passover, the weather was overcast and miserable," she said, "I translated a message from the British Intelligence that an SS killing squad would be moving up toward the high mountain village of Avastella and the monastery of Santa Ava dell Stelle, where many refugees and the families of our fighters were hiding out. It was also close to the spot where the English airdropped our supplies. Not only was it essential we stopped the Germans from reaching Avastella, we learned that same morning that this was the same unit under the command of one Capt. Stanislav Braun, a particularly vicious commander, who had murdered or taken away every Jew in Ceneda, including *mia famiglia*. Yes, the vengeance of hell boiled in my blood.

I wanted nothing more than to kill each and every one of those Nazis—but I was just a girl."

While Jake listened intently to Dolcetta, his palms and fingers grew sweaty with fear. He had known from studying the covert parts of transcripts of Eichmann's trial, that Braun and Eichmann had come up the ranks of the Gestapo together. Jake had also seen and remembered enough of that rugged landscape, even now eighteen years later, to understand the terrors of what his love had to contend with. She went on to describe how her unit set an ambush above a narrow ravine, where the direct road to Avastella ran on the western slope of the mountain. But she was not allowed to join with them. Instead, she and one other partisan, Ferruccio Fresia's adult son, Rinaldo, were sent by bicycles to a lookout post high up along the road on the opposite eastern flank of the mountain. And calling it a road was generous at best. This path was actually little more than a dirt track used primarily by shepherds to move their flocks between summer and winter pastures. It climbed up along an extremely winding and dangerous route with over thirty hairpin turns and was just barely wide enough in places for a vehicle to pass through without falling off the cliff.

"Rinaldo had already lost an eye in an earlier battle that had killed his wife, Lucia, so I was tasked with being the lookout," she continued. "From our vantage point, which was at the bombed-out ruins of an old stone farmhouse and barn situated just before a severe 90-degree turn in the path, I could see the entire valley below to a distance of some fifteen miles with my binoculars. I spotted the German convoy approach a "Y" in the road at the valley floor, and as we expected, it turned left toward the western flank and directly toward the ambush our compatriots had set. The Germans had a jeep-like command car in the lead, followed by two troop transports. We estimated that there were about thirty troops altogether, but when Rinaldo tried to radio that information to our compatriots across the valley, our equipment would not work."

"*Dio mio*," exclaimed Jake, "What did . . .?"

But Dolcetta raised her hands and bid him wait. "Just then, as the Germans started to drive up the western flank, there was a break in the clouds and a Messerschmitt doing reconnaissance flew over the valley. It must have spotted the ambush because moments later the convoy turned around. It went back down to the "Y," and then headed up our side. Although it was the longer way around, we had nothing here to stop the Nazis from reaching Avastella, which had been left undefended.

"We estimated that it would take the Germans just under an hour to reach our positions and if they got past us, Rinaldo and I both knew Capt. Braun would, if given the chance, slaughter everyone in Avastella. We had to get word to the village and fast. With our radio not working, Rinaldo decided to chance it and see if he could get back up to Avastella in time to issue a warning. He was a far stronger bicyclist than I. Before the war Rinaldo had often raced in the Giro d'Italia. Rinaldo left me behind with what few weapons we had and the admonition to "stay safe," while also exhorting me to do what I could to slow them down if possible.

"Rinaldo set off for Avastella, racing as fast as he could over open exposed terrain. But then I heard the groan of that Messerschmitt's engine. Moments later, through my binoculars, I watched as the pilot of the ME-109 spotted Rinaldo on an open stretch and gunned him down with a quick burst of fire."

Standing up from the kitchen table so as to better animate her story, Dolcetta then described to Jake how she retreated to the defensive bunker they had prepared in the sub-basement of the collapsed stone barn. She inspected her meager armory: one Browning machine gun, a brand-new British-made bazooka, and a single contact land mine. From the observation slit in the bunker, she had a clear view of the road in front of her. Just to the right of the ruins there were the remnants of an archway that had once marked the entry to the farmstead. The road split in two just before the archway. The right fork went through the arch as the road continued to wind up the mountain, while the left fork, meant primarily for sheep and goats went outside the arch, behind some bushes and then teetered perilously close to the cliff, before narrowing precipitously into a small path that went downhill into rugged pasture land.

"I waited until the Messerschmitt finally left, then hurriedly ran out to the arch with the contact mine. My adrenaline must have been pumping like mad. With my bare hands I quickly dug out a hole for the mine on the exact spot where I guessed the tires of the lead vehicle would pass. After covering it with enough dirt, twigs and leaves to camouflage its presence, I retreated to the bunker and checked my two weapons. I waited and waited and waited, until at long last, just as dusk was settling into the hills, I heard the convoy approach. It was moving quickly, probably, I imagined, to reach Avastella before nightfall. The jeep was first, then the two troop transports. One machine gun, one contact mine, one bazooka, and one fifteen-year-old girl to stop a squad of hardened and bloodthirsty SS troops.

"In thirty seconds, it was all over. The front driver's side tire of the jeep hit the mine, blowing it up and backward. The driver of the first troop transport immediately swerved to the left to avoid the jeep, but it was moving too fast to stay in control. The truck went sailing over the cliff, its gas tanks exploding as it crashed down the mountain. I raised the bazooka and targeted the gas tanks of the other transport and prayed that my aim would be true. Just as I was about to pull the trigger, their Capt. Braun, who had been thrown out of the jeep, stood up, with gun drawn and blocked my view. But when that bastard who had murdered my family started screaming at his troop to fire at me in the bunker, I pulled the trigger.

"I saw the expression of horror on Capt. Braun's face as the rocket passed right through his heart and exploded upon contact with the truck, blowing it and everyone aboard to the hell they deserved. And then, it was over. Everything went silent and still. I didn't know what to do or think. My heart was pounding. Finally, I grabbed the machine gun and went back outside to check for survivors. They were all dead, what was left of them. I scratched a Jewish star on a shell casing and left it atop the remnants of Braun's body.

"The partisans never left me out of the fighting again. Word of what had happened eventually spread far and wide. The six-sided star scratched on a bullet casing became my calling card. The SS command dubbed me Queen of the Night and posted huge rewards for my capture or proof of death. But I continued to outsmart and disappoint those bastards time and time again. And when the war ended a year later, I had personally gained my vengeance—the wrath of holy hell that Mozart composed—on over five hundred Nazi soldiers, including all those who were on the troop train you photographed years ago on our way to Ceneda with Lt. Foxx."

"Oh," she continued, "That wedding band Enrico now wears, the one Ferruccio's granddaughter gave to him back in Ceneda, that was Rinaldo's ring. And Greta's ring, that was Lucia's. After her death, Rinaldo had worn hers on his left pinkie next to his wedding band so they would always be together. I recovered them on my return to Avastella that night, and after the war I gave them back to the Fresias."

Dolcetta put her hands out in front of her and turned her palms over so they faced upward. "In war it's easy to feel virtuous killing so many of one's enemy, but in peace, do you know what it is like to know there are five hundred families just like mine that will never see their loved ones again?"

Jake shook his head. Though his intelligence units had always been close to the front lines, he had never experienced actual combat. He had never even fired a gun in anger. Jake knew well that for each and every horrific moment in war he had witnessed or photographed, such as those survivors of Dachau, his Dolcetta, his sweet and loving and kind Dolcetta, had experienced terrors and nightmares on a geometric scale that he did not, could not, and would not pretend to understand. He shared those thoughts with her and confessed that he was only worried about how this news of a possible sighting of Danielle would affect her.

Dolcetta, both laughing and crying, came over and hugged him. "I love you, Jake, but you need not worry about me. It's taken time, yes, and I admit it was difficult and I put you all through a lot in the past, but I've accepted that Danielle is gone. You, you and Manny, Abe and Rosa, you are my life, my home, my every joy. You are my family now. Come what may, do you really think the girl they once called the Queen of the Night would be upset to learn Danielle's true fate?"

Chapter Ten: Songs of Seduction

Even Later that Night, January 4, 1786
The Palace of Baron Raimund Wetzlar von
Plankenstern, Vienna

Mozart . . . Of course, Mozart found a pianoforte in one of the antechambers off the grand ballroom of Wetzlar's palace, and all alone and seemingly lost in his own thoughts, he began to improvise variations on his own "Piano Concerto in D Minor."

Meanwhile all of the other guests—Adriana and I included—were far away and off in the ballroom listening and dancing to a small ensemble composed of musicians from the opera orchestra who were playing some new music based on a *danza alla tedesca*—a dance in the style of German peasants—considered by some in Viennese society to be rather scandalous as the partners held each other close with one hand clasped around the other's waist.

Much as the masks and disguises of Carnevale in Venice gave license to erotic behaviors normally forbidden in Catholic society, so too, this dance was a delightful form of foreplay of which Adriana and I fully indulged. And these pleasures appeared to be universally appreciated by all those couples similarly entangled, including Joseph II and Nancy Storace. And if His Majesty approved of the *Der Walzer*, as the dance was apparently known in the Austrian countryside, then all Vienna went along.

Pressed snug against each other, I could take the measure of Adriana's every curve and feel the warmth and softness of her flesh. My one hand caressed the small of her back and hips, and she for her part held me so tight that our thighs brushed teasingly against each other's as we floated around the dance floor.

We were both pleased to be able to hold each other in such romantic contact whilst in a very public eye, even as we edged ever more into the darkened corners of the room. Our bodies—and temperaments—were such perfect fits, a condition that felt preordained, that I could not help but imagine that we had always been together and would always remain as such. And how was it that I was falling for this diva? Was it the look in her eyes as our faces brushed each other's? Or the little endearments she whispered in my ear? Or the way she caressed my back? Or how she pressed her breasts against my chest? These were surprising emotions, ones I had not felt with any woman in the fifteen years since my spirits were crushed by Zina.

After Adriana discreetly steered us behind a pillar, we shared our first kiss. It was deep and warm and satisfying and we lingered, we lingered that is until I heard Mozart noodling away on that fortepiano. He was now playing variations on several themes he had composed for our heretofore secret opera. I recognized chords and sequences from the opening and various choral segments, no small feat for a non-musician such as myself who barely knew one note from another. I was a scribe, a man of the pen, a man of words. I left the music to my magician friend, Signor Mozart.

"Come," I said to Adriana as I led her by the hand into the antechamber. "This is why we are here."

A small crowd, including Salieri, Catarina Cavalieri, and the young tenor, Michael Kelly—who had also just performed in our opera hours earlier—had begun to gather around Mozart as he continued with his improvisations. The intimately sized room was filled with a variety of couches and sedan chairs that circled his piano. Mozart's reputation as the greatest pianist in the empire was as outsized as his fervent desire to produce an opera was frustrated.

"So that's Mozart?" Adriana inquired. She was only recently arrived in Vienna after singing on stages in Milano and Venice and had yet to meet many of the luminaries of music in our capital city. "You must introduce me."

"Oh, I shall," I said as we linked up with Salieri, Kelly, and Cavalieri.

Soon, joining Mozart out of seemingly nowhere, was the Baron Wetzlar himself with his guitar and then, a violinist, whom I pointed out was the master composer and conductor, Joseph Haydn. With Haydn was a nine or ten year-old boy, Johann Nepomuk Hummel, whom I knew to be a live-in student of Mozart's. Young Hummel was a musical prodigy that Mozart had brought into his home to teach. Hummel set up their music stands and then stood by to turn pages. As soon as the musical score was in place, Wetzlar and Haydn joined with Mozart on a wild and vibrant Fandango that I recognized immediately as being from the namesake wedding march of our opera.

The music was so rousing that it brought an ever-growing crowd of spectators into the room, including Joseph II, Nancy Storace, Count Orsini, Prince Lobkowicz, Baron von Swieten, and a host of other notables. Joseph II, of course, seated himself and Nancy on a divan directly in front of the musicians. In his more formal role as lord chamberlain, Orsini positioned himself directly behind the emperor, where, like a sheep dog guarding his flock, he could observe all and control access to His Majesty.

I, too, eyed the crowd as the trio played, noting who was and wasn't there. When they finished the wedding Fandango, Mozart, Wetzlar, and Haydn immediately segued into an extended instrumental version of our *"Deh vieni, non tardar"*—"Oh Come, Do Not delay." When I observed a delighted Joseph II tapping his fingers in time to the music, I nodded to Mozart. He in turn winked at Storace. Abruptly our diva stood up from the divan and then turning to face the emperor she began to sing at full voice and as seductively as possible:

> *Come, do not delay, oh bliss,*
> *Come where love calls thee to joy.*
> *While the night's torch does not shine in the sky.*
> *While the air is still and dark and the world quiet.*
> *Here murmurs the stream, here sports the breeze,*
> *Which refreshes the heart with its sweet whispers.*

Though taken aback at first, Joseph II, his face blushed red, clearly enjoyed having Nancy sing directly to him. Our emperor was a widower twice over, and what lonely monarch wouldn't have been charmed by her attention in front of his entire court.

> *Here flowers smile and the grass is cool;*
> *Here everything invites to the pleasures of love.*
> *Come, my dearest, and amid these sheltered trees,*
> *I will wreath thy brow with roses.*

But instantly, just as she finished her last line, this sweet moment of affection was shattered by the bellowing voice of one Francesco Benucci, the star of my Martin y Soler opera and the singer Mozart and I wanted to play our Figaro.

"Ah, to trust women is sheer folly!" Benucci stepped out of from the audience and pointed at Storace.

Everyone in the room was stunned into silence, particularly since there were rumors about Vienna that Benucci was also having an affair with Storace. Yes, our Nancy was a popular diva in Vienna. Even Michael Kelly, a sweet lad who often served Nancy as her beard, prepared to jump in-between the two to defend Storace.

Joseph II was equally startled, which gave Mozart his next cue. His little trio immediately began to play our Figaro's "Apite un po' quegli occhi"—"Open those eyes a little," as Benucci began to sing:

> *Just open your eyes, you rash and foolish men,*
> *And look at these women; see them as they are,*
> *These goddesses, so called by the intoxicated senses,*
> *To whom feeble reasons offers tribute.*

The gathered assemblage relaxed, now understanding that this piece was all part of a prearranged comedy and not just some deranged singer attacking the emperor's mistress.

> *They are witches who cast spells for our torment,*
> *Sirens who sing for our confusion,*
> *Night owls who fascinate so as to pluck us.*
> *Comets who dazzle to deprive us of light.*

As Benucci continued singing, Paisiello came around, wanting to sit on the divan beside Joseph II, but the emperor waved him off. His Majesty turned a knowing eye toward me and motioned for Adriana and me to join him on his couch instead. I also quickly noted that Paisiello was wearing not a vermillion cloak, but a blue one I now recalled he had been wearing earlier at the opera. Our second brigand, the one who escaped and was Casti's cohort in crime, had to be someone else altogether different, whom, I could not begin to imagine.

> *They are thorned roses, alluring vixens,*
> *Smiling she-bears, malign doves,*
> *Master of deceit, friends of distress*
> *Who cheat and lie, who feel no love, and have no pity.*
> *The rest I need not say for everyone knows it already.*

When Benucci finished to a great round of applause, Joseph II turned toward me, "So, Signor Da Ponte, is this the trifle you spoke of earlier this evening?"

"May it please you, Your Majesty," I said with a bowed head.

No sooner did the emperor reply, "It does indeed," than Storace stepped forward again and in the most plaintive voice, she began her aria, the same one Mozart had been whistling on the ledge an hour earlier, "Porgi Amor."

> *Oh Love, bring me some relief*
> *To all my sorrows, and for all my sighs!*
> *Either give me back my loved one,*
> *Or in mercy let me die.*

The sheer beauty of her voice, and Mozart's piano music along with Wetzlar and Haydn's accompaniment awed everyone in the antechamber. All who listened felt not only the true pain of her sorrows but also the absolute poignant beauty of the piece. Even such jaded veterans of the opera stage, including Catarina Cavalieri and my Adriana, had tears well up in their eyes.

But for reasons of our own, Mozart and I were focused on an audience of one: the Emperor Joseph II. It was his reactions above all that we were concerned about. Our goal all along was to have him seduced by the music before we ever said a single word about our secret opera. And there was not a better woman in all Austria to pull this off than Storace. When she encored her last line, "Or in mercy let me die," I witnessed even the ever world-weary Joseph II wipe clear his eyes.

Mozart, Wetzlar, and Haydn however gave them no rest. As soon as Nancy finished, Benucci launched into our most comedic piece, "Non piu andrai," a song he fully played for laughs. And there were many that came wholeheartedly from the assemblage around us.

No more, you amorous butterfly,
Will you go fluttering round by night and day,
Disturbing the peace of every beauty,
A little Narcissus and Adonis of love.

Storace gleefully stood in for the character of Cherubino in our Figaro as Benucci grabbed a hat and sword from one of the palace guards and thrust them into Nancy's hands—and she played the comedy to perfection as we knew she would.

No more will you have those fine feathers,
That light and dashing cap,
Those curls, those airs and graces,
Those womanish rosy cheeks.

Benucci sang with the greatest of animation and power his full-bodied voice could project.

Among soldiers, by Bacchus!
A huge moustache, a little knapsack,
A musket on your back, a saber at your side,
Your neck straight, your head erect,
A big helmet, or a big head dress.

And Nancy played the role of the silent new solider with an innocence and charm that kept the mood in the antechamber light and cheerful.

Lots of honor, very little pay.
And instead of the fandango,
A march through the mud.
Over mountains, through valleys,
With snow, and days of endless heat,
To the music of trumpets,
Of bombards, and of cannons,
Which, at every boom,
Will make bullets whistle past your ear.
Yes, yes, on to victory!
On to military glory!
On to military glory!"

When Benucci came to the final passage, which he sang out with his stentorian lungs, the effect was electricity itself, for the whole of the audience in the antechamber, as if actuated by one common feeling of delight, cheered, "Bravo! Bravo, Maestro! Viva! Viva grande Mozart!"

And although that was exactly the reaction we had dreamed of, Mozart was far from done. Before the thunderous applause had died down, Benucci humbly stepped aside and we then heard the high pitched, almost angelic voice of young Hummel singing, "Voi Sapete," accompanied solely by Wetzlar's guitar:

> *You ladies who know what love is*
> *See if it is what I have in my heart*
> *All that I feel I will explain*
> *Since it is new to me, I don't understand it."*

The entire audience fell into a hushed silence as they listened intently to Hummel's pleading voice of innocence, a state of being that those gathered around only knew from distant memories.

> *I have a feeling full of desire,*
> *Which now is pleasure, now is torment.*
> *I freeze, then I feel my spirit all ablaze,*
> *And the next moment turn again to ice.*

Adriana, close beside me on that divan, lifted up my hand in hers and kissed it tenderly in response to the singing, and for the moment I too felt like Cherubino with unexpected desires rising up. Yes, I craved that woman—and she knew it.

> *I seek for a treasure outside of myself;*
> *I know not who holds it nor what it is.*
> *I sigh and groan without wishing to,*
> *I flutter and tremble without knowing why.*

Joseph II, too, was moved and whispered aloud, "Oh poor child."

> *I find no peace by night or day.*

But yet to languish thus is sheer delight.
You ladies who know what love is,
See if it is what I have in my heart.

"Beautiful," said Joseph II to me, "absolutely beautiful. And you wrote this?"

"Then it pleases Your Majesty?"

Joseph II's smile and affirmative nod was all I needed to know as he added, "Later, later you will tell me more?"

"Assolutamente, Your Majesty, assolutamente."

Mozart and his trio then returned to his instrumental variations on the Figaro wedding choruses. After a few bars Benucci and Storace began to first sing again, but not any of our actual lyrics, just a steady rhythmic, "La, lala, lala, lala ..." in time to the music. They used their arms to encourage the entire room to join in and soon, the antechamber was filled with a delightful round that was repeated many times. I watched with pleasure as Joseph II, Adriana, Salieri, Caterina, Paisiello, Michael Kelly, and even the stodgy Count Orsini all joined in, "La, lala, lala, lala ... "

The singing continued until at last Mozart's ensemble returned to the stirring Fandango. Benucci and Storace paired off and began to dance as if they were indeed two passionate newlyweds madly in love with each other, a performance many about the room suspected held more truth than fiction.

Effortlessly they segued into the duet between Figaro and Susanna that was to be the opening of our opera, "Cinque, dieci, venti, trenta," but to prevent anyone from guessing the origin of our opera, we had Storace and Benucci substitute their own given names instead—and this might have been the only mistake we made that evening, for off in a corner of the room, I spotted Storace's husband, John Fisher, staggering in as if drunk. I crossed my fingers and hoped for the best.

Benucci sang as he pretended to measure the room:

"Five, ten, twenty, thirty, thirty-six, forty-three..."
Storace mimed putting on her wedding bonnet.

Yes, I am very pleased with that;
It seems just made for me.
Take a look, dear Francesco,
Just look at this hat of mine.

Benucci turned adoringly toward her.

Yes, my dearest, it's very pretty,
It looks just made for you.

Benucci and Storace came together hand in hand as they sang in unison while repeating over and over again the final chorus. And that enraged her real husband, the inebriated Fisher.

Oh, this morning of our wedding
How delightful my dear one
Is this pretty little hat
Which Nancy made herself.

What had been a perfect presentation rapidly dissolved into total chaos as Fisher, screaming and shouting, charged at Benucci and Storace. At first everyone thought it was part of our little act, but no. Caught unawares Mozart, Wetzlar, and Haydn froze and stopped playing. Had we snatched defeat from the jaws of victory?

Fisher, being the cowardly bully that he was, swung first at his wife and caught her full on in the chin, knocking her down before charging headlong toward Benucci. The singer sidestepped the drunken husband, which allowed the palace guards to dive into the fray and they wrestled Fisher to the ground and held him at sword point.

To His Majesty's credit, Joseph II ran to comfort Nancy while most of the assemblage fled the antechamber for the Grand Ballroom and a return to the soothing sounds of the opera orchestra playing "Der Walzer."

In a few minutes, it was all over. Joseph II ordered that Fisher be arrested for assault and jailed at the Hofburg Palace.

As a footnote, not long after, John Fisher was expelled from the Austro-Hungarian Empire, and his three-year marriage to Storace was annulled by a cardinal of the Catholic Church—the Cardinal was of course, a cousin to His Majesty.

Nancy, who sported a wicked bruise on her cheek, was more startled and shaken by the assault than hurt. Wetzlar offered her the comfort of one of his upstairs guest rooms for the night, and Michael Kelly was assigned to chaperone and guide her there, a role the pretty tenor had undertaken more than once in the half-dozen years the two singers had known each other. The only question that ran through my mind was this: After Kelly escorted her to safety, which of her lovers—Joseph II, Benucci, or Mozart—would discreetly arrive to comfort her for the balance of the night? Had I a year's pay in gold, would I wager it all on Mozart? Assolutamente.

Once all those matters of health and jurisprudence were settled, Joseph II had me sit beside him on the divan to discuss my "trifle." Orsini dismissed everyone else from the room, though he himself remained behind.

Adriana was the last to leave and reluctantly so. After she curtsied before the emperor, I blew her a kiss.

"A dopo, amore mio," I said.

"*Certamente! La bella luna brilla ancora,*" she said in reply with a kiss of her own. "*A dopo.*"

When she was gone and the room quiet, Joseph II wasted no time in getting down to business. "Now that I've both heard and witnessed your little trifle—and I don't mean your *La Ferrarese*," he added, penning a nickname that would soon stick to Adriana. "I want to know what your opera is going to be about. But wait . . . Even before that, I must confess that I've long been concerned about Signora Storace's infatuation with Mozart. Tell Your Majesty what you know."

"It's the music, Your Majesty, she loves his music," I hastily interjected, wondering where Joseph II was going to take this train of thought, even as I suspected Mozart and

Storace were upstairs, undressing each other, perhaps even directly above us.

"Don't interrupt the emperor," said Orsini.

Joseph II waved Orsini off; he was far more affable and at ease in regular conversation than his chamberlain allowed. "Of course, it's the music. *Es war wunderbar.* But Benucci, is he . . . he and Storace? That would be of some concern."

"I know nothing of these matters, Your Majesty. But they're actors, they are all actors who can 'pretend' anything, and you know what theater people are like," I replied, hoping he had no lingering suspicions about Mozart's infidelities.

"Yes, theater people, vagabonds with voices," he went on. "If not for the beauty and pleasure of their work . . . My God, what is opera? Yes, these theater people sing about rape, murder, sexual obsessions, infidelity, eternal damnation, kidnapping, births out of wedlock, gambling, secret identities, and war between the classes, and those are just our comedies."

"Indeed, Your Majesty, without these conflicts, there is no drama, and without drama there is no comedy. The best comedies . . . "

Joseph II interrupted before I could finish. "As you and Herr Mozart well demonstrated tonight, the best comedies are . . . " He paused and then repeated himself. "The best comedies are what?"

"Your Majesty, the best comedies are born from conflict, which is why Mozart and I have adapted our trifle from a play that Count Pergen has banned for the German theater stage, *The Marriage of Figaro*.

"What!" exclaimed Orsini with great indignation. "You presented banned material, right here, this very evening to His Majesty? We should have you arrested, exiled, or sent to the galleys for such an affront."

"Hold, Orsini, hold," said Joseph II. "There was nothing offensive in what we heard tonight, but Signor Da Ponte, that is quite a risk you took, *non è' vero?*"

"It was simply this, Your Majesty. In adapting Beaumarchais's original play into a libretto," I said, reminding him that an opera is about what people feel as expressed in song, "I was easily able to remove all of the dialogues and plot twists that would offend. In our comedy, as you yourselves witnessed tonight, there is only joy, sadness, passion, laughter, and love wrapped in some of the most enchanting music our ears have ever been fortunate enough to hear."

"That may be so, but I am constantly buffeted by my counselors who consider that our liberalizations under my Edit of Tolerance have gone too far and are the cause of an ever-increasing degree of civil disorder and disturbances. Why just tonight alone, in addition to Mr. Fisher's brutal assault on Signora Storace, my royal carriage was pelted with debris, one of Wentzler's servants was nearly raped, and Signor Paisiello informs me that the Abbé Casti was beaten and robbed by two masked men. And now you would have Count Pergen's rulings overturned?"

"I know nothing of those other matters, Your Majesty," I said, though in truth my hands were in all of them. "I am but a simple poet, one who treasures the value of words written well and music magnificently measured for the enjoyment of you and the company of your court. In my humble estimation, our libretto accomplishes that without dishonor."

"You are persuasive, Signor Da Ponte, but no more so than Herr Mozart's music. It was indeed enchanting. Send your libretto around tomorrow. I will read it. We do have an opening available at the Burgtheater in May, yes Orsini?"

"Yes, Your Majesty," said Orsini, "But how can you approve of such effrontery?"

"Hold, Orsini, hold," repeated Joseph II. "I did not say I approve of Mozart and Da Ponte producing *The Marriage of Figaro*. I said I would read the libretto and then and only then render judgment."

"Thank you, Your Majesty," I said, not trusting Orsini for a moment. I suspected he would do all he could to undermine our endeavor. "We serve to honor you and your court."

"You are welcome, Signor Da Ponte. The glory of this night is yours however. Now go, go. You have scored two victories already. Go," he said waving me off the divan. "Go, go. Go find your La Ferrarese and make it three victories before the moon vanishes. *Abbiamo vinto!*"

Chapter Eleven: Celebrations

Lunchtime, Thursday, May 25, 1962
The Café Mozart, New York City

Mozart... When Jake met Dolcetta for lunch at the Café Mozart on 39th Street near Park Avenue, it was to celebrate the sixteenth anniversary of her arrival in America. Though little more than a neighborhood eatery in midtown Manhattan, the café was a favorite spot they had frequented often. Not only was it halfway between their respective offices, it was also fairly close to the Metropolitan Opera House. The walls were decorated with portraits of the composer and his librettist Lorenzo Da Ponte, as well as autographed photos of the many stars who had performed in Mozart's operas at the Met. It even featured a unique, one-of-a-kind classic Wurlitzer jukebox that had nothing but recordings of Mozart's music. For a dime you could play the entire *Little G Minor Symphony*, which in fact was what they heard when they walked in the door.

It was a delightful spring day, and because the Memorial Day holiday that marked the true start of summer in the city was coming up, the restaurant was relatively empty.

The owner, Leo "Leporello" Ponziani, who claimed descent from the first singer to perform that role in *Don Giovanni*, had a chilled bottle of prosecco from Vittorio Veneto waiting for them at their favorite table in the back room.

Dolcetta, who had her hair pulled back in a ponytail, both surprised and pleased Jake by wearing a new turquoise shirtwaist dress that resembled the one she had changed into the day they had first met in Ceneda in 1946.

Jake also had a surprise for Dolcetta. Their first letter from Manny—an Aerogram from Vienna—had arrived at Jake's office just that morning.

In the post, which typically for the times took over a week to wend its way from Vienna to New York, Manny described the various adventures he and Pandorea had experienced since arriving there with Greta and Enrico Foxx—a world which bore little resemblance to the world Da Ponte had described in the diaries they had been translating. As Jake and Dolcetta sipped their prosecco and dined on Café Mozart's signature dish, Wiener schnitzel, Jake shared the contents of the letter from their son.

First up, Manny described the Foxx's luxury penthouse apartment at *Kartnerstrasse siebzehn*—seventeen—where he and Pandorea would be staying for the summer. Although the Foxxes' building was purportedly originally constructed sometime in the 1300s—yes, it was that old—the penthouse apartment was fully renovated and modernized. While originally a cluster of servants' quarters, their suite now encompassed the entire fourth floor. It even had a walk-up sunroom and porch on the roof that offered up some of the best views to be had in all Vienna. A few blocks to the north were the famous spires of St. Stephan's Cathedral, the very church where Mozart married Constanze some 180 years earlier, and where Manny went on to describe how he and Pandorea—inspired no doubt by the moment—both fell to their knees and exchanged love vows of their own.

The apartment's grand parlor, which held two of Greta's Bosendorfer pianos back-to-back, also overlooked the restaurants and shops of the *Neuer Markt*, places where Mozart had reputedly frequented. On the ground floor was a coffee house, the Café Venezia, where Beethoven premiered his *Opus 132 String Quartet* and where Manny figured he would spend many an afternoon between classes. A few blocks past St. Stephan's was Mozart's old residence on *Domgasse*, the place he lived when writing the scores for both *The Marriage of Figaro* and *Don Giovanni*. Diagonally across the back courtyard on *Rauhensteingasse* was another one of the composer's many residences in the city, the Mozart *Sterbehaus*, the one where he died in 1781. Five blocks south on Kartnerstrasse was the Vienna Opera House and a few more blocks from there to the west was the Hofburg Palace where Emperor Joseph II had lived. Adjacent to that was the Burgtheater, the old court opera house where Mozart had frequently performed.

On their first night in town, Enrico and Greta Foxx even took them out to dinner at one of the still-existent restaurants where Mozart, Da Ponte, Casanova, and even Beethoven were known to dine, *Zu Den Drei Hakken*, where they had their first taste of authentic, in country, Austrian Wiener schnitzel.

Two days later Enrico took them over to the *Musikverein*, Vienna's premier concert hall renowned for its almost perfect acoustics. There, Greta Tedesco Foxx, as soloist, performed Mozart's piano concerto No. 20 in D Minor, K466, with the Vienna Philharmonic. The next morning the kids began their opera studies at the Vienna Academy of Music. In addition to various master classes in voice, performance, and acting, the goal for all the students was to perform once in *The Marriage of Figaro* at the *Theater An Der Wien*, just before the summer's end.

After that, provided Manny and Pandorea were able to get visas to cross into Czechoslovakia, their student program was to be joined by two others in Prague at the Estates National Theater. There, the three opera schools would perform their respective pieces for a student opera festival. Their Vienna Academy would do *The Marriage of Figaro*. The Prague Conservancy would perform *Don Giovanni*, and a class from St. Petersburg in Russia was scheduled to put on Mozart's *The Mercy of Titus*.

Unfortunately, given the Iron Curtain and the Cold War tensions between Russia and the West, obtaining those visas was questionable. Consequently, despite their exceptional talents, Manny and Pandorea were not cast as the leads in *Figaro* but rather in secondary roles: he as Bartolo and Pandorea as Marcellina. Although Manny wrote of his disappointment, Jake was pleased to read of their assignments. He and Dolcetta agreed that to fully understand the brilliance of what Da Ponte and Mozart had achieved in *Figaro*, one had to view and comprehend the opera from the perspective of not just the leads but by the supporting characters as well.

As he and Dolcetta continued to dine, Jake could not only picture the two kids working through the Sextet in act 3, in his mind's eye, he could actually visualize them singing it in full costume.

Bartolo/Manny:
There stands tua madre.
Figaro:
Not my nurse? Mia madre?
Bartolo/Manny:
Tua madre.
Count:
Sua madre?
Don Curzio:
Sua madre?
Figaro:
Do I hear right?

Marcellina/Pandorea:
> *And there stands tuo padre.*

She runs to embrace Figaro.

Marcellina/Pandorea:
> *Dearest son, in this embrace*
> *Recognize tua madre.*

Figaro (to Bartolo/Manny):
> *Padre caro, do the same,*
> *Do not leave me longer here to blush.*

Bartolo/Manny:
> *Do not let conscience*
> *Stand in the way of your desire.*

He embraces Figaro.

Don Curzio:
> *He's suo padre, she's sua madre:*
> *The wedding can't go forward.*

As the images faded from Jake's imagination, he shared with Dolcetta that, all in all, it sounded like a great start to summer. She as well could not have been more pleased for the kids.

After lunch—and after the two of them finished the bottle of prosecco—Jake offered to walk Dolcetta back to her office near the UN headquarters. It was a splendid spring day, perfect for a stroll. Walking hand-in-hand, Dolcetta led the way, deviating ever so slightly from her usual path so that they would pass by *La Casa Sicilia*, the Italian pottery store where Marietta had bought them those espresso cups.

Both were pleased when they saw through the storefront window, the rows upon rows of floor to ceiling shelves filled with beautifully colored ceramics of every shape and design. There were dishes, cups, bowls, platters, wall hangings, lamps, sculptured figures, flowerpots, pitchers, Saracens, floor tiles, and wall tiles—all brightly decorated and often hand-painted in riotous displays of traditional and classic patterns.

"I want them all," declared Dolcetta as they started in. "We'll redo the house, upstairs and down and pretend we're home again."

"Of course," obliged Jake. "But couldn't we start small? Maybe a few cereal bowls?"

"Certo!" said Dolcetta.

When they walked in, a young dark-haired woman—one of two people behind the counter, the other being an older gentleman—called out to her in fluent Italian but marked by a guttural Sicilian accent. "*Oh, ciao Angeli, come sta?*"

The older man followed as well, "*Ah, Signorina Gemelli, il tuo ordine è proprio qui.*"

Dolcetta was totally startled, and flipped back and forth between Italian and English, "What? My order is ready? *Non capisco.* I don't understand? *Quale ordine?* What order? I've never been here before."

The two sales clerks were equally confused. The young woman pointed at Dolcetta's forearm. "*I tuoi numeri?*" They're gone?

"Her numbers?" asked Jake, first in English and then in Italian, "*I suoi numeri?* There must be some confusion."

"Oh, excuse me," said the older man in English. "I mistook you for another . . . " But then he stopped dead in the middle of his sentence and just stared dumbfounded toward the doorway at the front of the store.

"*Dio mio!*" the young woman proclaimed, suddenly reverting back to Italian, "*Ce ne sono due. Devi essere sorelle.*"

"*Mia sorella?*" asked Dolcetta. "My sister?"

"*Sua sorella?*" asked Jake.

"*Sua sorella!*" insisted the older man.

"*Mia sorella?*" repeated Dolcetta.

"*Sua sorella,*" said the younger woman. "Angeli Gemelli. She must be. She's standing right there."

Dolcetta and Jake both turned around to look toward the front door. There stood a woman, a near mirror image of Dolcetta, in a turquoise shirt waist dress with her long brown hair pulled back in a ponytail.

"*Sua sorella*," exclaimed Jake. "It is Danielle!"

"*Mia sorella?*" said the woman in the doorway, her face gone white with a look of total shock.

"*Mia sorella*," repeated Dolcetta, as tears, the happiest tears of a lifetime, flowed from her eyes. "*Mia sorella gemella, 9213474.*"

Dolcetta's and Danielle's embrace of reunion in the doorway of *La Casa Sicilia*, was filled with such emotion, joy, disbelief, tears, kisses, and clinging that Jake still considered it to be a perfect work of art, the Olympic gold medal and world champion hug of hugs, one that could never, ever be surpassed anywhere, anytime by anyone. In an instant he watched two decades of incredible pain, suffering, torment, loneliness, and anguish in the hearts of these two sisters simply vanish forever. He saw a sparkle of light, a beacon of joy, hope, and inspiration in both their eyes so bright and inextinguishable that even the two store clerks who witnessed their reunion began to cheer and applaud.

As Jake continued to watch in awe of that first hug, he thought of Mozart and the infinite beauty of the finale *tutte* of *The Marriage of Figaro*, where the chorus of voices soared toward the heavens with expressions of joy:

> *Then let us all*
> *Be happy.*
> *This day of torment,*
> *Of caprice and folly,*
> *Love can end*
> *Only in contentment and joy,*
> *Lovers and friends, let's round things off*
> *In Dancing and pleasure,*
> *And to the sound of a happy march*
> *Let's hasten to the revelry.*

Yes, Jake knew, if one looked deeply into the works of Mozart and Da Ponte, there was a lyric for every emotion.

Afterward, Jake and the two sisters, each bubbling over with an unmeasurable joy, retreated back to the Café Mozart and over another celebratory bottle of prosecco, *Le due sorelle* shared their stories.

Danielle began hers with a tale of amnesia, blessed amnesia. She recalled waking up sometime in the summer of 1945 in a US Army field hospital somewhere in southern Germany, not remembering her name, or where she was from, or how she had gotten there. Speech at first was difficult. She had had some command initially of her native Italian but had extreme difficulty recalling enough of her school-girl English to be able to converse with the doctors and nurses who tended to her. Confusion ruled her day.

Fortunately, at the hospital, there was a combat pilot, George Cosentino—Giorgio, she called him—an Italian-American Jew, who had also been wounded in the closing days of the war. Giorgio's family was originally from Venice, and because he spoke fluent Italian, he became her de facto translator.

Danielle then described how only then did she learn that she had been unconscious for almost two months, the likely cause being a high fever from typhus, compounded by extreme exhaustion and malnourishment. The only identification the staff had for her was the Dachau Concentration Camp number 9213474 tattooed on her arm and a single black and white photograph found in a pocket of her ragged dress. It was a picture of twin girls—her and a sister—and on the smudged inscription on the back that appeared to be, "Gemelli, Angeli." Consequently, she and everyone else at the hospital presumed that was her name.

She did not know her real name was Danielle Spinoziano and not Angeli Gemelli, until she sat down with Jake and Dolcetta at the Café Mozart, a shock no less seismic than the reunion itself.

"My health," she said, "in the military hospital was still precarious and it would be another couple of months before they would consider me strong enough to be repatriated—that is if they could figure out where I was from and who might be my relatives. During that time, Giorgio and I became close. He was so sweet. We would sit for hours together, he trying to help me recover my memory and me . . . Well, I tried to block the horrid visions that did come to me of life in the concentration camps."

Much as she wanted to, Danielle told Jake and Dolcetta that she could recall nothing of consequence that would have helped her be reunited with whatever family she may have had. The Red Cross tried to match her up with possible relatives but found no Gemellis anywhere that might have been *famiglia*. And only now, two decades later, did she understand why.

Giorgio's leg injury precluded him from staying in the military, and when he was scheduled to finally be shipped home to Brooklyn in September of that year, he proposed marriage.

"Of course, I accepted. I had come to love Giorgio; he felt like family, like one of us immediately, and I had no one else in the world to turn to. Whatever village I had come from, whatever people I may have called my own, were all dead to me," Danielle said to her sister and Jake.

But then Danielle started to laugh. "I accepted his proposal but with one caveat: That I be allowed to keep my full name, Angeli Gemelli, so that if ever any one from our family was still alive, they would be able to find me. Little did I know the difficulty that would cause."

"Si, yes," said Dolcetta, hugging her sister again, "We were momma's *Gemelli angeli*, her twin angels. That's why she wrote that on the back."

"Oh," Danielle let out a huge sigh before continuing, "I have no memory of her or our father or our home. All I see is a gray cloud when I try. Did anyone else survive?"

"*Solamente io,*" said Dolcetta. "Just me . . . and you!"

"And unfortunately for both Giorgio and me, he was shipped back to the States abruptly and without even being able to say goodbye, much less marry."

"*Dio mio,*" exclaimed Dolcetta, "What did you do? That's horrible."

"Alone, feeling abandoned, and with no other known family, I found myself being shipped out to a string of Displaced Persons or DP camps. The first I don't remember. The second was in southern Germany near Munich, a horrid place named *Landsberg am Lech* that had previously been a concentration camp. That's where I discovered I was pregnant by Giorgio. But there was no way to reach him. All I knew was that he lived somewhere in Brooklyn."

Danielle also had made attempts to locate Gemellis in Italy but that was obviously doomed to failure. "I could remember nothing of where I lived, and this picture . . . " She pulled a reprint of that photograph out of her wallet. "This picture of the two of us twins was my sole link to the past. And those who did see it and tried to be helpful could only suggest what I feared most: that you, my twin, had probably been murdered in one of Mengele's experiments on human Guinea pigs."

"But here I am!" exclaimed Dolcetta. She hugged her sister yet again. The two of them could not stop embracing each other.

"Then the boy I met at the opera?" asked Danielle.

"My son, Manny . . . Emanuele Conegliano," said Dolcetta.

"He's gorgeous," said Danielle.

"Oh, thank you," said Dolcetta.

"He was so confused. He saw me kissing Giorgio," Danielle laughed and then said, "He must have imagined it was you having an affair."

"And your child?"

"Ah, my Gaelle, Gaelle Gemelli. She's home in Israel."

"Israel?" asked Jake.

"Yes, Israel. After she was born in 1946 at the Landsberg DP camp clinic, I decided to forgo Europe for Israel. In Cyprus we joined up with a group of other Jewish refugees who sought to reach Israel by freighter. That ship was the *SS Exodus*, and those desperate refugees aboard, well, that was me," she added, referring to the novel and movie of the same name. Both had both been huge blockbusters in the States. "And not long after I arrived in Israel with baby Gaelle, the War of Independence began. The Arabs attacked us from all directions with the intent of annihilating every Jew they could not drive into the sea."

She described how she—much like Dolcetta—had to learn to fire military weapons. An unintentional combatant, she used them in self-defense when her apartment complex outside Jerusalem was attacked. Soon thereafter she was assigned to help protect a newly built Israeli airstrip near Herzliya. There, by a miracle of miracles she was reunited with Giorgio.

"Giorgio, who had never given up trying to find me, had joined with a number of American war veterans who had volunteered to pilot fighter planes against the Arab states. We were married between his combat sorties."

After the war ended, they settled in Tel Aviv. Giorgio, who was an engineer by training and an entrepreneur by nature, was instrumental in helping the young Israeli Air Force develop low-tech, low-cost alternative combat systems. His inventions helped turn the tide in the second Israeli war for survival, the Suez War with Egypt in 1956. One invention was a specially designed tailhook on old fighter aircraft that could rip out the telephone lines that the Egyptians relied upon to communicate with their troops. A second and even more critical one was his placement of a rear-mounted machine gun on the tail of the old P-51 Mustangs the IAF had acquired as secondhand US war surplus. This tail gun enabled the old prop-driven planes to shoot down the much faster MiG jets the Egyptians had obtained from Russia. "And now," she said, "Giorgio is working on some top-secret early warning system that could detect hostile Arab air attacks."

Danielle told them that they still lived in Israel, and would be returning there soon. It was only when her husband's business brought them to the States two or three times a year that they stayed in their Manhattan pied-à-terre. It was for the apartment that she had ordered dishes from *La Casa Sicilia*. She then pulled out a picture of Giorgio and her daughter, Gaelle, to show them.

When Jake noted that Giorgio's features were not unlike his own, so much so that they could have been brothers, Dolcetta joked that they probably were related, given how many women their ancestor, Lorenzo Da Ponte, had slept with in Venice. Even the translation of his public diaries described his depositing any number of illegitimate children at the orphanages of La Serenissima.

Gaelle was about the same age as Manny, and she too could have been passed off as Manny's sister. Gaelle was in an advanced medical studies program at the Technion in Haifa and, unfortunately, had not joined Danielle and Giorgio for this trip.

Over the next few weeks before Danielle and Giorgio returned to Israel, *Le due sorelle*, the two sisters, spent as much time together as possible getting to know each other all over again. Jake met Giorgio and took an instant liking to him, and the two couples dined out together several times and even caught a performance of *Cosi Fan Tutte* at the Met. They sat with Abe and Rosa in their private box and watched their favorite, Roberta Peters, sing the role of Despina. The reunion worked wonders for Danielle, and she even began to recover bits and pieces of her memory, both the good and the bad.

At dinner at their apartment one night—coincidentally the night the Israelis finally hanged Eichmann—Jake and the two sisters went through the genizah trunk, hoping some of the pictures and records would stir her memory. She remembered their great-uncle, Rabbi Geremia, but still blocked all recollection of the rest of the family who were murdered or dragged off to the camps.

"It's too painful," Danielle finally confessed. "I suspect my heart must have instructed my brain in what to forget. You can only imagine the horrors we experienced. Perhaps it is better this way."

Jake then asked both Danielle and his own wife, Dolcetta, how it was that they managed to survive intact through all they had endured.

"Love and fortitude," Danielle answered first. "Somehow," she continued, "I stayed strong in my heart because of the love and affection that my family, especially Uncle Geremia, shared with me when we were growing up. Even when my memory of other matters failed, I remembered Geremia's voice, his words, his wisdom, much of which he shared through song."

"Yes," chimed in Dolcetta, "Geremia sang often to us and mostly opera."

Danielle continued, "Certo! Geremia would sing or play a piece such as Figaro's *cavatina* in the first act and then ask us what it meant."

"And not just in the context of the opera," Dolcetta added seamlessly, as if she and Danielle were one mind and one person in two separate bodies, "But in life—just as he did in Ceneda, Jake, when he played 'La Ci Darem la Mano,' for us."

Jake nodded, remembering well that day, a day—and a lesson in fundamental humanity—that forever changed his life.

"What did Da Ponte intend? What life lessons could we learn from this?" said Danielle.

"This was our bible, our Torah," said Dolcetta.

"As composed by Mozart and written by Lorenzo," said Danielle.

And then Jake watched in amusement as the two sisters both jumped up and began to dance and sing the *cavatina* in unison as they must have as children:

If my dear Count,
You feel like dancing,
It's I
Who'll call the tune.
If you'll come
To my school,
I'll teach you
How to caper.
I'll know how...
But wait,
I can uncover
His secret design
More easily by dissembling
Acing stealthily,
Acting openly,
Here stinging,
There mockingly,
All your plots
I'll overthrow.

"Passion, Geremia would say," added Danielle, "is what comes from love. And if you have love for life in your spirit, then you should be passionate about what you do . . . "

"Who you are, and what you believe," said Dolcetta. "It gives us the strength to fight injustice whenever we are able . . . "

"But to be wise enough to be like a willow tree. To bend and flex in the wind when necessary . . . " said Danielle.

"But to also be a Figaro, brave enough to act and smart enough to know how to overcome one's enemies," added Dolcetta.

"This is what he taught us, love and fortitude, and a lifelong desire to be resilient," said Danielle. "To be a rock, like Fiordiligi," and the two sisters began to sing yet again:

I stand as a rock
Against all winds and tempests!
My soul will always be strong
In faith and in love.
My constancy consoles my grief,
And only death can change
My heart's affection.
You, ungrateful creatures,
must respect my example of fidelity,
Let it extinguish
Your false audacious hopes!

"And what matters, is this life. That's the secret, Geremia would add. There is no heaven and there is no hell, only the unending today," said Dolcetta.

"What we do today, is our only concern. Love, respect for others . . . " added Danielle

"Justice, courage, decency, wisdom," confirmed Dolcetta.

"And when Geremia was challenged by anyone over questions of whether there was a life after death, he said this," offered Danielle, but Dolcetta answered first.

"It is only because each one of us is a conscious creature, we are fundamentally incapable of imagining a state where there is no consciousness, where there is no life, where there is no continuation of our very being."

"So, to fill that gap," Danielle jumped in, "that emptiness in our inability to comprehend anything outside of our own thoughts, humans invented the concept of an afterlife, of heaven, hell, of purgatory, of God and of the devil."

"And when faced with unspeakable horrors, especially during the war," said Dolcetta.

"We would act as we believed best, for we had love and fortitude."

The sisters embraced and then turned to face Jake. "That is how we each survived," they concluded in unison, "Just like Figaro, just like Fiordiligi. We survived."

Danielle then asked Jake and Dolcetta, "When you translate more of Da Ponte's *Secret Diaries*, please send them to me. This is our heritage and something I want to share with Gaelle. She should know well where she comes from."

"Certo," said Jake. "Are we not all Da Ponte's children?"

Chapter Twelve:
A Descent into Hell

The Next Morning, Thursday, January 5, 1786
The Palace of Baron Raimund Wetzlar von
Plankenstern, Vienna

Mozart . . . I was dreaming of the libretto I had written for Mozart and needed to soon deliver it into the hands of the Emperor Joseph II for his approval, but Count Orsini in the guise of a snarling watchdog was blocking my way. No matter which way I turned, I could not get past this guardian.

This was not just any libretto but the one for *The Marriage of Figaro*. Yes, *Figaro*, the one based on a now-banned play. Yes, the one with Count Almaviva pounding on his wife's bedroom door.

Yes, I was sound asleep and in the middle of this nightmare when I first heard that noise. What had started as gentle taps grew exponentially louder until I awoke enough to realize the door banging was not from any nightmare.

Instead, it was Mozart himself, calling, "Lorenzo, Lorenzo, wake up. Open up, open up."

So much for Figaro, the count, and the diva of my dreams, Adriana Ferrarese del Bene, whom I noticed—most happily and appreciatively—was asleep beside me in the bed.

Where was I? Oh, yes, with my head pounding from a night of excess, I struggled to remember what had happened and how I ended up here, wherever here was. La Ferrarese and I had danced *Der Walzer* until dawn. And somehow, yes, somehow, we ended up in a bed in the guest wing of Wetzlar's palace. Yes, I had succumbed to her many charms; that was it, and oh, how my head hurt.

Throwing on a nightshirt, I went over and unlocked the door. Mozart stood there with Celestina, the uniformed servant girl we had rescued the day before. His face was reddened and puffy from his night of excess, and I can only say he looked as wretched as I felt. The servant girl carried a tray laden with a set of ornate Italian style espresso cups and a matching coffee pot.

Beyond their profiles in the doorway, I saw a clear blue sky in the glass windows that lined the hallway of Wetzlar's palace. From the angle of the view downward, I guessed we must have been on the fourth floor. Outside and below the back of the estate was a market square, *Judenplatz*, I calculated. Last night's snow flurries, which had coated the entire city of Vienna, were as yet undisturbed.

Dio mio, it was still early morning, and I had probably not slept more than an hour or two at most, if that, especially considering that I had a vague but sweet memory of making love with Adriana in that bed until we both collapsed with exhaustion.

"*Che cosa?*" I asked of Mozart, too groggy to even want to try to comprehend what they were doing here at such an early hour. All I desired was to be able to crawl back into bed with Adriana and sleep, but that was not about to happen.

Before Mozart could answer my question, Adriana sat upright in bed. As with most of the divas I had known, she was a bit of an exhibitionist, and though naked with her breasts proudly on display, she asked the same question, "*Che cosa?*"

"It's Mozart," I replied as cheerfully as possible. "You said you wanted to meet him, and, by Jove, here he is. He's even brought coffee."

I made a hasty introduction of Adriana to Mozart and vice versa while the servant girl filled all three cups. Oh, coffee, blessed coffee.

Unflustered, Adriana never missed a beat. Despite her nakedness, she stood up, extended her arm out to Mozart with the grace and dignity of a ballerina and said, "*Piacere mio.*"

Mozart, with even greater fanfare, bowed and kissed her hand. "The pleasure is all mine."

Of course, it was, as it would have been for any healthy male. At age thirty, Adriana had as perfect and statuesque a figure as any woman I had ever known.

My exquisite diva immediately snatched an espresso off of Celestina's tray. Adriana bolted it down in a single gulp before sitting back down on the bed. "More." She was rather insistent. "More. If we are here for coffee, give me more."

"Si, Signora, si," said the obliging and deferential servant girl.

Mozart and I each took one of the cups as Celestina refilled Adriana's.

Concurrently I asked again, what was going on.

"It's the man in the vermillion coat," answered Mozart. "Wetzlar's guards found him drunk and asleep in one of the back gardens. They locked him up for safe keeping in a storeroom off the wine cellar. Wetzlar insists you, me, and the girl all come down to identify the brigand, if we can."

"*Adesso?*" I asked. The espresso did little to stop the pounding in my head.

"Yes, now. Wetzlar's waiting for us."

I turned around toward Adriana, wanting only to slide back into bed with that luscious womanly body of hers and find comfort in her arms until the moon rose again. Who was this woman, this goddess whose spell had intoxicated my senses? In truth, I was smitten, absolutely smitten, and for the first time in fifteen years I could imagine that this woman might be the one to make me abandon my profligate ways. Fully contented by the spell her allures cast over me, I could certainly visualize myself coupled with her indefinitely. Some might consider that rash and foolish behavior for an abbé such as I was, but the catalogue of my previous failings said otherwise.

Yes, to this day I confess I remain the same *spiritoso ignorante* I was as a youth. And while it is true that my list of past infidelities could have filled volumes, I readily admit I still understand nothing of the substance of real love, nor how it was that Adriana, this lovely creature, had somehow pierced my flesh with her teeth and claws. I only knew I wanted her.

"I must go," I finally declaimed as I gathered up my clothes and began to dress. "Shall I see you again? Later perhaps?"

"Si, certamente!" she exclaimed with an assuredness that pleased me to no end. "Call for me this evening. Do you know the stagecoach stop on Kartnerstrasse?"

"By the Wilden Mann Gasthaus? Yes." I answered. Indeed, I knew this inn at Kartnerstrasse siebzehn rather well. My tiny garret of an apartment was on the uppermost floor, the fourth, in the old servants' quarters. On the street below was a rundown coffeehouse and the carriage-stop for coaches arriving from the south, including the spas of Baden. In fact, Mozart and I were due to meet the returning Constanze there later that afternoon.

"Excellent, yes. Call for me then at the Wilden Mann Gasthaus at Kartnerstrasse siebzehn." Even the way she articulated her words excited me. "You will find me at the grand suite on the second floor, at home of Luigi del Bene, *mio marito.*"

"Your husband?" I said, with a bit of shock in my voice. Yes, I was caught off guard, the new love of my life, the woman I had already conceived of marrying, had a husband?

"Certo!" she laughed upon seeing my distress. "Oh, don't worry, he's back in Milano. Good heavens, Lorenzo, we women have so little chance to amuse ourselves, we must take it as it comes."

I wondered, while kissing her goodbye, was it too soon to reveal I lived upstairs? She slid back between the covers as I went out the door with Mozart and Celestina. Oh sleep, blessed sleep. I wanted it, but she got it.

Upon leaving, as I shut the door behind us, the door directly opposite opened ever so slightly and Nancy Storace's face appeared in the crack. Nancy held Mozart's top coat out for him. She too was absent even a shred of clothes. Mozart leaned in, kissed her lips to the satisfaction of both parties, and grabbed the coat before Nancy closed the door once more and disappeared from our sight. Yes, I thought, I should have wagered all on Mozart; he and Storace were a sure bet.

Thus, Mozart and I followed the servant girl back down the hallways of Wetzlar's palace. He began to whistle again, this time it was one of our tunes from last night, "Open those eyes a little," and I began to sing along—softly at that hour—with a self-deprecating variation:

If we only open our eyes, we rash and foolish men,
To look at these women; and see them as they are,
Goddesses, we call them with our intoxicated senses,
And to whom our enfeebled reason offers undying tribute.

"You didn't know she was married, did you?" asked Mozart, who certainly picked up on my surprise.

"No, I did not. But I had greater expectations for this diva. A future together perhaps."

"You expected fidelity in a woman? How delightfully naïve of you, Lorenzo. While everyone condemns women for being so fickle, I excuse it as a necessity of the heart," Mozart said to me, "Are not all women like that? Cosi fan tutte. Should they behave differently than we, the men they often disparage? Of course not. A lover who finds himself deceived by these comets that dazzle should blame only his own folly."

"Your solution?" I asked.

"Surrender—but with a smile—to these night owls or they will pluck you to the bone. Do not lose hope my dear Lorenzo. From all appearances it seems La Ferrarese is yours into the foreseeable future. For me, much as I might wish it were not so, do you imagine my Constanze behaves any differently, or is any more faithful than I?"

Given that was a question between men to which there was no correct answer, I said nothing. But, yes, I did know better. Since my first night years ago in Venice, I had come to know, not only the flesh of scores of women but their thoughts, fears, emotions, and desires as well. Yes, I should have known better.

With that, we soon began our descent deep into the bowels of Wetzlar's palace. We left the gilded hallways and ballrooms behind for the rough-hewn stone passage ways with dirt floors beneath the palace that felt as if they were chiseled out of the very earth itself. After traversing a network of subterranean passageways, we found Wetzlar and several of his guards waiting for us outside the locked door of one of his wine cellars.

"The drunk's in there, asleep," said Wetzlar. He waved Celestina forward to look through a barred observation window at the man with the vermillion coat. "Is that the man who attacked you?"

"Yes, sir," she informed us.

"Do you know him? Have you ever seen him before?" inquired Wetzlar of Celestina.

"Never before last night, sir."

Mozart was next. He looked in, but quickly shook his head. "I cannot say one way or another. All I saw was the color of his cloak as he ran off."

I followed and looked in, expecting to see little I would recognize other than the vermillion cloak, but that expectation was soon shattered. I did indeed know the man lying there even though his face was pockmarked and swollen like an alcoholic. It was Girolamo Tiepolo of Venice, the wastrel twin brother of my former lover, Angela Tiepolo, an ally of the Casti family, the betrayer who knew all our secrets going back to the night Zina stabbed the commendatore, and the man responsible for my expulsion and banishment from the Veneto.

On this last point, I should elaborate. Though I loved my life here in Vienna, I must confess that I would have never willingly abandoned my homeland, the Veneto, so long as there was the least bit of hope that I would find a means to be restored to my beloved Zina. Yes, revenge is as much an aspect of Venice as its canals and gondolas. Girolamo Tiepolo, who long sought his against me for my role in helping Zina escape, finally obtained it seven years ago in the summer of 1779 and in so doing destroyed my prospect of ever seeing Zina again—again, as in forever.

There exists in Venice at strategic points about the city, these *boche dei leoni*, hollow stone lions with open mouths that any citizen can use to post a letter of denunciation of any other person to the Council of Ten. In June of that year, one such anonymous declaration of adultery was made against me in which it was claimed that I, a converso Jew, had brought the Christian faith into disrepute by seducing another man's wife, Anzelotta Bellaudi, and fathering her children. Though the first claims were true and the last one false, such behaviors were not only common in La Serenissima, they were, in that era, perhaps the norm.

I had in fact modeled myself after the one man who epitomized the epicure's life in Venice: Casanova, who, though twenty years my senior, had become a true and good friend. He taught me that if I wanted to "fly with the eagles," that is to achieve success and prosperity in a world run by aristocrats, then all I had to do was to "fly with the eagles." "Dress and act as a gentleman," he would advise. "Be intimidated by no man and no rank." Thus, my priestly duties and abbé's robes were limited to Sunday Mass and confession. For the other six days of the week, I wore regal suits and my life revolved around gambling halls, opera parties, and the myriad of masked balls in La Serenissima. And it was there, on those occasions, that I often engaged with fine wine, excellent food, and exquisite women.

When first apprised of the accusations and a scheduled hearing before the *Esecutori contro la bestemmia*, a commission set up in the Middle Ages to monitor public behavior, I considered them frivolous and ignored them.

But the charges and accusations, mostly written in Girolamo's handwriting, continued to flow into the lion's mouth. Truth mattered not. I was blamed and held accountable for such nonsense as dressing too fashionably, leering at women in church, that I went straight from sleeping with parishioners to saying mass before my congregation, that I gambled in houses of ill repute while wearing my abbé's cassock, that I was previously expelled from my seminary in Treviso for immoral behaviors with a Jewess, and that I was still now living in sin with the married woman, Anzelotta Bellaudi.

Well, if pressed, I would confess many of the accusations had occurred, but I never imagined anyone in La Serenissima would have ever taken such offenses seriously.

Finally, the *Esecutori* decided to act and they scheduled a full trial. Though I laughed off the claims against me, my friends and fellow writers, such as Caterino Mazzolà, warned me not to disregard this summons to court. But I did. I continued to ignore the court until—and fortunately—Casanova, who was more closely connected to the inner circle of power in La Serenissima, insisted I flee Venice immediately. Casanova, perhaps more than any of my other friends, understood that throughout all the world, the application of justice and jurisprudence was routinely unequal. Those who aligned with the prevailing powers went unpunished, while those whose presence was more problematic—such as a converso priest—were always judged harshly. If convicted I risked imprisonment in the Leads, the same prison at the Doge's Palace where Casanova had been incarcerated before his now famous escape some thirty years earlier.

Having learned to trust Casanova during my years in Venice, I took his advice. Tossing away my priest's robes, I fled that very night. Tried in absentia and found guilty based on Girolamo's testimony, I was subsequently officially banished from Venice as well as all lands and territories under its dominion for a period of fifteen years. If found in the Veneto during that period of time, I would be subjected to seven years imprisonment in the Leads.

Penniless and forced to flee afoot from my homeland, I wandered like Moses, my only manna from heaven the many maidens I met upon the way. I remained a nomad for several years until I finally arrived in Vienna with Mazzolà's letter of introduction to Salieri. Here, in the heart of the Hapsburg Empire I presumed myself safe, but in finding sanctuary, I found myself further and further away from the one true passion of my life, the Rabbi's daughter, Zinabella Spinoziano.

For all these troubles, I held that disreputable wretch lying on the floor of the wine cellar, Girolamo Tiepolo, responsible. I shared the relevant portions of my story with Wetzlar, Mozart, and the servant girl.

When I finally finished my narrative, Celestina, could not help but ask me in a small, polite and deferential voice, "You're him, aren't you, sir?"

"Him, who?" I asked her.

"The Jewish priest, the one from Ceneda," she said.

Mozart, certainly puzzled, repeated her words, "A Jewish priest?"

"Who are you?" I asked her. "How do you know this?"

"You hid in our apartment the night the commendatore was murdered."

"I did?" It was no struggle to remember the night I had slept with Zina in the Venetian ghetto on a bed of straw. It was a hovel of a home belonging to Zina's older cousin and her daughter—and then it struck me: "You? You were the little girl?"

"*Si, mia madre è Signora Ricca Graziano.*"

"Ah, but you're a 'Grahl,' now, yes?" I asked.

"My father, who's a traveling merchant, changed our name to Grahl in order to hide our Jewishness."

And suddenly it all made sense. The Casti clan with help from Girolamo was still in the business of revenge. And, if true, none of us were safe.

Wetzlar fully understood that decisive action needed to be taken to put an end to the machinations of the Casti clan in Vienna. He ordered his guard to have Girolamo transported in chains to the prison at the Hofburg Palace, where he would face further punishment from Joseph II's magistrates.

As the four of us started away down the corridor, Mozart repeated his question, "A Jewish priest? How did I not know this?"

"There are many things you should not, nor need not know, my dear Mozart," said Wetzlar in response, "especially when lives are at stake."

"Jews, conversos, Catholics, and Protestants, what does it matter?" asked Mozart. "Why all the secrecy? What is the risk? Are we not all children of the same God?"

"Wherever Hebrews have traveled amongst Christians," I said, "there has always been blood on the tracks—ours, not theirs." Only after those words left my mouth did I realized what I had just confessed, not only to Mozart, but to myself as well. Yes, beneath this title of abbé, of priest, of converso, of "New Christian," in my heart, I remained the same Jew I had been since childhood—and it brought tears to my eyes.

"I still do not understand, why, why is it this way?" Mozart asked. He was sincerely puzzled by our discomfiture at existing on the fringes of a Christian world.

It was a question I had avoided answering my entire life, but not Wetzlar.

"Come," said the baron. "If you want to comprehend the plight of Hebrews in Europe, I will take you through the gates of hell itself, and then maybe, just maybe, you will begin to understand the daily struggles Jews endure in order to survive in a hostile Christian world."

And he did. Wetzlar lifted a lantern from a wall mount and then led us down a perpendicular corridor. At the end of the corridor was a heavy wooden door that he unlocked and then opened. Out of the darkness, a burst of noise hit us, a sound unlike any other I had ever heard in my life. It was as if off in the distance, deep into the bowels of the earth, hundreds of voices were screaming in pain.

"What is that?" I asked.

"Some say it is the tears of God," Wetzlar answered, "But others say it's merely the sound of air and water rushing through the sewers. I believe it is the howls and screams of our ancestors who died here."

His words sent a chill through me, and I could see it also visibly upset Celestina. Although not often noted in histories of the Middle Ages, most everyone in Jewish communities knew well the record of the various persecutions that had occurred throughout Europe going back to Roman times when the Emperor Titus was blocked by the Senate from marrying Berenice, the Queen of Judea. When you grow up as part of a minority, such knowledge was an intimate part of your heritage, as much a part of your being as your skin—and nothing becoming a converso could ever erase. In 1421, according to an account called the *Wiener Gesera*—the Vienna Persecutions, some 1,400 Jews were murdered in an Austrian orgy of hate. Was this the place, I wondered as Wetzlar led us forward.

Inside the doorway were a number of other lanterns. Wetzlar lit three more and gave each of us one. Holding our lights up high, Wetzlar led us down a few rough-hewn steps and into what appeared to be catacombs. The roof was rounded and the walls were supported by endless rows of arches along the side walls. On the stone floor were hundreds of six-sided Jewish stars drawn with a sort of red chalk, which also appeared to be relatively new. Some of the stars were large, three or four feet across and others, many others were small, about half that size. One could not walk without stepping on the stars.

"What is this place?" Mozart asked, "I have never seen anything like this in Vienna before."

"Hell, hell on earth," said Wetzlar.

The baron went on to explain that when his workmen were expanding his wine cellars and digging a new line into the city's sewer system, they broke through a wall and discovered several layers of intact but abandoned catacombs that ran underneath the *Judenplatz*, which he noted was directly above us. Lying haphazardly about in those passages, he and his workers found the skeletal remains of hundreds of people—men, women, and children judging from the bones and scraps of decayed clothing—all of whom, according to the *Wiener Gesera*, had committed suicide to escape the brutal torture being inflicted upon them by their captors.

Wetzlar told us that his workers along with a local rabbi had carefully reburied the skeletal remains in the crypts that lined the passage way we were now walking. And in tribute to the dead, the workers then sketched six sided stars with red chalk to mark each spot where bodies had been found. The large ones represented fallen adults, the small stars, children. The discovery, which Wetzlar had kept most secret from all but his trusted friends in the Hebrew community, did indeed confirm the accounts described in the *Wiener Gesera*. Even Mozart, the only non-Jew amongst our quartet, was visibly moved to tears by this account.

As we walked over the many stars, one could not help but feel terror at the thought that each marking represented a Hebrew life brutally cut short, but the worst, Wetzlar said, was ahead of us.

At one point he had us cross a small bridge over a deep crevice in the earth. Wetzlar went first, followed by the girl and then Mozart. I was last. From below I could hear the ever louder roar of an underground river, no doubt part of the natural flow of water from the mountains that passed under the city and toward the Danube less than a mile away, but to me it sounded like the screams of the condemned crossing the River Styx. And then I thought I heard the voice of a woman calling to me from that abyss. Was it Zina's?

"Leave the dead to sleep," it said. "Take the hand of the living. Laughter returns at daybreak."

I shook my head, as if to remove the cobwebs of confusion, but the voice came back again, this time ever more insistent, "Listen, time is short. Take her hand."

Whose hand, I wondered, and then I heard Zina's voice echo one last time, "Never forget, never forget, never forget who you are."

Mozart turned around toward me. Had he heard it too? He spoke softly, reverentially—but his body verily shuddered as he did so, "One day I will capture this horror in music. I must. And you will help me."

I nodded as if in a solemn agreement, and thus the seeds of a thought were born that would eventually find maturation in the overture of *Don Giovanni*.

After crossing the bridge, Wetzlar led us up a stone stairway that veered off to the right. Ahead of us, at the end of the existing tunnels, were the remnants of the synagogue itself where the worst of the atrocities had occurred. The site was fully underground and filled in with rubble but it was easy to see the remnants of burnt bones protruding from the dirt: Not just any bones, these were Jewish bones, Jewish skulls, Jewish skeletons.

Wetzlar then told us the sordid details of the *Gesera*: how Duke Albrecht V of Austria, who was then fighting a war against the Hussites and their religious heresy, fell deeply in debt to bankers and money lenders, most of whom were the Jews then living in Vienna. To escape his debts, the duke falsely condemned the Hebrews before an uneducated peasant populace that was all too willing to go along with his anti-Semitic rants. He claimed we Jews participated in the ritual murders of Christian children so as to use their blood for the Passover ceremony—an event that has never happened in physical reality, only in the vivid imaginations of fearful, ignorant, and hostile people.

Thereupon Duke Albrecht ordered first the expulsion of the less prosperous members of the community. These poor souls, men, women, and children, were stripped of all their possessions, except for the clothing on their back, and they were placed in open boats in the middle of the Danube without oars, shelter or food. Set adrift, those that survived the turbulent waters were carried downriver toward Hungary. Many drowned, some starved, others were beaten

back from where they landed and forced to sail on. They were indeed the lucky ones.

The duke next ordered the arrest of the remaining Jews, all of whom were locked up inside the synagogue. Their homes and property were seized and added to the duke's own estate. Albrecht then had the Jews tortured, purportedly to force them to accept baptism, but in truth it was to compel them to reveal where they had hidden the rest of their valuables. The hundreds of stars we walked upon represented those Hebrews who chose suicide over submission.

Even so, Wetzlar went onto explain, there remained some 200 to 300 Jews who had endured the torture but refused to be baptized. On March 12, 1421, those surviving Jews were burnt alive inside the synagogue. When the fires were over, the remnants of the building were pulled down and the entire square was filled in with dirt and rubble. In all some 1,400 Jews were killed, maimed, or exiled.

Celestina fell to her knees in tears. I knelt beside the poor sobbing girl, but when I went to comfort her, I realized she was holding in her hands a blackened rib bone, that of a child. Yes, to be born a Jew is to know one essential truth: religion—theirs and ours—was the principal source of hatred in the world.

Mozart, in response to her tears spoke up but most softly, as if not wanting his voice to add to the history of violence we were witnessing, "I have watched my own poor mother, ravaged and tortured by illness for weeks on end, die before my eyes. And, I have seen the arbitrary cruelty of cardinals, priests and papists, but never this, never this savagery. This is indeed a hell on earth. Our only grace is that it happened, what, three hundred and fifty years ago?"

"Yes," both Wetzlar and I said simultaneously.

But when Mozart in his naivety added, "Thank God that in our Age of Enlightenment such barbarity no longer occurs." Wetzlar stunned us all with a spontaneous burst of laugher, a burst of derision so powerful that it shook the very dirt from the earthen walls about us and echoed up and down the catacombs. The last time I had heard anyone roar so loudly, it was Casanova at the docks on my first night in Venice.

When the echoes finally died down, Wetzlar said in a mock prayer to whatever gods may have been above and could hear us, "Forgive him, Lord, for this holy innocent knows not of what he speaks. Mozart, my dear sweet friend, hatred and cruelty never go out of fashion. What we have seen here, has, yes, happened in the past, but know even here in an enlightened Austria, it stews daily in a cauldron of ignorance and it will reemerge once again in the future in some new and ever more hideous form."

Mozart's face blanched white as a ghost as he made the sign of the cross and then in a whisper said a prayer, the Ave Verum Corpus:

Hail, true Body, born
Of the Virgin Mary,
Having truly suffered, sacrificed
On the cross for mankind,
From whose pierced side
Water and blood flowed:
Be for us a foretaste
Of the Heavenly banquet
In the trial of death!
O sweet Jesus, O holy Jesus,
O Jesus, son of Mary,
Have mercy on me.
Amen.

Even if we scream "No, never again!" I thought, so long as our world is populated with frail, imperfect humans, such hatred, cruelty, and barbarism will haunt us all the days of our lives.

"Please, sir," a plaintive Celestina asked of Mozart, "if ever you should compose another mass, please let the voices of these lost souls be the requiem we hear."

Tears flooded Mozart eyes. His lips moved but he could not speak, only nodding yes.

Celestina then brought the bone fragment to her lips and kissed it. Afterward, she carefully reburied it in the soft dirt, before turning to look directly at me. "Abbé, with your permission, may I tell you about Zina?"

Chapter Thirteen: The Marriages of Mozart

Thursday, May 25, 1967
The Lorenzo Da Ponte Banquet Room
at the Café Mozart, New York City

Mozart . . . Jake was endlessly proud of the fact that most music scholars cite the three operas of Mozart and Da Ponte as perhaps the greatest collaborations between composer and librettist in the history of that art form—and each one of the three, features a wedding. Thus, when his son Manny and his future daughter-in-law, Pandorea chose a theme for their wedding to celebrate their heritage, it had to be the "Marriages of Mozart."

They had insisted it be held at the Lorenzo Da Ponte Banquet Room at the Café Mozart on the twenty-first anniversary of Jake's return to America with his war bride, Dolcetta. The hall, which resembled an Italianate palazzo in the style of *Figaro*'s Count Almaviva, was upstairs from the restaurant. The wedding party dressed in period costumes straight out of *Don Giovanni*. For the entertainment, Jake contracted with a musical group consisting of a string quartet, a pianist, a soprano, and a tenor, appropriately named, "The Cosi Fan Tutte Ensemble." And what would they perform that night in addition to the traditional mix of dance music? Every love song and wedding march from the three operas.

To honor the families of the bride and groom, the proprietor, Leporello Ponziani, not only imported cases of prosecco from Vittorio Veneto and Nero d'Avola from Sicily, he also had his chefs prepare for the main course Dolcetta's wartime recipe for *Carbonara Gemelli Ebraico*. For the wedding cake—the culinary hit of the evening—Leporello had gone down to Ferrari's in Little Italy to order a traditional Sicilian layered cake. It began with a crostata di pistacchio base, which then supported three *Cassata Siciliana* upper layers, each made from ricotta-filled sponge cake covered over with icing, almond marzipan, and candied fruits.

Officiating at the nondenominational ceremony would be none other than the eighty-one-year-old but still spry Father Beccavivi of Ceneda, who again wore Geremia's red beret and rabbinical *tallit*. Father Beccavivi had flown in from Italy accompanied by that once curious young girl, the now thirty-year-old, Olivia Fresia. A highly successful business woman and one of Ceneda's leading citizens, Olivia not only transformed her grandfather's repair shop into a successful Fiat dealership, she was also heading up the drive to have a statue erected in honor of Emanuele Conegliano, a.k.a. Lorenzo Da Ponte, in her hometown.

The wedding also occasioned Manny's godparents, Greta and Enrico Foxx, to fly in from Vienna, and they too could not have been happier to see the young couple they had chaperoned five years earlier now tie the knot. Manny, who while in Austria had come to consider his godfather Enrico an important career mentor in the intelligence field, honored the former lieutenant by asking him to be his best man at the ceremony.

In fact, following the wedding and honeymoon, Manny, who by now had completed his PhD in International Studies while continuing to minor in music, would be starting his career—in secret—as a field agent at the CIA Headquarters outside Washington, DC. However, publicly, for all anyone knew, Manny had been signed by a talent agency, the Amadé Artists International, as a bass-baritone opera singer, a role that would allow him to travel the world while covertly handling delicate espionage missions. It was no coincidence that Amadé Artists International also represented his godmother, Greta Tedesco Foxx, as a touring solo pianist.

Since their student program in Vienna five years earlier, both Manny and Pandorea, who had earned her PhD in Library Science and Administration, had continued to hone their operatic skills at advanced programs in New York; Santa Barbara, where they attended the summer program at the Music Academy of the West; and at the Ojai Music Festival, where they performed under the direction of famed conductor, Lukas Foss, in one of his experimental programs that incorporated music from *Don Giovanni.*

Back in New York—and while still in school—both interned at the Met and occasionally sang in the chorus, which was an enormous source of pride for not only Jake and Dolcetta, but Manny's grandparents, Abe and Rosa, as well. That a grandson of poor immigrants performed at the Met on the same stage where Abe had installed lighting and sound equipment verily thrilled Abe and Rosa. They made a point of bringing their friends and attending each and every concert in which the kids sang.

After graduation, Pandorea decided against a career in opera. She had instead landed her dream job in Washington, a mid-level administrative post at the Library of Congress. To assist the kids in their move to the nation's capital, Jake and Dolcetta made their wedding present a hefty down payment on a small house in Takoma, a quiet northwest DC neighborhood.

As their gift, Pandorea's parents, Frank and Marietta Cornetti, were sending the kids on a two-week honeymoon to Sicily, where they owned a cliff side cottage above the Mediterranean at Capo San Marco, just outside Sciacca.

The men in the wedding party—Enrico, Jake, and Frank—all wore formal tuxedos based on Venetian *tabàro* outfits sans masks and hats. Enrico Foxx even went so far as to wear the sword he had earned as an officer in the Coldstream Guards. The women, including Dolcetta and Marietta, all wore multicolored Carnevale gowns. Olivia reprised her role as the flower girl. Mia Brancato, a friend of Pandorea's from the Ojai Music Festival, served as her maid of honor.

Most of Pandorea and Manny's friends who attended the ceremony were those they had met through their opera study programs. Some were local New Yorkers. Other Music Academy friends, such as Mia Brancato, came in from California. And still others flew in from London, Venice, Vienna, and Prague. Two singers, Terese Burauskaite and Kazys Skirpa, even arrived from as far away as St. Petersburg, Russia.

Jake looked about the hall for the three missing people he and Dolcetta had expected to arrive from Israel: Danielle, her husband Giorgio, and their twenty-one-year-old daughter, Gaelle. Gaelle, who was currently doing her mandatory service with the Israeli Defense Forces, had obtained leave from active duty to be able to attend. The night before, Jake and Dolcetta had received a telegram from Danielle warning that their travel plans were in doubt and their flight out of Tel Aviv might be delayed due to unforeseen circumstances. "Hope to arrive in time, but may be late," it read.

In the five years that had passed since the sisters were reunited, Dolcetta's visits with her sister had been limited. With Danielle in Israel, it was only when Giorgio's business—that of covertly procuring high tech military equipment for Israel's outnumbered armed forces—brought them to the States did they stay in their Manhattan pied-à-terre.

As an intelligence expert, Jake was well aware of top-secret information beyond the news headlines that he could not share with anyone, not even his own family. Egypt, Jordan, and Syria were poised to attack, leaving the Jewish state on the brink of yet another possible war for its very survival. The state-controlled propaganda arms of the Arab countries, all still smarting from their two prior defeats against the Israelis, were clamoring for their armies to complete the extermination of the Hebrews that Hitler began. Both sides had been maneuvering troops into position on their respective borders for weeks now, and at any moment the bullets could begin firing in anger. With the Russians backing the Arabs by providing new tanks, transports, and jet fighters, Jake was deeply concerned about the chances of Israel surviving yet another assault.

Now it seemed that this latest crisis might very well prevent Danielle and her family from flying to New York.

As the wedding party began to gather beside the chuppah, the Cosi Fan Tutte Ensemble played and sang variations on a wedding chorus from the opera of that same name:

> *Everything now, my dearests,*
> *Accords with your desires.*
> *Joy grows and spreads*
> *Throughout your veins.*
> *She is so beautiful!*
> *He is so handsome!*
> *What lovely eyes!*
> *What attractive lips!*
> *Clink glasses and drink!*
> *Drink and clink glasses!*
> *In those glasses and thine*

> *May every care be drowned,*
> *And let no memory of the past*
> *Remain in your hearts.*
> *Blessed be the bridegroom*
> *And his lovely bride!*
> *May a kindly heaven smile on them,*
> *And, in the way that hens are,*
> *May they be prolific*
> *Of progeny to equal them in beauty.*
> *Surely here's the promise*
> *Of every joy and perfect love!*
> *And all the credit*
> *Goes to dear Mother Italia.*
> *Repeat that joyful music,*
> *Renew that lovely song,*
> *And we will sit here*
> *In highest mirth and glee.*
> *Drink and clink glasses!*
> *Clink glasses and drink!*

When they finished, Father Beccavivi began the ceremony in his native Italian, a language almost every one of the hundred or so guests in attendance understood as they were all either opera singers or aficionados. "Wishing you every happiness, I come to honor you both and celebrate your spiritual divinity. Blessed is the bridegroom and his lovely bride. May a kindly heaven smile on them."

The priest then turned to Enrico, "Lieutenant, may we now have the rings that symbolize the unity of two lovers as one heart?"

Enrico held out the two wedding bands. Manny slipped the first one onto Pandorea's finger. She took the second one, but before she put it onto Manny's ring finger, she kissed his Conegliano pinkie, the little one that marked his heritage as a descendant of the first Emanuele Conegliano, Lorenzo Da Ponte, a gesture that made Jake smile.

Father Beccavivi resumed, "By these word as spoken by me and in the eyes of your beloved friends and family, may the following be joined in matrimony: Signorina Pandorea Cornetti with Signor Emanuele Conegliano. The bride is a daughter of Siracusa, Sicilia, and New York; the gentleman, a son of Ceneda, Vittorio Veneto, and this great city as well. In honor of all we hold sacred, it is my privilege to pronounce you husband and wife."

Everyone cheered, "Bravo!" and applauded as Pandorea and Manny kissed.

Never let it be said that opera people do not know how to party. As the Cosi Fan Tutte Ensemble began to sing and play Verdi's *Brindisi*, Enrico Foxx drew out his saber from its sheath and with a single, powerful whack, he sliced off the top of a bottle of prosecco. As the bubbling wine gushed out, Jake filled the first two glasses and passed them on to the bride and groom.

The ensemble tenor sang:
Let's drink from the joyous chalice
Where beauty flowers ...
Let the fleeting hour
To pleasure's intoxication yield.
Let's drink
To love's sweet tremors—
To those eyes
That pierce the heart.
Let's drink to love—to wine
That warms our kisses.

In a matter of moments the entire banquet room was a swirl of couples dancing and toasting the bride and groom. Jake found Dolcetta and swept her onto the dance floor. Enrico and Greta the same, as did Abe and Rosa, Frank and Marietta, Manny and Pandorea, and a dozen other couples. And when the ensemble reached the tutte, the entire assemblage joined them in song.

Tutte:
> Ah! Let's drink to love—to wine
> That warms our kisses.

The ensemble soprano and Tutte:
> With you I would share
> My days of happiness;
> Everything is folly in this world
> That does not give us pleasure.
> Let us enjoy life,
> For the pleasures of love are swift and fleeting
> As a flower that lives and dies
> And can be enjoyed no more.
> Let's take our pleasure!
> While its ardent,
> Brilliant summons lures us on.

Tutte:
> Let's take our pleasure
> Of wine and
> Singing and mirth
> Till the new day
> Dawns on us in paradise.

It was only later, after the party was well underway, did Danielle finally appear at the doorway—alone, harried and out of breath—but in costume, one nearly identical to her twin sister.

As Jake and Dolcetta went over to greet her with enthusiastic hugs, Danielle offered up an apology that ended on sobering note.

"At the last minute, just as we were boarding our flight, Giorgio and Gaelle were called back by the Israeli Defense Forces. War is imminent and both must serve."

Her words confirmed Jake's deepest fears. As he scanned the room filled with a blessedly joyful wedding party, he could only ponder what paths must Jews continue to take to survive in an endlessly hostile world?

Just then, Father Beccavivi approached the three of them and asked Danielle in Italian, "Do you recognize me?"

Danielle appeared perplexed, her memory working overtime.

Finally, the priest added a clue "I'm from Vittoria Veneto, Ceneda. Your home. I knew you when you and your sister were little girls, teenagers."

Danielle stared deeply at his face, the strain of the past obvious, before finally answering, "Were you my Uncle Geremia's friend, yes? But I cannot remember your name. I'm sorry."

"*Nessun problema. Sono padre Beccavivi*," said the priest. "Welcome. May the love you feel here be forever your true home."

"*Grazie, Padre*," said Danielle.

Father Beccavivi turned to Jake and Dolcetta. "The bride's father, Signor Cornetti, tells me that you two have been busy translating Da Ponte's *Secret Diaries* into English. *È vero?*"

Jake laughed, "Yes and no."

Deciding to let Jake continue to answer the priest, Dolcetta said, "I want my sister to dance with my son on his wedding day," and she led her Danielle away to the dance floor.

As the music flowed on behind them, Jake explained to Father Beccavivi that the translations were very much an off-and-on project, one they only undertook on the rare occasions both he and Dolcetta had time to do the work together. "My ability to actually read Italian is still rather abysmal," Jake confessed. "And Dolcetta's written English is perhaps as stilted."

He continued to explain to Father Beccavivi that in order to actually produce a translation that was both accurate and literate required their combined skills and again, only when the time permitted—a rarity in their hectic lives.

Dolcetta would do the initial translation of each page, line by line, into English and then Jake would go back and smooth out her work into a more readable and graceful English. Their task was further complicated by the fact that many of the pages were in bad condition, others were missing entirely, the ink was faded and Da Ponte's handwritten script was often illegible. In the two decades since they were in Ceneda, Jake confessed they had barely gotten through a third of the diaries, and he had no idea when or if they would ever finish.

"At the rate we're going, it will probably fall to our grandchildren to finish, he added. "Why do you ask?"

"I read them many years ago when the ink was not so faded," said Beccavivi, "I wondered if I might be of some help."

"You read them?" Jake was surprised. "When? With Geremia? After the war?"

"No, much earlier, 1905, with Father Adriano." said Father Beccavivi. "You do know that Geremia was given the diaries by his cousin Adriano, when he passed away just after the war ended."

"Yes," said Jake. "Wasn't Adriano a distant cousin? And a Da Ponte?"

"Indeed, yes, and when I was a young man at the seminary in Ceneda, Father Adriano was also my Latin and Italian grammar teacher. I knew him well. His grandfather was Lorenzo Da Ponte's nephew."

"Well, we could always use some help," said Jake, "Especially as there are at least three, maybe four questions about the diaries that I don't understand at all."

"Ah, what are they? Perhaps I can assist you."

"Thank you, Padre. That would be lovely. My first question is the most basic. Why do the *Secret Diaries* even exist?"

"A good question. Go on," said the priest.

"Okay. Next, is why are the *Secret Diaries* so very different from the memoirs published back in the 1920s? Truly, there are accounts and stories that appear completely opposed to what is stated in Elisabeth Abbott's work. I do not understand why that is the case."

"Of course, and . . . "

"Yes, and third, Geremia had promised to tell us the night before he died, how was it that the *Secret Diaries* ended up in back in Ceneda. By all accounts Da Ponte was already a resident of New York City when he wrote his memoirs."

"True, enough," said the priest.

"Oh, and fourth, I know Da Ponte and I are somehow related, but even with Geremia's genealogical charts, I am not certain how exactly. Will the diaries help make the connection?"

"Ah, all very good topics for an inquiry," said Father Beccavivi, "Let me begin by answering your third question, which may also inform your others. The story as Father Adriano once explained to me and later confirmed by Geremia was this: Da Ponte wrote his memoirs when he was living in New York City—and probably not very far from this restaurant. You New Yorkers may know more about this than I do, but in Da Ponte's era, Jews were shunned in New York. They were pariahs. Anti-Semitism among the very New Yorkers Lorenzo was involved with was part and parcel of their lives."

"Even now," said Jake, knowing full well the discrimination Jewish immigrants had faced in the city before and after the Second World War, "even now there's many a Jewish immigrant who has changed their name to avoid overt hostility. Just as Graziano once became Grahl, Smiligs became Smiths, Danishefskys became Daners, and Lipschitz became Lefferts."

"Yes, you're right. Names are as much a costume as Da Ponte's priestly robes for protecting one's identity. Now imagine poor Lorenzo, struggling to make a go of it in a strange country with nothing but his wits and talents to build upon. Being Italian was exotic enough for that time. Very few New Yorkers even knew that he was Catholic, much less a priest, and might I add a married one at that. I don't believe he ever spoke of religion publicly. And so, when Lorenzo first shared early handwritten drafts of his memoirs with one of his friends, a Mr. Moore, he was cautioned about discussing his Hebrew heritage. Apparently, Mr. Moore, who taught Oriental and Greek literature, as well as divinity and biblical learning, at a seminary of the Episcopal Church, believed that Lorenzo would be shunned by the very society he had cultivated if they had learned that he was a Jew."

"Why am I not surprised?" said Jake. "This drama of hate never seems to end, does it?"

"No," replied the priest. "We have seen it all too often in all of our lives to pretend such hatreds do not exist in the hearts of what we believe are otherwise civilized people."

"It's a hard world we live in, Father. After all we have seen in this bloody century of ours, how could I condemn any Jew for changing names or wearing a costume or becoming a converso, if that path enables them to survive?"

"Certo," said Father Beccavivi. "But sadly, this notion that Da Ponte could not tell the truth in his memoirs frustrated him—but he understood exactly what Mr. Moore warned him about. Lorenzo removed everything from what I call 'the public diaries,' before publishing them that indicated he had been born a Hebrew. I imagine this also involved rewriting certain segments as well to protect others in his narrative, which is why what you are reading is inconsistent and occasionally contradictory with Elisabeth Abbott's translation."

"That makes sense."

"Now, when Da Ponte finally passed away, Mr. Moore followed Lorenzo's instructions and sent the *Secret Diaries* that told his true history back to his family in Ceneda, along with a letter that described Lorenzo's final burial. Adriano showed me Mr. Moore's letter once some fifty or sixty years ago. Have you not seen it folded into the volumes with Lorenzo's yad that Mr. Moore also sent back?"

"I have the yad, which we use whenever we read the diaries, but, no, not the letter. Maybe it's still buried in the genizah trunk."

"Or more likely, crumpled to dust," said Father Beccavivi, noting that when he read it, it was already stiff and brittle. "Now, let me tell you what I know of his family and how you are possibly related to Signor Da Ponte."

"Good, I was hoping you might shed some light on that."

"And yes, it will all become clear long before you finish the diaries." Father Beccavivi went on to explain that there were three known principle family lines of descent, as well as what he called the "unknown number of unknown family lines," due to Lorenzo's profligate ways in Venice. "The recognized lines begin with the Catholic Da Ponte family, principally from his one surviving brother and his many half-siblings born after his father's remarriage."

"By that you mean the marriage of his father to that Catholic woman, Orsola Pasqua, when Lorenzo was fourteen?" said Jake as he glanced out toward the dance floor and saw Danielle with his son, Dolcetta with Enrico, and Pandorea with her father, Frank.

"Yes," Father Beccavivi told him, before continuing to explain that there were also the two known Jewish lines, the Spinozianos and the Coneglianos that derived from Zinabella Spinoziano and her children.

"Oh," exclaimed Jake, "then she did have more than one child with Da Ponte? I have been wondering that since I read the epitaph on her tombstone the day we buried Rabbi Geremia."

Father Beccavivi demurred. "Yes, you'll see, the diaries explain all of that. But a more important link is that pinkie condition you Da Ponte men all have. Even the 'public diaries' mention the many women Lorenzo slept with, who gave up their infants born out of wedlock to the orphanages of Venice."

"*Dio mio*," laughed Jake. "Then there's more of us out there?"

"*Chissà*? Who knows, maybe two centuries later half of all Venice can claim to be his descendants. But find a man with your hands, and he's probably a cousin," teased the priest.

"Are there any other surprises?" said Jake. Out of the corner of his eye, Jake spied Greta walking toward them.

"I can't say," answered Beccavivi, "It's too many years ago."

"Thank you," Jake said just as Greta gestured toward him to join her on the dance floor,

"Ah, my friend, read on. Da Ponte's life will startle you at each and every twist. Yes, you must read on, my friend, but for now, dance." With that Father Beccavivi ushered him to join with Greta. The priest then broke out into song, a recitative from *Cosi*.

> *In your glass and mine*
> *May every care be drowned,*
> *And let no memory of the past*
> *Remain in your hearts.*

Oddly for Jake, the timbre and pitch of the priest's rich baritone recalled a déjà vu, a flashback, the voice of that horrid Abbé Luigi Hudal, the priest and later bishop at Santa Maria Dell'Anima. One of the greatest frustrations of Jake's career at the CIA had been his inability to get the agency to act quickly enough on his reports that proved Bishop Hudal ran the "Ratlines," a series of underground safehouses at various monasteries that facilitated the escape of Nazis to South America and the Mid-East. Though Jake's research, along with Enrico's at MI6, clearly implicated Hudal, foot-dragging by the Allies allowed the bishop to escape prosecution prior to his death from natural causes. The end of the Hudal investigation also marked the end of his work chasing former Nazis. Now it was the Russians who were the great threat.

Greta reached for Jake. With her long hair swirling like Botticelli's copper-haired goddess, she pulled him toward the dance floor, another déjà vu gesture that instantly reminded him of that moment decades ago in Ceneda when she kissed him goodbye. As they wrapped themselves in each other's arms for a slow dance, Greta rested her head on Jake's shoulder and whispered in his ear, "Your wife is dancing with my husband."

"Si, certo," replied Jake. "Should we be jealous?"

"You do know about them, don't you?" asked Greta.

"What?" asked Jake.

"At Aviano," said Greta. "Before Treviso, yes?"

Jake did not know what she was alluding to, and if there had been something between Dolcetta and the lieutenant back then, it was ancient history. He shrugged and said as much. Very much in the present, he and Enrico had more pressing concerns as both were involved in trying to uncover the identity of a Russian operative, they code-named Osmin, after a character in Mozart's *Abduction From the Seraglio*. Osmin had been brutally torturing and killing covert allied agents, mostly women, who worked both sides of the Iron Curtain.

"You do know, Jacopo Conegliano, that I am still madly in love with you?"

"Assolutamente," he whispered back as he mused—and not for the first time—about how his life would have turned out differently if not for those two flat tires.

"But I am more madly in love with my godson and his mother," Greta added, "I adore Manny as if he were my own son. And Dolcetta Zinabella Spinoziano Conegliano is the finest, most outstanding woman I have ever known. You are one lucky man."

"Assolutamente," repeated Jake. He kissed Greta on the cheek and quoted a line of Ferrando's from *Cosi*: "It was love, that powerful god, who drew me there in search of her."

"*Anch'io*, with Enrico," said Greta. "We four are blessed. To the God of love." She returned Jake's gesture with a kiss on his cheek.

Just then the music stopped and there was the clanging of a knife against a water glass calling for everyone's attention.

Manny and Pandorea stood by the chuppah. Manny had the band's microphone in his hand but put it down when he realized with his deep and powerful voice, he had no need of further amplification.

"To echo a speech of Don Alfonso in *Cosi*, 'I would speak, but my courage fails; my lips stammer. I cannot say the words which stay locked inside me.' From my Aunt Danielle, I have just learned that my Uncle Giorgio and my cousin Gaelle, a cousin whom I have yet to meet in person, have been called by their command to the battlefield and cannot be here to celebrate this day of joy with us. As most of you know well from the nightly news, Israel is once again at the brink of war, a war for its very survival, a fact that breaks my heart, knowing full well that Pandorea and I are the children of such conflicts, as are many of you. Our lives are not comedies, nor are they songs. Still, to honor Giorgio and Gaelle, and my parents, and Pandorea's parents and everyone else gathered here, Danielle, Enrico, Greta, Olivia, Father Beccavivi, all of whom stayed resilient in the face of overwhelming horrors and confronted their fates with the greatest of courage, we would like to dedicate this one song. It's not Mozart, it's not Da Ponte, just a little Puccini, if you can stand it, but good Puccini."

With that Manny and Pandorea began to sing:
Nessun dorma!
Nessun dorma!

And spontaneously everyone in the room joined in with a sound that rocked the ages and left not a dry eye in the house.

> *Even you, oh Princess,*
> *In your cold room,*
> *Watch the stars,*
> *That tremble with love*
> *And with hope.*
> *But my secret is hidden within me,*
> *My name no one shall know,*
> *No... no...*
> *On your mouth, I will tell it,*
> *When the light shines.*
> *And my kiss will dissolve the silence that makes you mine!*
> *No one will know his name and we must, alas, die.*
> *Vanish, o night!*
> *Set, stars! Set, stars!*
> *At dawn, I will win!*
> *Vincerò!*
> *Vincerò!*

Chapter Fourteen: Diamonds in the Snow

Monday, January 5, 1786
The Streets of Old Vienna

Mozart and I agreed. As much as I wanted to hear from the servant girl about Zina, my first obligation was to deliver our libretto for *The Marriage of Figaro* to the emperor before the sounds of Mozart's music had vanished from his royal ears.

It mattered not that it was still snowing when I left Baron Wetzlar's. There were perhaps four or five inches on the ground as I made my way over to the Hofburg Palace to see Joseph II. The streets of the city were slick, slushy, and slippery, which made me grateful for the walking stick I had pilfered from the costume room the night before. My goal at the Hofburg was to avoid the court chamberlain, Count Orsini, and place the libretto directly into His Majesty's hands lest the emperor's guard dog shred our manuscript before Joseph II had the opportunity to read our version of Beaumarchais's work.

Still, all in all, I was in a cheerful mood and why not? My luck had changed and good fortune was at hand. Not only had I been victorious last night with my libretto for

Martin y Soler's successful premiere of *Il burbero di buon cuore*, the emperor had loved the sampling of music Mozart and I had put together for *The Marriage of Figaro*. Martin y Soler was eager to work with me again and so apparently was Salieri. And I consummated my new romance with La Ferrarese. "*Abbiamo vinto!*" Although the New Year was less than a week old, 1786 might well prove to my most successful yet.

My spirit of enthusiasm grew ever more when I encountered Paisiello just outside the Hofburg complex. I was entering as he was leaving, but nonetheless, he made the effort to heartily congratulate me for *Il burbero di buon cuore*.

"Tell me," he asked, "Might you have a libretto or a story for me?"

"Perhaps," I replied, never being one to turn away the possibility of work, especially since my salary as the Hapsburg court poet covered little more than my basic expenses. The commissions and profits we garnered from the sale of libretti and opera tickets were essential for all working artists, including Mozart and me. How else could we maintain even the pretense of a social life in Vienna commensurate with the aristocrats we, by necessity, partied and dined with? Clothes, wine, and women were costly to maintain. The noble classes had their land and estates to generate endless flows of wealth, whereas all we had were our wits—and those, despite our best intentions, often failed us in times of need—but not last night.

"Those songs you wrote for Joseph II yesterday, brilliant, just brilliant," said Paisiello. "And your presentation with Mozart, Haydn, and Wetzlar, a superb trick of the trade. I wish I had conceived of such a tantalizing performance like that myself. Yes, just brilliant. You and I, we should dine one night soon, *non è' vero?*"

"Si," I nodded, "Indeed I would like that."

"Long overdue. And you'll share some of your ideas for libretti with me, yes?" Paisiello asked.

"Of course," I said, though certainly not expecting anything to materialize, much less Paisiello actually meeting me for dinner. Promises packaged in such flattery were often offered but rarely delivered. And if he did, I suspect it would be merely to steal my ideas and toss them off to his friend, Casti. Paisiello was, after all, like Orsini, one of the abbé's close friends. Court life was just a game of appearances, and nothing Paisiello said would I ever be foolish enough to trust as genuine. Ultimately, in the fawning politeness of Vienna society, it was critical to survival to never forget that "my enemy's friends are also my enemies."

"You do have some notions for future stories, yes?" Paisiello asked, perhaps sensing some hesitancy in my voice.

"If it was easy crafting good plots with great characters," I replied, "then any illiterate peasant from the fields of Bohemia would be harvesting ink and paper just to transmute them into silver and gold." Yes, finding appropriate material for an opera was truly a challenge. Many were the days I wandered like Quixote through the shelves of booksellers in search of ideas.

"I'm sure you will find me one of exquisite quality," And then as if on cue, having spent enough time being as polite as a courtier before a maiden, Paisiello abruptly changed the subject. "Beastly weather, this snow, isn't it?"

I nodded.

"Bravo, Da Ponte, bravo! Find me something, a diamond in this blizzard, and I will reward you in kind." Paisiello wrapped himself tighter in his cloak and headed off into the blowing snow without even a last glance back.

Inside the Hofburg palace, I announced myself to one of the emperor's servants and in a matter of minutes I was directed to the wing where Joseph II held court. But instead of finding His Majesty awaiting my arrival, I was instead met by the man I dreaded most, Count Orsini. Surprisingly, the Lord Chamberlain and head of the Burgtheater, greeted me most warmly. Orsini's good cheer and kindly demeanor was a stark contrast to the snarling canine he had shown himself to be at Wetzlar's the night before. First Paisiello, now Orsini. The espoused friendship of such men made me fearful.

"Ah, Da Ponte," Orsini proclaimed as he clapped me on the back. "How wonderful. Come sit with me. Brandy?"

Though as suspicious of his assault of kindness as one would be of a smiling executioner with a sword, it was never too early on a chilly winter's day to be warmed by a shot of brandy from the Hapsburg's private cellars. I accepted his hospitality.

"I see you have brought us the libretto for *The Marriage of Figaro*. How wonderful. I cannot wait to read it."

"*Veramente?*" I asked, somewhat leery of this unexpected shift in Orsini's attitude. Why, I needed to know, was he being so nice?

"But of course, yes, I'm anxious to peruse your pages. You have proved yourself most worthy as our court poet. Why even this morning, Paisiello met with His Majesty and verily raved about your work. He wants you to present him a new libretto. That is quite an honor, Paisiello himself."

"So he tells me. We chatted on my way in."

"And you will find something for him? Now that would truly please His Majesty."

I nodded, though in truth, I was desperate for solid story ideas that would serve the current mood of the opera *cognoscenti* who demanded a precise and delicate blend of drama, comedy, and song in each creation. The days of Opera *Seria* that were once dominated by the likes of a Metastasio had long passed. No one cared anymore for works about the Greek gods or classical heroes such as the great poet's *The Mercy of Titus*, or even Mozart's *Idomeneo*, which my friend had composed for the court of Munich six years earlier. Far more in vogue were works such as my *Il burbero di buon cuore* —*The*

Good-Hearted Curmudgeon—an *Opera Drama Giocoso* whose roots derived more sustenance from the Italian street theaters of the *Commedia dell'Arte* than the great works of antiquity.

"And Salieri too," added Orsini. "Our Kapellmeister was beside himself with praise when we returned to the palace last night. Salieri noted how far you have come since he first hired you—worth every one of the emperor's kreutzers, he declared."

"I'm honored to know he believes I've earned my pay."

"Oh, ever more. And Martin y Soler reports that the two of you already have another opera in the works for us, yes?"

"Ah, si," I replied, unsure of why Orsini was being so solicitous. "We hope to have *Una cosa rara*, ready for this spring season. If not then, perhaps in autumn."

"*Eccellente, eccellente.*"

"But what of Abbé Casti?" I inquired. "Is he not writing for these composers as well?"

"No more, indeed, no more. The good Abbé Casti announced to His Majesty just this morning that at his age, he can no longer tolerate the chilly winds of our Vienna. He left on the morning coach so as to return immediately to the sun and warmth of Venice where he has an offer to write for La Fenice."

"*Non è vero?*" I said with some surprise, wondering if Casti's decision had more to do with a blow from the walking stick I held in my hand than the snows outside.

"Si, indeed, there is much work ahead for you this year, Signor Da Ponte. Now, if you will leave that libretto for *The Marriage of Figaro* with me. . . . " Orsini stretched out his hand toward me.

"But," I argued, keeping the pages out of his reach, "Joseph II specifically asked me to present it to him, myself."

"*Mio caro*, Lorenzo, I admit my reactions last night were, shall we say, a bit overwrought. Yes, too much wine for me so late at night. And though you did catch His Majesty and me unawares, your fear and hesitancy are uncalled for. We love your work. This morning, however, the emperor is preoccupied with critical matters of state and cannot be disturbed. If you want him to approve this libretto of yours, you must certainly leave it with me," Orsini insisted.

"Did you not value Mozart's music last night? Surely you were smiling, singing and enjoying yourself," I said, stalling for time to plot my next move in this chess match.

"Ah, si, very much so. His Majesty and I are both enthusiastic supporters of Mozart's *concerti*. Such a wonderful pianist and composer, he is. Vienna is fortunate to have him here."

"But what of his songs? Did they not please you sufficiently?"

"*Sì, certo, ma Mozart è tedesco. Non un italiano, come te e me.* How can a German-speaking composer possibly write for my Italian opera stage? Mozart needs to apply himself to what he does best, composing for and playing the pianoforte."

"But you did like his music last night, everyone did, yes?"

"*Mio caro*, Da Ponte, please, you must understand. I hold nothing against Mozart. But what has he done? *Idomeneo*, an opera *seria* in the old style? Or *The Abduction from the Seraglio*, which is little more than a German singspiel? Come, Abbé, let us be frank here. Like a mule who believes himself to be a stallion, our Herr Mozart is reckless and headstrong. Yes, he's a man who all too often climbs out on a ledge. And, mind you, if Mozart does that too frequently, the man is eventually going to fall out of His Majesty's good graces. Must Joseph II see a servant of his made happy while His Majesty is left to sigh? Or shall Mozart possess a treasure while the emperor's desires are in vain?"

Orsini's comment made me wonder if the Count knew about Mozart's affair with Storace. Had he seen us outside

Storace's window? And was this remark a veiled threat delivered inside a compliment, one I needed to alert Mozart about?

"But his music?" I replied, "Does it offend?"

"In His Majesty's eyes, Mozart the man, his manners, and his music are mightily inseparable. At a moment when your own career begins to soar, why tie your wings to such a weight as he? There are only so many fledglings an eagle's nest can hold."

"I mean no offense, but given your predilection in regards Mozart, is that not all the more reason why I should hand our libretto directly to His Majesty?"

"You come from a headstrong and stiff-necked stock, Signor Da Ponte," said Orsini, no doubt a jab at my Hebrew heritage, "and I have strived to be most patient with you in this regard, but please, listen and listen carefully. I like you and I like your writings, but when it comes to those pages you hold in your hand, I am His Majesty, I am his chamberlain, I am the representative of His Royal Highness. In giving it over to me, you are indeed giving it over to the Emperor."

"But Joseph II asked . . . "

"There are no 'buts.' Do not fail to realize that Joseph II's world does not revolve around his subjects. Mozart was not born a bold enough fellow to cause His Majesty torment nor to indeed laugh at his discomfiture. On the contrary, you and Mozart and every other artist in our opera theater must submit to and orbit around our emperor.

"The Hapsburg Empire is a vast world with millions of subjects who speak more than a dozen different languages. We have a war with the Turks on one border, threats from Prussia to the north, and danger from revolutionaries within. All those politics must be taken into account in every ruling Joseph II makes. Now, listen carefully, Mozart's music might be acceptable and your libretto might, and I stress, might, pass muster, but consider what you have done and what you have started with: a play that has already been banned. His Majesty does not make these decisions in abstraction or merely to confound a playwright. The survival of the Hapsburg Dynasty and the weight of his ancestors' memories rest upon his shoulders."

"But with all certainty, Count, I have removed or replaced every aspect of the theater play that could possibly offend His Majesty, and you, yourself, have acknowledged the beauty of Mozart's music," I replied. "What is wrong with that?"

"And that, exactly, is the problem. Your libretto may be wonderful, and the music of Mozart could soar toward the heavens with as much intensity as one of his piano *concerti*, but in so doing, you create the false illusion in the eyes of the public that *The Marriage of Figaro* is acceptable literature. You unwittingly undermine our efforts to maintain civil order and public decency. Beaumarchais's play was banned for good cause. That is the danger we, that is Count Pergen and I, must guard against. That is why if you wish to continue as the court poet, and if you want my support against your rivals . . . And if you want to work with my composers, and if you want to have your libretti performed on my stage, with my singers and musicians, and, must I add, if you, my dear abbé, wish me to continue turn a blind eye as you flout all the Holy Orders of our Church and sleep with my divas, then I suggest for the very last time, you turn that libretto over to me."

Five minutes later, in a perplexed state of mind, I was back out on the streets dodging snowdrifts and a chilly wind. What was I to do? Fight Orsini on behalf of Mozart and our *Figaro*, or stay gainfully employed and romantically satisfied? Either way, I knew with absolute certainty, I had best find a basket full of new and splendid ideas to satisfy Vienna's hunger for vibrant operas or my shooting star of a career would burn out as quickly as it had been launched.

Just past the Lobkowicz Palace as I was crossing into the *Neuer Markt* on my way back to Kartnerstrasse to meet Mozart, I decided to detour toward Zimmermann's Booksellers, Purveyor of Rare and Unusual Editions. In the years since my first arrival in Vienna, the proprietor, Herr Jarrell Zimmermann, had assisted me in rebuilding my personal library with volumes of Shakespeare, Plato, Dante, Plutarch, and Cervantes, among many others. If there was indeed a diamond in the rough to be found, Herr Zimmerman was the man.

Nearing the front door, I heard a loud and familiar laugh coming from inside. Through the window I saw none other than my old friend, that tall patrician gentleman, the Chevalier de Seingalt himself, Casanova, sharing an exchange with the proprietor, Herr Zimmermann.

"I'd know that laugh anywhere," I declared as I walked in and shook off the snow from my coat. Both men greeted me warmly. Casanova had aged greatly in the eight years since I had last seen him on the night I had fled Venice. His hair had gone totally white, his cheeks were gaunt, sunken, and lined with age. Herr Zimmerman offered me a glass of Brunello from a bottle he and Casanova had been sharing, which I readily accepted.

"What brings you to Vienna?" I asked.

"These," Casanova replied, pointing to a pile of books on Zimmerman's work table.

Atop the stack was an exquisite edition of Metastasio's *Collected Stories and Poems* that seemed all too familiar. It was bound with carefully worked hides dyed in a deep maroon hue and embossed with golden lettering and decorations. Yes, it was indeed the volume my father had once restored for a bishop in Milano and was in Mozart's hands when we first met at the Teatro San Benedetto.

"That's Mozart's!" I said with some surprise, "And the bookbinder who restored that volume was none other than my own papa." I opened the book to the page I had ruined and showed them my handiwork.

"Yes, indeed," said Casanova. "I rescued it the night of the Teatro San Benedetto fire. Mozart had left it by the bed in Angela's office, but I have not seen our young *genio* since. Herr Zimmermann and I were just laughing about that ink stain that obscured the ending of "The Lovers' Descent." After Signor Giulio seduces his friend, Fernando's wife, Dona Flora, does she stay with him? Or does she return to her Fernando who has, in a delicious turnabout, seduced Signor Giulio's wife, Dona Dora? Will we ever know?"

"I asked Metastasio that very question when I met him just before he died," I said.

"Metastasio, you met him? How fortunate. What was his answer?" asked Herr Zimmermann.

"I told you, he died." And my answer set the two men laughing again. In truth I had met the great poet almost immediately upon my arrival in Vienna several years early. Bedridden at the advanced age eighty-four, Metastasio's health was rapidly failing, and he passed on only days after our encounter.

"And now you've taken Metastasio's place? I understand you're the court poet with a hit opera to boot," said Casanova.

"Yes," I stated firmly, proud to know that in the eyes of an old friend my star was ascending.

"You've done well for yourself, my friend," acknowledged Casanova.

"*Eh tu?*" I asked.

"Well, as for me, the adventures of my youth are all but ended. I now find gainful employment and lodging as the librarian for Count Waldstein. I am installed at his castle at Dux just outside Prague."

"But what brings you here to Vienna? A woman, no doubt?"

"No, my friend, at this age, I live in quietude and solitude and rarely am I so fortunate as to have a damsel in distress to rescue. Even now I'm here on the count's business, to buy and sell books for his collection—and to deliver the Metastasio back into Mozart's hands."

"That I can do for you," I said, explaining to Casanova and Zimmermann, not only about my projects with Mozart and how I was to meet him shortly at the Café Bruno on Kartnerstrasse, but also my frustration with having to leave our libretto for *The Marriage of Figaro* in the hands of Orsini.

"I knew Orsini when he was but a pup in Milano. Officious to a fault," said Casanova, "and therefore, easy to bribe. Sometimes you must butter the bread of such men. But," he paused and assumed a thoughtful demeanor, "I've often found that an alternate strategy of using a woman to go around him will prove infinitely superior."

When I told him about Storace, Casanova replied, "So much the better. Your diva is the emperor's mistress and Mozart's as well? Your *Figaro* will be produced, of that I have no doubt, but only if you gentlemen engage the young lady to do your bidding. And then show patience, my friend, patience."

Which led me to ask Casanova if he had truly abandoned romance.

"Alas," he said, "My Henriette has died, the only woman I have ever truly loved. And if there was but one mistake in my life that I regret, it was not making her my bride when I had the chance. Who can say how many years of joy we might have shared together? In the end, is not true love life's only real virtue? Isn't that the point of that Beaumarchais's play you seek to turn into an opera? Figaro and Susanna? Marcellina and Bartolo? Barbarina and Cherubino? Even the count and contessa? Now that I am an old man whose fires burn low, I merely tend books for the count. And oh, Herr Zimmermann believes I should write my memoirs."

"Which will probably outsell the Bible," chimed in Herr Zimmermann. "In the secret heart of every woman is a desire to be loved by a Casanova, and in the heart of every man is a dream to be Casanova. Yes, my shop here would sell out every copy the day those memoirs are published."

"Herr Zimmerman is too kind," said Casanova, "But in his words there's a lesson for you, my friend. Find that passionate affair, find that ineffable *Doña Deseable* who sets fire to your heart and never let go until you have both burnt to the ground with naught but your ashes to spread about."

As Casanova spoke of passion, I had to ask, "What of La Serenissima's Queen of the Night? What has been Angela Tiepolo's fate?"

My question set him laughing again, "With age and poor health working against Angela, she was forced to humble herself in service as a lady-in-waiting to your friend, Signorina Matilda Wider, the one you called your Dona Brunetta."

"How so?" The thought of such a reversal occurring would have been inconceivable a decade earlier.

"The fire at Teatro San Benedetto was the beginning of the end of the Tiepolo family wealth. By the time the new opera house, La Fenice, was built, the Tiepolo clan had fallen deeply in debt. Angela, compelled to find a wealthy husband, played her typically risky game of setting multiple suitors off against each other. In the past that had been a successful strategy, but this time that tactic caused her to lose all, including the family palace on the Grand Canal."

"This turnabout surely must have satisfied my Dona Brunetta."

"Indeed," said Casanova. "Angela's humiliation was ever the more so when Matilda, as the newly married Duchess of Mantua purchased the old Tiepolo home in Venice, thus forcing Angela into servitude in the very palace she had once lorded over."

I then told him about last night's incident with the Casti clan, wherein Girolamo and the Abbé Casti had attacked Wetzlar's servant girl.

"The Casti family," he said, "is still enraged over the unsolved murder of the commendatore. Bribes from the Casti clan would have easily motivated Girolamo to assist in what has apparently become an ever-spiraling blood feud. Girolamo fell even deeper into poverty than Angela, and as such is ever more destitute and vulnerable."

Remembering well that the dagger Zina used to kill the commendatore had belonged to Casanova, I asked, "No doubt, one more reason for you to find shelter and quietude with Waldstein at Dux, *non e' vero?*"

"Assolutamente," replied Casanova. "No sense bloodying this suit. I have all too few in my closet as is. And you? Having now produced one successful opera, can you sustain such good fortune?"

"Everyone from Paisiello to Salieri and Righini to Martin y Soler wants a libretto from me, but I am bereft of ideas."

"How can that be? A man of your wit and resources?" Casanova pulled a book out of the middle of his stack. "Have you tried Boccaccio's *Decameron?* Why even Metastasio's "Lovers' Descent," was derived from several of Bocaccio's hundred tales. Turn that story of dual infidelities into an opera, my friend. It's a perfect comedy of errors, overconfidence, and the inevitabile victory of our unchecked libido to cause havoc—something we can all relate to, *non e' vero?* Or this," he said, handing me another volume off the stack of books.

It was a play, *Don Juan and the Stone Guest.*

"What is this," I asked?

"The original Don Juan story," interjected Herr Zimmermann, "Written by a Spanish monk, Tirso de Molina, in 1616. Have you read it?"

"No, but you think it worth the effort?" I asked Casanova.

"*Certo*, why even the French playwright, Moliere turned it into a comedy a century ago."

"Hmm," I uttered as I considered the volume, already an antique, bound in a blue leather cover with embossed gold lettering.

"And consider this," added Casanova. "Tirso de Molina's family was, like yours, conversos, who also struggled with our Christian precept of love and found it unsatisfactory."

"How so?" I asked.

"As St. Augustine once asserted," continued Casanova, "When humankind accepts the utterly unselfish love of Jesus Christ, your elaborate body of Jewish law becomes redundant and unnecessary. Christian love, the good saint claimed, will always elicit the right behavior spontaneously. Unfortunately, the issue, as de Molina demonstrates, is that a Christian society that depends on moral consciousness has no defense against a predator who has none."

"And this is a comedy?" I asked incredulously.

"*Assolutamente*, Signor Da Ponte" asserted Casanova, "But remember this, my friend, if I may give you yet one last piece of advice before we part again: the only artists who get away with telling the truth without losing their heads are the court jesters."

Chapter Fifteen: A Night to Remember

Tuesday Evening, January 27, 1976
The Kennedy Center, Washington, DC

Mozart, this Tuesday evening was the anniversary of Mozart's birthday, and to celebrate, Jake was off to see a production of Mozart's *Don Giovanni* at the Kennedy Center in Washington. He was to escort his daughter-in-law, Pandorea, who was now almost nine months pregnant with her first child. Manny was cast in the dual roles of the commendatore and Masetto for the run of the show. Given Pandorea's growing immobility and discomfort, Manny had procured the entire Box Thirteen for her and Jake so that his wife would be able to move around at will and rearrange the extra chairs, if necessary, in order to make herself comfortable during the more than three-hour performance.

Although Manny had performed as the commendatore numbers of times overseas, tonight's opening was the first time he had done so at home in the United States. Why now? There were changes afoot at the CIA, with Bill Colby retiring and George H. W. Bush coming in as the new director. Field agents, such as Manny, had been summoned home—while remaining under cover—to receive new instructions, and thus his talent agency, Amadé Artists International, had him booked for the role in *Don Giovanni*.

Jake, following protocol, never discussed his work with his son, but in fact he was in town for the same reason. He had flown in on the Eastern shuttle from La Guardia earlier that afternoon in order to catch Manny's performance before beginning his confidential planning sessions the next day at CIA Headquarters. Dolcetta, who had a busy schedule herself at the UN, was unable to join him for the trip, much as she would have loved to see her son perform. The trip was particularly poignant and bittersweet for Jake as it also marked the very first of Manny's American performances that neither Abe nor Rosa would attend, as both had passed away the year before. Jake had even caught a glimpse of the Hebrew Cemetery in Queens where they were buried when his flight lifted off from La Guardia.

With global terrorism on the upswing, countermeasures were on the agenda of every American intelligence agency during this bicentennial year. The Baader-Meinhof Gang was implicated in bombings in West Germany; Osmin was still killing and mutilating allied agents; and Arab saboteurs were creating havoc in the territories Israel had captured in the Six-Day War of 1967. Add to that, the Olympics were scheduled for Canada in July, only four years after the massacre at the 1972 Summer Games in Munich, in which the Palestinian terrorist group, Black September, had taken eleven Israeli athletes hostage before killing them just as a rescue was being mounted.

After Jake picked up his backstage pass at the box office, he meandered through the bowels of the Kennedy Center to find his way to his son's dressing room. As Jake neared it, he could not but help overhear Pandorea helping Manny run through his lines. Although Pandorea had long since abandoned a career in opera, she remained possessed of a magnificent mezzo soprano voice. The kids, as he still thought of them, were singing Zerlina and Masetto's parts from the end of the first scene of act 2. Entranced by the superb quality of their duet, and just loving the affection for each other that was so apparent in their voices, Jake purposely waited outside the open door. He would not interrupt until they finished.

Masetto/Manny:
> *Oh, oh, my head is broken,*
> *Oh, oh, my backbone, my shoulder.*

Zerlina/Pandorea:
> *Did I hear some speaking?*
> *I thought it was Masetto!*

Masetto/Manny:
> *Oh, dear Zerlina,*
> *Zerlina dearest, come help me!*

Zerlina/Pandorea:
> *What has happened?*

Masetto/Manny:
> *The villain, the base assassin*
> *Has left no bone unbroken.*

Zerlina/Pandorea:
> *Oh, dear, what can I do! Who?*

Masetto/Manny:
> *Leporello, or else some friend, that looked exactly like him.*

Zerlina/Pandorea:
> *The wretch! Did I not tell you that your jealous*
> *And most unruly temper would surely bring you*
> *Before long into some trouble?*
> *Where does it hurt you?*

Masetto/Manny:
> *Here.*

Zerlina/Pandorea:
> *Besides, where?*

Masetto/Manny:
> *Here and also here.*

Zerlina/Pandorea:
> *Is nothing else the matter?*

Masetto/Manny:
> *Yes, there's something with this foot,*
> *And this elbow, I cannot bend it.*

Zerlina/Pandorea:
> *Come, come; if that's the worst,*
> *There's no great harm done.*
> *Come with me home to supper,*
> *And give your faithful promise,*
> *you'll nevermore be jealous;*
> *Those bruises can be cured,*
> *where love is zealous...*
> *Come, shall I tell thee,*
> *How what befell thee,*
> *Soon can be cured*
> *By my potent charm?*
> *No garden grows it,*
> *Though it abounds,*
> *Like furnace glows it,*
> *Yet none 'will harm,*
> *All guard and cherish it:*
> *Gold cannot buy it,*
> *Say, wilt thou try it*
> *Soft it is and warm.*
> *Has thy wit flown,*
> *Hear, how it throbs within,*
> *It's all thine own,*
> *Ah, it's thine alone.*

When Jake finally walked into the dressing room, he found Pandorea kissing Manny on the cheek while he rested his hand on her stomach. Manny was feeling the heartbeat of their yet-unborn child. Although the kids had settled on

"Israele Conegliano," as their son's formal name after their distant ancestor, both had already nicknamed him "Yael," for short.

After warm hugs and greetings all around, Pandorea presented Jake with a present wrapped in plain brown craft paper.

"What is it?"

"A surprise, of course," said Pandorea. "Go ahead, open it."

Jake did just that. Inside the package was an antique edition of Tirso de Molina's play, *Don Juan and the Stone Guest*, bound in blue leather with embossed gold lettering.

"I love it," Jake declared. "Thank you. But how ever did you find this?"

"Even we librarians have our confidential sources. After reading your last translation of Da Ponte's *Secret Diaries*, I was determined to procure a copy of *Don Juan and the Stone Guest* for you. And you'll need to thank both Greta and Enrico as well. When I tracked down this volume to a bookseller in Vienna's *Neuer Markt*, the Foxxes were able to pick it up for me and forward it here."

Jake again thanked Pandorea for the effort she had put into finding this copy. "Have either of you read through it yet?"

"Not me," said Manny, "But she's had it propped up on her stomach for weeks now to read."

"True enough," Pandorea confessed as she stroked her own waist. "Our little Yael probably knows the entire play by heart."

"Do I need wait until my grandson is born to ask him what he thinks?" asked Jake of Pandorea. "Or will you share your thoughts about de Molina's version with me?"

"Certainly," but before she could answer, the backstage lights flashed a warning that the performance was to commence shortly. Pandorea and Jake each gave Manny a good luck hug and then headed out into the hallway.

As Jake then assisted Pandorea to the elevator that would bring them up to the private box seats, she continued, "My sense of the play is that it's a satire on the Church, with Tirso secretly mocking Christian dogma."

"How so?"

"In de Molina's eyes, his Don Juan is a devout Catholic who does not doubt that repentance and forgiveness through confession will save his soul regardless of the crimes and sins he's already committed. Consequently, Don Juan calculates that he can revel in his evil and licentious life without hesitation; all he needs for absolution is to repent later."

"So, what you're saying is that Christianity can produce a Don Juan who revels in evil, precisely because he believes in heaven, hell, and the sacraments of the Church?"

"It's not me that's saying it; it's Tirso de Molina's thesis."

"But even in de Molina's play, isn't Don Juan dragged down to hell by the Stone Guest? Would that not be a sign of divine justice? A sort of all's well that ends well?" asked Jake.

"No, I think not," Pandorea said. "No, I believe Tirso's point is this: 'If a farcical supernatural intervention is the only tool that rids a society of its psychopaths like Don Juan or Don Giovanni, then de Molina's not-so-subtle message is that Christianity has a fundamental flaw, that through its very design, it is incapable of ridding itself of evil.' "

"Do you truly believe that?" Jake asked, "That such evil exists? That's rather cynical, isn't it?"

"You're asking a Siciliana if evil exists?" laughed Pandorea as they reached Box Thirteen. "You lock your doors at night, yes?"

"Of course. Doesn't everyone?" said Jake, who then realized his answer won the argument in her favor.

"That's my point. Evil is a constant in our lives. You, you and Manny both, you've spent your whole lives locked in combat against real evil, yes? First Hitler, Mussolini, and the Holocaust, then escaping Nazis, the Cold War, and now

Arab terrorism? Isn't wrestling against the darkness such evil fosters the very foundation and motivation of your careers?"

"Point well taken, but I'm no hero. Most of my work involves sitting behind a desk."

"And that's one of the things I love about Manny. He's a fighter. He sees what's wrong in the world and endeavors to make it right." Pandorea, who was obviously uncomfortable, eased herself into a chair. "He loves working in the field . . . and being able to sing."

"Even with the baby? Last we spoke, Manny said he's planning on coming in from the cold and working on analytics at HQ."

"You know Manny. He changed his mind again after that last bus bombing in Jerusalem. 'If we don't stand up, who will?' he said. He even cited your frustration with Bishop Hudal escaping justice. 'Never again is now.' "

"This concerns me," said Jake, knowing too well the dangers Manny faced overseas. "He's going to be a dad. There are other means to fight the good fight without being on the road half the year. Yael needs a father."

"I agree. But much as I love Manny, this is the one and only issue that we're divided on. 'Wait,' he tells me, 'just a little bit longer, a few more years.' "

Pandorea sighed with discomfort and then asked Jake to turn one of the extra chairs around so she could raise her legs and rest, which he did. She then continued, "Getting back to Mozart and Da Ponte, do you believe they were consciously writing social commentary when they put together *Figaro* and *Don Giovanni*?"

"No, absolutely not," replied Jake immediately and with certainty. "That's just my opinion, but it's a question I've wrestled with since we first began translating the diaries. Da Ponte and Mozart both had a full understanding of how human emotions create and drive drama. They knew how conflicting needs and desires intersect to build tension and propel stories. You feel it in every aria. They understood the necessity of crafting plots with grand villains that compelled their heroes to grow ever stronger until they are able to overcome their crises. But almost to a fault, Da Ponte and Mozart were never, ever overtly political. They were just two working stiffs—talented ones of course—who wanted to make great operas, with stories that entertained and held an audience's attention. It was their job, albeit one they were each passionate about, but ultimately it was a way to earn a living and as my mother said more than once, a way to put food on the table. No shame in that."

"But what about in their personal lives? Weren't they both, especially Da Ponte, fighting against evil? Evil in the form of greed, corruption, professional jealousy, and even anti-Semitism?"

Just then, the lights flashed again.

"Yes, but only if you consider living your days in secret, as Da Ponte did, undercover and in costume as a priest, a form of fighting," answered Jake.

"And that's the same answer your son gave me when I begged him to stay home," she said as the theater went dark and the overture began. "He claims his most important work is done covertly."

Jake did not respond as they settled back in their seats and focused on the stage below. He knew Manny was essentially a courier, and yes, the work he did was vital, but he feared his son had an inflated sense of importance about his work—a dangerous flaw for a covert agent and that troubled him, especially when Osmin was still lurking out there. And that there was nothing Jake could do about it, troubled him ever more.

As they listened to Leporello's opening aria, Pandorea began to grimace. And when Don Giovanni and Dona Ana wrestled through their first duet, Pandorea's first spasm began. Her breathing turned heavy and measured as she struggled to control the pain.

When the singer-actor playing Don Giovanni made his mock sword thrust into Manny in his role as the soon-to-die commendatore, Pandorea cried out in pain. Fortunately, her anguished cry was hidden from the audience behind her husband's on-stage baritone voice.

Commendatore/Manny:
> *Help, assistance, all is ended!*
> *Oh, to die alone unfriended,*
> *Vile assassin, thou hast undone me,*
> *Heaven protect and guard my child!*

Pandorea abruptly gulped hard and dropped her legs off of the extra chair. Embarrassed, she turned to Jake in a strained and anguished whisper, "My water just broke. But it's two weeks early . . . "

She groaned as another contraction hit. "He's coming!"

"It's time," said Jake. "Your Yael's a precocious child. Why am I not surprised?"

"But . . . the hospital . . . " Pandorea abruptly stopped mid-sentence as she realized Yael was indeed on his way. Now.

"It's too late. Let's get you comfortable."

Jake helped her lie down on the floor, using his topcoat as a pillow to support her head. He then ducked out into the hallway for a moment, returning quickly after insisting one of the ushers call for paramedics.

He held Pandorea's hand and as best he could, he helped coax her through another round of contractions. Pandorea, who knew the music of *Don Giovanni* by heart, even tried to hum along with the music to calm herself. It was an effort that reminded Jake of the day Manny was born at Mount Sinai Hospital in Manhattan three decades earlier.

It was October 12, 1946, and their taxi to the hospital was stuck in bumper-to-bumper Columbus Day Parade traffic in New York. Dolcetta's contractions were intermittent but powerful, and she did everything she could to be brave and keep calm. She even began to recite out loud in English the full recipe for her *Carbonara Gemelli Ebraico* as a sort of birth mantra, "One pound of gemelli; a pot of water heavily saaaaaaalted," her voice rising and falling on the spasms. "Four tomatoes, cut into chunks; two eggggggggs beaten," and so on, as they made it to Sinai for the delivery. As they exited the cab on the way into the emergency room, the cabbie waived the fare, thanked her for the recipe, and wished them well.

Meanwhile, back live from the Kennedy Center for the Performing Arts, Pandorea's birth spasms peaked again during Elvira's first aria, and then slowed all the way through Leporello's rendition of the catalog song, when at last, the paramedics arrived.

One set up a privacy screen while another prepared Pandorea for the final delivery. Yael began to descend out the birth canal just as Don Giovanni and Zerlina sang their duet, "La ci darem la mano" and he popped out with a cry that was once again masked from the rest of the audience by Dona Elvira's shout.

Dona Elvira:
Stop! Leave her, you vile seducer!

The paramedics quickly tended to both mother and child. Then, wrapping Yael in a blanket, they passed the boy to his grandfather. To the end of his days, Jake would swear that his grandson, Yael, opened his eyes, raised his head and looked around, first at his mother, next at his grandfather, and then finally the opera stage below where his father, Manny, was now singing as Masetto. Little Yael's eyes sparkled as and he smiled most contentedly. And, no, it wasn't gas.

And thus, on the 220th anniversary of Mozart's birth, Yael Conegliano, the seventh-generation descendent of Lorenzo Da Ponte, had his premier performance at the Kennedy Center in the middle of the first act of his ancestor's most famous opera.

Chapter Sixteen: Kartnerstrasse Siebzehn

January 5, 1786
Café Bruno, Vienna

Mozart was both furious and frustrated when I told him about Orsini. Another two inches of snow had fallen on the city before I reached him at the old Café Bruno at Kartnerstrasse Siebzehn. The inclement weather already had my friend anxious about when the coach carrying his wife, Constanze, and their infant son from the spas at Baden would finally arrive. It was now over an hour behind schedule. The Café Bruno occupied one half of the ground floor of my apartment building, the Wilden Mann Gasthaus, while the stagecoach stop and livery servicing it occupied the other.

Mozart sat at a table beside a window, drinking a Barbera d'Alba red wine, watching the snow pile up. "We're doomed," he said, drumming his fingers against the glass. "My father had predicted all this correctly when he said these Italians hate me and are not to be trusted, especially Orsini. What are we to do?"

I did not hear him at first, distracted as I was by the thought that my latest flame, Adriana Ferrarese del Bene, lived in the grand suite directly above us. How many times had I eaten here not knowing La Ferrarese was upstairs? Was she there now? What was she doing? What was she wearing, if anything? What about Luigi del Bene, *suo marito*? Did he matter? And what would our future be together, if I did indeed call on her later this evening? I poured myself a glass of Barbera, emptying the bottle that Mozart had already made a serious dent in.

"What are we going to do about Orsini?" Mozart repeated, ever louder.

"Oh, sorry," I apologized for being absentminded.

"Are you hungry?" asked Mozart. "I ordered some sausages and potato pancakes for us, but they still haven't come."

Though the Café Bruno was never famous for its service in the best of times, I dined there frequently due to its proximity to my apartment on the top floor, which had no kitchen. The café was a pretty rundown affair in need of a major overhaul, and matters had only gotten worse since the proprietor, Herr Bruno, had passed away a few months back. Poor Frau Bruno had neither the skill, money, or staff to stay atop matters.

"Yes, I'm starving," I declared, realizing I hadn't eaten since Wetzlar's party last night and it was now mid-afternoon. "I ran into an old friend, Casanova, on the way over here from the palace. He had some ideas that might help us circumvent Orsini. And he asked me to return this to you." I pulled the Metastasio out of my satchel and handed it over to Mozart.

"Oh, my God," declared Mozart, "Where did he? How did he find this?"

"The bed in Angela Tiepolo's office, night of the fire at Teatro San Benedetto. He snatched it on the way out."

"Ah, my birthday," Despite his dark mood, Mozart could not help but smile as he no doubt recalled his first intimate encounters with the female gender of our species. "Angela Tiepolo brings me to her office to propose a performance contract but instead lifts her skirts and presses herself onto me as a birthday present."

"You accepted her gifts, yes?"

"*Natürlich*," laughed Mozart. "And only to have Matilda Wider repeat the gesture at her home after we escaped the flames. Your poor Dona Brunetta was so shaken by the fires, I could not in good conscience refuse her. Fortunately, everyone else at the Wider mansion, including my father, was asleep, thus allowing me to enjoy the fruits of my birthday well past midnight."

"Bravo," I said. Although Mozart had by now already known of my entanglements with those identical two women that very day, I had always refrained from telling him of my third tryst of that same night with Zina. Yes, Zina, whose dulcet voice I could hear in my imagination. Yes, Zina calling out to me as she had down in the crypts below Wetzlar's palace: "*Never forget, never forget, never forget who you are.*" Zina occupied a special place in my heart, one elevated above gossip or conversations of conquests.

"Oh, yes, Angela Tiepolo and Matilda Wider," said a momentarily cheered Mozart. "We lived out Metastasio's 'Lovers' Descent' that night, didn't we?" Mozart returned to the ink-stained page. "And this is the very volume you said your father bound in leather, yes?"

"Certo," I replied.

"Please," said Mozart as he passed the book back over to me. "You keep it. I've lived without it for fifteen years, and it holds greater significance for you than me. Perhaps with Metastasio's help you'll find us another idea for a libretto after Orsini crushes *Figaro* under his feet."

"All is not lost," I said, "I'm reading this." I showed him the Tirso de Molina edition Casanova had given me.

"*Don Juan and the Stone Guest?*" mused Mozart as he perused the book. "Intriguing, but what of our *Figaro*? How can we save it?"

I shared Casanova's twin ideas of either using bribes with Orsini or engaging Storace to win over the emperor.

"Bribe Orsini? We're too poor for that and he's too rich to succumb." By now both our bellies were growling. Mozart finally called out, "Frau Bruno, where's our food? And more wine."

"It's coming," the widow Bruno called back. "Soon, Herr Mozart, soon."

"And Storace? Nancy Storace?" questioned Mozart, the alcohol feeding his anger. "Casanova suggests we use Storace to go around Orsini? Why do that? Divas are temperamental enough without giving them even more power over our libretti. Joseph II should approve our work based on its own merits and not the mendacity of a woman. No one writes characters as well developed as you, my friend. And my score?"

It was true. No one in Vienna, or all Europe, composed music as brilliantly as Mozart. "It should be so," I said, "but haven't we both learned by now the world does not respond to merit, only gain. Should we first give in order to receive?"

Grumbling under his breath, Mozart rebelled at that suggestion as the widow brought over another bottle of Barbera for our table. She opened it with a distinctive pop before refilling our glasses.

He and I wrestled back and forth over our strategy for salvaging *Figaro*. In the end, we drank a lot of wine, Mozart far more than I, but could settle on no plan.

Just outside our window, two of His Imperial Majesty's soldiers arrived at the coach depot on foot. Between them was a prisoner in leg and hand irons.

"Oh, look who's there," I said, pointing. The unlucky convict was none other than Girolamo Tiepolo, twin brother to Angela, the siren of La Serenissima who in one night had seduced us both.

"Good," said Mozart. "Wetzlar told me that the poor fool is being exiled back to Venice under chains. No doubt they're waiting for the coach from Baden to turn around and head back south."

"Casti's gone too," I said. "He left on the morning stage for the Veneto."

"Good riddance all. Now what about Casanova's plan? Do you honestly believe Storace could persuade Joseph II?" Mozart asked, reopening our debate over tactics. "Or maybe we should have bribed Orsini with Casti's own purse, yes?"

"But you gave that away," I said.

"Yes, a king's ransom. Oh, poor *Figaro*.

Just then, the door to the kitchen on the far side of the café opened. At last, our dinner . . . There it was on a tray carried by none other than that servant girl, Celestina, the one we'd rescued the night before.

"What is she doing here?" I asked Mozart.

"Oh, her. Wetzlar had me escort her over here to meet with you about this Zina woman. The girl won't feel safe until those swine who attacked her are gone," he said as he pointed outside to Girolamo.

"Yes, but why is she bringing us dinner?"

"Look at this place," said Mozart. "It's chaos. When I ordered our meal from poor Frau Bruno the old lady was in tears, desperate for help. So, the girl jumps up and volunteers. Said she's worked in kitchens her whole life. I let her go. What else was I going to do if we're to eat before Wetzlar's ghosts drag us back to hell?"

The girl reached our table with a platter of sausages and potato pancakes at the same moment the coach from Baden, half buried in snow, finally arrived outside. Even the four horses pulling it were covered in white. The livery team sprang into action. One handler began unloading the luggage, another unhitched the horses, while a third groom brought around a fresh team.

"Sit," I told her. "Sit with us and eat."

The girl hesitated, so I pointed out the window to where Girolamo waited beside the two guards.

"Oh, no," she exclaimed, her face went white with fear.

"Don't worry," said Mozart as he stood up, "He's in chains and will be gone as soon as they turn the coach around. Take my seat, eat my portion. I'm leaving too. My wife has returned. Finally!"

The girl, whose hands were trembling, did so reluctantly, never taking her eyes off of Girolamo.

Mozart's wife, Constanze, was the first one off the coach. In her arms was their infant son, Karl. Franz Xaver Süssmayr, Mozart's twenty-year-old assistant, was next.

"Will you speak to Storace?" I asked Mozart as he threw on his winter coat and gathered his things up to leave. "It may be our only hope to save *Figaro*."

Mozart shrugged. "For now," he insisted, "No more talk of Storace. My Constanze is here. It's time to make more babies—or she'll be tempted to do the same with Süssmayr." He threw a few coins on the table for our lunch and exited.

I watched through the window as Mozart raced to greet his wife and child. Never had I seen a man so happy to embrace his family. That was Mozart: passionate about his wife when with her, forgetting about her when not. Taking her hand, Mozart and Constanze walked off in the direction of his apartment on Domgasse, leaving Süssmayr to tend to the luggage now being unloaded.

As the fresh team of horses was hitched in place, a new pair of coach drivers climbed into their seats. The soldiers quickly boarded Girolamo, and in a matter of minutes, there was nothing more outside our window other than the dreary aspect of falling snow.

"You've naught to fear," I told the girl, explaining that the Abbé Casti, her other assailant, had also left Vienna.

I bade her eat. The girl thanked me again for rescuing her the night before. As we dined on the meal—one the girl had apparently cooked and delivered herself—she asked permission again to tell me about Zina. I nodded consent. After a sip of wine, I sat back in my chair to listen.

"A year ago, just before Passover," she began with some hesitation, "my mother, Signora Ricca, the woman who hid you and Zina the night Zina killed the commendatore . . . "

"Yes," I nodded.

"She and my father, John Grahl—he's a traveling merchant—they were called away on business to London. My parents were concerned about my remaining in Venice alone. The Casti clan had been seeking out and attacking any one they suspected was connected to the murder of their commendatore. Fearing for my safety, my mother arranged for me stay in Ceneda with Zina and our Spinoziano cousins. I arrived just in time to help Zina prepare the dinner. Rabbi Baruccio led the Passover Seder."

"You know him, Rabbi Baruccio Spinoziano? He's still well?" I asked, remembering well Zina's father and his words of wisdom with great clarity.

"Yes," she said.

"A good and wise man."

"Certo," she said. "As I was saying, it was especially cold and foggy that night. A light rain mixed with snow flurries and the streets were icy. Zina had me build up a huge fire in the Spinoziano hearth to both cook the holiday meal and keep the house warm. There were perhaps ten of us there that evening. The rabbi had just come to the first of the Four Questions—'Why is this night different from all other nights?'—when we all heard a commotion outside that included the sound of horses on the cobblestone, a rare event in the ghetto, especially at that hour when the gates are supposed to be locked. Baruccio turned to Israeli Conegliano, who at just thirteen was the youngest boy in the family."

I stopped her there. "Who is this Israeli Conegliano you speak of?"

My question startled the girl, who answered with surprise, "Your son, of course."

"My son?" I said, dumbfounded. "My son? What son?"

"Barbarina's younger brother. Your son, Zina's son. My cousin. I thought you knew . . . " her voice trailed off.

"I have a son?" And then and only then did I realize that my tryst with Zina on the floor of Signora Ricca's hovel had led to the birth of a child, my son. I stammered, "I . . . I did . . . I did not know. Tell me about him."

The girl went on to describe Israeli as an especially bright, precocious boy, very tall, handsome, and muscular for his age who was fond of singing and opera. And though he had aspirations of being a poet and writer, he excelled at chopping wood and splitting logs for their fires.

"And Barbarina, my daughter, was she there as well?" I asked, remembering the young girl who had attended to Angela and me the night the commendatore died.

"Of course, and with her fiancé, Marco."

"Fiancé?"

"Yes, they finally married this past summer in Ferrara and even now she is expecting her first child."

It troubled me how little I knew of these people, my own children. I silently cursed my father, Gaspare Da Ponte, for his converting us to Catholicism. The cross I still bear created a rift and barrier between me and the people I should know and love. I then and there made a vow to destroy this harness, this travesty, that religion had imposed upon me. Some way, somehow, I would find the means to be reunited not only with Zina but with my children and now grandchildren as well. Yes. Nothing was going to stop me.

The girl continued, "Just as Rabbi Baruccio asked Israeli 'Why is this night different from all other nights?' the door to the house burst open. Two riders stood there, swords drawn. I recognized them immediately from their uniforms as members of the Casti clan. The first one, the *capitano*, strode forward and demanded we turn over Zinabella Spinoziano—the 'woman with the scar'—while his lieutenant barred the door and stood guard."

A chill ran through my body as I feared the worst for my Zina. Even my hands began to shake as the girl continued.

"Zina was on the far side of the table, tending a kettle of soup over the fire. She spoke without fear 'By what right do you come here to our seder? If it is to join us in peace, put down your swords and sit. I will feed you as guests, but if it is me and me alone you want, then come and take me. I will not resist.' Everyone else in the room remained silent as the capitano walked around the table and began to approach Zina. 'I come by the right and strength of this sword,' he said. 'We seek no further harm to anyone, if you return with us.' He switched his sword to his left hand and reached out for Zina with his right, 'Come with me . . . '

"She said, 'yes, of course,' but what happened next defied all expectations. Even before I understood what had occurred, Zina flung the pot of boiling soup into the capitano's eyes. Blinded, the capitano screamed in terror and dropped his weapon. Zina instantly turned and fled out of the house through a back door. Simultaneously Israeli grabbed the sword and in a single swift motion lopped off the capitano's head as easily as if he had been splitting logs. Full of bravado, Israeli shouted at the *tenente*, the lieutenant, 'By the right of this sword, prepare to die.' "

"He did that? My son did that?"

"Yes, but it was a foolish jest. The tenente quickly realized that this thirteen-year-old boy was no match in a duel for a trained warrior. The tenente began to advance. He would have killed Israeli if not for Marco grabbing an ax and Rabbi Baruccio a pitchfork. As they closed ranks around Israeli, we all heard Zina outside mount one of the horses. As she started to ride off, the tenente quickly turned and raced out after her. He leapt onto his steed and the race was on. We watched them gallop out the open ghetto gate until they disappeared into the rain and fog."

Trembling for Zina's safety, I asked, "What then?"

"Zina rode hard and fast up the *Via Giudecca* past the cemetery, but not fast enough to lose the tenente. The dense fog rising up from the ice flows in the River Meschio, hid both horse and rider from her view. She could hear him close behind, gaining on her, but whenever she looked back, she saw nothing. Closer and closer came the sound of the tenente's horse. In a panic, Zina veered off the *Via Giudecca* and onto a trail that led to the top of *Monte Cervino*. She pushed the horse to go as fast as possible and drove it headlong right over the cliff. Now airborne, she leapt off the horse and tumbled into the half frozen river below. As Zina hit the water, she could hear the screams of the startled tenente as he fell to his death. We found his ice-covered body the next morning impaled upon the rocks."

"And Zina?" I asked breathlessly.

"She and the horses all survived, but Zina had broken both of her legs in the fall. Weighed down by her clothes, she was unable to pull herself safely ashore at the beach. The icy rapids carried her back toward town. It was there that your father, Gaspare, rescued her from drowning under the water wheel that powered his shop."

I was stunned. "My father rescued her?"

"Yes," he carried her all the way back home to the ghetto by himself. He stayed only long enough to see that she was taken care of properly. It was the first and last time any of us in the ghetto saw or spoke with him."

"I'm surprised he did that much. And how is Zina now?"

"She caught pneumonia," said the girl, "and died three weeks later."

"Zina is dead?" I was horrified, stunned, dumbfounded, and speechless. Although it had been years that we'd been apart, I never imagined not seeing her again. My world collapsed in on me. And then I thought I heard a woman's voice calling to me from that abyss of darkness. Was it Zina? "Leave the dead to sleep," it said. "Take the hand of the living."

Chapter Seventeen: Kartnerstrasse Siebzehn Revisited

Wednesday Morning, April 9, 1986
Café Venezia, Vienna

"Mozart would have sat right there by the window, drinking his wine, waiting for Constanze," said Greta, as she, Jake, Dolcetta, and their now ten-year-old grandson, Yael, entered the Café Venezia for their first-ever breakfast in Vienna. "And Da Ponte would have been right there across from him."

Greta, whose lengthy copper-red hair still gave her the appearance of Aphrodite in Botticelli's *Birth of Venus*, remained as lovely, gracious, and trim as any woman half her age. She led the four of them to a table on the spot by the window where some two hundred years earlier Mozart and Da Ponte debated about how to save *The Marriage of Figaro* from Orsini's hands.

For Jake and Dolcetta, this two-week trip to Vienna was their first excursion to Europe since they had left Ceneda back in 1946. But, as fate would also have it, Dolcetta knew it would also probably be her last. Just before New Year's, Dolcetta had been diagnosed with heart disease, which coincidently occurred only months after Danielle had been similarly diagnosed in Israel. The impact had been life-changing for Dolcetta. Pandorea's mother, Dr. Marietta Cornetti, was not only her cardiologist but also one of her closest friends. Although Marietta told Dolcetta that with proper medication, moderate exercise, and eating carefully, she had a reasonable chance of living a normal life span, Dolcetta disagreed.

She had seen the disease weaken her own mother and aunts before the war. Now that Danielle had the same diagnosis, Dolcetta was convinced the illness was hereditary and the effects inescapable. Although she agreed to follow her physician's instructions, she was convinced that the span of her life would no longer be measured in decades, but months and years. She recalled the advice Geremia had given both her and Jake the day they met: "Happiness occurs when one understands and accepts the laws of nature and then experiences the peace of mind such knowledge brings." Dolcetta vowed to find peace and tranquility in the embrace of family, regardless of whether the hours accorded her on this earth were to be short or long.

Her courage in the face of trauma inspired Jake. He too was determined to make whatever time they had together the best years of their lives. Although Jake and Dolcetta had always been near perfect partners in marriage with nary a fight or disagreement between them, they were ever more so now, sweeter and kinder and more attentive to each other. Jake could not imagine a greater communion or stronger bond of love than that which they now shared. Dolcetta was also determined to spend as much time as possible with Yael, her only grandchild—time she and Jake both knew from reading the *Secret Diaries* that their ancestor, Lorenzo, was barred by the cross from having with his family. Thus, her first decision after the diagnosis was to retire early as a translator at the State Department's UN office.

Jake and Dolcetta adored Yael, and he also adored them. Much like his sword-swinging namesake, Yael Conegliano was an especially bright, precocious, and handsome boy known for his smile and a sweet, all-knowing twinkle in his eyes. Jake was doubly pleased that Yael's parents had formally named their son, Israeli. The naming honored Zina and Da Ponte's son, Israeli, who not only had saved Zina's life by killing the Casti capitano but who also proved to be the missing link that directly connected Jake to Da Ponte, himself.

Since Yael's birth at the Kennedy Center, Jake and Dolcetta had made it a point to visit him as much as possible and be a known presence in his life. This was particularly important since Manny, their son, who continued to perform in operas around the world while covertly doing the business of the CIA, was often absent from home. Jake kept a raft of shuttle tickets from La Guardia to Washington on hand and together he and Dolcetta would fly down to DC every few weekends.

As might be expected of a boy with the Conegliano pinkies, Yael grew up loving opera and all things Mozart. Instead of playing cowboys and Indians or *Star Wars* and aliens, Yael's imaginary heroes were composers and librettists, divas and tenors, producers and impresarios. He'd often entertain his friends by inventing opera-style stories or by regaling them with tales from the *Magic Flute*. Yael even named his pet parrots Papageno and Papagena. Each morning before heading off to school he would sing to them, playing both the baritone and soprano parts of the duet in the original German and the parrots would sing along.

Papageno:
  Pa-pa-pa-pa-pa-pa-Papagena!
Papagena:
  Pa-pa-pa-pa-pa-pa-Papageno!

The parrots:
> *Pa-pa-pa-pa-pa-pa-Papagena!*

Papageno:
> *Bist du mir nun ganz gegeben?*

Papagena:
> *Nun, bin ich dir ganz gegeben!*

The parrots:
> *Pa-pa-pa-pa-pa-pa-Papageno!*

Papageno:
> *Nun, so sei mein liebes Weibchen!*

The parrots:
> *Pa-pa-pa-pa-pa-pa-Papagena!*

Papagena:
> *Nun, so sei mein Herzenstäubchen!*

Beide:
> *Welche Freude wird das sein,*
> *Wenn die Götter uns bedenken,*
> *Unsrer Liebe Kinder schenken,*
> *So liebe, kleine Kinderlein!*

The parrots:
> *Pa-pa-pa-pa-pa-pa-Papageno!*

Papageno:
> *Erst einen kleinen Papageno!*

Papagena:
> *Dann eine kleine Papagena!*

The parrots:
> *Pa-pa-pa-pa-pa-pa-Papagena!*

Papageno:
> *Pa-pa-pa-pa-pa-pa-Papagena!*

Papagena:
> *Pa-pa-pa-pa-pa-pa-Papageno!*

The parrots:
> *Pa-pa-pa-pa-pa-pa-Papageno!*

For his age, Yael had grown tall and muscular. Bilingual, just like his parents, Yael devoured books and new experiences with an independent hunger and drive that surprised even his grandparents. Though he had aspirations of being a writer and librettist, he excelled at athletics with a particular fondness for fencing inspired, no doubt, by his love of *Don Giovanni*.

So, when Jake and Dolcetta accepted Greta and Enrico's invitation to join them in Vienna for the two-hundredth anniversary performance of the *Marriage of Figaro*, it was a natural to bring Yael along. Their stay with the Foxxes in the Kartnerstrasse siebzehn penthouse, was also the perfect opportunity for Jake and Dolcetta to kick back and experience a city primed to salute Mozart at a pace that accommodated her illness. As the penthouse occupied the entire fourth floor, including Da Ponte's old cubbyhole of an apartment, the Coneglianos could not help but feel that much closer to their ancestor. Although the floor plan for the apartment had been modified numerous times over its life, the guest bedroom that Yael was to stay in was the same space where Da Ponte had once lived. That thrilled their grandson to no end.

By bringing Yael with them to Vienna, it also allowed Manny and Pandorea to have a vacation of their own, something that had been lacking in their marriage. Despite Pandorea pleading for Manny to "come out of the cold," Manny continued to insist that he best served his country by remaining on the road and under cover. Manny and Pandorea went off to stay at the ranch of their friend, Mia Brancato, a place that sprawled among the avocado orchards and mandarin orange groves of Ojai. The small spa town in central California, which was once used as the setting for Shangri-La in the 1937 film *Lost Horizon*, was a perfect paradise and getaway for a couple desperate for time together.

Although the highlight of Jake and Dolcetta's trip was to see *Figaro* later that evening from Greta and Enrico's private box at the Vienna State Opera House, the Foxxes had in addition lined up an ambitious Mozart-themed tour for them through the city. There would be a visit to the Mozart House Museum on *Domgasse*, where the composer wrote both *Figaro* and *Don Giovanni*. They also had reserved seats to see the German translation of Peter Shaffer's play, *Amadeus*, which was on stage all month at the original Hofburg theater—the same one where Mozart and Da Ponte had climbed out on a window ledge to hide from Emperor Joseph II. Greta had also used her connections to arrange for Jake to take Yael over to the *Theater-an-der-Wien* to watch a closed and private dress rehearsal of *The Magic Flute*.

Enrico and Greta also bought tickets for Jake and Dolcetta to a Mozart-themed Grand Ball at the Kursalon Hall sponsored by the British Embassy and Enrico's former unit, the Coldstream Guard. Ballroom dancing was one of the few activities Dolcetta could engage in without putting undue stress upon her heart. Greta had promised to not only take Dolcetta shopping for a gown to wear to the ball, but to also treat her to the finest hair salon in all Vienna. Greta confessed that her elegantly coiffed red locks would be gray and ragged if not for the grace of her stylist. Greta's gift to Dolcetta was for her ailing friend to experience that magical transformation as well as a spirit-booster that Dolcetta readily welcomed.

But before all those adventures ahead, there was still that first breakfast to be had at the Café Venezia. For simplicity's sake, they allowed Greta to recommend a sampler of delights along with their respective beverages. With its menu of fabulous cakes, coffees, tarts, and pies, the Café Venezia promised to be a delicious introduction to the city of Mozart, Da Ponte, Haydn, Beethoven, Brahms, and Strauss.

While they waited for their order to arrive, Yael spotted children walking into a shop across the street.

"Aunt Greta, is that a toy store?"

"Assolutamente," she replied. "A very special one that even sells puppets from *The Magic Flute*."

"Wow, cool," said Yael, his eyes lighting up. "*Nonna*, can we go there?"

"After breakfast," replied Dolcetta.

And Jake? Jake tried to envision Mozart and Da Ponte sitting across from each other, oh so many years ago. Since Dolcetta's diagnosis, their work together on the translations had been put on hold. Jake had read ahead of Dolcetta as best he could, but unfortunately many of the remaining pages in the Vienna portion of the *Secret Diaries* were damaged, missing or illegible, which made his translating these pages without her help extremely difficult.

Jake also struggled to understand how it was that Mozart and Da Ponte had persuaded Joseph II to allow *Figaro* to be performed. Even the film version of Peter Shaffer's *Amadeus*, which had won the Academy Award for Best Picture a year earlier, got it wrong. Shaffer eliminated Da Ponte entirely from the script, a move Jake thought most ironic: a playwright edits out the existence of most important character in Mozart's opera career, the writer, the librettist, who made those performances possible. It also surprised him how few opera lovers even knew Da Ponte's name.

When their waiter finally arrived with their dishes, Yael, who was still studying every detail of the menu, abruptly asked, "Pops, why does the menu read, 'Café Venezia?' Didn't you say it was called Café Bruno in the *Secret Diaries*?

"Wait," said Dolcetta. "Before anyone says another word, taste this first." She lifted a forkful of her crostata di pistacchio for Yael to sample.

"Wow, Nonna, it's awesome," exclaimed Yael.

Dolcetta then did the same for Jake. "When have you ever had this before?"

Jake nibbled at the cake and then licked his lips as if sampling a rare vintage wine that pleased, one he had tasted

in the distant past. "You served it to me once before . . ." Jake froze, choked up by the memories flooding back to him. "We had it the morning Geremia died."

Dolcetta nodded. "It's my family's secret recipe. Most cooks, especially Sicilianos, make crostata with crème or ricotta. My mother's special ingredient was to use yogurt instead, just like this one. How did her recipe end up here in Vienna?"

"Ah," said Greta, speaking to all three of her guests. "You're not the only ones to do some research. I have the answer to each and every one of your questions."

"Speak," said Dolcetta to their hostess.

"Do you recall the servant girl in the *Diaries*, the one called Celestina?" Greta asked.

"Zina's cousin?" said Yael, who practically knew the *Secret Diaries*, by heart—except the racy sections Jake and Dolcetta kept from him. "Celestina is the girl who was with Zina at that Passover dinner, right?"

"Yes, her full name was Celestina Nancy Grahl," said Greta. "And do you remember the money Mozart and Da Ponte gave to her?"

"After Abbé Casti attacked her?" Yael both asked and answered hurriedly. " 'A king's ransom . . . Enough gold and silver to buy Richard the Lionheart's freedom.' And they made her promise to 'spend it wisely and show kindness to others.' "

"You have an excellent memory," said Greta.

"Certo," Yael replied with pride and in fluent Italian. *"Ho aiutato il Nonna e il Nonno a tradurre i diari."*

"Yes, he has been helping us translate," confirmed Jake. "His command of Italian is better than mine."

"Allora va bene," replied Greta, impressed at Yael's effortless use of Italian. "Well then, it turns out that Celestina used the money Da Ponte and Mozart had given her to buy the café from the widow, Frau Bruno. Celestina fixed up the restaurant and renamed it the Café Venezia."

"Cool," said Yael. "That's really cool. So, our cousin owned this place?"

"Certo," repeated Greta.

"And my mother's crostata di pistacchio recipe?" asked Dolcetta. "She brought that here too?"

"Si," said Greta. "It turns out that when Celestina purchased the café, she made the Spinoziano family's crostata di pistacchio its signature dessert dish. It became all the rage in Vienna."

"So, Café Venezia was a success?" asked Jake of Greta.

"To this day," said Greta. "Celestina used that money wisely. And did you notice the motto," she added, pointing to the café's logo on the napkins. It was a German phrase under the café's name: *Zeigen Sie anderen Freundlichkeit*. "Show kindness to others," Greta translated.

"Remarkable," said Dolcetta.

"The inn has always been popular," said Greta. "Even Beethoven used the café to premiere his *Opus 132 String Quartet*. But you need not worry, the owners of the café have kept the recipe for the crostata di pistacchio a secret for the last two hundred years."

"Wow, two hundred years," said Yael, who was all too soon distracted again by the sight of other children walking into that toy store across the street. "Nonna, can we go there, now?" he asked his grandmother.

"Of course," said Dolcetta. "Finish your breakfast first though."

As soon as Yael wolfed down the remnants of his croissant, Dolcetta relented and led him across the street. Greta immediately turned to Jake, and feeling great concern about Dolcetta's condition, pressed him for an update.

Jake gave her a full and extensive answer, the good, the bad, the indifferent, and then concluded by saying, "Visiting with you and Enrico helps. Walking in Da Ponte and Mozart's footsteps helps even more. And experiencing

Vienna with Yael, that's the best medicine of all. It would be a cliché to say she's fighting as hard as she can—that's all true—but she is doing it her way, the Dolcetta way, which is to find sweetness and pleasure in each and every moment she has left."

"Months? Years? What are you thinking?"

"I don't think," Jake said with a shake of his head. "It's too painful imagining life without her. But Dolcetta, she has an astonishing simple, clear attitude. My girl is determined to live her days in joy and peace until it is time to kiss us all goodbye."

"Remarkable, she's just remarkable. I love that woman," said Greta, who then turned serious. "Enrico won't tell you this, but he's been struggling himself as well."

"What?" Jake asked. "What's going on?"

"Never let him know I told you, but he's in treatment for prostate cancer."

"Oh, dear, I had no idea. Why hasn't he . . . "

"You know the Brits—keep a stiff upper lip. Never show emotions, never show weakness, never miss a day in the office. But it's been exhausting for us both."

"Why doesn't he retire? He's old enough."

"Code name Osmin," she answered. "He won't quit until they nail Osmin, especially after the frustration of seeing Abbé Hudal escape justice. Osmin is Enrico's great white whale, his *Moby Dick*. He's obsessed. Besides, Enrico can't imagine not working. He put it into his will that if he dies at his desk, he wants to be embalmed right there in the embassy, with pen in hand, so no one accuses him of taking a day off."

"And you?" Jake asked, but then immediately withdrew the question. "Never mind." In the intelligence business, no one ever asked "How was your day at the office," even if he was concerned about her safety as a touring artist and espionage agent.

Greta nodded in a silent assent that said both nothing and everything. She then turned her questions back to the *Secret Diaries*. "I've read the translation that took us as far as Zina's death. You do know more, yes?"

"*Un po*," said Jake. "Dolcetta is determined that we get back to the translations after this trip, so I don't have any actual pages to share yet. But what I can say is this: the story of Zina's death had truly caught Da Ponte unawares. That night he went into shock, genuine shock. Da Ponte would later write about how he abruptly left the Café Bruno and walked aimlessly around the snow-covered streets of Vienna for hours, not knowing where he was going or what he was even doing. He felt as if the news of her death had ripped from his chest the very spark of life that sustained him. By the time it grew dark, our poor Lorenzo was heartsick, numb, and half frozen. When at last, he finally returned to Kartnerstrasse siebzehn, he trudged up the stairs. Only when he reached the landing for the second floor, did he remember his promise to visit La Ferrarese, little as he felt like having company," continued Jake as he looked directly into Greta's eyes. "The prospect of a woman's warm embraced comforted him. He knew he needed someone, if not Zina, then perhaps Adriana."

"Of course," said Greta, returning his gaze. "What good is a wounded man without the consolation of a woman's touch?"

"Yes, from what I was able to translate, Da Ponte found the del Bene apartment. He knocked and waited. Nothing. His eyes teared up as he remembered Adriana's last embrace earlier that morning, her arms, her breasts, her sweet voice, her long, flowing hair. He knocked a second time and finally heard stirring from inside. Ah, at last, he thought. Expecting La Ferrarese's smile to greet him, he instead got her sleepy-eyed chambermaid. The servant informed our poor Da Ponte that Adriana had gone out and was not expected home until late."

"Oh dear," said Greta, "The old boy's really having a bad time of it then, yes?"

"So it would seem," said Jake. "I try to imagine Da Ponte, feeling totally crushed, despondent, and probably even a bit dizzy and lighted-headed. I see him, dragging himself up the stairs to his own flat on the top floor . . . " Jake paused. "I still can't believe that you two own Da Ponte's old apartment. And you gave the room to Yael last night. He's blown away. The coincidence . . . all these years."

"History is one of the charms of Vienna," said Greta, "Especially when you realize Kartnerstrasse siebzehn was already hundreds of years old when Da Ponte lived there. Manny stayed there, too, when he and Pandorea were in school. Unfortunately, we didn't know about the Da Ponte connection back then."

"Manny would have loved knowing he slept in the room that had once been the home of his forefather, the great Emanuele Conegliano. There must be some generational magic about it."

"Assolutamente. You Coneglianos are definitely a unique species, a world apart from the rest of us. But what about our poor depressed Da Ponte? What happened when he returned to his room?"

"Well, yes . . . When Da Ponte unlocks the door to his apartment, he describes in the diary the blackness inside as being as deep and impenetrable as his sadness. Before reaching for the candle and matches he keeps by the door, Da Ponte waits for his eyes to adjust to the darkness. Suddenly he hears a rusting off in the corner by his bed," Jake pauses. He looks directly into Greta's eyes.

"And?" asks Greta. She returns his gaze with a firm intensity. "Tell me true."

"Well, as you might imagine, Da Ponte freezes, startled and taken aback by the noise. Is it a mouse, a rat, or an apparition? And then, once more he hears that voice from the catacombs call to him, 'Time is short. Take her hand.' Is it the wind again? His imagination? Or Zina's ghost? His eyes fill with tears, making it ever so much harder to penetrate into the bleakness before him. He fumbles in the dark for that candle, hoping beyond hope he might see his beloved one last time—even if she's just a phantom from the spirit world. He lights a match, but the spark of flame only serves to blind him yet again. 'Come, my darling,' the voice suddenly urges. It is a smooth, seductive soprano voice, one that abruptly blows out the flame. 'Come, my darling, come soothe the pangs of our innocent love.'

"A woman's bare arms surround him. He feels her flesh. Her hair brushes his face; her breasts push up against his chest. Are they real? He finds her lips—a warm invitation to love and compassion. He kisses them a thousand times as they tumble onto his bed."

Part Three
Prague

Chapter Eighteen: Leopold the Second

Sunday Night, October 14, 1787
The Estates National Theater, Prague

Mozart, a fidgety Mozart showing the strain of his own expectations, acknowledges the applause from the audience before sitting down at his pianoforte in the orchestra pit. I watch my friend take a deep breath to gather himself as he prepares to conduct our opera. It is a command performance ordered by our Emperor Joseph II to celebrate the wedding of his niece to Crown Prince Anton of Saxony. The twenty year-old bride whom we must please, the Archduchess of Austria, Maria Theresia, is the daughter of the emperor's brother, Leopold II.

Even as I write these discreet diaries about the true events of our lives, I need to digress for one moment. Much noise is already being written by scholars, musicians, and critics about the outsized influence Mozart's father, Leopold Mozart, purportedly had on his gifted son. During our time together, Mozart never met my father, nor I, the elder Mozart, who died this past May. Lacking any direct knowledge or wisdom to add to such discourse, I will say no more about the effect that senior generation may have upon ours.

I will, however, suggest that the more impactful, if not downright fearful influence upon Mozart's life—and mine—is to be made by a different Leopold, Leopold II. This Leopold is not only the father of the bride, he is the royal next in the line of succession to become the emperor of the Austro-Hungarian Empire. And he is most notable as a man who despises opera.

In sad truth, much as Mozart and I may have fancied ourselves as so-called independent freelancers, we are still artists in servitude to the whims of the Hapsburgs. And tonight, under the ever-present shadow of the royal family, our immediate future as artists is inexorably linked to the happiness of Leopold II's daughter. The young bride, Maria Theresia, is ensconced beside her new husband, the crown prince, in the royal box directly across from where I sit between Mozart's wife, Constanze, and two of Mozart's close friends from Prague, Madame Josepha Duschek and her husband, Franz Duschek. And no, it requires only one quick glance at the expression of boredom and disdain on Maria Theresia's face to realize the prospects for our success tonight are at best, slim. Even Constanze, now seven months pregnant, senses the tension in the theater. As she looks down below at her husband, she shares his anxiety. Constanze makes the sign of the cross and then, clutching my hand, she squeezes the blood out of my fingers. I say nothing, especially as Josepha, who first met Mozart in Salzburg long before her marriage to Franz and his to Constanze, seems equally distraught and is squeezing my other hand.

How had all this come to pass? How is it that after all of our hard work and efforts, our fate, our careers, our livelihood, hang in balance on the whims of a twenty-year-old archduchess who is very much her father's daughter?

A mere two or three weeks earlier, my life seemed grand, successful, and without worries. Mozart had gone off to Prague to prepare our opera for the stage, while I remained behind to complete work on three other libretti, one each for Salieri, Martin y Soler, and Antonio Brunetti. In the past year alone, there were twenty-two operas performed in Vienna and six, yes six, of the most successful were mine. I wrote libretti for all of the leading composers. Commissions poured in, my fame grew, money was plentiful, and I continued to enjoy a most discreet lover in Adriana Ferrarese del Bene. Indeed, La Ferrarese was even the star of one of the hits I had written, and she was soon to star in yet another. Though I still longed for a true romance and partnership, I was content enough at being delightfully satiated in secret by my diva whenever her husband, Signor Luigi del Bene, was out of town. And it was our good fortune that Signor Luigi's businesses required him to reside in Milano most months of the year.

Adriana and I were in fact enjoying a late breakfast at the Café Venezia after a particularly languid morning together in bed. The postal coach had apparently just arrived with a dispatch for me from Mozart in Prague, which Celestina delivered to our table. With no desire to interrupt the sanctity of our morning, I set it aside.

"Aren't you going to open it? What if it's important or some terribly bad news?" Adriana asked.

"All the more reason than to let it hold," I said.

"Or good news worthy of a celebration?" she countered.

"If that be the case, then later we'll toast with champagne and dance 'til dawn."

My reply pleased her. If nothing else Adriana was terribly fond of the party life.

We took our time, sipping our coffees, nibbling our crostatas, which were oh so heavenly, and chatting about nothing. It was these simple pleasures that appealed most to me, simple pleasures that let me dream of how our life might someday be, if only Adriana could shed that nuisance of a husband.

We were well into our second cup before the conversation slowed and Adriana prodded me again, "Open it. I am dying to know what Mozart wrote. Perhaps it is some nasty gossip about the royals."

"Mozart does not gossip about anyone, especially the royal family."

"Yes, yes, I know, I know, Mozart doesn't tell tales, but they do—about him. To hear those women talk, he's bedded more of them than Casanova. Come, read it already."

At her urging I picked up the envelope. "If you insist, but knowing Herr Mozart, all he is going to write to me is about how desperate he is for our opera to succeed. He needs the money."

Indeed, while I was experiencing my most successful year ever, Mozart had been in a funk for the better part of the last eighteen months. Our *Marriage of Figaro* was at the root cause of his despair. Let me explain. As it turned out, Joseph II did give his blessing to my libretto over Orsini's objections. And I will proudly add that the emperor's approval was based entirely upon the merits of my script. Yes, we had succeeded without recourse to a bribe for Orsini or a seduction by Storace. Nonetheless, the path to production still proved to be perilous.

Simply put, the final preparations and the dress rehearsal were an unmitigated disaster, one that Mozart laid at the feet of the Italian cabal. He firmly believed that the conspirators opposed and undercut him at every turn. Remember, the theater was controlled by Orsini; the production staff, the musicians, and most importantly the singers were all in his employ. Sabotage was everywhere: musicians muffed their parts, singers forgot their lines, scene changes were delayed, and even the wardrobe mistress sent the players out in the wrong costumes.

If, however, I had learned nothing in all my training as a priest, it was this: I knew how to instill fear into the hearts of miscreants, a fear so powerful that each would immediately reform their own behaviors. Theater folk are by their very nature vain and narcissistic. One by one and in secret I met with each of the participants and had them peer into their own reflections in an old tin mirror I carried around in my satchel. And so, it was not the wrath of some all-powerful God I showed them but rather their own frail egos and reputations. If they were to fail once more on opening night in front of Emperor Joseph II, the humiliation arising from such disasters would not fall on Mozart, the target, or Orsini, the perpetrator, but on each of them as individuals.

And so, *The Marriage of Figaro* opened the spring opera season in Vienna's Burgtheater on May 4, 1786, a day that for Mozart ranked as a rare operatic triumph. Numerous arias and duets were encored to thunderous applause, so much so that Joseph II ordered limits on the number of encores for all future productions.

Unfortunately, however, *Figaro* closed after a mere seven performances. Why? It was apparent from the reaction of the aristocrats who normally fill the boxes at the Burgtheater that mocking the foibles of their noble class, which our opera did in spades, was no path to success in Vienna.

Mozart was devastated. Yes, he had finally gotten an opera performed, but it had garnered him nothing. After *The Marriage of Figaro*, Mozart's status as a composer of Italian language opera was little better than before. By contrast, my next opera with Martin y Solar, *Una cosa rara*, became the popular hit of the season with over twenty-five performances.

So frustrated was Mozart by the betrayals around him that he considered relocating to London, as Michael Kelly and several others from our opera family planned to do early in the new year. Mozart begged me to consider going with him. Given how poorly his composition had been received by the aristocratic audiences of Vienna, at first even I was hesitant to commit to working with him again. But I did.

Despite his lack of commercial success, when it came to talent and genius, Mozart was clearly first. All the others I wrote for—including Salieri, Martin y Soler, Vincenzo Righini and Giuseppe Gazzaniga—ran a poor second.

London indeed would have been our new home had not stunning news come to us from one Pasquale Bondini, the director of opera at the Estates National Theater in Prague. His word gave us both renewed hopes. Though in the capital city of Vienna, *Figaro* failed to achieve the success we believed it merited, the common people of Prague, a relative backwater in the Hapsburg Empire, had apparently loved it. Night after night, a local opera company played it to sellout crowds. It was the biggest opera hit that city had ever experienced. Even on the streets, laborers, merchants, and princes alike were singing its tunes, including "Non piu andrai" and "Dove sono." Based on its success, Bondini commissioned Mozart to produce a new opera for Prague that would open the night of October 14, in celebration of the marriage of Leopold II's daughter.

Recalling my Tirso de Molina volume *Don Juan and the Stone Guest* and inspired as well by our journey into the ghostly tombs below Wetzlar's Palace, Mozart and I agreed to create a new Italian language adaptation, *Il dissoluto punito, ossia il Don Giovanni*, or simply *Don Giovanni*. Though confident that I could easily write the libretto, I struggled at first trying to grasp the nuances, the subtle whys and wherefores of our dissolute lead character. What was it that the fairer sex saw in a Don Giovanni? How was it that all manner of women were drawn like moths on a hot summer night to be consumed by the fires of passion our Signor Giovanni lit?

Mozart had proposed a dinner of research. "Let's invite your friend, Casanova, and Storace, along with Magda and Mora," two uninhibited women from the chorus, whom we both knew intimately. "Let us ply them with wine, sit back, and just listen to what they say and how they act."

We all met at a Gasthaus, *Zu den Drei Hakken,* on *Singerstrasse* not far from Mozart's house on *Domgasse* and did just that. We dined well, drank aplenty, laughed, and talked much. From the memoirs he was now writing, Casanova regaled us with explicit tales of love, sex, and intrigue. The more titillating the talk, the more Magda and Mora were attracted to my aging but still most charming libertine friend. I observed all with interest, as Casanova was, in my initial estimation, the closest living model for our *Don Giovanni.*

We continued this amorous and enjoyable discourse until Storace abruptly broke into tears. She inexorably altered the course of our conversation by announcing that she had had a miscarriage and because of her own dissolute life, she did not know who the father was. Storace added that the emotional strain of juggling her affairs and the court intrigues of Vienna were simply too much for her. Consequently, she was returning home to London. When Mozart ventured to console her, I gathered it was time for me to exit.

After leaving the restaurant, I returned home alone to work on the libretto for *Don Giovanni.* Not so for Casanova. Inspired, my aging lothario of a friend departed with the two young nubiles, Magda and Mora, clinging to each arm. His adroit maneuver left Mozart—the ever amorous Mozart—alone to pursue his affair with Storace. Yes, his wife, Constanze, was away again in Baden, not that it mattered a wit to Mozart. Her presence would have only altered his technique and timing. Mozart's seduction of Storace, our prima diva for *The Marriage of Figaro*, struck me then and there as identical to the manner in which he slid Angela Tiepolo away from me in Venice, when we first met there on his birthday during Carnevale of 1771. I realized then, that Mozart himself, not Casanova, would be my true inspiration for the character of *Don Giovanni.* Yes, in truth, it was Mozart whom I pictured when I wrote the lyrics for "La che darem la mano."

As fortune and necessity would have it, I worked nonstop all that summer on three operas simultaneously. In the morning it was *Axur, King of Ormus* for Salieri. After lunch it was *The Arbor of Diana* to star Adriana for Martin y Soler. And in the evening, it was *Don Giovanni* for Mozart. In between, Celestina or one of her waiters from the café would bring me up food and wine. Celestina—when she had the time—was indeed a great help beyond just bringing me sustenance. She had a lovely and innate sense of story, so much so that I would on occasion runs lines past her. And late at night, when my labors were finally complete, La Ferrarese would slip into my room and together we would spend the night entwined as one. Yes, it was a grueling schedule that did not let up until *The Arbor of Diana*, was ready for the stage.

Soon thereafter I placed a completed libretto for *Axur*, into Salieri's hands and my friend, Mozart, carried *Don Giovanni* off to Prague.

Now was the time to finally open Mozart's letter and share with Adriana all that he had to say. Indeed, inside his brief note, Mozart pleaded urgently for me to race to him in Prague as quickly as possible. Apparently, all the preparations for our opera were in total chaos, and he once again blamed the Italian cabal for undercutting him. The singers, whom he declared were lazy and undisciplined, had not learned their parts. Set construction was way behind schedule, the production managers were often absent, and the musicians . . . well, let's just say they were a poor lot, scarcely equal to the rigors of a Mozart score.

"Mozart wants me to meet him in Prague as soon as possible? Seems *Don Giovanni* needs my help."

"Will you go?" Even in a question, Adriana's voice warmed my soul. Oh, if only we could shed her husband, Luigi, from our lives.

"Yes, the premiere is in two weeks. I'll take tomorrow morning's coach out."

"So soon? And leave your other work behind?"

"What choice do I have? It's Mozart," I said affirmatively.

"Yes, Mozart," replied Adriana with disdain. "Always Mozart. Why worry about a failure? That's what he is. And what about *The Arbor of Diana*? My premiere is just ahead too," she added, staking out a defiant position. Like many a diva, she often assumed the role she played, that of a Greek goddess, was indeed who she was in real life.

"Why don't you come with me first? A week in Prague, we'll have fun."

"Truly, Lorenzo, you shock me. I begin rehearsals in three days. And even if I did not, why do you imagine such things? How can I travel to Prague with a priest for a week of . . . Never mind."

"What are you saying?" I asked, perplexed by her reaction.

"I am married. Did you forget?"

"Of course not. But that troubles you still?"

"Yes," she insisted. "It's easy enough to dismiss the snickers of gossips when I am seen about Vienna with you, my librettist, but Prague? *Dio mio!* To be seen there cavorting with a priest? Now that would be a scandal, one a lady in my position can ill afford. Luigi del Bene is my husband and I intend to stay married. *Capisci?*"

"I do, I do understand."

Abruptly, Adriana stood up. "No, you don't. You never have. When I perform as a goddess, the theater is my empire, and the stage my throne. Never doubt Diana's pride blazes within me and though the smile upon my face seems to promise peace, there are thunderbolts in my heart that can make earth and heaven shake."

"Yes, you're a goddess on stage, queen of your empire," I fired back, "but I wrote those lyrics. Without them, what are you? Divine royalty? No, you're nothing, nothing but an empty mouth in search of words to sing."

In a huff Adriana stormed out of the café. I let her go. It was hardly the first time my diva exited stage left after some sudden disagreement. Truly, Adriana's temperament had become even more volatile than that of my first lover back in Venice, Angela Tiepolo. What was it about such fiery women that lured me in? Perhaps I too was just a moth drawn to love's fires—a moth who dreamt it was a man, a man immune to such immolation.

As one might imagine, she did not come up to my room that night. I slept alone. But the next morning she relented. When I went downstairs to board the early morning stagecoach for Prague, Adriana was there with her sweet kisses to wish me *un buon viaggio*. And just as the coach was about to depart, Celestina arrived with a hamper full of food from the Café Venezia. She sent me off with enough delights to sustain me on the three-day journey to the Bohemian capital city.

When I arrived on the 8th of October, Mozart, a very distraught Mozart, met me at the stagecoach stop beneath the clock tower in Prague's old town. He was still grumbling about the Italian conspiracy. He had my bags taken over directly to the Duscheks' estate, Villa Bertramka, where he and Constanze were staying, but me, Mozart dragged over to the Estates National Theater to witness yet another disastrous rehearsal.

Yes, it was chaos. I'd never seen an opera theater so dysfunctional.

"Two days," Mozart said, "Joseph II decreed that we have two days to prepare *Don Giovanni*. And if it is not ready for a full dress rehearsal by then, the emperor has ordered that the company perform *The Marriage of Figaro* for the wedding party instead.

I laughed a humorless laugh. "So, our beloved Emperor Joseph II believes *Figaro*, an opera about rape, infidelity, kidnapping, births out of wedlock, secret identities, and war between the classes, is appropriate fair for a newly married royal couple?"

"Yes, he loves the music," said Mozart. "It's a nightmare. It's either *Figaro* or a half-baked *Don Giovanni*."

"Let me see what I can do," I told my despairing partner.

I spent the next forty-eight hours at the theater investigating every aspect of the show to the point of exhaustion, never leaving even to sleep or eat. Those necessities of life I grabbed backstage whenever there was a spare moment to nap or dine. From the singers to the managers to the backstage laborers, the opera performers of a provincial Prague were just not that good. Most were barely above the level of amateurs, and few would have ever qualified to work in Venice or Vienna. I found no conspiracy, no Italian cabal to ruin poor Mozart, none whatsoever. What I discovered was perhaps worse, the simple incompetence of a regional company. And as such they were immune to fear or even the wrath of a vengeful God.

What they did know and know well, however, was the opera they had been staging for over a year, *Figaro*. Therefore, in the end we surrendered to circumstances. The premiere of *Don Giovanni*, was pushed back several more weeks to the 28th of October.

And so, now, the real drama begins as Mozart sits down at his pianoforte to conduct *The Marriage of Figaro* for the twenty-year-old archduchess of Austria, Maria Theresia, and her new husband, Crown Prince Anton of Saxony.

Our first act moves along tolerably well at best, though I'm certain I see both members of the bridal couple cringe when Count Almaviva's initial attempt to seduce Susanna is played out on stage. My hopes, however, for a successful outcome are revived when our Figaro sings "Non piu andrai" to a wildly enthusiastic crowd that immediately demands an encore.

The second act, however, brings the royal bride, Maria Theresia, to the breaking point. When our countess on stage sings "Dove sono," and laments about how Count Almaviva's love for her has gone cold in favor of other affairs, Maria Theresia grabs her husband's hands and drags him out of the theater.

My heart sinks, as does Constanze's and Josepha's. Fortunately, Mozart, with his back to the audience, will not know of this disaster until the end of the opera two hours later.

The next morning, I board the coach to Vienna, where I hope to return as a moth, blind to the fiery tempest that is my Adriana. And Mozart? Poor Mozart, disheartened by yet another mishap, he must remain behind in Prague until he premieres our *Don Giovanni*.

Chapter Nineteen: The Velvet Revolution

Late Friday Afternoon, November 17, 1989
The Estates National Theater, Prague

Mozart and Da Ponte's opera, *Don Giovanni* did finally open at the Estates National Theater in Prague on the night of October 28, 1787. And although Mozart had been suffering from a run of theatrical mishaps and disasters, *Don Giovanni* was not one of them. As the winds of fate would have it, the opera turned out to be a rousing success in Prague, not only then, but forever more. That much, Jake knew.

This afternoon, over two centuries later though, the show would not go on. The Estates National Theater was empty with the exception of Jake and British Cultural Affairs Attaché Enrico Foxx. Enrico had bribed a guard to let them in, but only after Jake insisted they go there after leaving Prague's Central Hospital. In fact, all the theaters of Prague were empty as were the schools and university campuses. Only a few blocks away, fifteen thousand protestors demonstrated against the ruling Communist regime, clogging the old town area. Their calls for an immediate countrywide general strike had the riot police out in force on *Národní* Street that bisected the city.

Not only was the Estates National Theater one of the oldest classic opera houses in all Europe, it had only a few years earlier served as the primary filming location for *Amadeus*, the Academy Award–winning motion picture about Mozart. Now it was Jake who stood in the dimly lit theater beside a tarnished brass plaque on the floor of the orchestra pit. The plaque marked the very spot where Mozart sat at his pianoforte when he conducted *The Marriage of Figaro* and later the premieres of *Don Giovanni* and his *The Mercy of Titus*. Jake stared up at the stage's opening set, which was the two-story tall exterior of the commendatore's villa. He struggled in his own mind to comprehend what had happened there the day before. He could not. His senses were reeling. He'd had no sleep. His body and mind were exhausted. And his emotions felt like they'd been put through a laundromat's spin cycle.

Enrico hobbled over to the left side of the stage. He now walked with a cane not unlike the silver-headed one Da Ponte had used to clobber his rival, the Abbé Casti. The former lieutenant who once resembled Errol Flynn, was now a pale but determined shadow of his former self. To Jake, the tap, tap, tap of Enrico's cane on the wooden floor sounded like a clock ticking its last beats. Yes, it was clear his friend's battle against this disease would not end in victory. But that news was secondary. There was a pool of dried blood on the floor just below a smashed electrical panel.

"Code name Osmin," said Enrico. Even his voice had aged. "This is where he died, this is the spot."

"Tell me again, tell me everything, tell me how it all unfolded. Please," begged Jake, his eyes watered up and his heart felt as hollow as their long-sought victory. "I need to know."

Jake recalled Enrico's opening words over a secure phone to him just twenty-four hours earlier when he was still in New York, "We got Osmin, but we paid a price. How soon can you get here?" Jake flew out immediately from Kennedy, direct to Prague on a British Foreign Service jet Enrico had arranged.

That was yesterday. Now, with an effort that revealed just how weary Enrico had become, the aging spymaster climbed down from the stage and then, like an old pensioner, he settled into one of the musician's chairs to sit opposite Jake. "I don't . . . I don't know where, where to begin." Gone from Enrico's voice was the ever-efficient and direct manner of a former officer of the British Coldstream Guard.

Jake waited patiently as his old friend caught his breath and then finally continued.

"As you well know, after years of false hopes, our team finally had a nearly conclusive set of leads as to Osmin's true identity. Each one of the assassinations of our female agents behind the Iron Curtain all had sexual overtones, brutal overtones: rape, torture, and even genital mutilation. Two KGB suspects, one a woman, the other a man, had both been detected upon their arrival in Prague from Budapest ten days ago. My team, which had been tracking another assassination attempt in Budapest . . . " Enrico paused, he was shaking, hesitant to go on.

This triggered Jake to ask, "Greta? Greta was there, wasn't she? Was Greta the target?"

Enrico inhaled deeply and calmed himself before answering, "Yes, but she's okay. Greta knew the protocols and extracted herself in time."

"*Dio mio*," said Jake. "They broke her cover? They know her identity?"

"Yes," confirmed Enrico. "And so, when we got Greta back to Vienna, she had Amadé announce her retirement as a performer. She's done. And after we wrap up here, so am I."

"I'm glad, glad for both of you," Jake said, his thoughts however were focused elsewhere.

Enrico continued. "My team determined that one or the other, if not both of these deep KGB plants, was most likely our Osmin. I flew up from Vienna immediately and met our crew at the British Embassy. We began to assemble an 'observe and snatch' plan. You may know the suspects, Terese Burauskaite and Kazys Skirpa."

"Terese and Kazys? The opera singers?" Jake was incredulous.

Enrico nodded. "Why not? We use singers as spies, the Russians use singers as spies."

"Good grief, they were at Manny's wedding." Jake was dumbfounded. "They're Osmin?"

"Yes, a ninety-nine percent certainty. Do you remember that summer, twenty-five years—no, twenty-seven years ago—when Manny and Pandorea were still teenagers? They performed *The Marriage of Figaro* for the Vienna Academy of Music at that Prague Festival, yes?"

"Of course," said Jake. "Manny was furious he was shunted aside and had to play Dr. Bartolo instead of Figaro because of the uncertainty of him getting a Czech visa. That changed his career and his life."

"Terese Burauskaite and Kazys Skirpa were students in the Russian Academy class from St. Petersburg that was there as well."

"Deep plants? KGB assassins?" asked Jake, wondering where all this was leading.

"Yes. And it was Manny who first raised suspicions about them."

"He did? Manny? How so? That's not his area."

"Three of his Iron Curtain contacts—all women—were murdered these past two years in cities where he was performing: Belgrade, Riga, and Dresden. Terese was performing in the first, Kazys in the second, and both were in Dresden. Manny said that whenever he was in the same opera as either one of them, something, something he could not quite put a finger on, always felt off. Opera companies are like little families. The intensity of production pulls performers together quickly, with their emotions, their love lives, and often their politics on full display. Yet between rehearsals neither Terese nor Kazys would socialize with the rest of the cast—or each other. That alone was an anomaly. On a hunch, Manny went back over years of performance records and found that in a vast majority of cases, one or both were in the cities where agent deaths or assassination attempts occurred."

"*Dio mio*," said Jake. "He never said a word to me about this. But, how could he?" Jake answered his own question.

"No, he couldn't. He sent it all up through chain of command."

"And the Osmin killings? Those could have been coincidental, but you confirmed his suspicions, yes?" asked Jake.

"Our veteran staffers were skeptical at first, but after twenty years of frustration, we were willing to look everywhere and anywhere. Finally, after much review, the analysts back home in London gave his thesis a high probability score. We alerted our field agents and interceptors and soon enough they all confirmed his theory as having a high probability of being accurate."

"I see. He did good work then?"

"Yes, and as soon as we learned that Terese and Kazys were both scheduled to open a new performance of *Don Giovanni* in Prague this month, we set up a 'decoy and trap' that was originally intended to play out later this month during the run of the show. We even had Amadé Artists arrange for Manny to join them in his role as the commendatore."

"You brought Manny in? Why? And after Greta? He's just a courier," said Jake.

Enrico shook his head, "No," a gesture that stunned Jake to his core.

"Manny's been engaged in covert interagency field work for years now. He's been as focused as any of us on this project to nail Osmin. He could just never tell you. You,

you and Pandorea, you and Dolcetta, you were all so against Manny being on the road, that he never said anything—not that he could if he wanted to."

"*Dio mio*," gasped Jake who went silent with disbelief. Even though he had spent his entire adult life in the intelligence field, even though he thought he knew well his own son . . . He struggled; Jake just could not reconcile this new reality with all he thought he believed. And Dolcetta, how would her heart, wounded as it was, ever be able to handle this?

Enrico reached around with his arm to console Jake. "I'm so sorry."

"What happened? You must tell me how it went down," asked Jake, half-afraid to hear the answer, yet desperate to know the full truth about his son.

Enrico nodded. His face was ashen. "Of course. Their *Don Giovanni* production was to open tonight. Yesterday, last night that is, was to be the final dress rehearsal. Hours earlier, around noon, Manny and I met together for the first time since we'd each arrived in Prague. We had drinks and lunch a few blocks from here at the Americky Bar. It was strictly social, just me and my godson, the opera singer. We had not briefed him on the particulars of the mission yet; that was to come later. Manny was again set to play the commendatore, while Terese was booked in the role of Dona Elvira and Kazys was to play Don Giovanni. Manny did not know we had confirmed his suspicions regarding his costars, nor had he previously met the 'bait' for our trap, Nadia Zoros, a young Bohemian Jew, who was to play Dona Anna. Nadia is one of our top counterintel field agents and a karate black belt to boot.

"The Americky, which is just a few blocks from the theater, has always been a popular meeting spot for artist, writers, and theater people. In recent months it had also become a hangout, a sort of informal headquarters for students and others opposed to the Czech Communist regime. This largely unorganized democracy movement had been hoping to push the government for months as it teetered on the edge of collapse—all part of the Glasnost phenomenon that had been building all summer.

"And by noon yesterday, the bar was packed and noisy. We had to shout to have even a simple conversation. Many of the performers from the opera company were there, all scattered at different tables and in their separate cliques. A particularly boisterous group of students, along with some of the members of the *Don Giovanni* cast and chorus, were crowded around a piano singing a wild proliferation of protest-type songs. They were led by our plant, Nadia Zoros. The tension in the bar was palpable as Nadia led the crowd in everything from John Lennon's 'Imagine,' to 'La Marseillaise.' They were countered and heckled by supporters of the regime so much so that it felt as if we were on the set of *Casablanca* watching the Nazis and the Free French rail at each other. At first the heckling was good-natured, but as the singers grew ever louder and more strident, the hecklers became increasingly disturbed and impatient with the protest group. The hardliners were there in force, as were the ubiquitous agents of the Czech secret police. But first and loudest among the hecklers was Kazys. He was seated a few tables away from our booth and he had been drinking heavily."

"Before a rehearsal? Not typical behavior for a baritone or a KGB assassin—if he was one," said Jake.

"True enough," said Enrico. "Though I said nothing to Manny, it had me wondering as well. On one hand, if he was in fact our Osmin, he'd certainly be more discreet and reserved. But anything is possible. These are indeed strange days, with the Soviet empire crumbling right before our eyes. And Kazys—who is not Russian but Lithuanian—might well have felt he was witnessing the end of his career as a deep cover KGB agent. I presumed nothing, but noted everything."

"Of course, but what about the other one, Therese Burauskaite"?

"Yes, also a Lithuanian national. She was there at another table with several members of the chorus, at least one of whom we already suspected was a Czech undercover police agent. They sat, ate, and drank as if nothing out of the ordinary was happening. Manny described them, 'as still as a pair of herons waiting for fish to spear.' Their very quietude made me suspicious.

"As the tension increased, Nadia Zoros called out to the room and said she would play something everyone could agree upon: 'Ma Vlast, My Homeland' by Smetana. It worked. As Nadia played the melody on the piano, everyone across all political stripes began to hum along. That seemed to calm things down. But just when you think the tension had dissipated, Nadia starts talking over her playing by telling a story. It's the tale of how her grandparents sang a song to this melody as they were marched to the death camps by the Nazis. She then segues into the 'Hatikvah,' the Israeli national anthem, which as you of all people know derives from the same melody."

> *As long as within our hearts*
> *The Jewish soul sings,*
> *As long as forward to the East*
> *To Zion, looks the eye—*
> *Our hope is not yet lost,*
> *It is two thousand years old,*
> *To be a free people in our land*
> *The land of Zion and Jerusalem.*

"Well, the 'Hatikvah' was too much for Kazys. He leapt up from his table and screamed at Nadia, 'You fucking Jewish bitch!' The bar went silent. Everyone froze. 'You cunt, you fucking cunt.' Kazys grabbed Nadia from behind and threw her backward to the floor, ripping her dress to shreds as if he was going to rape her right then and there. That was it for

Manny. Up in a flash before I could stop him, Manny spun Kazys around and decked him cold with a single knockout punch. Quickly, before anyone else—especially the secret police—could react, I hustled Manny out of there."

"You briefed him afterward?"

"I had no choice. That one punch threatened to upend our whole operation. But when I asked him why he took it upon himself to strike Kazys, your son had a very simple answer."

"Which was?" asked Jake.

" 'I had to do it. Never again is now.' " said Enrico, repeating Manny's words. " 'Or it's the Bishop Hudal all over again.' "

Jake understood his son's response all too well. Manny had grown up in the shadow of the Holocaust and had heard all the stories and all the nightmares firsthand from his parents. The slaughter of six million Jews was not merely an academic fact for Manny or any of the Coneglianos; it was personal. It was their family. And Manny, who had grown up with a partisan fighter for a mother and an intelligence agent for a father, was determined to confront anti-Semitism whenever and wherever it reared up. Never again would he allow this to happen.

Enrico continued, "Everyone in the opera world knew Manny was an Italian-American Jew. Manny claimed that if he had failed to confront Kazys that would have been ever more suspicious. He had to stand up."

"You continued with the mission?"

"Yes, but there was still a full dress rehearsal to perform that night, with Kazys, with Nadia, with Therese, and with all the rest of the cast, many of whom had been at the Americky Bar that afternoon."

"*Dio mio*," said Jake. "Madness, just madness."

"Yes, but the show must always go on, right? We had our team placed covertly in and around the Estates National

Theater before Manny and the other performers returned. As Manny's guest, I was seated up front in an otherwise nearly empty auditorium.

"The rehearsal began normally enough. First the orchestra performed the overture as vibrantly as if it was opening night. Then their Leporello, in full dress costume, sang his opening aria. His finish was the cue for Nadia as Dona Anna and Kazys as Don Giovanni to appear at the top of the palace staircase. They fought with each other just as Mozart and Da Ponte scripted. Initially the wrestling between Nadia and Kazys appeared as normal and typical opera actions. But soon Kazys' rage became obvious. His hitting and bashing of Nadia came with an intensity that clearly went beyond stage acting. In response Nadia reacted as if Kazys had in fact raped her. She used her fingernails to rip off Kazys' Don Giovanni mask with such force that she drew blood. And even as the orchestra played on, their singing reflected that violence. It was blood-curdling and violent:

Dona Anna/Nadia:
Unless you kill me,
Don't imagine that you'll escape!

Don Giovanni/Kazys:
Madwoman! Your shouts are in vain.
You'll never discover who I am!

Leporello, from off-stage:
Oh, God, what shouting,
My master's in trouble again!

Dona Anna/Nadia:
Help, servants!
Come and kill this traitor!

Don Giovanni/Kazys:
Shut up, you bitch,
And tremble at my feet!

Dona Anna/Nadia:
Help! Traitor!

Don Giovanni/Kazys:
> *You stupid bitch,*
> *You'll rue this day!*

Dona Anna/Nadia:
> *Help! I'll track you to your death!*

"As in the script," continued Enrico, "Manny entered in his role, her father, the commendatore. Nadia retreated to the wings of the stage. When Manny drew his sword—a fencing foil actually—to confront Don Giovanni, the hostility between the two men filled their respective lyrics with a rage that rang all too true."

Commendatore/Manny:
> *Leave her be, you bastard,*
> *Draw your sword and fight with me.*

Don Giovanni/Kazys:
> *Go away, old man,*
> *It's not my habit to kill fools.*

Commendatore/Manny:
> *Afraid of me?*
> *Is that your excuse to run away?*

"Kazys then drew his foil," said Enrico, "With a look of vengeance in his eyes. This was not acting."

Don Giovanni/Kazys:
> *Beware my anger, old man!*
> *Prepare to die.*

"The duel commenced in earnest as scripted," said Enrico. "As the two actors fought with their fencing foils, one of the orchestra's percussionists stood just behind the curtain, stage right, clanging together two real swords to enhance the sound effects of the battle. Therese, waiting for her eventual entrance as Dona Elvira, stood beside the percussionist.

"But the duel between Don Giovanni and the commendatore quickly turned into something else when Kazys whipped his foil across Manny's neck and drew real blood.

Manny, whose costume included thick gloves, stood there, stunned. He wiped his neck, but when he saw the blood on his gloves, he cursed under his breath at Kazys, 'You bastard.'

"Kazys then ripped the safety tip off the end of his foil and went at Manny in all seriousness. Manny fought back in a fury.

"Manny was by far the superior swordsman. He stayed on the offense and backed Kazys up, all the while shredding Kazys' clothes with his sword thrusts. Manny's goal was humiliation, not harm. Manny's strikes and parries were so powerful, he finally knocked Kazys' foil away. However, before Manny could bring his opponent to yield, Therese—still waiting in the wings—snatched one of the swords away from the unsuspecting percussionist and flipped it to Kazys.

"A foil was no match for a sword and so suddenly Manny was on the defensive. Kazys drove Manny back across the length of the stage."

Don Giovanni/Kazys:
> *You fucking Jew-bastard!*
> *You dare mess with me?*

"At this point the poor conductor finally realized that his actors were totally out of control. He stopped the music. The conductor called for order, but the duel, now a violent life-or-death clash, went on. Everyone in the cast and crew came out from the wings to watch what was going on. I too rose from my seat and made my way toward the stage.

"Kazys' repeated sword thrusts eventually snapped Manny's foil in two. With Manny now defenseless, Kazys plunged his sword into Manny's gut. But when Kazys pulled it out and tried to strike again, Manny twisted aside and grabbed the tip of Kazys' sword with his gloved right hand. He clamped his left hand on Kazys' right. Though bleeding from his wound, Manny used his superior strength to push the edge of the sword blade back toward Kazys' neck."

Commendatore/Manny:
> *You invited me to dine, Don Giovanni!*
> *Here I am!*

"Caught off guard by the strength of Manny's grip, Kazys desperately tried to wrestle free. Manny pushed harder and harder against his opponent, moving the blade ever closer to Kazys' exposed flesh."

Commendatore/Manny:
> *Yield!*

Don Giovanni/Kazys:
> *Never!*

"Kazys pushed back against Manny with all his strength, which was exactly what Manny was counting on. He had Kazys wound up as tightly as a coiled spring."

Commendatore/Manny:
> *Then you are doomed to hell.*

"And then, abruptly, Manny like a judo master, dropped backward to the stage and using Kazys' own force against him, he flipped the KGB agent over his head and into a 360-degree somersault. His move hurtled Kazys and his sword directly into the transformer box.

"The sword shorted out the junction box, which burst into flames. Kazys' screamed in terror as fifty thousand watts jolted his body. Yes, his soul was dragged down to the hell that bastard deserved. His screams were as bloodcurdling as anything I'd ever heard in the war. Plumes of fire flared all around his body. The stench of burnt flesh was unbearable. His corpse continued to throb wildly until the crew cut the main power, at which point his body fell backwards onto the stage.

"But then Therese grabbed the other sword and ran toward Manny. On pure instinct I walloped her across the face with the silver head of my cane. Therese crumpled like a sack of potatoes. Later, my agents snagged her before she could flee the theater. We disappeared her fast—all the way to an interrogation cell in London.

Just as that was happening, Manny sang out to me as he struggled to stand.

Commendatore/Manny:

Yes! Now must my soul take flight.

"Barely alive, Manny collapsed beside Kazys. My team ran Manny out of there and off to the hospital ER. Once he entered surgery, I called you."

When Jake, in New York, got that call about his son, he dropped everything and raced as fast as he could to the airport. On the limo ride over, he placed calls to his family, the first being Pandorea. He dialed her home number, but it was Yael who picked up first.

"Hey, Pops, how are you?" Yael's light and cheery voice, that of a prepubescent thirteen-year-old, was a stark contrast to Enrico's grave tone.

It caught Jake off guard. "You're home today, not in school?" Yael was enrolled at Potomac Prep, a private school in DC for gifted students who were expected to enter top academic colleges, two, or three years early.

"Did you forget? Thursday is independent study day. I've been working with Nonna on the diary translations," said Yael.

"That's your project?" Jake had in fact forgotten that Dolcetta's retirement work had been to forward her rough draft translations of the *Secret Diaries* to Yael so their brilliant grandson could polish them up. Jake himself had long stopped work on the translations. "Which section are you working on?"

"The last book, the one Great Grandpa Da Ponte called 'Prague.' Nonna and I did the chapter, 'Leopold the Second,' together but for my independent study project, I'm doing the entire translation of the next chapter, the one on 'The School for Lovers,' by myself, start to finish. Nonna sent me copies of the original pages. It's pretty cool."

"That's great," said Jake, barely able to focus on Yael's response to his question. "Is your mom at home? I need to speak with her."

"Yeah, sure Pops. She's outside in the garden."

Jake heard Yael place the phone down and call out the back door for Pandorea. When she picked up the receiver, Jake asked her to take the call in another room, away from Yael. Jake tried to be upbeat when telling her than Manny had been hospitalized after an injury at the theater, but trembling in his own voice betrayed him.

"How serious?" she demanded. "What happened?"

"I don't know. I am flying directly there immediately. He's in surgery, but Enrico is there watching over him," he added, but that bit of news set Pandorea off even more.

"Enrico? MI6? CIA? Then this is not an opera injury?"

"No. They caught Code Name Osmin, but Manny was wounded in the operation."

"Operation? What operation? He's a courier, for God's sake. Damn him." Pandorea was livid. That which she had feared most had come to pass. For over a decade she had been pleading with Manny to come out of the cold, and now this. Try as Jake might, nothing he said could calm her down. He let her rant and rage at him over the phone until she broke down in tears and could speak no more.

After that call, he placed one to Pandorea's mother, Marietta, who was still Dolcetta's cardiologist. Marietta, now semiretired herself, was at home on Long Island when Jake finally got through to her. After describing to her what little he knew of Manny's condition, Marietta understood exactly why he was calling and said as much.

"Don't worry, Jake," she said, "Give me about half an hour. I will . . . "

"She's at the beach house," interrupted Jake. Though Jake and Dolcetta still had the garden apartment in Queens, in recent years they spent more and more of their time at their beach house in Huntington overlooking Centerport Bay on Long Island's north shore.

"Then give me an hour—Ceneda Lane right off Washington Drive, right?" said Marietta. "I will drop by the house and pop in to see Dolcetta. If you give me that time, I'm certain to be there when you call and break the news to her. I can even stay the night."

Jake thanked her and hung up. Before dialing home to speak with Dolcetta, he waited several more hours until well after his British Diplomatic Corp jet leveled off on its direct flight to Prague. When he was finally certain that Marietta had indeed had more than enough time to get over to the beach house, he placed his call.

Dolcetta was her typically chatty self when she answered, filling him in on the local events of the day and how Marietta had just dropped by and how they were planning a walk on the beach to the lighthouse and how the two of them might catch a film in town after dinner at their favorite restaurant, the Moorings, and how, if Jake was home in time, they could pick him up at the train station and he could join them, and what time would he be home? Jake let her go on until she finished sharing all the news of her day. Only then did he finally tell Dolcetta that Manny was injured in Prague and still in surgery. At first, Dolcetta was more stoic than he had expected, but he could hear the distress in her voice even as she tried to remain brave.

"He's a soldier," she said. "He knew the risks," and then Jake heard her collapse in tears as the phone fell and bounced on the floor.

Jake waited. He could hear Dolcetta wailing and Marietta talking but the words and sounds were indistinguishable.

Finally, Marietta picked up the phone. "You still there, Jake?"

"Yes."

"I gave her a shot, a sedative," said Marietta. "You go take care of Manny. Don't worry about Dolcetta. We'll get her through this. And I'll stay here with her as long as necessary."

All through the balance of the flight nothing calmed or reassured Jake. He thought of Manny in surgery, of Dolcetta sedated, of Pandorea in rage, and of Yael in blissful ignorance. He tried to distract himself by reading, but when that didn't work, he tried to sleep but found it near impossible. He tossed miserably in his seat until it was time to buckle back up for their landing. Although it was just past midnight at home in New York, it was dawn, local time, in Prague when Enrico met him outside customs. Jake was a self-proclaimed basket case. A British embassy limo raced them back into town.

Their first stop was the hospital. Manny had been in surgery for over nine hours and was still in critical condition. That sword thrust had damaged multiple organs and he had lost a lot of blood. The surgeons monitoring Manny's condition kept him in intensive care. At best Manny was still touch and go. If necessary, they were prepared to rush him back into the OR.

Enrico and Jake paced and fretted for over an hour before the surgeons would allow Jake to see Manny and then only for a minute. When at last Jake entered, he saw his son's pale and bandaged body hooked up to an array of monitors, oxygen, and multiple drip lines. Manny was barely conscious. His eyes were dim and glossy but they lit up when he saw Jake. He wanted to speak. Jake leaned in.

"I got him," Manny whispered. "I killed the Abbé Hudal."

Chapter Twenty:
The School for Lovers

Tuesday, October 28, 1788
Café Venezia

Mozart loved Prague and the people of Prague adored Mozart, but Constanze, seven months into a difficult pregnancy, was never comfortable there. And after suspecting that Mozart had perhaps engaged in something more than merely flirting with their hostess, Madame Josepha Duschek, Constanze wisely insisted she and Mozart return home to Vienna.

Given my own predilections, I never pass judgment on the infidelity of others. Still, I too had my suspicions about Mozart and Josepha. Why? I knew only too well my friend's amorous nature. Mozart had an uncanny knack for detecting in females that which most men could not: a woman's hidden, repressed, or camouflaged hungers *d'amore* that verily begged to be satiated. It was for that reason I acknowledged previously that Mozart and not Casanova was the man who inspired my characterization of *Don Giovanni*.

Yes, Josepha was the kind of woman of beauty and grace that Mozart often fancied. Not only was she effortlessly charming and witty, Josepha was a talented singer and the doyenne of all things musical in Prague. All it took was a single glance at Franz Duschek, the awkward and fumbling composer she was married to, a man twenty-five years her senior, to know he lacked the finesse and necessary skills to please a young lover. And Josepha? Did she live among us as a saint? Or was she made of bone, flesh, and skin and therefore, a flirt? Who can say?

I must confess that during my brief stay in Prague, I neither saw nor heard the slightest evidence that would have confirmed Constanze's suspicions.

More important, however, than Mozart's romantic affairs—or mine—was the shadow cast over our lives by the Hapsburg monarchy. Yes, much had happened since the premiere of *Don Giovanni* in Prague, some good, some bad, and some simply devastating. I recount them all in these diaries so the reader can understand not only the immense pressures we endured, but how we struggled to bear up under them.

First, I would happily recall those bits of good news that brightened our winter. After word of *Don Giovanni*'s success in Prague had reached Joseph II, the emperor rewarded both of us. His Majesty presented me with a handsome stipend, more gold coinage to add to my ever growing coffers. Those extra funds inspired me to rent a new and far more fashionable apartment on *Heidenschuss* just off the *Graben* in the very heart of Vienna. And it was there I was at last able to entertain Adriana Ferrarese del Bene far more discreetly and in an elevated style not only befitting my diva but my own aspirations as well. Preserving the secrecy of our trysts was ever more critical whenever her unsuspecting husband, Luigi, was in town. Quite annoyingly, this had become so much more often.

And to Mozart, Joseph II awarded my friend something he had long sought, a title as the official court chamber musician. This post included a small but stable annual salary that enabled Mozart to obtain a new apartment back inside the city walls. One needs to understand that Mozart's profligate spending on clothes, servants, wine, parties, and gambling often outstripped his not insignificant income. Regularly running up huge debts, Mozart was forced to move frequently during his family's sojourn in Vienna. In good years, he was able to rent prestigious quarters, such as their lodgings on *Domgasse* where we had worked together on *The Marriage of Figaro* and *Don Giovanni*. But in the bad times, when those debts outraced his earnings, Mozart and Constanze would suffer the humiliation of taking lodgings beyond the city gates. The outer suburbs were judged places no self-respecting member of court would ever countenance.

Following Mozart's investiture at the palace, Joseph II then made what we thought of at the time as his most significant gesture of respect and benevolence: our music-loving emperor ordered that Orsini slot our *Don Giovanni* into the Hofburg Theater so that it would open the spring opera season. Though Orsini was none too thrilled to book another opera written by that "Jewish priest," as he had begun to call me, our outlook heading into the new year of 1788 could hardly have been better.

Finally, the last bit of good news that showered down upon the Mozart family arrived on the 27th of December. Constanze gave birth to their first daughter, Theresia Constanzia Adelheid Friedericke Maria Anna Mozart. It was a Christmas present of unsurpassed joy for Mozart's household, and it was one that all of his friends joined in celebrating. Many a bottle of wine, prosecco, and spirits—some might say too many—were hoisted and emptied in honor of the young child.

But then as the calendar carried us into the New Year, our tides of good fortune began their ebb away from us. Regrettably, Joseph II and his brother, Leopold II, had entered into a military alliance with Russia. That treaty in turn had led to war on the eastern front of the empire with the Ottoman Turks. Although Mozart and I were the type of artists who by necessity had scrupulously avoided politics, politics did not avoid us. Only days before the premiere of *Don Giovanni*, Joseph II, already ailing and in ill health from a bout of malaria, was called away to war.

In his absence, we had no protection from the Italian cabal that controlled the theater. On May 7, 1788, *Don Giovanni* opened in Vienna. Despite our opera's overwhelming success in Prague, the reception at the Burgtheater by the aristocratic audience we had expected to come and come again, was at best lukewarm. After a handful of performances, we were done.

That was May. June began with even more despair. Mozart's daughter died of a sudden fever. Tragically, her name—Theresia Constanzia Adelheid Friedericke Maria Anna Mozart—proved to be longer than her life. Mozart and Constanze were devastated. No parent is ever prepared to witness the burial of a child, particularly one they treasured and loved so dearly. It had been Constanze's fourth pregnancy in five years, with only one son, Karl Thomas, surviving.

There was a simple funeral held for the child a short coach ride away at the St. Marx's Cemetery in Währing northwest of the city. A small number of Mozart's friends and family attended. I recall seeing Constanze's mother, Cäcilia; two of her sisters, Sophie and Aloysia; as well as Mozart's assistant, Franz Süssmayr. Salieri, along with Caterina Cavalieri and our mutual friend, the poet Caterino Mazzolà, represented the court opera company. Our proprietress of the Café Venezia, Celestina Nancy Grahl, was among those attending, as was a new acquittance, the actor and impresario Emanuel Schikaneder, who had only the month before opened the *Theater-an-der Wein*, a new performance house just outside the city walls. *Il mio amante*, Adriana Ferrarese del Bene was there too, but she was accompanied by her now seemingly omnipresent husband, Luigi. Needless to say, I kept my distance from them.

After the presiding priest from the local parish finished his prayers, two cemetery laborers began to lower the tiny wooden box containing the child's body. I looked across the open pit at Constanze, Mozart, and young Karl Thomas and saw the absolute total anguish upon their faces. My poor, poor friends . . .

Suddenly and most unexpectedly a wave of grief and despair swept over me. Tears streamed down my face like the rivers of Babylon. Dizzy and lightheaded, I feared falling into the grave and so quickly turned away from the other mourners. And then I ran. I ran away as fast as my feet could carry me. I ran past row upon row of headstones and tombs, until at last I came to a low stone wall that blocked my path. Exhausted and unable to go further, I sat upon the wall, which separated the Catholic cemetery from a Hebrew one on the other side, and tried to calm myself. What had happened to me? I tried to understand why my sense of desolation was so, so overwhelming. Why, why, why? I kept asking myself. The child, I barely knew the child in that box.

No, death was not uncommon among those so very young and frail. As a priest in Venice, I had officiated at many such a funeral for an infant. Why was this different? Why was I gasping and full of such fright and tears? As I struggled to understand, to make sense of my grief, I saw imagines of my own mother, whom we buried when I was but ten at the cemetery at the end of the *Via Giudecca*. And then I saw in my mind's eye a vision of what I imagined was Zina's tombstone. Standing beside the open pit that held Zina's coffin was Celestina; my daughter, Barbarina, whom I had only met that once; and my son, Israeli, whom I had never met. In my vision I saw our cousin and my two grown children each toss a handful of dirt onto their mother's grave.

And when my heart witnessed that sight, I completely broke down in the most anguished shower of tears and sobbing and wailing. Never in my life had I ever experienced such pain, such grief, such a sense of total despair and desolation, not even in the ghastly tombs beneath Baron Wetzlar's palace. It was not Mozart's child whom I mourned but rather the loss and absence of every one in my life I had truly loved. Yes, in all this world, for all my growing fame and success, I was alone, truly and despairingly alone and inconsolable.

How long I sat there on that stone wall, I do not know. That journey into the darkness of my own soul was only interrupted at last when I heard a woman's voice. One with a Veneto accent, calling to me ever so gently. I opened my eyes. Before me stood Celestina Grahl in a black mourning jacket and gown. Was it another vision? I rubbed my eyes. Yes, she was there, really there.

Celestina reached out toward me, a smile of compassion upon her young face. "Come, Lorenzo, come, take my hand," she said. "Let us leave the dead to sleep."

Accepting her hand in my own, I pressed it against my forehead, hoping the warmth of a woman's flesh would soothe my anguish. Then, in a voice barely above a whisper, for that was all I could muster, I said, "*Grazie, grazie amica mia.*"

"*Prego*, Lorenzo." Celestina pulled her hand back and pointed to the far side of the wall and asked, "What is this place?"

"The border between our past and the present," I said, turning to look with her.

"Those are Jews," she said, surprised.

"Yes, they are."

Inside the Jewish Cemetery of Vienna, known as the *Israelitische Kultusgemeinde Wein*, there was another group of mourners around another grave site. Above the sound of the wind blowing through the oaks, we both heard the distinct sound of a prayer, the "Yizkor," the Jewish blessing for the dead being intoned by a rabbi in Hebrew. "The human soul is a light from God. May it be your will that the soul of Emanuele enjoys eternal life, along with the souls of Abraham, Isaac, and Jacob, Sarah, Rebecca, Rachel, and Leah, and the rest of the righteous that are in Gan Eden. Amen."

We both listened, heads bowed and silent, until the rabbi finished.

"I miss the sound of Hebrew," said Celestina. There was a wistful yet distant tone buried in her words. "I miss the melody of my mother's voice singing her prayers on a Friday night as she would light the Sabbath candles. I miss *la mia famiglia.*"

"*Anch'io,*" I said. "*Anch'io.*" For in truth I knew who I was: a Jew from Ceneda, one who survived and perhaps even prospered by masquerading all these years as a priest. I was no more a Catholic than the rabbi who had chanted the "Yizkor."

Celestina offered up her hand to me again, "Come, Lorenzo, come, *mio cugino.* You, you are my family."

"Si, grazie," I replied as I again took the hand of this young woman whose jet black hair and dark eyes clearly marked her as a fellow member of our tribe, the descendants of Abraham and Isaac. "Yes, you're right, *mia cugina.* It is time for us both to find our way home and leave these dead to sleep."

Not long after the funeral Constanze and her son returned to the spas at Baden. There she would take the cures to console herself yet again from the grief she had suffered. My poor friend Mozart, left alone to mourn in Vienna, took to drinking, gambling, and flirting with the wrong sort of women. Understand that our social world in Vienna was at its core, no different than a small town. If Mozart did not know what he was doing, everyone else did—a situation that was often the root cause of his troubles. As for myself, I saw little of him over those weeks as I was once more fully engaged in writing libretti for several other composers of note in town, but the gossip, stories, about Mozart? I ignored them as best I could.

In August came the ever more devasting news about the costs of war. The battle against the Turks was indeed a substantial drain on the finances of the Hapsburg's empire. Through his chamberlain, Count Orsini, Joseph II announced that as a necessary cost-cutting measure, the Burgtheater would be shuttered and our Italian Opera Company would be disbanded at the end of the year.

My first response to this impending disaster that threatened to undercut my entire life and livelihood was to surrender the apartment on *Heidenschuss* and return to my humble room at Kartnerstrasse siebzehn. Adriana was none too pleased with my relocation back to our same building. Her husband was now at their apartment on Kartnerstrasse more or less permanently, as his business interests in Milano had shriveled up. Concurrently his return to Vienna had the same impact upon our assignations.

As I squirreled away in my hovel contemplating my future—if I indeed had one—it became ever clearer that sooner or later my affair with La Ferrarese would also reach its finale. Though I was not prepared to give her up just yet, change was definitely coming with the winds of autumn that had begun to swirl through the city. Was it the sound of London beckoning me to her opera theaters?

It had been a tough season for Mozart as well. When we finally sat down together at our table by the window at Café Venezia, the strain of it all showed on his face. It had been a year since *Don Giovanni*'s premiere in Prague. If the past had not proved taxing enough, the pending demise of the opera business in Vienna was a precipice neither one of us wanted to fall off.

"London, London is calling us," were also the first words out of Mozart's mouth. "We need to relocate to London."

I did not disagree. "That would be my plan as well."

Celestina, who was serving a group of well-coiffed society ladies at the table adjacent to us, could not help but overhear.

She turned to us and asked with a derisive tone to her voice, "London? You two? Why would you ever want to live there? My father, John Grahl, who's been to England on many a trip, says it's cold all year with a chill that never leaves your bones. In winter, he says, it's the fog that seeps into your skin, carrying with it the black dust of coal fires. And in the summer, whenever it rains, that dust turns to a muddy paste that stains your clothes and fills your lungs. The sun never visits the city and the food, well, it's inedible. And their wine, if you can find any, is an undrinkable swill. Why Herr Grahl even declared in one of his letters to my mother and me that English cuisine *e' un ossimoro*, an oxymoron, especially if you compare it to Venice, Vienna, or Prague. If you move there, you'll both starve to death."

"I was there as a child," said Mozart. "It's not all that grim."

"And we'll starve if we stay here," I said. "No music, no opera, no bread,"

"What are you talking about?" she asked.

"You are aware the emperor has ordered the theaters to close down before the new year?" I asked her.

"*Certamente!*" replied Celestina. "In my little café I hear everyone and everything. There's not a bit of gossip I haven't heard before it's pronounced and published as news by the press." All of that was probably true, as in a mere two years, my entrepreneurial friend had transformed the Café Venezia into the one eatery where all the *beau monde* of Vienna loved to congregate.

"Consider Michael Kelly and Nancy Storace," said Mozart, "Ever since they returned to London, both are doing quite well for themselves. The theaters are open year-round, there's lots of work for librettists and ample opportunities for composers."

"And none of them are dependent upon the whims of an emperor," I added. "English theaters are not run by the king or by the court; they're controlled by businessmen who know how to turn a profit."

"And Kelly claims their opera houses are always full," said Mozart. "Everyone attends, not just lords and ladies, but merchants and laborers as well, and yes, even the little people of London line up to buy tickets."

"Ah, but you two, you'd have to wrestle your way in, start all over. You're both too old to do that."

"Our friends there will help," said Mozart.

"Your friends?" laughed Celestina. "In Vienna those actors were your friends only because they needed you. In London, pfft! You'll be groveling. Why leave Vienna, when everything you need already exists right here?"

"Here? Vienna? After Christmas there is no 'here,' here anymore," insisted Mozart. "Joseph II's proclamation is our death sentence. He might just as well have us hung on the gallows."

"Wait," I said to Mozart. "Celestina may be on to something. What are you talking about when you say everything we need is already in place?"

"Of course, it is. You two are just so shortsighted, you cannot see the grand view. Look around and count your blessings; the Burgtheater, the actors, your singers, the stage hands, your impresarios, they're all here. What you lack is investors—and even they already exist in spades."

"What are you saying? Tell me more," I insisted, for truly I could sense that Celestina was on to something.

"*Ascoltami*," she said. "Listen to me. When I bought the old Café Bruno, it was with the money you both gave me. You were my patrons. Your kindness enabled me to take the old bones that were here and rebuild something new and fresh, a place everyone in Vienna wants to come to, to see and be seen, to drink and dine on meals so divine the gods are jealous."

"And so, you are suggesting what precisely?" Mozart asked, ever more curious as I was to know where Celestina was heading with her arguments.

"Why go to London, when you can bring the London business model here." She laughed at us. "Investors? You need capital, right? Look around. Your patrons, the ones that fill the boxes at the Burg, they're right here in my café. Every day, every night. If Joseph II closes the theaters for austerity's sake, where will these lords and ladies go to promenade? To the *Naschmarkt*? The Prater? Heiligenstadt? No, no, and no again. The emperor may turn his back on gaiety but *la haute société*? No never. If you offer up great opera on a grand stage, the Viennese will all be there."

"A business? That's it," I declared. "*Dio mio. Sei un genio*, Celestina. Bring us your finest bottle of prosecco and three glasses. We celebrate. Together. I have a plan."

A few weeks later when Joseph II returned briefly from the front, Mozart and I arranged for a private audience with him inside the Hofburg Palace.

"London? You would abandon me for London?" asked Joseph II. The emperor was not only incredulous, it was one of the few times I had seen him verge on anger in our presence.

"With all respect, Your Majesty," I began tentatively, "is it not Your Royal Highness that is abandoning us, your most loyal servants, by shuttering the opera house?"

"My friends, I cannot sustain the opera company during a war," said Joseph II. "Are you aware the wages of three divas alone cost as much as a hundred grenadiers and I dare say the grenadiers give better service. Have you no concept of how expensive it is to battle the Turks?"

"Certainly, we do, Your Majesty," Mozart replied. "But we too must provision our families. If not, we shall die as surely as if we had been further casualties of this Turkish War."

"And it is not only for our sakes," I added. "When we consider all of the hundreds of artists, singers, laborers, musicians, and craftsmen employed, why just imagine the ruin that will rain down upon their people as well."

But Joseph II cut us both off with a wave of his hand. He was clearly annoyed at being forced to confront the wreckage his closing of the opera house would create. "Gentlemen," said Joseph II, "I am truly sorry. You two know more than most the esteem I hold for my musicians, but I simply cannot throw kreutzers at singers to the detriment of my troops."

"But Your Majesty, just as much as if we had been refugees escaping the dogs of war, everyone associated with the opera company will be forced to flee Vienna. Everyone will scatter to Venice, Prague or London, unless . . . "

Joseph II cut me off again, which was my plan. "Unless what?"

"Unless this. We can save the opera if we take the financial burden out of your hands and turn it into a privately administered business."

"A business?" he asked.

"Yes, a business," echoed Mozart.

"All we need to ensure its success, is for you to gift us the use of the Burgtheater," I said.

"How so?"

I began to explain. "Everyone who is anyone in Vienna considers a box at the Hofburg Theater a social necessity. The woman, whose family owned the Teatro San Benedetto in Venice, confided to me once that opera was commerce disguised as spectacle. She did not mean the play upon the stage. It was rather more about those affairs in the boxes that fascinated her far more. Who was there, who was wearing what, who was with whom, who was sleeping with whom, and what deals, exchanges, and other transactions that could be negotiated. Yes, it was for her an entirely commercial venture, one that on the surface seemed to be all about the stage, but in her reality, it was the jewels, the champagne, the card playing, the gambling, and the assignations that mattered. Where else, she insisted, could our noble aristocrats, our foreign ambassadors and dignitaries, and the ever-growing number of wealthy, aspiring bankers, and merchants show off their rank, their riches, and parade their women? Yes, let us not forget those women of Vienna, those feather-plumed fowls who are the true arbiters of society. As much as Viennese culture needs a venue to thrive, that venue must be the opera house."

"Well, Da Ponte, all that may be true, but the expenses are enormous. Have you any idea of what it costs the crown?"

"Indeed, I do, Your Majesty. Look here."

I pulled three sheets of paper out from my satchel upon which I had composed a battle plan of our own. Yes, before Mozart and I had walked into the emperor's chambers, we had done our homework. On the first page I gave an exact accounting of all the costs to operate a full years' worth of opera performances. On the second page, I detailed precisely how those costs could easily be covered by a subscription campaign that sold in advance the rights to all of the Burgtheater's premier seats and private boxes. On the last page I had a list of all the patrons—the *crème de la crème* of Viennese society—who had committed to buying those seats along with the names of several bankers, including our friend, Baron Wetzlar, who would control the finances.

Joseph II examined the papers with great care. "Fascinating, absolutely fascinating and brilliant. Signor Da Ponte, you never cease to astonish. What more do you require from me?"

I pulled out a fourth document. "Your royal signature and seal granting me the use and full control of the Burgtheater on behalf of the Italian Opera Company."

"And Count Orsini, what is his role in your scheme?"

"None, Your Majesty. Your royal chamberlain would be liberated from his labors at the Burgtheater. And without the distraction of those despairing divas and temperamental tenors we all know that he hates, Count Orsini would be free to serve Your Highness ever so much more effortlessly elsewhere," I replied.

"Excellent, indeed excellent. Consider it done," he said, then asking, "But confess to me first, who was it that tried to lure you to London? Certainly not Michael Kelly. It had to be a woman. Storace?"

Mozart shrugged. "Storace?"

"I do miss her . . . her voice," said Joseph II, "But if you had gone to London, that little coquette would have betrayed you as well, Mozart, mark my words."

"Your Majesty?" I exclaimed loudly to deflect Joseph II's attention from my partner, less the emperor change his mind about signing our agreement.

"A faithful woman has never existed and never will," said Joseph II. "And if either of you expected Storace . . . Well, how delightfully naïve. I'd not expect that of two such gentlemen as you."

"You speak to the converted, Your Majesty," I replied. "One might as well try to catch the wind in a net than trust the fidelity of a woman."

"Good, excellent," said the emperor as he put signature and seal to our contract. "And will you gentleman now compose a new opera for our theater?

"Our search for suitable material never ceases, Your Majesty," I said.

"What shall it be? Another *dramma giocoso*?" asked Joseph II, "I understand your disappointment with the reception for *Don Giovanni*, but the opera was divine. Possibly, just possibly even more beautiful than *Figaro*. But such music is not meat for the teeth of my Viennese."

"Give them time to chew on it," said Mozart. "They'll come around."

"Perhaps. Well then, hear me," said Joseph II. "Let me share a notion I've long had, one inspired equally by Storace's affairs and Metastasio's tale, 'The Lovers' Descent.' You do know it? The one where a brash young man tempts the fidelity of his best friend's wife and is in turn cuckolded?"

"Assolutamente," I said.

"Infidelity?" asked Mozart. "You'd like an opera about the infidelity of women?"

"Yes, of course. One where their fidelity is tested," replied Joseph II. "There's your conflict. Right there."

"*È possible*," I replied.

"Signor Da Ponte, aren't you the one that told me every good comedy needs conflict to make the plot succeed?"

"Yes, indeed, Your Majesty."

"So, aren't they all?"

"All what?" I asked, though I knew full well His Majesty's intent.

"Wanton, unfaithful," he declared. "Storace, Caterina Cavalieri, and that hot-tempered soprano you admire, Adriana Ferrarese del Bene. Of course, they are. Why even your Dr. Bartolo in *Figaro* said it aloud, 'Cosi fan tutte,' thus all women are."

"Unfaithful?" Mozart bowed graciously before Joseph II with an exaggerated sweeping gesture, "And if that is Your Majesty's wish, thus it shall be."

I nodded agreement, "Yes, an opera wherein the fidelity of women is tested. A comedy."

"*Wunderbar*," said Joseph II. "And if the libretto pleases, I may yet design to be your patron. No war lasts forever."

Mozart and I smiled at each other before thanking the emperor. And in that moment of sweet, hard-earned victory came the spark that transformed Dr. Bartolo's throwaway line from our *Marriage of Figaro* into our next collaboration.

When I returned alone to Kartnerstrasse siebzehn, I stopped at the Café Venezia to seek out Celestina. I found her working on her accounts in the back of the kitchen in a small space that served as her office and bedroom. She looked up, surprised to see me.

"Da Ponte? *Che cosa?*"

"Thank you," I said.

"For what?"

"I just came from the Hofburg. The emperor loved your idea."

"I don't understand. My idea?"

"Yes, of course, turning the Italian Opera Company into a business. You saved my life, my career. It was a touch of brilliance."

"Oh," she seemed surprised. "You, you and Mozart once saved mine. Twice actually," she added, waving her hands about to indicate that she meant the money for the restaurant. "I was just returning the favor and showing kindness as my two best customers taught me."

"Would you then allow me to express my gratitude by taking you out for the finest dinner and champagne to be had in all Vienna at *Zu Den Drei Hakken?*"

"*Assolutamente, mio cugino*," she replied as she stood up and brushed her fingers through her hair. "But no desserts afterward, Lorenzo, I am not going to sleep with you."

I nodded. And off we went. Yes, there was a lot to admire about Celestina Nancy Grahl.

Chapter Twenty-One:
La via della Giudecca

Saturday Morning, January 27, 1996
Casa della Luna, Ceneda, Italy

Mozart, yes, Mozart, for seven years, the very mention of Mozart had meant misery for Yael Conegliano. Same for Da Ponte and the diaries. Yes, ever since his father had died performing *Don Giovanni* in Prague, Yael's mother, Pandorea, had banished the mere mention of either Da Ponte's or Mozart's names from their lives. Seven years. Seven years of his mother's rage. What had been love, became hate; what had been joy, became sorrow; what had been the story of his family, became a reoccurring nightmare of despair.

That Yael Conegliano's life was intricately linked to both of these men had become ever more challenging and problematic. That was his first thought in the morning when he woke up alone after his first night at Casa della Luna, a B&B just outside the old Ceneda ghetto, and heard the cathedral bells calling out the hours. He counted the chimes, wondering all the while, why was it he had agreed to come here on this, his twentieth birthday? *Uno, due, tre, quattro, cinque, sei, sette, otto.* Eight o'clock. Still early. He'd rather be asleep, tired as he was from yesterday's drive all the way up from Ferrara on local roads that were buried in a dense fog. Why was he here? Yes, Pops, his grandfather Jake, had asked Yael to meet them here, but Yael was not sure why he agreed. He could have said no, but he didn't.

Yes, he was Da Ponte's seventh-generation descendent. Yes, he shared the same birthday—today—as Mozart. Yes, he was born during a performance of their *Don Giovanni*, but no, damn it, his father died performing that same opera. And Manny's death and his mother's anger over it, when Yael was just thirteen, forever altered his life.

At his dad's funeral at the Hebrew Cemetery in Queens, New York, Pandorea had announced to the family—no, "announced," was too soft a term—she declared in no uncertain terms that she was done with anyone and everyone who lived a life so covert that they could not speak about what they did at work at a family dinner. She was done with spies, done with the CIA, done with Washington, done with her in-laws, done with the diaries, and done with anyone who had worked in the intelligence field, including Manny's godparents, Greta and Enrico. Yes, done, finished, *finito*. She had quit her job at the Library of Congress and was moving to California, specifically to her friend Mia Brancato's family ranch in Ojai, and taking Yael with her.

In a matter of weeks, Yael's entire life abruptly changed. In the middle of his school year, Yael was ripped apart from his friends, family, and everything he knew and plopped down into a guest house in the middle of an orange orchard on Ojai's east end. Mozart and Da Ponte were not welcomed, neither was their music. Nor were Papageno and Papagena, his pet parrots, nor his *Magic Flute* puppets, nor the *Secret Diaries*.

"Channel your energies elsewhere," demanded his mother. Yes, Pandorea was in full retreat in this small town known for little more than being a haven for spiritualists, farmers, private schools, rustic country living, and bored teenagers. Though Manny's life insurance and pension set her up for life, Pandorea took on two part-time school librarian jobs. The first was at Ojai's Aldous Huxley Academy, a prep school for talented and gifted students, and the second was down the road and up the coast at Montecito University. Pandorea enrolled Yael at Huxley and when he graduated high school at sixteen, he went on for a combined bachelor's and master's degree at Montecito.

Yael may have been gifted but he was also indifferent. The circumstances of his father's death had robbed him of all which he had loved: his grandparents, his music, opera, his family heritage, and his translation work on the diaries. He cruised through Huxley and aced his college classes, but with a minimum of interest and effort. When not in classes, he busied himself on the Brancato family ranch picking oranges and working as a busboy, waiter, and cook at the family restaurant with the same name on the eastern edge of town.

He dated occasionally, but never seriously. Though many a young woman was attracted to this handsome, talented young man, his mother's persistent rage scared him off having any significant relationships. Yael drifted from one affair to another, never really caring what the outcome would be. For the most part, he remained isolated and alone.

His saw his grandparents only rarely, especially as Pandorea would never even make the least effort to welcome her in-laws when they were there. Add to that, Nonna Dolcetta was in poor health, and Pops was reluctant to come alone.

When Yael finally graduated Montecito, magna cum laude, in May of 1995, he was lost and without a clue as to what to do next in his life. Nor did he care. His professors encouraged him to go for a doctorate, but no, nothing felt important or worth the effort. Sensing his ennui, his other grandparents, Marietta and Frank Cornetti, suggested he join them for the summer at their cottage at Capo San Marco outside Sciacca in Sicily, which he did.

He spent July and August with them, touring bits and pieces of the island in their old Fiat Tempra wagon—Cefalu, Enna, and Erice and the Greek ruins at Selinunte, Agrigento, and Segesta—but mostly he walked the beaches and spent time collecting sea glass. When his grandparents asked why sea glass, he would answer simply, "Because it is meaningless."

When Marietta and Frank returned to the States in September, they let Yael stay on at the cottage in the hope that perhaps with time alone, he'd find himself. Yael worked occasionally at a local pizza joint as a bartender and again dated sporadically, but not really caring who he saw, what their names were, or for how long they stayed together.

And then the letter from Pops came, the one asking Yael to join them in Ceneda for a special ceremony on his birthday in January. He couldn't decide if it was worth the effort. More out of boredom than anything else, he flipped a coin, an old Roman one he had found along the beach that depicted the Emperor Titus, the Roman ruler who besieged Jerusalem and later built the Coliseum. The coin was probably worth a fortune, but Yael didn't care. Flipping it relieved the pressure of thinking about or justifying his choices for the day, an exercise he somewhat sarcastically began to call, "The Mercy of Titus." The coin toss came up heads and so Yael said yes. He committed to celebrating his twentieth birthday in Ceneda, the village where his ancestor, Lorenzo Da Ponte, was born.

At first, Yael could not even find Ceneda on the map until he remembered that the name had been changed to Vittorio Veneto. No one in his family had had the courage to ever go back and face the nightmares of the Holocaust in

Ceneda since Nonna Dolcetta had left fifty years earlier. Why now, he wondered?

Nonetheless, after New Year's Eve, he locked up the cottage and headed out in the Fiat. He had three weeks to reach Ceneda, but unable to decide which route to take, he consulted Titus. Tails; he started with the longer southern route across Sicily.

At the end of his first day's drive he found himself in Siracusa at a small hotel, *La Via della Giudecca* in Ortygia, the old part of the city. The hotel took its name from the street it sat upon. How ironic, Yael thought as he checked in, to be staying at the "Street of the Jews," when he was probably the only one within a hundred miles. Yes, in this regard, the Nazis had succeeded. Their destruction of Hebrew communities all across Europe, had indeed left them *Judenfrei*.

Yael rested up in Siracusa for a few days and though he wandered aimlessly and without intention, he did manage to find the apartment where his Cornetti grandparents had lived before the war. It was now a popular puppet theater that used nearly life-sized marionettes. He considered attending a performance, but when he discovered that the next show was *The Magic Flute*, the prospect was too painful. He turned away and left.

The theater was just off the *Piazza del Duomo*, the site of a Roman Catholic cathedral that had been built into the very walls and pillars of a Greek temple, and that fascinated him. Although Yael defined himself as a totally secular Jew, he found himself drawn inside the apse, if only to witness the spot where for three thousand years people had continuously come to celebrate their spirituality.

But this awakening inside of him did not last long. Reverting back to a state of indifference, he found a café that night, wherein he found *una ragazza*. Together they found a bottle of Nero d'Avola and ultimately, of course, they found his bed at *La Via della Giudecca*.

In the morning while the young lady was washing up in the restroom, Yael once again, flipped the Titus coin. Heads and he'd stay on; tails, he'd leave. It came up tails.

He kissed *la ragazza* goodbye and later that day, he caught the auto ferry out of Messina for the mainland. Each morning he followed a similar pattern: heads or tails, this way or that. Such was his ambivalence about his journey that he relied upon "The Mercy of Titus" to make his decisions. Regardless, he steadily moved northward, wandering, drinking, eating, and philandering. He passed through the countryside of the Italian boot, then Naples, then Rome.

Yael saw the Coliseum through his rearview mirror, remembering from his history courses that it was indeed the Emperor Titus who ordered it constructed by Jewish slaves captured after the fall of the Second Temple—no doubt, including our *famiglia*. While leading the Roman armies in Judea, Titus had taken a lover, the Jewish Queen Berenice. But when Titus sought to bring Berenice to Rome and make her empress, he was opposed by conservative forces in the Senate. How different the history of the world might have been, Yael wondered, had a Jew become a coregent of Rome? And if Titus had stood up to the Senate, would there have been two thousand years of anti-Semitism?

North out of Rome, he zigzagged off the Autostrada and through the Apennines, grateful for the four-wheel drive Fiat wagon that allowed him to climb the frequently snow-covered mountain roads. Yael stayed in small *pensiones* and *agriturismos* and flirted with whatever women he met: young ones, old ones, country girls, city girls, blonds, and brunettes, falling in love every other day before moving on. He'd drink Brunello in Montalcino and devour pasta in Perugia, and then charm a local *ragazza* or two to keep him warm for the night. None of it mattered.

He headed through Arezzo and Firenze, and on through Bologna, seeing the sites, sleeping with women, but more often than not, nothing felt real. Nothing, that is, until "The Mercy of Titus," led him to Ferrara. He found a hotel in what a guidebook called the "hip" section of town, just east of the *Cattedrale di Ferrara*. The hotel, he quickly discovered was in fact inside the former ghetto. "Of course," he thought. "Where else would Titus have me land?"

When he headed out for his evening's adventures, he passed the city's last surviving *Tempio ebraico*. On the outer wall was a memorial plaque in honor of the members of the congregation—one hundred in all—who had been murdered in the Holocaust. He had seen similar memorials in the former Jewish ghettos of Cefalu, Siracusa, and Firenze, usually on streets called the *Via Giudecca*, or the more formal, *La via della Giudecca*, but thought nothing of it. But this was different. For the first time, it felt personal. Why?

Near the top of the list were two Coneglianos, Bruno and Giulio, whose names were chiseled into the stone. He didn't know who they were, but it had been a mantra of Nonna Dolcetta when he was growing up, that if you meet a Conegliano, treat them as family—they probably are. Yael also recalled from reading in the *Secret Diaries* that his ancestors, Barbarina and her husband Marco, a Conegliano, had moved from Ceneda to Ferrara and had a son named Giulio as well. He tried to imagine how Bruno and this Giulio had died in Hitler's "Final Solution." An image of the two men being led to the gas chambers, flared up in his mind's eye. They were naked, stripped bare, as they were shoved forward by their Nazi guards and their Kapo collaborators, but Yael could see their hands, their Conegliano pinkies. Yes, they were family.

Suddenly and without warning, an involuntary shudder ran through his body. He couldn't think, his mind went blank. He felt faint and clutched at the plaque for support. But then, a wave of uncontrollable dizziness took over. Vertigo. His head spinning, his body trembling, Yael sank to the pavement. He curled up into a fetal position and he began to sob. Tears, uncontrollable torrents, flooded out from his eyes and they would not stop.

No, they did not stop until Yael heard the voice of an old woman, a passerby, speak to him, first in Hebrew, which he did not understand. And then in Italian, "*Non dimenticare mai, non dimenticare mai chi sei.*" And then in English, "Never forget, never forget who you are." When he looked up to see her face, there was no one there, just a phantom, a phantom with a scar, but his heart knew. His heart knew it was the ghost of Zina calling him home to Ceneda.

Yes, they were family, these were his people, this was his history and for the first time in seven years, Yael Conegliano felt alive—but it hurt like hell.

Around the same time Yael was waking up at Casa della Luna in Ceneda, his grandfather Jake cleared his baggage through customs at Venice's Marco Polo airport and exited the terminal.

Out front, Jake spied a brand new lipstick-red BMW 328i convertible sedan with its top down, this despite the fact that it was a chilly morning in January. Sitting there, her crimson Aphrodite hair blowing in the wind, was Greta Tedesco Foxx, appearing as much the goddess in Botticelli's *Birth of Venus*, as when they had first met. Today however, no ragged coat, no torn stockings. Greta wore an Italian designer fur coat and a black Armani silk pants suit. Her crystal blue eyes sparkled in the glare of the early morning sunlight. When she saw Jake, she pretended to fluff her hair and preen as she had decades earlier while sitting in the back seat of Lt. Foxx's jeep.

Jake dropped his bags to the pavement and let out the loudest cat-call whistle he could muster. They both started to laugh, no doubt remembering how far they had all come from the day they first met. Greta quickly exited her BMW and gave Jake a warm but brief hug. It had been three years since they had last seen each other at Enrico's funeral.

"And where's my girl, Dolcetta?" was her first question when they pulled apart.

"Right here, wait a minute." Jake turned around, looking first at the door of the terminal and then at his bags. He reached into one, a leather knapsack, and pulled out a beautiful hand-painted Italian pottery urn. On one side was a golden sun over a mountain dotted with emerald, red, white, and turquoise flowers. On the reverse was a deep indigo sky dotted with silver stars and a portrait of Dolcetta dressed as the Queen of the Night. Beneath her picture was a simple inscription. "*Purtroppo, amori miei, devo andare via adesso.*"

Greta lifted the urn from Jake's hands and kissed Dolcetta's lips. Tears trickled down from her eyes. "Oh, I miss my girl."

"*Anch'io,*" said Jake as he retook the urn and put it back in his knapsack.

They both sighed and hugged again, but this time Jake verily collapsed into Greta's arms for support. A flood of tears rolled down his cheeks. She just held him close until the sobbing stopped. Greta, who had loved Dolcetta as much as Jake, understood the pain of loss.

When he finally recovered, Jake, a tad embarrassed, thanked her in a half whisper that said more about his grief than any words could have expressed. Quietly and subdued, he loaded his suitcase into the back and then climbed into the passenger seat with the knapsack in his lap.

"You don't want to drive?" Greta asked, dangling the keys in front of him.

"Not with these rain clouds in my eyes. And my heart's still pounding," he answered.

"Amen," said Greta. She lifted a gold chain that hung around her neck and kissed the larger of two wedding bands that hung from it. "It's hard. I still miss Enrico. It never goes away, especially when I wake up in the morning. There's not a day when I don't think about him."

"Si," nodded Jake.

Greta slid into the driver's seat, started the engine and hit the switch to close the roof.

"No fresh air this trip?" asked Jake, trying to elevate his own mood out of sadness.

"Assolutamente, no. Not freezing my buns off again. And it provoked too many complications the last time around," answered Greta.

"Oh, yes," said Jake reflecting back. "But still, I glad you're here now. There's no one else's shoulder I'd rather cry on."

"Dolcetta's orders. My girl would not have it any other way. The last time we spoke, she insisted I be the one to drive you to Ceneda. She knew."

Before Dolcetta had passed away peacefully the prior September at their Long Island beach house, she had made lists, long and highly specific lists of final requests. True to her nature and how she wished to be remembered, some were, as she joked with Jake, "dead serious," others, clearly comic and lighthearted and touched by an affection for all those she had loved. Jake, ever the adoring husband, and now the bereaved widower, was determined that her wishes be executed just as she had desired. Even now, the thought of pleasing her brought a smile to his face. It was, after all, the only way he knew to push through the grief of having lost his partner, his lover, and his best friend.

First and foremost, Dolcetta wanted to return home to Ceneda by having her ashes scattered from Monte Cervino into the Meschio River on the anniversary of the day she and Jake had first met. For her, it represented a victory over the hate that had driven her away. Dolcetta had insisted, however, that not only the day, but their entire journey of return, be one of joy and remembrance. Let her remaining friends and family gather and have them sing those songs from the operas that had sustained her as a partisan. After all, she declared, we won, they lost, we celebrate.

Secondarily Dolcetta wanted her return to Ceneda to be the instrument that brought Yael, her only grandson, back into the family fold. She knew from speaking with Marietta of Yael's aimless indifference to life. Dolcetta insisted Jake do all he could to ensure that Yael was there. She'd take care of the rest, posthumously if necessary.

On the 26th, Jake had boarded a flight from Kennedy to Venice with her urn packed into his carry-on knapsack. As soon as the seatbelt sign was turned off, he pulled her out of the bag and slept the entire way with his Dolcetta cradled in his arms. It was a peaceful rest, filled with sweet and romantic dreams.

Greta—also following Dolcetta's instructions—had driven down from Vienna the day before so as to meet Jake at the terminal and then make the drive to Ceneda together.

"You have the directions?" Jake asked Greta.

She laughed at Jake's question and echoed her response from decades earlier, "*Non sono una navigatora, Sono una pianista,*" and then she handed him an envelope from Olivia Fresia. "It's up to you now to get us there. Olivia wrote everything out."

Jake opened the envelope, which included a map and specific instructions that would take them directly to Casa della Luna, the same B&B where Yael had checked into the previous night. Olivia, now Olivia Fresia Bianchi, owned the place they would all be staying. Francesca Bianchi, one of Olivia's daughters, and her fiancé Mario were the on-site managers.

"Looks like the A-27 takes us straight there. Shouldn't be more than an hour. But, oh, there's a note here from Olivia that warns us to be careful of fog on the roads as we get closer to the hills."

"*Va bene, il mio navigatore,*" said Greta. "I trust you'll get us there."

She then pulled an unmarked CD from her purse and set it into the car's player.

"What is it?" Jake asked as they pulled away from the terminal.

"Another one of Dolcetta's last wishes. She sent it to me last summer with specific instructions not to listen to it until our drive to Ceneda. Here goes. *Avanti.*"

The music kicked in just as Greta turned onto the highway. It was instantly recognizable to both of them: the overture from *Cosi Fan Tutte.*

Dressed, showered, and shaved, Yael found his way from the third story back to the stairway leading down to the breakfast room on the second floor of the B&B. Just as he started down, he saw a young woman with long dark hair, hug an older woman goodbye and then head down the stairs to the first floor.

The older of the two women, who was fashionably coiffed and dressed, had a classic Italian face. She was perhaps in her late fifties. The woman looked up at Yael when she heard him come down the stairs.

"*Buon compleanno*, happy birthday, Signor Conegliano," she said. "And welcome, I'm Olivia Fresia Bianchi."

"*Grazie*," said Yael, a bit taken aback. "How did you . . . "

"The whole town knows who you are," she added.

"Really?" Used to the anonymity of his travels, especially with women, Yael was even more surprised by the very notion that he was a celebrity in this small town.

"Well, perhaps not everyone, but you and your family are the first Coneglianos to visit in fifty years."

"Oh," said Yael, not realizing till now how unusual his appearance in Ceneda actual was.

"Coffee's there," she said pointing to a Nespresso machine on a sideboard. "Help yourself. And the crostata is divine. You must try some. Mario is a superb cook."

"*Grazie*," replied Yael as they both heard the crunching sound of a car on gravel coming up the fog-shrouded driveway. Olivia glanced at her watch.

"But, if you'll excuse me, I have other guests to prepare for." Olivia nodded goodbye and headed down the stairs.

Watching her walk away, Yael did not quite know what to make of Olivia nor her Casa de Luna. Whenever his grandparents had spoken about her, they had always called her "Olivia, that curious girl," this despite the fact that she was apparently a highly successful business woman who not only owned the B&B but also a string of auto dealerships. He'd met her daughter Francesca and her fiancé, Mario, when he had checked in the night before. Both seemed warm and very sweet, and they greeted him with the same *abbraccio*—embrace—as if he had been family.

Yael looked around the common room. When he had arrived yesterday, it was already dark and he had not had a chance to see any of the rest of the Casa de Luna before heading up to his room to sleep. The B&B was built around an old restored farmhouse. The common room, with its beautiful stone work and arched ceiling, had once been the barn loft. On the one side there was a fire roaring in a massive stone hearth that helped take the damp chill out of his bones. On either side of the fireplace were arched window casements that overlooked a gravel courtyard and the driveway. The mists were so dense he could barely see where he had parked his Fiat. On the other interior walls were paintings and portraits, replicas, no doubt. He recognized a copy of Zina's portrait, the one he recalled seeing in Pops' apartment in Queens when he was a kid. There were also several of Mozart and Da Ponte, including one of his great-ancestor as a newly ordained priest. Da Ponte couldn't have been more than twenty in that one.

He made himself a cup of espresso and after setting it on the dining table, he went back over to the sideboard. There was food aplenty spread before him, from fresh local cheeses to baked breads and pastries. He used the cheese cutter—a piece of wire stretched between two wooden handles—on a round of gouda before cutting himself a slice of the crostata.

Tasting the crostata di pistacchio, he was instantly thrown back to the Café Venezia in Vienna when he was but ten. It was identical—and perfect. He savored every bite. After he finished and had gathered up every last crumb, he went over to the Nespresso machine for a refill. It was then he heard the tap-tap-tap of a woman in high heels no doubt coming up the stairs. Yael turned and looked over his shoulder as a strikingly elegant woman with long, flaming red hair tumbling over her fur coat, entered.

"Oh, my God," he said half aloud, "Aunt Greta." Though Yael had not seen her since that trip to Vienna when he was but ten, he recognized her straight off. He left the coffee behind and ran to greet her.

"Yael?" she called out, almost more of a question than a statement.

"*Sì, sì, sono io*," he said as he embraced her. "I didn't know you were coming?"

Even in her high heels, Greta had to stand on her tip toes to kiss Yael on both cheeks. "*Buon compleanno*, I would not miss this day for all the world." Greta then leaned back and looked from Yael's face to the portrait of the young Abbé Da Ponte. "*Dio mio*," she declared. "Turnaround, you look exactly like him."

Yael did. As he looked and examined Da Ponte's face more closely, he realized, yes, he had seen it before—every time he looked in a mirror. Yael could have posed for that portrait of Da Ponte and no one would have been the wiser.

"Mom would hate that," he said, somewhat downcast. "Ever since Dad died, she's hated everything about our family. I didn't even tell her I was coming here. She thinks I'm wine-tasting in Tuscany."

"That must be hard for you, keeping secrets from her." Greta moved toward the fireplace, warming her hands.

"Yeah," said Yael. Completely deflated, he sat back down at the table. "Mom used to say that the one Conegliano family trait she hated the most was keeping secrets. And," he said, pointing back to the portrait of Da Ponte, "she blamed him for starting it by pretending to be a priest. I'm sorry about her; she's always angry."

Greta sat down opposite him and took one of his hands in her own. "No, you mustn't be. There is no need to apologize. I knew your mother very well. When Pandorea was young, she even lived with us at Kartnerstrasse for the summer. She wouldn't be angry without cause."

"What do you mean?" asked Yael. The concept of his mother's rage being justified had simply never occurred to him.

"We—and by that, I mean all of us, your father, Nonna Dolcetta, your Pops, Uncle Enrico and me—we all chose this life of secrets and spies. Your mom didn't. And worse yet, your dad . . . well, let's just say that he too kept more secrets from her than he wanted. And when he died, a part of her died as well. That hurts."

Yael looked at Greta in total astonishment. "*Anche tu?* A spy? But you were *una pianista*. I heard you play in Vienna."

She shook her head, "*Mezza mezza*. I was recruited as a spy by MI6 when I was seventeen."

"You?" Yael still couldn't believe it.

"*Io*. The war was on. My father, a church organist, had been drafted into the Italian army and as best we knew he died somewhere on the Russian front. One of his old friends, aware of how desperate my family was for money, found me a job as a warm-up pianist for the opera singers at La Fenice. I loved it . . . I loved it until the Nazis took over in '43. They were coarse, brutal pigs. I hated them but could never show it. The *Partigiani*, who were working with the British, asked me to flirt with the German officers at the opera house and report back on what I saw and heard. At first it was little things, like where they were staying, what their routines were and such. But then as other agents were found out or executed, the *Partigiani* recruited me to step up and become a real spy. The work became harder, more complex, and far more dangerous."

Yael was still aghast. He simply could not conceive of any of this. "Was Uncle Enrico, was he part of that? Nonna said you met during the war."

"Yes, he was my contact and handler, but we never met face to face until after the war. His team also ran supplies to your Nonna Dolcetta and her *Partigiani* group."

"Why did I never know all this?"

Greta nodded in the direction of the Da Ponte portrait. "Secrets were more than a family tradition. It was how we all survived, even Da Ponte in his day."

"But after the war?"

"After? Our countries needed us and we continued to serve. First it was uncovering the escape routes that Fascist sympathizers such as the Abbé Luigi Hudal had established that allowed Nazi officers like Eichmann to escape to South America and the Middle East. And even before we finished that work, a new enemy appeared—the Russians—so we all kept on serving."

"Are you still?"

"No. The man your father killed in Prague, Kazys Skirpa, he and one of his allies, Terese Burauskaite, almost trapped me a month earlier in Budapest. Manny's actions may have well saved my life, but once I was exposed, outed as a MI6 agent, I had no choice but to retire."

"How? Why? Why did you all choose this?" I don't understand why anyone would want to live their entire life in secrets and shadows."

"We only half chose. Our roles were thrust upon us by the times we lived through. But just like your Nonna Dolcetta at Avastella, for us it was kill or be killed."

"You? You did that too?" Yael was still struggling to wrap his mind around these revelations.

"Yes." Greta pointed to the wire cutter next to the round of gouda cheese on the food table. "That cutter is also a garotte." She mimed wrapping it around someone's neck and forcibly pulling tight. "Twice," she added, holding up two fingers.

"My God," exclaimed Yael, taken aback. He simply could not picture the elegant pianist sitting across from him as a killer.

Greta took a deep breath and shook her head. "I've never told anyone that before, not even Enrico." Now it was her turn to struggle before she could continue speaking. "It wasn't glorious or heroic, nothing like the movies . . . " She looked directly at Yael, eye to eye and spoke slowly, deliberately but with conviction. "It was terrifying . . . and horrible . . . and bloody. I cried my eyes out the first time, but it steeled me for the second time, and if necessary, I would have done it a third, fourth, or fifth time."

"Truly?" asked Yael, sincerely trying to understand the depth of Greta's commitment.

"Si," she answered without hesitation. "Yesterday, today, or tomorrow, if need be. We stood up because we had to. And your dad, he was cut from the same cloth. He gave up the prospect of being a major opera star to serve his country as an undercover agent. But he too could never share the details of what he did with anyone, including your mom. Of course, she knew he was CIA, but no, Manny could never speak of what he did, not his assignments nor the details."

"Thank you, Aunt Greta, I really appreciate this." Yael said as he pointed up at Da Ponte's picture. "I am just beginning to understand what motivated that man."

"Now you've stumped me," said Greta. "How so?"

"My great-great-grandfather, etc., Lorenzo, he was born a Jew, Emanuele Conegliano, right here, right here in

Ceneda. And to survive the cruelty of anti-Semitism, he dons that costume. Suddenly he becomes the Abbé Da Ponte. But in his heart, he remains a Jew. He lives his entire life under cover. And only in the *Secret Diaries* does he tell the truth."

"*Si, capisco,*" said Greta. "And now that you understand him, maybe now you can also forgive your mother? She's wounded and has suffered a lot. And the only cure for that sort of pain is your compassion and love."

Before Yael could answer, his grandfather Jake came up the stairs with Olivia. "Ah, you're both here!"

Chapter Twenty-Two: La Rinascita di Emanuele Conegliano

Thursday, August 5, 1791
Ceneda, Italy

Mozart was never a fan of my mistress, Adriana Ferrarese del Bene, and often chided me about my long-running and more-often-than-not tempestuous affair with her. However, after Mozart observed Adriana's vocal agility when she played Susanna in the Vienna revival of *The Marriage of Figaro*, he decided to cast her in the role of Fiordiligi for our next piece together, *Cosi Fan Tutte*. Yes, La Ferrarese had the voice, the range, and the ability as an actress to portray both Susanna and Fiordiligi on stage with a degree of credibility that won over audiences. And that was what mattered.

With Adriana as its star, the *Figaro* revival became not only the seat-filling, audience-pleasing hit we had always expected it to be, it was also a financial winner. The return on investment proved out Celestina's prediction that if I were allowed to run the Burgtheater as a business, the Italian Opera Company would be successful. Success meant power, and with power came influence. As a newly minted impresario, I selected the operas, picked the composers, and arranged for which stars were to perform with whom on the stage at the Burgtheater. If ever my light shone brightly, this was its apex. Why even Paisiello came hat in hand to beg me for a libretto and a slot in the schedule.

These were indeed good times for us. Neither Mozart nor I could have been happier. All of our work was now in vogue. In addition to *Figaro*'s new found success in Vienna, our *Don Giovanni* was fast becoming a popular sensation all across the continent. And, naturally, expectations were high as Mozart and I tweaked the final touches of *Cosi*.

It goes without saying that as the light of success shone on us, it inevitably threw shadows upon others. New enemies arose within the cliques and cabals that flourished backstage. Nonetheless, with Joseph II's support and blessings, we were easily able to deflect the barbs and arrows flung by our detractors.

Mozart and I both looked forward with great anticipation to the premiere of *Cosi Fan Tutte* on what was the eve of his thirty-fourth birthday. As was Mozart's habit and artistic preference, he was scheduled to conduct the first several performances himself. In addition to Adriana, we had a stellar cast that also included Francesco Benucci and his powerful baritone voice as her Guglielmo.

But in truth, in real life, my Adriana was neither a Susanna nor a Fiordiligi. She was their polar opposite, a hellion, a demanding diva without the morals, ethics, or the steadfast resolve of either of those characters she had portrayed. And I, more than anyone, knew this—even if I failed to act upon that wisdom.

It is an axiom of great literature that in order for audiences to cherish the stars they see on stage, their creators, that is the writers who fabricate those personalities, must also love these fictional creatures so as to imbue them with life. Through the artifice of my libretti, I had crafted the very personalities and traits that made women such as *Don Giovanni*'s Zerlina, *Figaro*'s Susanna and the Countess Almaviva, and *Cosi*'s Despina and Fiordiligi appealing to audiences.

Why and how, you ask, was I able to craft the very words that flowed out of their mouths in harmony with Mozart's incomparable scores? It was simple. These creations of mine succeeded because they embodied the particular traits I admired in the two women I had truly known as friends: my first love, Zina, and now our mutual cousin, Celestina. When writing my libretti, I drew upon their attributes of kindness, wisdom, humor, strength, quick wits, resourcefulness, honesty, and their zest for life.

Nonetheless, Mozart continued to challenge me in regard to my infatuation with Adriana. For example, during our *Cosi* dress rehearsal, Adriana complained about being upstaged by Dorotea Bussani, the actress portraying Despina. Mozart turned to me and asked bluntly, "Why do you persist with this La Ferrarese, when the woman you dream of is really a Susanna? You despise most everything about Adriana—except her bedside manners, true?"

I had to agree with Mozart. Though I had a deep-seated longing for a Susanna or a Fiordiligi, and I was tried and tested by Adriana's tirades, temper tantrums, and vanities, it was the pleasures of the flesh that held me in her thrall. I confess that even as I entered my forties, I remained a prisoner to my weaknesses.

The first crack in the jail cell of emotions that bound me to her as a slave occurred after the fourth performance of *Cosi*. The show had been a marvelous success, a sellout in part due to La Ferrarese's star turn as Fiordiligi. The reviews of her performances were in a word, fabulous, the best of her career. She adored the adulation and applause that came with fame, so much so that offstage it accelerated her transformation into an insufferable and self-absorbed diva.

Mozart and I were both with Adriana in her dressing room, reviewing notes from the show's performance, when Orsini came by. I had personally never witnessed the emperor's chamberlain so downcast and in despair.

"Joseph II has been taken ill," he said, "and I fear, this is his last. He will not recover."

Despite our personal difficulties with Orsini, Mozart and I shared the chamberlain's deep affection for Joseph II. The emperor had always been a good and kind monarch, particularly in regard to the opera company.

Mozart and I each expressed our regrets. Adriana, however, busied herself with her makeup and said nothing.

Orsini then told us that out of respect for the emperor, he had personally ordered that all theaters in Vienna, including the Burg, were to be shuttered.

When Adriana realized there would be no fifth performance, she had the audacity to accuse Orsini of closing the theaters just to spite her. In an incoherent rage, she berated the grieving chamberlain for ruining her career. Tears welled up in Orsini's eyes as she pounded on his chest. Joseph II, Orsini's closet friend was dying and all La Ferrarese could think of was, naturally enough, herself. It was a slight Orsini never forgave.

Joseph II died less than a month later. His brother, Leopold II, the man who despised opera, became our new emperor. After a respectful period of mourning for the deceased monarch ended, Leopold II delegated oversight of the Burgtheater to his wife, the Empress Maria Luisa. Recalling the fiasco of her daughter's wedding celebration in Prague, the empress was no fan of ours. Further she considered opera *buffa*, our forte, both crude and vulgar, and certainly not fit for the likes of her court.

That included our *Cosi Fan Tutte*, which ran for only another six performances before Maria Luisa strongly suggested that I remove it from the schedule. She deemed our

Cosi as far too licentious for people of good taste and virtue. I may have been the impresario that put operas on stage, but Their Majesties owned the house. *Cosi,* was canceled in favor of a stilted *ancien régime* opera *seria* from Salieri, a production more aligned with Her Majesty's prudish and autocratic personality.

With each passing week, Mozart and I were progressively moved to the periphery of power. As our stars began to wane, our enemies, particularly a new version of the old Italian cabal, gained ascendancy. But the Italians were not alone. Everyone who had witnessed our stars rise, took shots at bringing us down, particularly me, the Jewish priest, and with gusto. Subterfuge was indeed to be had in all quarters of the opera house.

And Mozart, well, he was a wreck. He was still consistently overspending well beyond his income. As his debts grew out of control, he regularly begged wealthier friends and patrons for loans so as to pay off prior loans. Adding to his stress, Constanze was pregnant yet again and terrified by the prospect of losing another child.

When Adriana's contract was up for renewal, I risked my own now fragile standing with the royal court to argue on her behalf with Orsini but to no avail. The wound she had inflicted upon him over Joseph II's death was still too raw. He openly declared that she was not to be forgiven. Without a contract, Adriana was soon dismissed outright. Shortly thereafter, she and her husband Luigi bid farewell to Vienna and returned to Italy. I confess to having no regrets when she finally left Kartnerstrasse siebzehn. My bed went cold, but oddly I found comfort in being released from the prison her arms had created about me.

With dismay, Mozart and I watched the state of the opera and its programming decline. We even heard rumors bandied about backstage that Orsini and Salieri sought to lure back the Abbé Casti. The avowed goal of that venture: to replace me at the Burgtheater as court poet, one they could more easily control.

As the cascade of bad news continued, I issued an appeal directly to Leopold II. My personal note to him, decrying the dismal state of affairs at the opera company, was intercepted by our enemies. My protestations, polite and respectful as they were intended, were twisted and turned by our foes into accusations of extreme disloyalty to the court, so much so that late in the spring of 1791, I was indeed, dismissed from my position. Salieri later informed me that I best conclude all my affairs in Vienna with haste. Leopold II was so enraged by my effrontery that he had issued orders that I was to be formally banished for life from the entirety of the Hapsburg Empire.

In no time I went from being a powerful impresario to a thrice-banned exile. As a converso I had been forbidden from associating with Jews, then I was tossed out of Venice for blasphemy, and now here I was on the verge of being booted out by the Hapsburg emperor.

When Mozart and I met at Café Venezia to discuss this latest sour turn of events, I declared openly, "London, we must move to London and with speed."

He heartily agreed. "What choice do we have?" he said.

"None," I replied. "We could be in London for their summer season."

"Perhaps by September—if the child is healthy," countered Mozart. Constanze's baby was due in late July. "Even better, October. Yes, let us meet you there in October."

"October?" I questioned. "So late? Surely you could travel before then?"

Mozart then confessed that Guardasoni, from the Estates National Theater in Prague had commissioned him to rework an old Metastasio Opera *Seria* for the September coronation celebration of Leopold II, our emperor, in his secondary role as the King of Bohemia. "It is one you know well," he added. "From the night we first met in Venice, *The Mercy of Titus*."

Twenty years had gone by since that extraordinary evening when I, as the newly minted Abbé Lorenzo Da Ponte first arrived in La Serenissima: I met Dona Brunetta; Zina stabbed the commendatore; Angela Tiepolo sheltered and seduced me; Casanova appeared as Homer; the cherub revealed himself to be Mozart as we spoke of Metastasio's tales of love, weakness and infidelity; the Teatro San Benedetto burnt down; and Zina and I escaped from its flaming roof into each other's arms. One night, one extraordinary night.

And now as the gates to this current chapter of my life were about to be slammed shut, I had to wonder if in fact I had learned anything at all about life, love, or women, or was I still that same naïve and lust-driven priest?

"So be it then, October," I replied.

"No, better yet, let us plan on meeting there in November," said Mozart, again reconsidering. "Schikaneder has a German Singspiel he needs me to complete for his *Theater-an-der-Wien*."

"November?"

"Yes, let us plan on meeting there in November or even December. Presuming you head there now, Lorenzo, you will be well situated by the time we arrive in December, yes?"

Reluctantly, I agreed. What choice did I have? Mozart had his assignments and I had what? Exile? We lingered at the café drinking more wine while sketching out preliminary plans so as to be able to conquer the opera stages of London.

When at last Mozart and I drained the last of our Barbera, he made to leave the café. He was anxious to go home and inform Constanze of his decision. He offhandedly declared, "That's it. The deed is done. There's truly nothing left for us in Vienna, is there?"

I disagreed. "There is my Susanna."

"Your Susanna?"

"Yes, my Susanna. The woman who has inspired me these past five years."

Mozart flashed one of those cheek to cheek smiles of approval that reminded me of the Cherub mask he wore so long ago. "Yes, go find your Susanna," he said as we shook hands and parted ways at the front door of the café. "You would do well to stay in her company. *Auf Wiedersehen, mein Freund.*"

"*Ciao, addio.*"

I watched Mozart walk down Kartnerstrasse towards St. Stephan's Cathedral, his hand waving to the invisible music percolating inside his head. When Mozart finally disappeared around a corner, I turned about and went directly to the kitchen office of Café Venezia.

Celestina, who was working on her accounts, looked up at me. "Lorenzo, what is it?"

I knelt down before her and asked, "Celestina Nancy Grahl, will you marry and be my wife?"

I could not help but think as she answered me, that she had long expected this question, for her answer came swiftly and assuredly, "Yes, Lorenzo, of course, but on one condition."

Thus, three months later, on the 5th day of August 1791, to honor and fulfill that one condition, we found ourselves, two exiles, back in the Veneto, on the very outskirts of Ceneda—home.

Our exodus from Vienna and our transition into our new life, however, had not come quickly or easily. Letters were sent, friends and family contacted, rendezvous arranged. Celestina sold the Café Venezia to our benefactor, Baron Wetzlar. Another old compatriot, Casanova, who was well schooled in the arts of exile and personal reinvention, arranged new identity papers for us both. These he had delivered in secret to Zimmermann's book emporium inside a faux Latin botany text titled, *Tradescantia Pallida—The Wandering Jew*.

Only days before my expulsion from the Hapsburg Empire was set to be enforced, everything fell into place. Celestina and I hired a small coach and left Vienna. We headed, not north to the English Channel, but rather south toward Italy. Given that I, as the Abbé Lorenzo Da Ponte, had also been banned from Venice and the Veneto, our only choice was to travel incognito using Casanova's forged documents.

Such travel was not without danger. Both Celestina and I understood that as conversos, we were forbidden by law to associate with or have contact under any pretext whatsoever with any other Hebrews. If caught, we could be sentenced to the whip, the pillory, indefinite prison, life as galley slaves, or hanging by rope until dead. But in order to ultimately return to the ghetto of Ceneda, we took that risk and traveled as Jews. It was one we did so willingly.

And so, to accomplish this, we donned yet another costume and cloak of secrecy. Our newly forged passports provided by Casanova identified us simply as, *La coppia sposata ebraica*, Celestina and Emanuele Conegliano. I wore the red beret Italian Jews were required to wear outside the ghetto and I let my beard grow to further mask my identity. Celestina wore the hooded cape typically adapted by Jewish women in that era.

Thus attired, we avoided all the major roads and towns. Instead, Celestina and I moved surreptitiously from one Hebrew community to another, until at last, after a journey of several months, we reached the woodlands just outside of the village of my birth.

However, sneaking into Ceneda undetected in order to fulfill Celestina's one condition would be another matter.

Our faces were both known well inside and outside the ghetto. And on a scorching summer eve, when many a villager would sit outside to escape the heat indoors, our task would be that much more difficult, particularly in a small town where everyone knew everyone else.

In order to avoid detection, we waited until near dusk when most families would be dining. Celestina wore a broad brimmed straw hat to shield her face and I pulled the beret down low over mine, hoping between that and my beard, I could succeed in moving undetected.

Driving our wagon neither fast nor slow, we approached town from the eastern end of the valley. Unfortunately, at this time of the day, the sun was directly in our eyes. As we neared the livery stable on the outskirts of town, we were both startled half to death when a man jumped out in front of us.

"Halt!" the man shouted.

Terrified, Celestina dug her fingernails into my right arm. Not wanting to arouse suspicions I stopped the wagon. My hands trembled as I tugged the reins of our horse. With the setting sun glaring behind him, it was difficult to distinguish the man's features. Reaching for the only weapon I had, my silver-headed cane with one hand, I shielded my eyes with the other. I could at last see a tall, muscular young man, waving his arms and wearing the red beret of a fellow Jew.

"Halt!" he repeated in a deep resonant voice.

The young man approached me and said that his donkey cart had lost a wheel, but that he need help getting his load of wine bottles into the ghetto before the gates were locked at night fall. He had already unhitched his donkey from the damaged cart that lay by the side of the road.

"Can you help me? And quickly? The sun is going down."

I looked at Celestina, who nodded agreement.

Jumping down from the wagon, I hurriedly assisted the young man in loading four cases of wine into the back of our cart. When we were done, I climbed back onto the left side of the bench seat. After the young man tied his donkey to the rear of our wagon, he then joined us on the right. Celestina sat between us in the middle. I urged our horse forward and we started off into town.

Still rattled and nervous, I asked the young man if he was a wine merchant, a question which made Celestina and the young man both laughed aloud.

Between their unexpected laughter and his answer, "No, it's a gift for my father. He's getting married today." I was thoroughly confused until Celestina spoke up.

"Lorenzo . . . " she started to say and then she changed pace and said, "Emanuele, meet your son, Israeli Conegliano. Israeli, this is your papa."

Her words set my heart afire. If we had not been racing to reach the ghetto before nightfall, I would have jumped off the wagon and embraced the child I had never seen before.

"Just drive, Papa," said Israeli. "And do not stop for anyone or any reason until we are inside the gates." He reached around Celestina and patted me on the back, a simple gesture that brought me untold joy.

Catching my breath and trying to settle my nerves, I asked, "What is the wine? Prosecco?"

"Yes, but only one case," said Israeli, "The other three are Dolcetto, a new red wine from a grape originally grown in the Piemonte, south of Torino, near Alba."

"Dolcetto? Is it a sweet wine?" I asked as "*dolce*," means sweet in Italian.

"No, but it has a sweet temperament," he said.

"Ah," said Celestina, "Perfect for a wedding."

"Si. It is the cantor's gift," said Israeli, referring to the man who joins with a rabbi in leading Hebrew congregations in psalms and songs.

"Who might that be, this cantor of Ceneda?"

"Your son," laughed Israeli. "And I know all your songs, all your operas." He let loose with Figaro's line from the opening of that opera in a voice nearly as rich, strong and powerful as Benucci's:

> *Ah, with our wedding day so near,*
> *How my dear fiancée loves*
> *This pretty, charming hat,*
> *That Susanna has made for herself.*

I was home, truly home . . . almost.

I followed Israeli's instructions as we zigzagged through the streets of Ceneda. Celestina and I were careful to avert our eyes from those we passed along the way. Not ten minutes later and not a moment too soon, we arrived at the southern ghetto gate where the night watchman was preparing to close the barrier and secure it for the evening. When the watchman saw us coming, he glowered and then with a clear display of impatience, he waved us forward. We were the last ones in for the night. The gates crashed shut behind us with a thud.

In the darkening light, we secured our rig outside the synagogue and followed Israeli in through a side door. He led us to the rabbi's study. Baruccio looked up at us and undoubtably recognized us both immediately, "Ah, Emanuele, Celestina, *Benvenuto a casa*. I see you have finally remembered who you are and where you have come from."

"Si. If only for one night," I replied. "By dawn, as you known, we must be gone, less we be discovered."

Rabbi Baruccio Spinoziano rose from his work table. His *abbraccio* embodied such love and affection that for one brief moment we both felt as if we had never left home.

"And do you know where you have yet to travel?" the rabbi asked.

"I do," I said.

"We both do," added Celestina, never one to be cast into anyone's shadow. "For one night, we are Hebrews. *Domani*, London. My parents await us there now.

"England, eh?" said Baruccio with a chuckle. "But I meant your spiritual paths. No matter, never mind. Wherever you go, whatever you become, wherever your fates lead you, may you both always find peace and love inside your hearts," said Baruccio. "Come into the sanctuary with me. Everyone is waiting."

The rabbi led us into the synagogue where there was already erected a chuppah of palm leaves and olive branches in front of the ark that held the Torah.

A young woman who very much resembled Zina called out to me. "Welcome home, Papa." It was Barbarina, my now twenty-six-year-old daughter who held a four-year-old boy on her hip. "Momma always said you would return to us one day. Now come and meet your grandson, Giulio Emanuele. He too has the hands of a Conegliano."

As I went to embrace them both, Barbarina added, "And this is my husband, Marco."

Words, even those of a court poet, cannot express how overjoyed and happy I was to finally be reunited—if only for this one night—with my family. I simply could not stop hugging and kissing them.

Under the chuppah, Rabbi Baruccio performed the wedding ceremony, Israeli sang the benediction, Barbarina acted as Celestina's bridesmaid, Marco stood in as my best man, and little Giulio served as the ringbearer.

When it was over, I kissed my bride. I was the happiest man in all the world, united with a woman to whom I would be a faithful and caring husband all the remaining days of our lives together—which would be many.

Afterward we returned to the main room of the Spinoziano house. In the *abbraccio* of *mia famiglia* we celebrated deep into the night. We began with the sparkling prosecco and finished with the sweetness of the Dolcetto. For those few brief hours, I came to know my family. I was in love, a love that would last forever.

It was already scorchingly hot when the sun rose early the next morning. Celestina and I breathed heavily in the dense humidity as we packed up our wagon with the remaining Dolcetto. When finished, we embraced each and every one goodbye. It was hard to let go.

"*Purtroppo, dobbiamo andare via adesso,*" I said as we boarded our wagon. We waived our last farewells and then headed out the north gate of the ghetto on the *Via Giudecca*.

The heat was relentless. By the time Celestina and I reached the Jewish cemetery atop *Montegiudecca*, we were verily dripping with sweat. The only relief was a cool breeze wafting up from the Meschio River, which ran beside the *Via Giudecca*.

We dismounted and placed a bouquet of flowers on Zina's grave.

Celestina used her straw hat to fan us both. "Did I ever tell you Zina's last words just before she died?" she asked.

"No."

Celestina started walking toward Monte Cervino. "First," she commanded, "Follow me."

I did, as she led me to the bluff over the river. There she stripped off her clothes and again, I followed until we both stood naked at the cliff.

She then told me Zina's last words: " 'Find Emanuele. And when you do, take his hand and never let go. He needs you and you, him.' "

Celestina entwined her fingers in mine, and never ever did a woman's touch feel so sublime.

And then, hand-in-hand forever, we jumped from the *Via Giudecca* into the cool, cool waters of the Meschio.

Chapter Twenty-Three: By the Rivers of Zion

Saturday Afternoon, January 27, 1996
Ceneda, Italy

"**M**ozart? Why this addiction to Mozart? Why is he so important to all of you?" Yael asked as he, Greta, and Jake, who had the leather knapsack holding Dolcetta's urn slung over his shoulder, followed Olivia out of the gravel driveway of Casa de Luna. Somewhere out there, beyond the dense and damp fog that filled the path before them, was town. "Da Ponte wrote thirty operas for eight or nine different composers. Only three were for Mozart."

"Ahh, they were not only his best, they spoke emotional truths, simple truths that everyone can understand and identify with," declared Olivia as she led them into a twisting warren of cobblestone alleyways. Walking was a bit of a challenge. The stones beneath their feet which had been worn smooth with age, were now slick with condensation. "Everyone in Vittorio Veneto sings them. Mozart and Da Ponte are beloved here."

"As they should be. And if not for Mozart, your Nonna and I would have never met," said Jake. "And there would be no, 'you,' no Israeli Conegliano, nor even an Emanuele Conegliano."

Just as he finished speaking, Jake suddenly slipped going round a corner. The knapsack banged against a stone wall. But Yael reacted quickly and caught his Pops before he fell. Nonetheless, everyone was alarmed that the urn might have shattered.

As soon as he was able to recover and stand erect, Jake looked inside. He breathed a sigh of relief. "She's okay."

"Hey Pops," said Yael. "Let me carry Nonna."

Jake hesitated, reluctant to let his Dolcetta go.

"Come on, Pops. It is my birthday," pleaded Yael, "And Nonna did invite me, right?"

"She did indeed," said Jake finally relenting. He handed the knapsack off to Yael.

"Up you go, Nonna. Don't worry, I'm going to get you to the river." Yael gave the bag an affectionate hug before slinging it on his back.

"Mozart, you ask? Why Mozart?" said Greta rhetorically, continuing their conversation. "It's true that all his music speaks to us, not just the operas. But did you know I was performing Mozart when I met your Nonna for the first time?"

"You were?" asked Yael.

Jake was also surprised as he reflected back. "Even I did not know that. Where and how? What were you playing?"

"It was a few days before our trip to Treviso. You do remember that, yes?" asked Greta teasingly. "Our first date?" She once again fluffed her hair and pretended to preen as she had decades earlier while sitting in the back seat of that jeep.

"Of course," said Jake, winking his eye.

Their exchange about a "first date," puzzled Yael, but he said nothing as Greta continued.

"I was practicing on the piano at Aviano's Officers' Club after lunch. A handful of soldiers were still around, scattered about the hall. There I was, working through the score for *Cosi Fan Tutte*. Just as I started in on the accompaniment for Fiordiligi's aria, 'Come scoglio immoto resta,' this voice, this absolutely incandescent soprano voice, starts up behind me. I dared not turn around to see who it was for fear of making a mistake. I just kept playing. I did not want to embarrass myself in front of such a vocalist."

Fiordiligi/Dolcetta:

> *Like a rock standing impervious*
> *To all winds and tempests,*
> *So stands my heart ever strong*
> *In faith and love.*
> *Between us we have kindled*
> *A flame which warms, and consoles us,*
> *Only death alone could*
> *Change my heart's devotion.*
> *Respect this example*
> *Of constancy, you abject creatures,*
> *And do not let a base hope*
> *Make you so rash again!*

"When we finished, the soldiers in the club stood up, clapping, cheering and yelling, '*Bravo, bravo, bravo!*' "

"I turned around and saw by the doorway, standing next to Enrico, this slim dark-haired young woman, this girl really, who could not have been more than seventeen or eighteen. Her face, her dark eyes, they were even more beautiful than her voice. Her hair was pulled back in twin braids. Under her worn overcoat she was wearing khaki trousers, combat boots, and an olive green military turtleneck.

"Enrico brought the girl forward to me and introduced her as, 'Dolcetta Spinoziano, the one the Germans called, the Queen of the Night.' "

"I could not believe it. Everyone in the Veneto had heard of this Queen of the Night, that fierce woman warrior whose guerrilla squads would appear out of the fog to annihilate hundreds of battle-hardened Nazi troops before vanishing once again into the mists like ghosts. She was legendary. And this beautiful young girl, this child with a voice that could woo the angels, this creature was that same *partigiana*. I was in shock.

"And when Dolcetta reached out her hand to shake mine, I ignored it and embraced her instead. I was in awe and in love and we've remained the closest of friends until," and then Greta began to sing, " 'Until death alone changed my heart's devotion.' "

"Enrico went on to tell me that he had gotten four tickets and two hotel rooms to see *The Marriage of Figaro* in Treviso on Sunday. He was taking Dolcetta and had also invited an opera-loving GI—your Pops," she said indicating Jake. "And did I want to go as this young corporal's date? Even though I had a crush on Enrico, I said yes without hesitation and off we went."

"Wait," said Yael. He stopped dead in his tracks just as they were about to turn onto the *Via Giudecca*. Yael pointed first at Greta, then his grandfather, and finally, the knapsack. "You went with Pops? And Nonna was with Uncle Enrico? What? What am I missing?"

"A pothole in the road and two flat tires," said Jake, smiling, "that was the calculus that changed all of our lives forever."

"Oh, did it ever," said Greta. "You must realize, Yael, that during the war, we were no older than you are now. We were starved for food, starved for fun, and starved for love and affection." Bemused by Yael's discomfiture, Greta kissed him on the cheek.

"*Dio mio*," offered up Olivia, also laughing and nodding toward Jake and Greta, "That's also when I first met these two. My grandfather was supposed to drive everyone to Treviso in his old truck but he could only take two at a time. Enrico and Greta were going first . . . "

"Right," said Jake. "Enrico commandeers my date and . . ."

But before Jake can continue, Olivia jumps in. "And then Greta, whoa, she turns around . . . and oh, right in front of us . . . she kisses your Pops goodbye in the rain. Ahh, I was only eight, but it was like watching *Casablanca*, the most romantic kiss I had ever seen. Even to this day, I still remember, oh yes."

"*Anch'io*," said Greta nodding.

"*Anch'io*," added Jake.

"Come on," said Yael. "You're all spoofing me? Is this some kind of *Cosi Fan Tutte* birthday gag? You're all just making this up, right?"

"No, it's all true," said Jake. "You could have been a redhead."

"Yes, we switched partners," said Greta, "Your Nonna Dolcetta often said, 'When God shaped our hearts, he made them capable of holding more than one great love.' Still, Dolcetta and I always agreed that in the end we each had found our best mates." Greta then sang from *Cosi*, as if imitating Dolcetta, "We shall keep the faith that we have pledged until the hour of our death."

"Oh, Dolcetta had the most beautiful voice," said Olivia as they passed through the arch that had once been the southern entrance to the old ghetto. The fog was even denser here. "She and her twin, Danielle, they were my babysitters. Often, they would sing lullabies to me, but my favorite was when they performed a duet as Papageno and Papagena." Olivia, who had a coloratura soprano voice, began to sing, " '*Pa-pa-pa-pa-pa-pa-Papagena! Pa-pa-pa-pa-pa-pa-Papageno!*' "

Yael abruptly stopped and collapsed against the old gate post, his face just inches below the ancient rusted out mezuzah. Vertigo again. Tears were streaming down his face as he too remembered Dolcetta singing to him as a child. The pain of loss, another death, wracked his body. He was trembling. "I'm sorry, I am so sorry. Forgive me, Pops. I should have been there. I should have been with Nonna when she died."

Yael felt Jake's arms engulf him. And the warmth of his grandfather's hug recalled how his grandparents used to snuggle him in the old Conegliano quilt. Now Jake was doing it again, holding him secure. No words were needed, no words were spoken.

Greta first and then Olivia joined in the hug. They were all misty-eyed. No one moved until at last Yael choked out the words, "I'm okay. Really, I'm okay. I love you all. I'm okay. Thank you . . . So," he said, gathering his strength once again, he changed the subject to hide his embarrassment, "so, this is the old ghetto, this is where we're from?"

"Si," said Jake. He then planted a kiss on his forefinger, which he afterward transferred to the old mezuzah.

Olivia then pointed through the nearly impenetrable mist to one of the restored apartments on the left side of the street, "*Benvenuto a casa*, Yael. That one is the old Conegliano house. Above it was the home of the Spinozianos. And to the left, where that tailor shop sits, that would have been the old synagogue."

"*Oh, Dio mio*," said Greta, remembering back. "That's where we all got married. Is there anything left?"

"No," replied Olivia. "The apartments and the synagogue have all been rebuilt, remodeled and reused. Whatever few remaining artifacts were left after the war, after Dolcetta left, well . . . Father Beccavivi and my grandfather, Ferruccio, they moved everything they thought important into storage in our old barn, the same barn that is now our Casa de Luna. And then, maybe twelve or fifteen years ago, Danielle's daughter, Gaelle D'Angelo, she and her husband, they came here from Israel. Together we sorted through all the relics. The important artifacts they sent back to the

Italian Synagogue of Jerusalem. Everything else was tossed when we built the B&B."

"And the old cemetery where we buried Rabbi Geremia?" asked Jake.

"Still there," said Oliva. "A little worse for neglect. But there are a few surprises. Come, I'll show you."

The fog, which was flowing downhill from the mountains north of Ceneda, continued to grow in density, so much so that they could barely see the paving stones beneath their feet, much less the old north gate of the *Via Giudecca*.

"Is it always this foggy?" asked Yael.

"No, it's the Sirocco effect," said Olivia. "In winter, the desert winds spin off the Sahara across the Mediterranean until they crash into the Alps just above us. Mix hot air, snow, and the sea and you get fog."

"Oh," said Yael, "kind of like the Santa Anas in Southern California?"

"I suspect so," replied Olivia as they passed out the north gate. "But watch your steps as we walk. It gets worse up here by the river."

The mists, which swirled ever more on *Montegiudecca*, were so dense they could not see the old Hebrew Cemetery until they practically stumbled over the tombstones.

"*Dio mio*," exclaimed Greta, "This reminds me of the staging for *Don Giovanni* at La Fenice. Where's our commendatore, Olivia? Any ghosts about?"

"Ghosts? With all the killings and battles here, of course there are ghosts. There are always ghosts in Ceneda," said Olivia. "Especially when the fog is locked in. Some claim to have seen the headless *capitano* stumbling around, others the lieutenant chasing after Zina. And still more swear they've seen the ghosts of Don Giovanni and the commendatore arm wrestling at the gates of hell. Me? No, I've never seen any ghosts myself, but before he died, Father Beccavivi swore that the ghosts of Ceneda are best viewed on a belly full of vino. But look over here. This is what I want you all to see. The formal dedication with the mayor and the city council is at noon tomorrow, and hopefully we have some sun by then."

Olivia led them past a marble bench to a brand new stone memorial she personally had erected to honor Ceneda's heroes, the *Gemelli Angeli*, Dolcetta and Danielle. The monument, which stood beside Zina's grave, was shaped like the twin tablets of the Ten Commandments. The left side was for Dolcetta. The top of the facade was engraved with a replica of the Jewish star she had worn her entire adult life, the one that was scratched onto a bullet casing. On Danielle's tablet, an equally sized Jewish star rose above, as if escaping, strands of barbed wire and the number, 9213474. At the memorial's base, below their biographical information, was inscribed in Italian the word for courage: *Coraggio*. Below that were the lyrics for the finale of Da Ponte's libretto for the *Marriage of Figaro*:

"Then let us all be happy. These days of torment, of caprices and folly, are finished. Only love can end it in contentment and joy. Lovers and friends, let's finish the hours off in dancing and pleasure."

"It's beautiful," said Greta as she turned up the collar on her coat against the wind, "But I'm freezing."

"Yes," said Jake. "It's everything you said it would be. I love it. Thank you, Olivia." Jake gave Olivia a warm hug and a kiss on the cheek. "But I'm chilled as well. We should get to the bluff."

"Si, certo," said Olivia.

As she, Greta and Jake turned toward the path to Monte Cervino, Yael lingered behind.

In truth, Yael loved the fog; he had loved it ever since he was a child growing up in Ojai, when moisture from the Pacific would be sucked inland and cool the valley after a 110-degree heat wave. He loved the way it refracted light, and he loved the way it muffled sound; he loved the way it obscured vision itself, and in so doing, disappeared the outer world. He loved the way it brought solitude and peace; he loved the way it made him feel safe from all the conflicts, anger, and hate of the outer world—and his mother. Above all, he loved the sense of quietude it brought to his soul—and right now, on this, his twentieth birthday, he needed that more than anything. Though he had loved the embrace, the distinct Italian *abbraccio* of family, he still felt alone, pained, and unsure of his future.

Yael scanned not only the monument, but the multitude of graves and headstones that bore familiar family names: Conegliano, Spinoziano, Palumbo, Graziano. His people, his roots, his past. The one missing was Da Ponte himself, who was purportedly buried in a Catholic Cemetery in New York in 1838, the city he had lived in for the last thirty-three years of his life. Pops had once even shown him the marker for Da Ponte at Calvary Catholic Cemetery in Queens near Kennedy Airport, but no trace of his ancestor's actual grave had ever been found.

When Yael looked up for his companions, the mist was so dense, he could not see them. Still he could hear their voices, muffled as they were by the fog. Yael hurried after them at a quick pace, lest he encounter another apparition. Once was enough. And he certainly was not about to share with anyone that Zina had appeared to him the night before in Ferrara.

He finally caught up with the others just as they reached the bluff over the Meschio. The river itself was half frozen. A dense cloud swirled upward from the waters. Yael imagined that it must have looked much the same as it had the night Zina led the *tenente—the lieutenant—*on horseback over the cliff.

Yael removed the urn from the knapsack and carefully passed it back to his grandfather. Jake opened up the urn and then handed a small scoop over to Olivia. She in turn gathered up some of the ashes. After first closing her eyes and making a silent prayer, she then began to sing variations on one of the countess's arias from *The Marriage of Figaro* as she sprinkled Dolcetta's ashes out over the river.

> *Where are those happy moments*
> *Of sweetness and pleasure?*
> *Where have they gone,*
> *Those vows of our past?*
> *Ah! If only my yearning for you*
> *Could bring back the joy*
> *Of this unchanging heart!*

After she finished, she passed the scoop over to Yael. He too said a silent prayer in honor of his Nonna before singing more of Da Ponte's lyrics from *Cosi*.

> *Oh, cruel fate!*
> *I would speak, but my courage fails,*
> *My lips stammer.*
> *I cannot say the words,*
> *Which stay locked inside me.*
> *It could not be worse.*
> *I grieve for you and for us all.*

Greta came next and she sang variations on the recitative that preceded Fiordiligi's aria, "Come Scoglio."

> *Begone, bold death! Leave this house!*
> *And with the unwelcome breath of tragedy*
> *I shall preserve her memory despite all fates*
> *Until my own death.*

When Greta was finished, Jake scooped out the remaining ashes and sang the words from another *Cosi* duet.

> *You friendly breezes*
> *Who have heard the*
> *Tenor of my grief,*
> *Repeated a thousand times,*
> *Oh please help carry my sighs*
> *To the goddess of my heart.*

After finishing off their farewells to Dolcetta, Olivia suggested they return to the warmth of the fireplace at Casa de Luna for some brandy.

Yael declined, wanting as he said, to spend some time sitting in the cemetery with *gli antenati*—the ancestors. He watched Olivia, Pops, and Aunt Greta head downhill until they disappeared into the mist. When they were gone, Yael followed the path back to the marble bench at the *Montegiudecca* cemetery.

He stared out at the tombstones surrounding him and, in his heart, Yael reached out to the past, to *gli antenati*. Zina was there with her eternal scar of courage. So was the buried wisdom of five generations of Spinoziano rabbis. His namesake, Israeli Conegliano, slayer of the Casti *capitano*, was there somewhere too, as were graves of five hundred years of other cousins and kin. Yael rubbed his hands together for warmth, and felt the blood that pulsed within. That blood connected him to each and every soul who rested there.

He called out aloud, pleas to the spirits of those forebearers: "Who am I? What am I supposed to be? What am I supposed to do? How can I survive and face this world?"

But abruptly—from out of the fog—came a ghostly soprano voice. It triggered a terrifying chill that rippled through Yael's body:

"They can't hear you. They're dead."

In a near panic, Yael searched the shadows. Where was the voice coming from? And then he saw a faint figure of a woman, a woman with a scar on her cheek, emerge from the mist. "Zina?" he called out in absolute disbelief at seeing her apparition yet again.

"Yes. Dolcetta invited me to dine with you," said this woman. Her face—and most especially her eyes—perfectly resembled Zina's portrait. "So, here I am."

"Again, another ghost?" stammered Yael, remembering his experience in Ferrara the night before.

"I don't think so," the woman said, as she brushed her hair away from her face. What Yael thought was a scar, disappeared. "I've been called many names, but a ghost? I don't think so. These are my people too."

"Who are you?" asked Yael as he realized this woman before him was very much living, breathing flesh and blood. "You scared the hell out of me."

"I'm Ziva. Ziva Gemelli D'Angelo. Danielle's granddaughter. And you, you must be Yael, *non è vero?*" She extended a gloved hand toward Yael. In her left hand she held a bouquet of flowers.

Yael shook her hand. "Yes, nice to meet you too," but couldn't recall ever hearing any mention of her name before, unless it was when he was still a child.

"*Anch'io*," said Ziva. She was a lean young woman in her early twenties with an easy smile. She had the sleek black hair of Spinoziano women along with intense dark eyes that would not let go of him. Ziva was dressed in black jeans, a wool topcoat over a snug-fitting sweater and a silk scarf. She carried a briefcase on one shoulder that had the pages of a musical score sticking out.

"I hope you don't mind me asking, but what are you doing here?" Jake asked.

"In Ceneda? Or the *Montegiudecca?*"

"Either, or."

Bemused, Ziva laughed at his question, but her eyes stayed locked on his. "I just told you, your grandmother, Dolcetta, she invited me. Wanted us to meet. Something about giving you a kick in the butt."

"Ouch," said Yael as he darted a glance at her black Ferragamo boots. "She really said that?"

"Assolutamente."

"Does Pops—my grandfather—know you're here?"

"Yes, in fact I saw everyone heading back down toward the Casa de Luna as I was coming up. And like you, I was wanting to visit *gli antenati* before the dinner tonight, but I don't talk to ghosts, except maybe Zina. That woman was awesome. I was named after her."

"Ziva, Zina? How's that?" asked Yael.

"My mom's a doctor, and, go figure, she wrote my name out like she was scribbling a prescription. The birth registry misread her handwriting." Ziva placed the flowers at the base of the twins' monument.

As she bent over, Yael noticed sheet music for "Queen of the Night" protruding from her briefcase. "Mozart, huh? You're a musician?" Yael asked.

"No, musicians fear me, especially the old men in the back of the orchestra. I'm training to be a conductor at *Il Conservatorio di musica Giuseppe Verdi* over in Milano."

"Whoa, that's impressive."

"It's easy for a woman to lead when you don't let little boys get in the way," she replied matter-of-factly.

Yael looked a little closer at the notations on the sheet music. "You're scoring "Queen of the Night" for three electric guitars, violin, cello, keyboard, and drums? Really?"

"Yes, along with a soloist and chorus. But tell me, what do you do?" she asked.

"I don't know, I haven't a clue," replied Yael, and then he pointed to the tombstones. "I was hoping they could tell me."

"These ancestors, they're tricky. Sometimes, when the wind blows, they'll whisper right here." She jabbed Yael's chest hard directly above his heart. "But only if you know how to listen—and how many men do?"

"I'm trying to learn," said Yael. He was becoming ever more intrigued by this Ziva. Her self-assuredness and strength were immediately apparent and so different from the women of his one-night stands. Yael did not quite know what to make of her, especially those eyes. They haunted him just as Zina's portrait did when he was a kid at Nonna

Dolcetta's house. "But it's getting cold up here. Can I treat you to a cup of coffee down in the village?"

Ziva glanced at her watch before answering. "I have a concert to prep for, but si, certo, if only for a few minutes. I'd love to. We are family."

"When is the wedding?" Greta asked Olivia. The two of them stood with Jake beside the fireplace of Casa de Luna while sipping the last of their brandy.

"April 14th, at the Cathedral, the week after Easter."

"*Va bene*," said Greta. She unhooked the gold chain that hung around her neck. "When you were but eight years old, you loaned these to Enrico and me. It is time I returned them. It would be my greatest wish that your daughter, Francesca, and her fiancé, Mario, consider these for their own wedding."

"Are you sure about that?" asked Olivia.

"Si, certo," said Greta. "Enrico and I enjoyed the happiest years of our lives while wearing these rings. But they belong here, in Ceneda with your family. This is their proper home. Your children deserve that joy."

As Greta then handed Olivia the gold bands that had once belong to Olivia's parents, Rinaldo and Lucia Fresia, Jake unconsciously touched the wedding band on his own finger.

Oh my God, assolutamente!" exclaimed Olivia, completely overwhelmed. "*Grazie mille.* They would love these." Unable to contain her joy, she hugged and kissed Greta effusively.

Off in the distance the cathedral bells rang out three o'clock. Olivia double-checked her watch. "Please excuse me. The dinner is at eight tonight, and I've much to prepare before then." She thanked Greta again before turning away and heading downstairs.

Jake and Greta both started upstairs.

"Your gifting the rings back to Olivia was a wonderful gesture but it surprised me. Are you certain you're ready to let go?" Jake asked.

"Enrico will always be with me, but it was time to say goodbye," said Greta with great assuredness. They reached the landing outside the doors to their respective guest rooms.

A wave of grief overwhelmed Jake as he again considered the wedding ring on his own hand. His look of sadness was all too obvious to Greta.

"You're not there yet, are you?" said Greta. She took his left hand in hers. Greta lifted it up to her lips and kissed the ring that had bound Jake to Dolcetta. "I loved her dearly too."

"*Dio mio*," replied Jake. "It's been four months now since she passed away. And every morning when I wake up—alone—I wonder when will I have the strength to follow through with the very last item on Dolcetta's wish list. It's one I am almost too embarrassed to share with you."

"Embarrassed? Jake? Come on, we're too old to be embarrassed. Out with it," insisted Greta. "Tell me what she said. Do that, and I'll share with you her last words to me, okay?"

"*Va bene*," Jake nodded. He then placed his hands atop Greta's shoulders and stared directly into her crystal blue eyes. Slowly and with great hesitation, he repeated Dolcetta's words, "*Il mio amore..., your heart can embrace... more than one great love... Abbraccia Greta.*'"

Jake leaned forward and then kissed Greta gently on both cheeks.

But when he started to draw back, Greta put her hands on his shoulders and held firm. "Not so fast, Jacopo Conegliano. My turn. Will you hear Dolcetta's last request of me?"

"Si, grazie," said Jake.

"'Abbraccia Jacopo. He needs you and you, him.'"

Jake pulled Greta back in close and inhaled her perfume—yes, still "*Escada.*" Their lips met once again, this time in full on communion. They each surrendered their past and wrapped their arms firmly around each other. Jake stroked Greta's still luxuriously long red hair. In that moment, all the world felt right and joyous. Only when the far off cathedral bells rang out the next quarter hour did their embrace finally end.

"*Vieni con me,*" whispered Greta as she took Jake's hand and led him to her room.

"Does your four-wheel drive work?" Ziva asked Yael. Their dinner party of eight, led by Olivia, was just about to enter *Olio e Limone*, a popular bistro in the heart of Ceneda's old town.

"Yeah," answered Yael. "Why do you ask?"

Before Ziva had a chance to answer, Olivia opened the front door and started to lead them toward a private room in the back. Suddenly and without warning, all the other diners stood up as if on cue, and began to applaud. Some called out, "*Buon Compleanno, Israeli.*" Others, "*Happy Birthday, Yael,*" and still others, "*Viva Dolcetta, Viva Danielle!*" Several of guests patted Yael on the back. A few reached out to shake his hand. The cheers did not stop until their party reached the back room and the doors closed behind them.

Inside the private dining room, the maitre d' seated them boy-girl-boy-girl, around a circular table. Ziva was to Yael's left, Aunt Greta to his right. Beside her was Pops. Beside him was Oliva, followed by her husband, Arturo, a winemaker, with Francesca and Mario from Casa De Luna rounding off their group. Although their wedding was still three months off, the young couple proudly displayed the wedding rings Greta had returned to Olivia that afternoon.

Yael, who was definitely not used to being a center of attention, was awed by the reception. "That was wild," he said to Ziva as the waiters began to deliver platters of locally grown and prepared antipasti. "I've never had a birthday reception like that before."

"Wait until tomorrow at the unveiling," said Ziva. "The whole of Ceneda will be there to see the monument. But if you have a four-wheeler, I thought afterward we might make the drive all the way up to Avastella. Olivia also paid to have a small memorial marker installed on the road where Dolcetta stopped the Nazis."

"I'd love to go, but I'm supposed to drive Pops down to Marco Polo for his red-eye flight back to New York."

"New York?" questioned Ziva. "Greta just told me, she and Jake were driving to Vienna."

"Pops and Greta? Vienna? Why?" It seemed inconceivable to Yael. He turned to Greta and Jake on this right. "Hey Pops, am I still driving you to the airport tomorrow? Or are you two . . . Ziva says you two are going back to Vienna—together?"

"Yes," said Jake as he reached for Greta's hand and cradled it in his own. "Change of plans. I was going to tell you."

"Does that bother you?" Greta asked Yael.

Yael fumbled. "Ah, no, it doesn't . . . No, it's fine. I'm fine."

Ziva spoke up, "If it's any consolation, you have my blessing. You two look cute together."

"Cute?" smiled Greta. "*Grazie tante.*"

Ziva nudged Yael with her elbow.

"Me too, you have my blessing too," Yael quickly added, a tad embarrassed. "It just . . . you just . . . you just caught me off guard. It's cool actually. Really cool. I'm happy you're going, that you're going together."

"Thank you," said Jake. "It means a lot to me, to us, to have your blessings."

"I love you, Pops. You too, Aunt Greta." Yael turned back to Ziva. "I guess I'm free. Sure, Avastella."

"Perfect," said Ziva. "We'll need your four-wheel drive in case there's snow up there."

Yael reached for one of the many bottles of red scattered about the table that were all from the Arturo Bianchi's winery and asked Ziva, "May I pour you some Dolcetto?"

"Assolutamente," answered Ziva, holding out her glass. "Dolcetto. It's not a sweet wine, but it has a sweet temperament," she added, as if quoting from Da Ponte's diary.

"You know the *Secret Diaries?*" asked Yael, as he filled her glass, and then his own.

"Of course! Your grandmother sent us every last page—that is until you stopped translating. Reading about Da Ponte and Mozart and hearing their music, that is what inspired me to become an opera conductor," answered Ziva as she sipped the wine and then hastily turned and called to Arturo across the table. "*Dio Mio*, Arturo, that is superb. Even better than the Dolcetto we see in Milano from Alba."

"*Grazie mille, Signorina,*" replied Arturo. "My goal is to put a smile on the face of everyone who tastes it."

"You've certainly succeeded," added Yael, who raised his glass in a toast to their wine hosts. "I love it too. Bravo."

His toast was echoed by everyone else at the table.

Ziva turned back to Jake, "So why did you stop? The translations?"

"Mom, she killed it along with everything Da Ponte," he answered. At the same time Yael found and pulled out the Titus coin from his pocket and began to nervously fumble it around in his right hand.

As he gave Ziva his history of what happened after his father's death and the trauma it caused, she compared it to her own struggles growing up in an Israel constantly beset by wars and terrorism. As they buried themselves in conversation, the waiters kept a steady flow of dishes coming to the table: cheeses, fruit, prosciutto, breadsticks, rolls, minestrone, orecchiette, gemelli, lamb, and ultimately, their main course, veal scaloppini.

But when Yael and Ziva were done comparing their past, Ziva brought the conversation back to the translations. "That was then. This is now. You're twenty. And frankly, I want to know what happens next."

"What happens next?" repeated Yael as if it were a question.

"Yes. The last translation segment I read was when Da Ponte and Celestina jumped into the River Meschio."

"I don't know what happens next. I haven't seen the diaries in almost seven years," said Yael. Almost unconsciously he started to toss the coin up and down.

"Oh, come on. Celestina and Lorenzo Da Ponte live for another forty years after Mozart dies and you don't know?"

Yael tossed the "Mercy of Titus" up in the air again, but before he could catch it, Ziva snatched it away with lightning speed. Yael looked at her, taken aback.

"We conductors are quick with our wrists. But now I understand why Dolcetta sent me to kick your butt," she added.

"Why?" asked Yael.

"You're still afraid."

"Me? Afraid? Of what?"

"Ghosts. Living ghosts, starting with your mother. You're afraid of her, her anger, of commitments and of becoming your own person, of being a Jew. *Dio mio*, you're a Conegliano. Think about all the struggles our ancestors went through: war, persecutions, the Holocaust. And each time tragedy struck, our people fought back. They stood up, or like Da Ponte, they damn well figured a way out. These were brave people, and flipping that silly coin of yours to make choices, that's the coward's way out. You dishonor them, you dishonor every *Ebreo* who rests on *Montegiudecca*." She tossed the Titus back at him with disdain.

All the while, as Ziva berated him, Yael could not keep his eyes off of her. Not only was he entranced by her manner and forthrightness, he knew instantly that she was correct. And when she finished kicking him to the curb, he confessed as much.

"You're right," he said, which brought a smile back to her face. "I've been weighing these things since I began the drive up from Sicily three weeks ago. But it wasn't until last night when I saw Zina in Ferrara..."

She stopped him right there. "You saw Zina in Ferrara? Do tell."

He described what happened to him beside the memorial plaque and finished with, "Zina called me home to Ceneda and said to 'Never forget who you are.'"

"And I thought I was the only one she spoke to," said Ziva. She took the bottle of Dolcetto and refilled Yael's glass. "Who knew ghosts got around that easily."

Yael turned back around toward Jake, "Hey Pops, you do still have the diaries?"

"Of course. They're at the beach house. Why do you ask?"

"I want to finish the translation. Would you send a copy when you get home?"

"Better yet," said Jake, "when you get back to California, I will send you the originals."

"And the genizah trunk?"

"Sure, if you want that as well. No one's looked at it in years."

"Cool," replied Yael. "Assolutamente!"

Just then, Olivia tapped on her wine glass with a knife and called for everyone's attention. It was time she declared for Yael's birthday gifts. Greta began by presenting Yael with two handmade, leather-bound journals crafted in the same style as Da Ponte's *Secret Diaries*. Arturo signaled for the waiters and they delivered a case of his winery's Prosecco di Conegliano to the table along with eight glasses and one more bottle of the same that had been chilled.

"Now to open it," said Olivia, "We have a special gift. Someone asked me this morning if any artifacts had been left behind when the old synagogue was remodeled. I lied when I said no. This present once belonged to your namesake, Israeli Conegliano. When the Rabbi Geremia Spinoziano died, my grandfather, Ferruccio, set it aside, hoping one day to return it to its rightful heir. That time is now." From under the table she pulled out the very sword that Israeli had used to slay the capitano two hundred years earlier. As she drew the blade out of its sheath, the steel sparkled as if brand new. "The prosecco and sword are yours, but only if . . . "

"I know," said Yael as he thanked her and took the sword from her hands. "I know how to do this." Though it had been over seven years since he had last wielded a sword in a fencing class, the stroke came naturally enough. With one quick slice against the glass neck, he opened the prosecco. As the bubbly flowed, Jake moved glasses underneath and filled one after another until everyone had theirs ready for yet another toast.

To the sound of "Viva Ceneda, viva Dolcetta, viva Israeli," they all drank.

"Now it's my turn," said Jake as he drew out two much smaller packages from his coat. "The first is from your Nonna Dolcetta." Jake passed it over to Yael, who opened the card first. Tears came to his eyes when he opened it.

"What does it say?" asked Ziva, "Tell us."

Yael turned and looked directly into her dark eyes, "*Coraggio, abbraccia il coraggio.*"

Ziva blew him a kiss. "*Va bene. Molto bene.*"

Yael then tore off the paper from around a small gift box. Inside was Dolcetta's Jewish star, the one carved into a bullet casing. Ziva helped him put it on around his own neck. With a look skyward, Yael blew a kiss to the heavens. "*Grazie mille, Nonna, te amo.*"

And then Jake passed him the second package and card. "This is from *gli antenati* by way of me."

Yael was rendered speechless by what Pops had written on the card. He placed it down and hurriedly Yael unwrapped the gift. It was the yad, Da Ponte's original, old tarnished brass yad.

Ziva picked up the card and read it aloud, "Never forget who you are."

"Thank you, thank you all," said Yael. "This is the best, most astonishing birthday ever. I will never forget it or all the kindnesses you have all shown me. For the first time in my life, I feel home. And I promise to make you all proud of me." Yael turned to his right and kissed Greta on the cheek.

But when he turned to his left to repeat the same gesture with Ziva, she turned her head at the last moment. His lips met hers for but an instant, a first kiss he'd long remember.

"But wait," said Ziva as she pulled back, "there's more." She lifted her conductor's baton from a coat pocket and pointed it at Francesca and Mario.

"Si, si," said Francesca and Mario. "We baked you a cake."

Suddenly the French doors between the private dining room and the main hall were flung open. A parade of waiters marched in to deliver plates and a massive crostata di pistacchio covered with the requisite twenty candles.

As Yael blew out the candles, he could see into the main dining room. All the tables had been moved to the side. Everyone who had been dining now stood assembled as a single choir. Off to one side, a musical ensemble consisting of three electric guitars, a violin, cello, drums, and keyboards, awaited their cue.

"*Dio mio*... Your Mozart band?" Yael asked of Ziva.

"Consider this my gift, the gift of music," answered Ziva. She stood up and positioned herself at the entryway between the two rooms. On her command, "Hit it, guys!" the band and choir began to sing "Happy Birthday," in alternating rounds of English and Italian.

When they all finished, Olivia rose from her seat and then walked out in front of the chorus. With Ziva conducting, Olivia sang a modified version of Mozart's "Queen of the Night" aria:

> *The vengeance of hell boils in my heart,*
> *Death and despair flame about me!*
> *If our enemies do not through us feel*
> *The pain of death,*
> *Then this will be our country nevermore.*
> *Dishonored may we be never more,*
> *Abandoned may we be never more,*
> *Destroyed never more*
> *All the bonds of nature,*
> *If not through us*
> *The enemy becomes pale!*
> *Hear, Gods of Revenge,*
> *Hear Dolcetta's oath!*

Olivia, who sang her heart out, hit the notes and trills perfectly and when she finished, the shouts went up again for "Viva Dolcetta."

And when those cheers subsided, Ziva conducted everyone in singing Verdi's "Va Pensiero."

> *Fly, thoughts, on golden wings;*
> *Go settle upon the slopes and the hills*
> *Where warm and soft and fragrant are*
> *The breezes of our sweet native land!*
> *Greet the banks of the river Jordan*

And the towers of Zion.
Oh, my country, so lovely and lost!
Oh, remembrance so dear yet unhappy!
Golden harp of the prophetic wise men,
Why hang so silently from the willows?
Rekindle the memories in our hearts,
Tell us about the times gone by!
Remembering the fate of Jerusalem
Play us a sad lament
Or else be inspired by the Lord
To fortify us to endure our suffering!

And when the choir finished, the real festivities began. The band kicked off another set of pure rock and roll beginning with an electronic version of "*La Chi Darem La Mano.*"

As various guests coupled up and began to dance, Jake and Greta, Olivia and Arturo, Francesca and Mario all moved out on to the floor and joined the party.

Yael reached his hand out to Ziva. "Shall we dance?"

"Assolutamente."

Chapter Twenty-Four: The Coda: New York, New York

Friday Afternoon, January 27, 2006
List Hall, the Metropolitan Opera House

"'Mozart? No, I never saw Mozart again.'"

Yael paused from his reading of the diary translations and looked out at the audience in List Hall. This was his very first public talk and book signing ever, and frankly, given that he had never done anything like this before, he was as nervous as all hell. There were perhaps 150 people who packed the theater, including opera aficionados, magazine editors, book reviewers, and Mozart experts. All had come to hear him read from and discuss the just-released *The Secret Diaries of Lorenzo Da Ponte*. A copy of the book cover was projected onto a screen behind Yael. His publisher, Cold Spring Press of Santa Barbara, where Yael still lived, had arranged for this event on the occasion of Mozart's 250th birthday in the Metropolitan Opera's Choir rehearsal hall. The book, which challenged conventional wisdom about Mozart's collaboration with Da Ponte—perhaps the most important in the history of opera—was already generating controversy because of its frank discussion of anti-Semitism.

Would anyone throw tomatoes at him, Yael wondered, or would they boo him off the stage? One op-ed in *Daily Variety* was already calling the book an elaborate hoax perpetrated by the bastardized descendants of Da Ponte.

Yael glanced over to the left side of the first row and caught the eye of his wife, the opera conductor, Ziva D'Angelo. Ziva, who sat with their seven-year-old daughter, Dede, knew just how to calm Yael down. A rising star in the opera world, Ziva had performed numerous times in front of similarly critical audiences, including *Cosi* at La Fenice in Venice and *Figaro* in Vienna. Using the type of subtle signal that only husbands and wives know, she lightly tapped the Jewish star that hung around her own neck with her index finger and then mouthed the word, "*coraggio*." That was all Yael needed, a reminder that Dolcetta's Jewish star, the one etched onto a bullet casing, hung around his own neck.

Inspired by her courage, Yael went on with his reading while sketches that illustrated Da Ponte and his life flashed continuously across the screen, " 'Before Celestina and I had even completed our journey from Ceneda, across central Europe and on to England, Mozart died in Vienna on December 5th, of 1791. We were devastated. Nonetheless we persevered. I went on to write and produce another nine libretti in London, but sadly, without Mozart's music, none of those works achieved any notable success. Nor did I . . . ' "

It had taken Yael the better part of another decade to finish the translations of all five parts of the diaries that his grandparents, Jake and Dolcetta had begun sixty years earlier on the night those two had first met in Ceneda. Although all three of them, Dolcetta, Jake, and Yael, were credited as the translators of their ancestor's diaries, Yael was designated as the editor. He had spent considerable time reworking the parts set in Venice, Vienna, and Prague into a unified whole, one that was consistent in tone and style with the final two portions about London and New York. The New York segments were by the far the longest, covering as they did some thirty-three years of Da Ponte's life. However, it was the "London" diary that presented the greatest difficulties. That entire volume had been water damaged and consequently numerous pages had disintegrated or were unreadable. Yael had consulted frequently over the phone with Jake, who was now living with Greta at the Long Island beach house, about how to treat these fragments. Their final decision was to only include that which they could clearly read and translate, and to footnote what other portions were missing.

Yael, who had had flown in from California with his family the day before the talk, had hoped that Jake and Greta would have been able to join them at the Met. Though Jake had considered making the drive into the city, in the end, all had agreed that the trip in and out of New York was more than he and Greta were up to at their age. Instead, after the reading, Yael, Ziva and Dede would drive out to Huntington and stay for the weekend to celebrate not only the book's release but Yael's thirtieth birthday. On the way there, Yael also planned to stop at the nearby Long Island Jewish Cemetery. A decade before, vast portions of the Jewish Cemetery in Queens, including the section holding the entire Conegliano family and the grave of his father, Manny, had been relocated to Long Island, and Yael had not as yet visited the new site. With these thoughts in the back of his mind, he continued to read from *The Secret Diaries*.

" 'Deeply in debt and pursued by creditors, I fled to America in 1805. Nonetheless, it was Mozart, or rather my collaborations with Mozart, that opened the doors of New York's high society to us, doors that would have remained barred had we simply been Italian-Jewish immigrants.

And, yes, in New York as in London, Celestina and I once again hid our Jewishness behind a façade of Catholicism. Had we not, we would have been shunned by a community where anti-Semitism was as much an accepted part of life as horse carriages, top hats, and shots of whiskey at every turn. And the key that unlocked that door of acceptance? A chance encounter in 1806 with a young professor of Greek and Biblical studies named Clement Clarke Moore. That encounter allowed our entrée into the rarified world of New York's elite. Our meeting occurred at Riley's Booksellers, on lower Broadway, just two blocks south of Union Square . . . ' "

"As some of you may know," said Yael as behind him, the video screen continued to illustrate each of his discussion points, "Riley's is now the present day location of the renowned —and dare I say, revered—Strand Bookstore. And Moore, Clement Clark Moore, is perhaps most famous for writing a jolly good poem that opens with these magical words, " 'Twas the Night Before Christmas." More importantly though, Moore was a professor at Columbia College—now Columbia University—and the son of Bishop Benjamin Moore. The elder Moore was the Episcopal bishop of the Diocese of New York and the president of Columbia.

"At the time of their first meeting, Da Ponte, ever the entrepreneur, was struggling to make ends meet. With Celestina's help, they ran what my grandfather and fellow translator, Jacob Conegliano, likes to call New York's first Jewish deli. It was in fact a dry goods and provisions store across the river in Jersey. They sold pots and pans, bolts of fabric, bars of soap, as well as all the fixings for a pretty fair Rueben sandwich; yes, you could buy cans of corned beef, sacks of rye flour, wheels of swiss cheese, sauerkraut by the barrel, kegs of dill pickles, and of course, tins of dried mustard powder. Though he and Celestina and their five children ate well, such a business was clearly ill-suited to Da Ponte's temperament. But he persevered—he persevered, that is, until he met Professor Moore. Clement, then twenty-seven to Da Ponte's fifty-seven, was fascinated by his encounter with this man who had not only collaborated with Mozart but had also known Casanova, the great Italian poet Metastasio, and the entire Hapsburg court, including its Emperor, Joseph II."

He continued reading.

" 'Moore and I conversed at great lengths about the classical and biblical roots of poetry, opera, and Italian literature. He professed a deep knowledge of the *Old Testament* and claimed to have read it in Hebrew. Moore was rather astonished when I informed him that not only had I done so as well, but that I also spoke and could write Hebrew as a native. When he asked how I had come to such a level of proficiency, I confessed in confidence that I had been born a Jew. Seeing the lock of dismay upon his face, I hastily added that I had been baptized as a Catholic little more than a year after my bar mitzvah.' "

Yael reached into the pocket of his sports coat and pulled out the old, tarnished yad that Da Ponte had used at his bar mitzvah and discreetly set it on the lectern before continuing.

" 'A dinner invitation quickly followed, one requesting that Celestina and I join the Moores at their estate, Chelsea, then the largest such property in lower Manhattan. Not surprisingly it came with one caveat: Clement Moore suggested—in confidence of course—that I make no mention of my Hebrew heritage in the presence of his father, the bishop, or their other guests.' "

"So, yes," said Yael with a subtle nod back at Ziva and Dede, "even in New York, early modern New York, a city we all now associate with the Statue of Liberty, immigration from every corner of the world, and a tradition of diversity and political liberalism, yes, right here, in the great melting pot of America, Jews were scarcely tolerated." The longer Yael spoke, the greater his confidence grew and the more the audience hung onto his every word. Although he had never been inside List Hall before, the Met itself felt like home. He had attended many an opera here as a child in the box the Conegliano family had kept since the 1930s when his great-grandfather, Abe, supplied the old Met with much of its lighting and sound equipment. And just a year ago he and Dede watched Ziva conduct an afternoon matinee of the *Magic Flute* on the occasion of their daughter's birthday. Dede—which was short for Danielle Dolcetta—was every bit a Conegliano, with deep dark expressive eyes and long black ringlets of hair that tumbled halfway to her waist.

"However," Yael continued, "through their acquaintance with the Moores, the Da Pontes were rapidly accepted into the uppermost echelon of New York's high society. Lorenzo quit the dry goods business, and for the next thirty years of his life, he became the premier promoter and teacher of Italian language, literature, and culture to these white-gloved, aristocratic American families. And Celestina? She was right there with him. An invitation to one of her traditional Italian feasts that featured the artfully renamed Carbonara Gemelli with braised pork and almonds or a crostata di pistacchio, was often the highlight of the social season. Through contacts Da Ponte maintained with friends and family back in the Veneto, he imported thousands of books, which he then used to expose his students to such Italian writers as Dante, Boccaccio, Machiavelli, Metastasio, Tasso, and Manzoni. In due course, Da Ponte not only became the first professor of Italian at Columbia, he was the first ordained Catholic priest to teach there, and perhaps most significantly in retrospect, the first Jew to teach there. Da Ponte later donated those volumes to Columbia and to this very day that collection is preserved on campus as the Lorenzo Da Ponte Library. And, I am honored to say that my other grandfather, Dr. Frank Cornetti, a professor of Italian literature at Columbia, served as the acting director of that collection at one point in his long academic career.

"So, I ask you all to picture Lorenzo Da Ponte . . . a child of Venice who grows up in an era when people wore masks and capes year-round. Much like the characters in his Mozart operas, Lorenzo spends his life shielding his true identity from those around him. And yet somehow, this chameleon, this creature of the theater, becomes an integral part, a building block if you will, in the cultural foundation of early modern New York. And in this great city of ours, Da Ponte counted among his friends New York's most privileged families: the Livingstons, the Hamiltons, the Duers, the Ogilbys, the Verplancks, the Onderdocks, and even the Bonapartes. Yes, Joseph Bonaparte, Napoleon's brother, the former king of Spain, who was then living here in exile as the self-styled Comte de Survilliers, was a frequent dinner companion of Da Ponte. Again, picture them together, inhaling an after-dinner Cuban cigar softened by sips of Courvoisier while discussing the state of the world from rocking chairs on the veranda of some fine estate overlooking the Hudson. It's a far cry from the ghetto of Ceneda . . .

"Lorenzo was also known and revered by many of the artistic giants of that era, the very men and woman who defined that emerging and distinctive American culture of the 1800s. These included Washington Irving, Samuel F. B. Morse, Williams Cullen Bryant, James Fenimore Cooper, and Henry Wadsworth Longfellow. In fact, Lorenzo and Celestina even watched as their youngest son, Lorenzo L. Da Ponte, married Cornelia Durant, the niece of President James Monroe. Still, through it all, none of them knew that Da Ponte, my seventh-generation ancestor, was in truth, a Jew born as Emanuele Conegliano.

"But not only was Da Ponte friends with these luminaries, he leaned on their influence and financial support to bring opera to America, which is one of the many reasons we are here today at the Met. Without Da Ponte's drive to showcase Italian opera, this building, this institution, might never have come into existence. The spiritual roots of the Met date back to May of 1826, when Da Ponte premiered his beloved classic, *Don Giovanni*, at the old Park Theater. In Lorenzo's private box at that first American performance sat Clement Clark Moore, Joseph Bonaparte, and James Fenimore Cooper, whose *Last of the Mohicans* would be published a few days later. In the next box over was William Cullen Bryant, who would write an enthusiastic review of the opera for his newspaper, the *New York Evening Post*.

"But through all of those years in America, the only one who did know of Da Ponte's Jewishness was his longtime friend and supporter, Clement Clark Moore. And it was Moore to whom Da Ponte turned when in 1838, he neared his eighty-ninth birthday. He wrote in the last few pages of his diary:

" 'My dear friend, Clement, the time of my passing from this earth surely approaches. In my dreams each night, I see the cast of players who have filled all the scenes of my life. They gather on the great stages of heaven to sing once more in the grand finale of this, my last act. Zina is there, as is Rabbi Spinoziano, Angela Tiepolo, Casanova, Dona Brunetta, Adriana Ferrarese del Bene, Joseph II, Nancy Storace, my Celestina, and of course, Mozart. They stand before a choir of every woman I have ever loved. And their voices are joined by all the immortals of my imagination: Figaro, Don Giovanni, Leporello, Susanna, Zerlina, Despina, and Fiordiligi. Soon the curtain will fall and I will join them to sleep and dream in this good earth.

" 'Knowledge, particularly self-knowledge, is something we Jews have always valued. It remains the one possession no one can ever take away from us. As a younger man I was taught that wherever we go, whatever we become, wherever our fortunes lead us, we can only find true peace inside ourselves. Therefore, we must know our own hearts, we must know ourselves, and if we must wear foreign vestments to shield our lives from the storms of hatred and bigotry that swirl about, we should do so as lightly as if these garments were but a jester's costume at Carnevale. This we shall do so until such days as we have the strength to reclaim our own fate and return home to ourselves.

" 'At the occasion of my bar mitzvah, I became a man, a Jewish man, a member of the congregation of Ceneda, for all the days of my life. That day, the Rabbi Spinoziano handed me a small brass yad to use when I read the Torah. I have kept it with me since then. It is forever a reminder of who I am, where I have come from, and where I have yet to travel.' "

Yael paused from reading the diary and again spoke directly to the audience as a photo of the brass yad appeared on the screen followed by ever more illustrative sketches and drawings. "Lorenzo Da Ponte died on the 17th of August, in 1838. An overflow crowd of mourners packed the funeral, which was held at the old St. Patrick's Cathedral on Mulberry Street. Clement Moore was among the pallbearers who carried his coffin to the cemetery behind the church. Da Ponte was laid to rest beside his beloved Celestina who had preceded him in death by some seven years."

Once again, Yael glanced over toward Ziva and Dede and considered how blessed he was to have found in them the strength and love that comes from family. "However," Yael said to the audience, "herein, lies the last great mystery about Da Ponte, one that remains unsolved to this day. The cemetery at the old St. Patrick's on Mulberry Street no longer exists. Its once vast and open sacred spaces are now at the intersection of Little Italy and Chinatown, close to where Ferrara's Italian Café sits. Were Da Ponte's coffin still entombed there, I imagine he could have reached a hand out from the grave for a cannoli and a cup of New York's finest cappuccino—but he's not there.

"Sometime around 1850, as New York City grew and land was needed for development, the old cemetery was closed. All the graves there were purportedly transferred and reinterred at the Calvary Catholic Cemetery in Queens. Although there is a memorial marker there in honor of Da Ponte, no trace of either his or Celestina's grave has ever been found there—or anywhere. Much like Mozart, Da Ponte's remains have vanished. It was only when I reached the very last few pages of the diary and read his note to Clement Moore, did I find a clue as to where he might possibly be buried. This I will share with you now."

" '*Purtroppo, figli miei, devo andare via adesso.* Unfortunately, my children, I must leave now. It is near time I depart to dream forevermore amongst the dead. It is my last and most final wish that after all the ceremony and pomp of my departure is over but before the sun has set three times, that my body and that of my beloved Celestina be reinterred at the Hebrew Cemetery of Manhattan and that this secret diary and my yad, which both represent the truths of my life, be sent to my son, Israeli Conegliano, the cantor of Ceneda and preserved there until such time as my family can safely be reunited.' "

"There is no Hebrew Cemetery in Manhattan," said Yael, "Nor have we been able to find any trace of Da Ponte's grave in any of the Jewish cemeteries anywhere in New York. So, one might ask, how do we know any of this is true? How do we know that *The Secret Diaries of Lorenzo Da Ponte,* is not one enormous fiction? Or a hoax, as has been accused? Let me suggest that there are four pieces of evidence to consider."

Yael held up both his hands, fingers stretched and spread out from the palms for all to see as an identical image flashed on the screen. "First is the DNA. Just as Figaro had his birthmark, my hands are those of a

Conegliano. Every male in our family line, from Da Ponte on down shares this anomaly. My grandfather, Jake, has it. I have it. And even my father, who was also named Emanuele Conegliano and whose grave we will visit later today, had these hands. If we can ever locate Da Ponte's final resting place, we may be able to extract enough DNA to prove the blood connections.

"Next, are the diaries themselves, which experts have confirmed were indeed written by Da Ponte's own hand. Then there is this." Yael lifted up the yad and used it to point toward a photo of the yad on the screen. At the tip of the yad was a tiny hand with an index finger pointing forward. "When Rabbi Geremia Spinoziano turned over the *Secret Diaries* to my grandfather back in 1946, this yad, the yad from Da Ponte's own bar mitzvah, was tucked inside the diaries. Consider this: For the entirety of his life as a converso, Da Ponte, never let go of this one last vestige of his Jewish roots. Through every triumph, through every tragedy, Da Ponte—or should I say, Emanuele Conegliano—carried it with him until the hour of his death."

Putting the yad back into his coat pocket, Yael continued. "The last piece of evidence that would have confirmed the truth of Da Ponte's story should have been the letter that Clement Moore sent to Italy along with the diaries and the yad. However, the last known sighting of that letter by Father Beccavivi of Ceneda occurred over one hundred years ago. And even then, Father Beccavivi described the paper that the letter was written upon as being in extremely fragile condition. For the past ten years, we've searched everywhere for that letter, starting in Ceneda. Unfortunately, there is nothing left in Ceneda of the Jewish quarter or of the old synagogue. The community there was wiped out in a raid by a German SS officer, Captain Stanislav Braun under the specific direction of the Abbé Luigi Hudal. Hudal, incidentally, was the same cleric who after the war established the

'Ratlines,' the escape routes and safe houses that allowed Nazis such as Adolph Eichmann to escape to South America.

"And if I can digress for one moment, I'd like to share something personal about my family. I grew up in the shadow of the Holocaust, I grew up despising Nazis, yet I am indebted to them for my very existence. Colonel Braun, who sent my wife's grandmother, Danielle, off to Dachau, was later killed by my grandmother, Dolcetta, when she was a partisan fighter," said Yael. His off-the-cuff remarks caught Ziva off guard. She bolted upright in her seat while putting a protective arm around Dede. "And then there is the Abbé and later Bishop Hudal, who conceived of the raid on Ceneda and was actively pursued, along with Eichmann, by my grandfather, Jake, during his post–World War II work for the CIA. If not for these two evil creatures, my grandparents would have never met. Nor would I have ever known the love of my life, Ziva D'Angelo, who sits right there." He pointed to Ziva in the front row and then continued. "She sits with our daughter, Dede, who represents not only the next generation of the Conegliano family, but also the next generation of Da Ponte's and Zina's descendants."

A copy of Zena's portrait, scar and all, appeared on the screen behind him. "Now," continued Yael, "most of whatever artifacts that survived the destruction of the Temple in Ceneda were sent to the Italian Synagogue of Jerusalem in Israel." Yael again pointed to Ziva. "My wife, who grew up in Israel and is fluent in Hebrew, and I went to the Italian Synagogue in hopes the letter had ended up in their collection, but to no avail. Back in Italy, we even explored the archives at the monastery at Avastella to see if Father Adriano or Rabbi Geremia had left it there after the war. No luck. Next, I decided to examine the genizah trunk that my grandmother Dolcetta had brought to New York as a young bride and had sat, unexplored, in their attic for fifty years. The genizah originally held a collection of sacred texts and papers that were no longer in use but that generations of rabbis in Ceneda had deemed too holy to destroy. Rabbi Geremia had added to the trunk all of the other papers from the Jewish community that had survived the war.

"To delve into the depths of the genizah, is to wander through nearly five hundred years of history—history that is in fact my family's history, one that not only dates to 1597 when my first known ancestor, Israel da Conegliano, settled in Ceneda, but in fact stretches back along all the *Via Giudeccas* of Italy to the Hebrew slaves brought to Rome and Sicily by the Emperor Titus after the destruction of the Second Temple in Jerusalem."

A photo of Yael's "Mercy of Titus" coin flashed on the screen. "During my search for that letter, I was often easily distracted by the many documents I found. One in particular captured my attention. It was the Passover Haggadah that had once belonged to Da Ponte's son and my namesake ancestor, Israeli Conegliano. It was easily dated by the blood splatters to the night he had killed the Casti capitano. As I turned its pages and reread the story of Passover, I found myself transported to that very singular ceremony and the events that led to Zina's death from pneumonia. However, when I raced to show the haggadah to Ziva, bits of yellowed paper fell out from the back of the book. It was the letter or rather, I should say, fragments of the letter Clement Moore sent to Israeli."

Yael pointed to the screen. There was a photograph in which the fragments of the letter were pieced together. "It was just over a year ago, December 24th of 2004, yes, the night before Christmas, just as I was completing a final edit of the *Secret Diaries*, that scholars at the Columbia and the Da Ponte Library confirmed that the handwriting you see there on the screen was indeed that of Clement Clark Moore.

"And that," said Yael as the screen changed once again, "brings us to the very final words of *The Secret Diaries of*

Lorenzo Da Ponte." Yael read the Italian and then translated it for the audience, "*Non dimenticare mai, non dimenticare mai chi sei*. Never forget, never forget who you are."

As they drove around the quiet lanes of the Long Island Jewish Cemetery in search of his father Manny's grave, Yael could not but be reminded that this coming August, Ziva was going to conduct multiple performances of Mozart and Da Ponte's *Don Giovanni* at the Estates National Theater in Prague, the very theater where his father had been killed seventeen years earlier.

"Are you okay with that?" Ziva had first asked him when her agency had booked her for Prague. Yael did not have an immediate response and hesitated to give one. Though he had seen her conduct in Venice and Vienna, he had never been to Prague. Yael had no idea how he would react to seeing what had been a reoccurring nightmare of his childhood—the commendatore's fall from a thrust of Don Giovanni's sword. As best he could imagine, his dread of going to the Estates National must have been akin to how Dolcetta had felt about ever returning to Ceneda.

"Yes," he finally told her, "It's time to chase away the old ghosts."

They had reached the cemetery's Avenue 'C.' The reinterred graves had been organized alphabetically and by family groupings.

"Does that 'C' stand for Ceneda or Conegliano?" asked Dede from the back seat.

Yael was about to say "neither," as he pulled the car over to the curb, but Ziva was one step ahead of him. "Both," she said to their daughter. "Just like Dede."

"Cool," said Dede as she popped out of the car. A long gravel walkway led to a cluster of tombstones about fifty yards away. Declaring she was going to find her grandfather's grave for them, Dede raced down the path.

"I'm proud of you," Ziva said to Yael as they exited the car. "You did well today. And no rotten tomatoes."

"Thank you," he said. Yael and Ziva put their arms around each other's waist as they started down the path. "Having you two there, made all the difference. Kept me smiling even when the questioning got tough." Yael repeated the words Rabbi Geremia had once told his Pops: " 'When you support, encourage and inspire others, then you will discover inspiration in your own life. And when you love and when others love and honor you, you create family and community. That my children, is Judaism.' "

Ziva turned and kissed Yael.

Yes, the talk had gone exceptionally well, the Q and A even better, so much so that the event ran over an hour long, with no one leaving their seats. And no boobirds, Yael was grateful for that. Every book he'd brought had been signed and sold. *The Secret Diaries of Lorenzo Da Ponte* book tour was off to an auspicious start.

"It's been a long day. Can't wait to kick off my shoes at the beach house and stare out at the sea," said Ziva.

"Likewise," said Yael. "When I spoke to Pops this morning, he told me that Arturo Bianchi had shipped them a case of his Dolcetto to help us celebrate."

"Ah, *va bene*," said Ziva, "There are few things more magical in life than sitting around that fireplace, sipping that beautiful wine, listening to Greta play a Mozart sonata, and seeing the look of sheer contentment on your Pop's face."

"Yeah, they're beyond happy being with each other."

"I found it!" Dede suddenly yelled. Ziva and Yael were still about 25 yards away. "I found Grandpa!"

They quickened their pace.

"There's two!" shouted Dede. "There's two graves for Grandpa!"

Yael and Ziva looked at each other quizzically, two? They hurried over. Yael's heart was pounding so hard inside his chest, it felt as if it were bumping up against the yad in his coat pocket.

Directly behind the tombstones for Yael's great-grandparents, Abe and Rosa Conegliano, there were indeed three more tombstones. The first, on the far left, Yael recognized from his father funeral. It read, Emanuele Conegliano, Born October 12, 1946, in New York; Died in Prague, October 18, 1989. Next to it, in the center, was a very old and almost illegible marker for Celestina Graziano Conegliano. And to the right of that, stood the second tombstone for Emanuele Conegliano. Equally, worn, stained and faded with age as was Celestina's, it read beneath the name, Born in Ceneda, Italy, March 10, 1749; Died New York City, August 17, 1838. Below the date was an inscription chiseled in Hebrew.

"Dio mio," exclaimed Yael as he collapsed to his knees atop the grave. "It's him. It's Da Ponte. No one is ever going to believe this. Can you read the inscription? What does it say?"

Ziva kneeled beside him. It was a bit of a struggle for her to decipher the chiseled script. But as she read the Hebrew and translated aloud, they both realized the quote was the last lines of the last libretto, *Cosi Fan Tutte*, that Da Ponte had written for Mozart:

> *Fortunate are those who are able to make the best of all adversity.*
> *Through all their trials and tribulations, they make reason their guide.*
> *What always makes others weep, is for them a cause for laughter*
> *And amidst the tempests of this world they will find sweet peace.*

Without thinking Yael pulled the yad out of his coat pocket and pushed it deep into the earth above the grave. "We're home," he said, "Safe at home. Sleep in peace and dream of Mozart."

The End

About the Author

Howard Jay Smith is an award-winning writer from Santa Barbara, California. *Meeting Mozart* is his fourth book. He was recently awarded a John E. Profant Foundation for the Arts, Literature Division Scholarship, the James Buckley Excellence in Writing Award. Smith is a former Bread Loaf Scholar and Washington, DC, Commission for the Arts Fellow, who taught for many years in the UCLA Extension Writers' Program and has lectured nationally. His articles and photographs have appeared in the *Washington Post*, the *Beethoven Journal*, *Horizon*, the *Journal of the Writers Guild of America*, and the *Ojai Quarterly*. While an executive at ABC Television, Embassy TV, and Academy Home Entertainment, he worked on numerous film, television, radio, and commercial projects. He serves on the board of directors of the Santa Barbara Symphony and is a member of the American Beethoven Society.

About the Illustrator

Zak Smith is an artist and writer who first came to prominence with his mammoth work, "755 Pictures Showing What Happens on Each Page of Thomas Pynchon's Novel *Gravity's Rainbow*," at the Whitney Biennial. His artistic pedigree and acute observation have landed him in high-profile shows from the Whitney to the San Francisco Museum of Modern Art, and his work has appeared in numerous major public and private collections worldwide, including the NY Museum of Modern Art; the Whitney Museum of American Art; Saatchi Gallery, London; the Carnegie Institute; the National Portrait Gallery, and the Baltimore Museum of Art. Zak Smith's books include *Pictures Of Girls* and *Pictures Showing What Happens on Each Page of Thomas Pynchon's Novel* Gravity's Rainbow. Zak holds a BA from Cooper Union and an MFA from Yale University. He lives and works in Los Angeles. He is represented by the Fredericks & Freiser.

About the Publisher

The Sager Group was founded in 1984. In 2012 it was chartered as a multimedia content brand, with the intent of empowering those who create art—an umbrella beneath which makers can pursue, and profit from, their craft directly, without gatekeepers. TSG publishes books; ministers to artists and provides modest grants; and produces documentary, feature, and commercial films. By harnessing the means of production, The Sager Group helps artists help themselves. For more information, please see TheSagerGroup.net.

More Books from The Sager Group

Mandela Was Late: Odd Things & Essays From the Seinfeld Writer Who Coined Yada, Yada and Made Spongeworthy a Compliment
by Peter Mehlman

#MeAsWell, A Novel
by Peter Mehlman

The Orphan's Daughter, A Novel
by Jan Cherubin

Miss Havilland, A Novel
by Gay Daly

High Tolerance: A Novel of Sex, Race, Murder . . . and Marijuana
by Mike Sager

Lifeboat No. 8: Surviving the Titanic
by Elizabeth Kaye

See our entire library at TheSagerGroup.net